THE MUSEUM OF HAPPINESS

Library of American Fiction
The University of Wisconsin Press Fiction Series

The Museum
of
Happiness

A NOVEL

Jesse Lee Kercheval

The University of Wisconsin Press

The University of Wisconsin Press
1930 Monroe Street
Madison, Wisconsin 53711

www.wisc.edu/wisconsinpress/

3 Henrietta Street
London WC2E 8LU, England

First published in the United States in 1993 by Faber and Faber, Inc.
Copyright © 1993, 2003 by Jesse Lee Kercheval
All rights reserved

1   3   5   4   2

Printed in the United States of America

Library of Congress Cataloging-in-Publication Data
Kercheval, Jesse Lee.
The Museum of Happiness : a novel / Jesse Lee Kercheval.
p. cm.—(Library of American fiction)
ISBN 0-299-18734-9 (pbk. : alk. paper)
1. France—Fiction.
I. Title. II. Series.
PS3561.E558M87   2003
813'.54—dc21   2003040184

This is a work of fiction. All characters and events are products of the author's imagination.
Any resemblance to persons living or dead is purely coincidental.

Terrace Books, a division of the University of Wisconsin Press, takes its name from the
Memorial Union Terrace, located at the University of Wisconsin–Madison. Since its
inception in 1907, the Wisconsin Union has provided a venue for students, faculty, staff,
and alumni to debate art, music, politics, and the issues of the day. It is a place where theater,
music, drama, dance, outdoor activities, and major speakers are made available to the campus
and the community. To learn more about the Union, visit www.union.wisc.edu.

ABOUT THE AUTHOR

Jesse Lee Kercheval was born in France and grew up in Florida. Her collection of stories *The Dogeater* won the Associated Writing Programs Award in Short Fiction for 1987. Her stories have appeared in magazines and anthologies including *Twenty Under Thirty: Best Stories by America's New Young Writers, Writing Fiction,* and *How We Live Now.* She teaches at the University of Wisconsin and lives in Madison.

for Dan Hughes Fuller

ACKNOWLEDGMENTS

THE AUTHOR IS grateful to the following persons and organizations for their support: James A. Michener and the Copernicus Society of America, the National Endowment for the Arts, the Dane County Cultural Affairs Commission, the Graduate School of the University of Wisconsin, the Wisconsin Arts Board, the Mary Ingraham Bunting Institute, and the Corporation of Yaddo. Thanks also to Jerome Stern who gave generously of his time.

Portions of this novel, in somewhat different form, have appeared in these publications: *Boulevard*, the *Carolina Quarterly*, the *Chariton Review*, *Fiction*, the *Greensboro Review*, the *Indiana Review*, *London Magazine*, and the *Massachusetts Review*.

THE MUSEUM OF HAPPINESS

CHAPTER ONE

IN THE MORGUE, Ginny Gillespie took a step forward and laid a finger on her husband Paul's cheek, touched a corner of his mouth where death had caught him blank-faced, too busy to smile or frown. His skin felt like wet rubber, like a hand hidden in a surgeon's glove. It was October 5, 1929. Ginny had only been married to Paul for three months.

An intern who'd been taking a nap on one of the old marble tables sat up. He saw a young woman with thick red hair cut almost viciously short, her dress starched and ironed the way nurses starched and ironed everything that touched their skin, and he took Ginny for what she'd been just months before, one of Jacksonville Memorial's nursing students. He didn't bother to stand.

Ginny was looking at Paul's bare feet. A sheet covered him from chest to ankles, but his feet stuck out as if his bed had come untucked. "Oh," she said, how horrible and ordinary it all was. Paul's second toe was longer than his big toe. Ape-toed, the girls at the academy had called it. How could she not have noticed that before? She felt someone beside her, the intern.

"I was there, you know," he said, leaning close, trying to impress her, "watching from the students' gallery. Just a routine hysterectomy, then, bam!" He smacked his hands together. "Dead before he hit the operating room floor—that first ovary still in his hand." Ginny felt her knees start to go, took a step back to steady herself. The intern checked his watch against the big chrome clock on the wall. "In my opinion," he said, suddenly professional, "Dr. Gillespie experienced a *massive* cerebral hemorrhage." He checked his watch again.

An accident of the brain, Ginny thought, using her father, Papa

Ben's, older medical terminology. Surprise! You've had an accident. And what had this accident done to the woman who was Paul's final patient? That was what Paul would want to know. Ginny turned to ask, but the intern was already gone, the heavy doors swinging behind him. Whatever happened, the woman would have to find a new doctor and Ginny was sorry for that. There weren't many doctors like Paul. She should know, what with her father a practicing physician and her mother a lapsed one.

A jet in the ceiling cut on. Ginny jumped back as the water streamed down. It fell in a fine mist over Paul, ran off the white skin over the arch of his nose, gathered in puddles in his ears. It was then Ginny felt the first push of the physical pain of grief. A fist shoved up and under her ribs, squeezing her heart, her lungs. For one terrible moment, she was sure she was going to be sick, be responsible for an awful mess some nurse would have to clean up. Paul wasn't sleeping down here in the morgue. He was dead, his flesh saved from rotting only by the slim grace of refrigeration. She closed her eyes and backed through the double doors.

In the hospital lobby, she thought she heard someone call out from beyond the empty benches, the pots of fish-tail palms, but she kept going, through the glass doors into the white Florida noon. At the corner of the building, Paul's car, a Reo, stood parked in the shrunken shade. She got in on the driver's side, the heat inside the car making the red hair on her arms stand up. She took a deep breath of the hot, leather-scented air. She was sweating but she felt cold, like after a summer swim in Indian Springs, when the water turned you so blue that even on the long ride home you shivered like a dog. She felt for the keys but they weren't in the ignition. She remembered that Papa Ben sometimes left his under the floor mat. She bent down.

"Mrs. Gillespie," someone knocked on the car window. "Mrs. Gillespie, please." She sat up, burning her wrist on the hot steering wheel. It was Dr. Thornton, the hospital administrator. She hadn't wanted to see him. She had imagined him taking command of her the way Papa Ben did his distraught female patients, making her lie down, frowning over her pulse. But now Dr. Thornton had caught her. He walked around the Reo as if to get in on the passenger's side, but Ginny slid across the hot leather seat and swung her legs out as he opened the door. She didn't want to sit in the front seat with Dr. Thornton like a couple of jazz babies. Dr. Thornton stepped back, off balance, holding a package wrapped in butcher's paper against his chest. The two times she'd seen Dr. Thornton when she was a student nurse, he had been up on a podium lecturing. Now she realized he was shorter than she was, wasn't even five feet tall. She stared down at the red worried wrinkles on the top of his head as Dr. Thornton shifted uncomfortably from one polished, thick-soled shoe to the other.

"I was worried," he said. "I was just about to telegraph your father."

"My father?" Ginny felt the muscles in her chest tighten.

"To be sure you had someone *rational* to advise you," Dr. Thornton said, as if to emphasize he'd had quite enough of the other Dr. MacKenzie, her mother.

"How kind of you," Ginny said. She lowered her eyes to Dr. Thornton's. Yes, he looked like a man who would telegraph: DAUGHTER A WIDOW. COME AT ONCE. Papa Ben would come out of spite, come to take her back to a house where her mother would refuse to say a word to her. She could almost feel the cool breeze of her mother brushing by her. She shivered. "Very kind," Ginny repeated and took a deep breath. Her crazy Aunt Fanny always said the trick to lying was to move fast. "But I've already talked to Papa on the telephone."

She watched as Dr. Thornton's worry lines smoothed, and the red trapped in them spread out across his scalp. He cleared his throat. "Well," he said scratching a foot across the gravel of the parking lot, "if I can be of any help with the arrangements."

Ginny understood. Dr. Thornton would know which funeral home was respectable enough for its name to appear next to Jacksonville Memorial's in Paul's obituary. It was not something she wanted to know herself. "Please," she said.

"Honored," he said and stood firm on both feet. The package in his hands crackled. "Oh," he said, remembering it, "Dr. Gillespie's suit, his keys from his locker, and the . . . things he had on. His nurse rinsed them out."

Ginny thought for a second that he was trying to give her the surgical gown Paul had worn, rinsed clean of blood, but that was hospital property. Paul would have had on underwear, but what? Then she realized. Paul had wet himself. Jehovah God, you die and pee in your pants, and you can't even apologize to the poor girl who has to clean up after you. She took the package by the string. "Thank you," she said.

Dr. Thornton asked if he could drive her home, but already assigned his favor, he didn't press her when she said no. She watched as he retreated across the parking lot, then she tore open the package. It was Paul's gray wool suit, too heavy for the weather they'd been having. The wool was damp from the wet underwear. Lanoline mixed with the scent of lye and sweat and a sharp cat smell, the ammonia of urine. Ginny's hands shook as she carefully picked Paul's keys out of his suit pocket. Then she pushed the soiled clothes into one of the trash bins at the corner of the parking lot.

Her hands were still shaking as she started the Reo, headed for the house. The inside of the car smelled like bay rum, like a living Paul. She thought of Paul standing in front of the mirror this morning tying his tie, the bay rum fresh on his cheeks. How could he be dead? After a lifetime around doctors, Ginny knew at forty-one Paul was not too young to die. No one was too young to die. But how could you have your coffee and eggs in the morning and be dead before lunch? She shook her head. She had gotten sick almost that quickly.

She had caught the influenza her second week in nurse's training at Memorial. One day she was bending over a patient, holding his head up as he struggled to breathe, and the next she was in bed herself. "I don't want to be any trouble," she told the head nurse as she was stripped and put in the high-railed hospital bed. What she meant was *please don't tell my mother*. When pneumonia set in, the hospital sent a telegram. Her mother came by the night train from DeSoto, and because his wife beat him there, Papa Ben wouldn't come at all.

So Claire MacKenzie found someone else to argue with. Paul. Ginny could still hear them, her mother the doctor and her future husband the doctor. Her mother, whose license to practice medicine in the State of Florida had been issued when a woman doctor was so rare it had all the *HE*s crossed out and *SHE*s inked in above, had abandoned medicine for a greater call. She was now an International Bible Student, not Dr. MacKenzie but Sister Claire, and in any argument she could call on Jehovah to back her up. Day after day, Ginny had awakened to find their two dark heads visible beyond the dim barrier of the pneumonia tent. Claire stood an invincible five feet. Dr. Gillespie was at least a foot taller, but the way he kept his head bent even when he wasn't examining a patient made him seem hesitant.

They stood at the end of her bed but faced each other as they argued their slow, ungiving points. Her mother wanted her to die. Clothed in the faith she'd discovered sixteen years before when she had heard Pastor Russell's lecture "Jehovah God's Plan for America," she stood fast on her biblical sureness and refused to allow her daughter to be transfused. It was the eating of human blood. The Bible forbade eating blood sausage, and this was much worse. Paul didn't see what God had to do with his decision as Virginia's physician that she should be transfused. It was a new procedure in cases like this but, in his opinion, the treatment of choice. He kept his tone professional, carefully unemotional, but Ginny thought she knew what he felt: *Poor girl, to die so young*.

Claire explained over and over, patiently, endlessly. Ginny was one of the 144,000 chosen, one of the Little Flock, baptized by Pastor Russell himself after the secret return of Jesus Christ. When she died, she would go straight to Heaven to help Jesus rule there forever—no waiting for the Resurrection of Life on the New Earth. For the Bible says "we shall not all fall asleep in death but we shall be changed, in a moment, in the twinkling of an eye." Her voice droned on and on until Ginny could no longer hear Paul's. Again and again *the little flock*, until she saw sheep in the room licking the edge of the tent, their pink tongues thirsty but friendly, their soft breath keeping time with the hissing of the oxygen. She was already passing on, turning from a thin stick of a girl to a fat young ewe. Fever became the close warmth of her new wool, curly, watertight, and safe.

Then, when she had about decided that it was more trouble to breathe than it was worth and the oxygen could stay in its bottle for someone else's use, she saw Paul's face. He was frowning, his forehead lined, as if each of her slow breaths caused him an exquisite sort of pain. She heard his voice again, and this time there was something new in it, something warmer than pity. Through the long nights when Claire was back at the hotel studying her *Watch Tower*, Paul sat with Ginny. His cool hand reached underneath the tent to press against her newly thin cheek or, checking her drowning heart, against a hot shrunken breast. On those nights, she looked at Paul's hand and thought, *This must be love*.

And so, Claire lost. "If I were your husband," Paul had said, stroking her damp hair, "I could give permission for your treatment." *Yes*, Ginny moved her lips. *Yes*. Rules were bent to save Jacksonville Memorial Hospital from the disgrace of student nurse Virginia MacKenzie's death. Paul married her.

5

"Hold still now," he said. With his own cool hands, he inserted the needle that carried the blood of strangers into her veins. He smiled at her as if she belonged to him, and she smiled back, thinking, *I am no longer my mother's daughter.*

Her mother had the same thought. She had sent a scripture card:

> He that loveth son or daughter more than me
> is not worthy of me.
>
> Matthew 10:37

Ginny parked the Reo, let herself into Paul's house. The house wasn't any emptier than it usually was, the big white-walled living room with its still-crated sofa and chairs, but now it would stay empty. Her eyes burned and she blinked, expecting tears, but none came. She walked through the living room to the kitchen, footsteps echoing on the tile floor. She pulled a chair from the wooden table, sat down. Her head ached. She poured herself a glass of iced tea, pressed the cool glass to her forehead. A month after Paul had married her, she was well. But Paul had other patients who needed him. So she'd moved into his big new house where the furniture he'd bought when he first moved to Florida stood packed in excelsior, and she waited. If her mother could wait so patiently for the end of the world, Ginny had reasoned, she could wait for Paul.

But now Paul was dead. Ginny sat up, held onto the seat of the chair. She felt as if time were ballooning out around her, shapeless and unfillable. What should she do? What first small thing could she do? She remembered Paul's body in the morgue, his feet bare, already slightly blue. She pressed her fingers to her eyes, still burning and dry. For now, her future could wait. Paul's couldn't. He needed to be buried.

But where? He'd told her he didn't have any close family, but she wasn't sure that meant no family. She took the glass of tea with her to Paul's study. She had never been in it. Paul spent little enough time there himself. She fought the impulse to knock but rattled the knob loudly as she opened the door. She set the tea glass on the desk and sat in the wooden swivel chair. It wasn't much different from her mother's study at home. The walls were bare, the desk and chair stood on the tile floor. But the bookshelves held only undisturbed rows of medical journals, no stacks of worn *Watch Towers*, no boxes of *Golden Ages* waiting to be taken door to door. The desk itself held no more clutter than a clock and a lamp. No Bible. Ginny turned on the lamp.

She opened the desk drawer. Maybe there were letters from cousins or uncles, from people who should be told, who would take from her this awful distinction of being the only one who cared where or even if Paul were buried. In the drawer was a packet of papers bound with red string. As she pulled it out, the doorbell rang. She rolled Paul's chair back and went to answer the door, the packet still in her hand. It was Mrs. Corbet, the next-door neighbor who had driven her to the hospital.

"Oh, very smart," Mrs. Corbet said, seeing the papers Ginny held. "Find out anything yet? No? Well . . ." She headed for the lighted door of the study, and Ginny followed like a guest. Mrs. Corbet sat in the chair. Ginny leaned on the desk. "I've been waiting for you to get done at the hospital and settle down to business." Mrs. Corbet took the packet from Ginny. "I know you don't feel like doing this now, but as my mother used to say, 'Hang all the pictures the day you move in, or you'll get used to blank walls.' " Mrs. Corbet couldn't restrain a quick nod toward the empty room beyond. "There'll be time enough for you to get used to what's happened. Believe me, I know." Mrs. Corbet was a widow too, though she was in her sixties and Ginny only twenty.

"What should I do?" Ginny asked, hoping for a small practical suggestion.

"Well, that depends," Mrs. Corbet said carefully, weighing Ginny's three months as Mrs. Gillespie in a fine balance, "on whether he left you any money or not." She held a knife to the string. "May I?"

Ginny remembered Paul telling her that Mrs. Corbet's husband had left her only a little money, but a good many run-down houses which she had moved across town on great wooden frames and rented out. A fine little business woman, Papa Ben would have called her. "Yes," Ginny said and Mrs. Corbet cut the knot. On the top of the bundle were stocks. Ginny could guess that from their heavy paper and engraved borders. "Before you came, I was looking for letters." Mrs. Corbet fanned the papers like cards across the desk. None of them were letters.

"This looks like a copy of the doctor's will," Mrs. Corbet picked out a long folded paper, opened it. "A new will too, for a bride."

Ginny took the will from her. It was new, dated July 12, 1929, a week after their marriage. *To provide for the care of my wife.* She read on. There were three bank accounts listed and some stocks, the house, the

Reo, instructions for selling the practice. She was amazed. She had done nothing to deserve these things that Paul had worked so hard for. Paul *must* have loved her. The black letters blurred, swam across the page. Ginny blinked; she was finally crying. It had been so hard to be sure. But he must have. He had married her, had saved her life, had made a will so she could live even if he did not. She pressed the stiff sheet of paper to her heart.

"Don't get that wet, dear," Mrs. Corbet said, holding her hand out for the will. Ginny looked at it one last time, then refolded it and gave it to Mrs. Corbet. She wiped her wet cheeks with the back of her hand. Surely if Paul had had any family, he would have remembered them in his will. Mrs. Corbet tied the will into a bundle with some of the stocks. Ginny touched it with one finger. Paul was all hers then.

"It looks like you had a good husband," Mrs. Corbet said. "He's seen to it that you can do as you please."

"As I please?" Ginny asked. That made her life sound like Aunt Fanny's game, Three Wishes, which she'd made up the summer when Ginny was eleven and visiting her at the State Hospital for the Insane in Chattahoochee. You could wish for anything you pleased. But even Aunt Fanny, who was in a lunatic asylum, never wished for anything that would really change her life—just candy, handsome visitors, and once, that her nurse would break a leg. Ginny, at that age still convinced by her twice-a-day Bible studies, thought she ought to wish for the Accomplished End to arrive, but Fanny said Armageddon wasn't part of the game. So Ginny had wished for a long voyage, a new, pretty name, a mysterious lover, though she couldn't really imagine any of those things.

"Dr. Gillespie's lawyer will have the true copy," Mrs. Corbet said, "and he's the executor too, so you'd better talk to him bright and early in the morning. No sense in waiting until he gets around to you." Mrs. Corbet pointed at the empty tea glass in its puddle of condensation. "Any more of that?"

"In the kitchen," Ginny said. "I'll get us some." Ginny left Mrs. Corbet adding up a long column of figures. In the kitchen she got down another glass. What should she do with Paul? Wherever he was buried, she would have to stay. How could she abandon him after what he'd done for her? She remembered her Aunt Fanny's exact words, "A big old handsome genie says you got three wishes. What do you want?" She closed her eyes. First Wish. Did she want go back home, bury Paul in DeSoto?

No. Not and go back to fighting with her mother, bargaining with Papa Ben for his protection. She'd had to do that all her life, even to do something as simple as take French at school. Ginny remembered passing Madame Duval's room at Dr. Love's academy, how she would stand outside and listen. She always felt those *Johns* turned *Jeans* and *Barbaras* made over as *Babettes* were really talking to her, trying to tell her things that couldn't be said in any other language. French was the language her Aunt Fanny had spoken when she taught in Martinique. A language for dreams, a language in which Ginny had never read the Bible. Every time Ginny looked up at the great map of the world that covered the front wall of the assembly hall at Dr. Love's academy, her eyes would search out the deep pink of France with its red heart, Paris. There, she thought, someone is waiting for me, standing in the station, checking every train.

"Why learn a foreign tongue when after Armageddon everyone will speak a new, grammatically simplified language?" her mother had said. But her mother's opposition got Papa Ben interested as it always did. He was only interested if Claire was not. Ginny had gotten used to that so long ago it seemed natural. Papa Ben paused over his breakfast long enough to take the gold pen out of his coat pocket and sign her permission slip with the flourish that he usually reserved for prescriptions on which Perkins' Drugs paid him a percentage. Her mother set her fork down on her plate so hard a chip went ringing off the gold edge.

Ginny poured the tea into the glasses. If not DeSoto, where? Did she want to stay in Jacksonville? Go back to nursing school? "Oh Genie, the Second Wish," Fanny would have said. She remembered the night, a week after she'd graduated from Dr. Love's academy, when she'd announced over dinner that she wanted to leave DeSoto, go to nursing school.

Her mother had listened, then leaned close. "Now, Virginia," she said, her tone reasonable. "You know perfectly well that there's no need for doctors and nurses anymore, no need for people like your father. Everyone who is saved will get a perfect, new body."

Papa Ben ran a hand through his coarse red hair. "What hospital were you thinking about, Virginia?" he'd asked. In the end, Papa Ben had arranged with Dr. Thornton for her training and bought her ticket to Jacksonville. Still Ginny couldn't quite believe she was going until she was standing alone on the platform with the ticket in her hand, her suitcase at her feet. Papa Ben often forgot promises. Her mother never forgot anything. But the Southern Crescent pulled in on time, and no one stopped her from getting on. As it rolled out of DeSoto, she saw the light in her mother's window, Papa Ben's big yellow and black Marmon outside Perkins' Drugs. Then the speed of the Crescent yanked that world away.

Ginny put the pitcher back in the Kelvinator. So she'd gotten what she wanted. She was out of DeSoto. But had she really wanted to be a nurse? She shook her head. No. She'd only imagined that in a well-ironed nurse's uniform she could face strangers, mirrors, her mother, crisply and efficiently. Ginny wiped her hands. One thing she knew for certain. If she wasn't going back to nursing school, then she didn't want to stay in Jacksonville. Didn't want Dr. Thornton to arrange a socially correct funeral, which, since she was now a wealthy doctor's young widow, might serve the double purpose of funeral and coming-out party, a chance for unattached doctors to get a peek at her before they came to call. They would come, Aunt Fanny would have said, like rats to sugar. Ginny had seen that happen to a young widow in DeSoto. She opened her eyes. No more doctors.

"Mrs. Gillespie . . ." It was Mrs. Corbet calling. It sounded like she was in the living room.

"Coming," Ginny answered, putting the tea on a tray. Mrs. Corbet was standing in the living room with a man in a dark green suit.

"Mr. McCue," Mrs. Corbet explained, "McMillan Funeral Home." She turned to the man, "Are you married to one of the McMillan girls?"

He shook his head. "Don't I wish," he said, tapping the side of his nose with a stubby index finger.

"Oh," Mrs. Corbet allowed noncommittally.

"Dr. Thornton sent you?" Ginny asked. Mrs. Corbet took tea off the tray and retreated to the study.

Mr. McCue nodded. "A nice little guy, Dr. Thornton."

She wasn't sure if the *little* was an assumption of familiarity or a joke about Dr. Thornton's height.

"Ah," Mr. McCue spotted the refreshments. He took the remaining glass of tea. "So kind of you to be a hostess under the present, sorrowful circumstance," he said, trying for that note of minor-key sympathy

Ginny had always imagined an undertaker would use. At the same time, he was drinking her glass of tea. "I was given to understand," he waved generally with his free hand, "that you'd need to come to some decisions in regard to funerary arrangements."

"My husband . . ." Ginny started.

"Nice room you've got here," Mr. McCue said, walking from the hall to the fireplace as if he were pacing it off. "Very commodious."

Ginny couldn't very well offer Mr. McCue a seat on one of the crates in the nice, commodious room, but she felt like she was trying to hold a conversation on a busy sidewalk. "Some more tea?" she asked. Mr. McCue raised his glass to show that it was still half-full. He was pacing off the room from the other direction. "Yes, but you'll want more. I'll bring the pitcher." Ginny fled to the kitchen.

What should she do? She was glad it was Mr. McCue she had to explain herself to and not Mr. McMillan, Sr., of the McMillan Funeral Home. She didn't think Mr. McCue would question the propriety, the table manners, of anything she decided. But what decision? She closed her eyes one more time, leaning over the table. She felt as if she were falling, spinning down from a height like one of Papa Ben's roller pigeons. Roller pigeons were supposed to fall, to come rolling down, wing over wing, until they were as close to the ground as they had the heart and breeding to dare, and for a great pigeon that was very, very close, close enough to get his wings dusty. Ginny wasn't sure she knew her way down and back up so clearly. She felt like one of the pigeons Papa Ben had ordered from a New Hampshire breeder which had gotten shaken so hard on the train. When he threw the first pigeon into the bright Florida sky, it flew high up toward the tall banking clouds and then came rolling down, a barrel with wings, down until it landed with a feathery thud on the sandy drive. Papa Ben had sent the pigeons up, one after another, and not one had the wit or the skill left to make its spectacular dive into a harmless morning thrill, to pull up before it joined its brood mates on the dirty white sand.

Ginny felt herself falling. She had tried to break away, pull up. She had come as far as Jacksonville, but Jacksonville wasn't nearly far enough. She was still falling. She held onto the table. The Third Wish. Where, where could she go to do as she pleased?

"Can I haul something into the parlor for you, Mrs. Gillespie?" It was Mr. McCue.

Ginny straightened up. "No," she said, "let's sit down here and talk. You don't mind, do you, Mr. McCue?" Mr. McCue looked around him, taking in the iron pots, the rough table, and looked as if he did mind, but he nodded and sat down at the table.

"So," he said as Ginny poured herself some tea, "the arrangements."

Ginny took a sip of tea. "Is it very difficult to ship someone, a body, I mean, on a boat or a train?" she asked, rolling the cool glass between her palms.

"Not too hard if it's not too far," Mr. McCue said. "Of course it's better when it's not so hot."

"How do people get bodies back from some place hot and far away then?"

"Well, the English, with all those deceased to get back home from India, usually cremate them. You know, then put the little bag of soot in a coffin and let it go at that." Mr. McCue rubbed his tea glass across the bridge of his nose. "Is that what you mean?"

"And cremation," Ginny pressed, "is it done here? Is it legal in Florida?"

Mr. McCue scratched his thumbnail across the grain of the table top. He could see where this was leading. Ginny saw it working across his face. Furniture still crated, eating in the kitchen, what else could you expect? "Yes, it's done sometimes. It's not illegal."

Ginny refilled Mr. McCue's tea glass. "Good, then I want Paul cremated, as soon as possible."

"There's papers to be filled out. That's the law," he said, dropping for good what Ginny was sure he thought of as his parlor manners. He went out to his car and when he came back, he dropped a legal form on the kitchen table without comment.

The form was headed *Declaration of Intent to Cremate Human Remains* with the subtitle *Florida Mortuary and Burial Act of 1928.* It gave Ginny a four-inch line for the justification of said cremation. Ginny paused, the point of the fat, black pen Mr. McCue handed her poised above the paper, then she wrote: *I am going to Paris.*

It just fit.

CHAPTER TWO

WHEN LENA KEPPI had been in labor thirteen hours, she opened her eyes and saw her mother-in-law Odile lift her baby from her. She saw Odile's webbed hand touched with her blood, then she saw her son's hand was webbed too. In that tiny hand, Lena saw her future. There had always been Keppis in Alsace, before Caesar, before anything. But she, fresh from Germany, full of plans for owning a house, a vineyard, anything, everything, would not get to stay. It was July 27, 1906.

As Odile held Roland out to Lena, her hand holding his hand, she saw what Lena saw. "It's better for you to go. No one has ever been happy here. It was a mistake even for us to have stayed."

Then Lena finally believed what everyone had told her about Odile Keppi, about the whole Keppi family—that they knew things they had no way of knowing. Lena looked at her son's closed eyes, afraid of what was behind them. When Roland opened his blue eyes and then cried, she held him away from her, refused to nurse him. He cried until the milk wept from her breasts, until his hair, which was as white and transparent as her own, took on the color of his swollen face and shone as red as a Scot's. Lena gave in to her son, but she made up her mind that one Keppi taking what she had to give was enough. She would not let her husband Max touch her again, though his hands were perfectly normal in every way. Lena refused to change her mind, although Max pleaded with her much longer than Roland had cried.

Even after Lena bound up her breasts, she did not relent. Once when she was talking to a German friend, she pointed at Max and Roland and Odile coming up the hill and said, loud enough for them to hear, "Look at them! They're not a family, they're a line of ducks!" It didn't matter that to please her Max spelled his name *Kepper* and spoke good German, not Alsatian dialect, even to Odile. Lena refused to think of him as German or as her husband. Gradually, Max lost the roundness of arm and face he once shared with his blond German wife. "Skinny as a mink," Lena said with disgust as she took in Max's trousers, as if his Germanness were melting away along with his stomach.

Then one Saturday in 1912, on Roland's sixth birthday, Max didn't come home. Two days later, Lena got a letter posted in Strassburg saying Max had joined the Kaiser's army to prove himself to her. "Who knew?" Lena said, and then she forgave him, although he was too far away training in Karlsruhe for this to do him much good.

Odile Keppi just shook her head. She couldn't believe she could raise a son so stupid that he *volunteered* for the army when there was going to be a war, when there was always going to be a war. Roland, following after her holding her skirt, shook his head too, maybe like a monkey, maybe because he knew what his grandmother knew. Odile was a Keppi who had married a Keppi. Her grandmother had had the Keppi hand, her great uncle, her great-great grandmother. People in that part of Alsace generally had long memories stretching back through several rounds of French and German occupations, but no one knew the past better than Odile. When Roland slept in her arms as she sat by her door, her webbed hand resting on his round head, his webbed hand tucked under a long, warm breast, they both saw armies rise from the mud only to sink down again. It was almost restful to see such things, asleep in his grandmother's lap, her breath warm on his head.

The idea of her son in the army upset Odile so much she stayed awake watching as the soldiers in her visions rose and fell. She tried to watch for faces she knew, for Max. She saw her husband Odilon, but he had died at home in their bed, not on the battlefield. She saw Henri Lahr, who had been her father's best friend, get shot in the neck, and her Uncle Jean, one foot already gone, being loaded on a wagon. That was old news. Uncle Jean had died falling down a flight of stairs years after his leg was cut off. She strained to see all the soldiers as they lay in the mud. It was so terrible for them to lie there alone, their mothers and wives as far away as heaven itself. It drove her out of her house. Roland went with her, holding tight to her hand. She went into houses up and down the hill, her webbed hand fluttering in front of her like a fan.

They should roll bandages, she told her neighbors, wash the walls down with lye, empty their parlors to make room for the beds—they would need beds. They should store food in the mine shafts. Sometimes she spoke in German, sometimes in Alsatian, sometimes even in her rusty schoolgirl French, which under German rule was dangerous. It wasn't always clear to her which war was coming, which war was past.

Finally, it was the authorities who came, two soldiers and a sergeant from Strassburg. "You can't go around saying there'll be a war, worrying people who have sons," the sergeant told Odile. "You have a son yourself serving the Kaiser. Why do you do this?" The sergeant had brought the two men with him because he thought from the reports they'd received from the woman next door that he had an important agitator to arrest. When he saw a skinny old woman helping a small boy fill mercurochrome bottles in the kitchen, he was sorry he'd come. But he had, so a report would have to be made, and he couldn't report that he had done nothing. He called Lena into the kitchen. How could she let her mother-in-law be such a bad example for her little son? Lena turned as red as the mercurochrome.

Roland didn't notice. The concentration it took to get the liquid through the neck of the funnel and into each small bottle cut him off from the world. When the last bottle was full, he pushed in the stopper and looked up. The sergeant had sent his mother to pack her son a change of clothes. There was a school for the children of soldiers, it seemed, and as far as the Kaiser was concerned, that was where Roland belonged. Odile Keppi looked at her grandson, his hands only slightly stained from the mercurochrome. What a fine scientist he would make! Because of this last thought, she kissed him formally on each cheek as if she were giving him a medal instead of hugging him good-bye.

One of the two soldiers took Roland's box of clothes. The other took his hand. Together they marched him to the train station, stood with him while the sergeant bought tickets. When the train came, the two soldiers helped Roland up into the car and sat beside him on one of the hard wooden benches. They let Roland sit by the window. The sergeant stood frowning at them from the platform. One of the soldiers waved as the train pulled out, but the sergeant didn't wave back. Roland held tight to his seat as the station slid backward, as the Protestant, then the Catholic, graveyard slid by. He pressed his face to the window as the hill under Odile's house shrank smaller and smaller until it was too small to see. The soldier next to him patted Roland's knee and cut him a slice of green apple.

"There, there," he said, and when Roland ate the sour apple without crying, "That's a good soldier." Outside Roland's window, green hills rose into steep vineyards, then dark mountains, but on the other side of the train the land was flat with wheat, stretching away to a single row of trees. "The Rhine," the soldier said, pointing at some spot past the border of trees, "and beyond the Rhine—Germany."

The train rocked the two soldiers asleep, their heads falling forward, but Roland kept watch all through the long afternoon. The train passed through town after town, each with two steeples, one Protestant, one Catholic, two sets of bells to ring in each hour. From a distance, any one of them could have been Hexwiller. Each time his heart rose a little, then fell. The train had not turned around. He was not home.

Because the men who took him from Hexwiller were soldiers, Roland thought they were taking him to his father. He often dreamed of Max. In one dream, he'd seen his father stop at the top of a flight of stairs to pat a strange boy on the head, and Roland knew his father did this because he had a son.

In the late afternoon when the train crossed a flooded river and stopped at a station that wasn't much more than a shed, Roland began to doubt that these men knew his father at all. The soldiers got off the train with him, and then one of them gave Roland's box of clothes to another man, a huge stranger. The stranger handed the box of clothes to Roland and walked away from the station without a word. One of the soldiers gave him a little shove, and Roland followed the stranger. They walked in silence. The road climbed a low hill. Roland stared at the man's broad back. He was wearing a uniform with braid and metal buttons like the soldiers', but he had a great beret flopped over his head like a slab of black bread. Just when the box became so heavy Roland was sure he would have to set it down in the ditch, leave behind his clean shirts that still smelled of Odile's house, the man in the beret turned onto a drive lined with trees.

From the first moment Roland saw the drive cutting between the two rows of trees, their trunks white as pillars, it seemed he had always been there, just there, just starting down the drive, the high iron gate waiting at the end, the branches overhead. When Drillmaster Erlanger reached the gate on that first morning, the leaves, still green with only a foreshadowing of yellow, roared over Roland's head in the wind like steam escaping from a train as it came into the station. Later when he marched, drilled endlessly back and forth on the drive, the red leaves fell with a sound like burning. Then came days when the bare branches, each twig coated in ice, popped and clicked like small arms' fire. But when he dreamed of the road, he was always frozen in that first moment at the head of the drive, too scared to hear anything at all.

The school was in a pair of three-story stone buildings beyond the gate. There had been a military school on the hill above the river ford since the time of Louis the Debonair, and from the beginning the school uniform had included the oversized beret. After the German annexation, the Kaiser's inspector of schools made the cadets wear sailors' hats with ribbons, the only German hats available, but one of the teachers had written to the inspector documenting the long history of the school cap. To let it be labeled a *béret* was to let the French steal the rightful cultural heritage of Germanic Alsatians. Besides, the school had hundreds of caps, enough for several generations.

Roland's first stop inside the school was a shed just inside the wall, the quartermaster's office. The fat man inside saluted the drillmaster. Then the quartermaster took the box of shirts away from Roland, shaking his head at his first sight of Roland's webbed hand. He handed Roland a pair of gray wool pants and a jacket with a fake collar attached so it looked like a cadet was wearing a shirt when all he had on was his underwear. Roland got to keep his own underwear and a nightgown Lena had cut down from one of Max's. He had to turn in his shoes, but all the boots he tried on were too big. "Here, Cadet Kepper," the quartermaster said picking out a pair, "stuff a sock in the toe." The last thing the quartermaster gave Roland was his beret. It was the practice for each boy to wear only one beret during his time at the school, and all the berets were the same size. The quartermaster rolled some newspaper inside the band before he put it on Roland's head, but still it swallowed him. One ear and his chin stuck out. From under this wool curtain Roland heard a sound like pebbles on glass. The drillmaster was laughing. "You'll grow into it, boy," he said. "They always do."

Drillmaster Erlanger took Roland back outside. A hundred boys had appeared from somewhere and were standing in formation. They all looked older than Roland. The drillmaster placed him at the end of the last rank, next to a dark-haired boy with ears as big as shoes. The ranks turned sharply on heel and to the left flank marched, and Roland managed to follow the big ears into the mess hall to what seemed like his place at the end of the last of the five long tables. Steaming bowls of cucumbers and potatoes and baskets of dark bread were passed from the quartermaster at the head of the table, boy to boy, down each side, but the food didn't get past the boy with the ears who seemed not to realize Roland was there. "Hello," Roland said. The boy turned and looked at him, breadbasket in hand.

"Don't let René Fuss snub you," said an older boy on the other side of the table.

"I," said Fuss, his ears turning as red as meat, "am one hundred percent German."

"Ha," said the older boy, "then what are you doing here, Bladder Ears?" Fuss put the bread down to make a fist. Roland grabbed at a piece, but Fuss caught his wrist. The fine skin between Roland's fingers shone as pale as butter against the bread's dark crust.

"Frog Fingers," Fuss said in what seemed to Roland an oddly friendly, even affectionate tone. "What do you know."

Roland's rank slept in a long attic room where each boy had a bed and a trunk and a picture of the Kaiser. Roland settled into the gentle valleys of his mattress, his body taking on the curled shape of all the boys who'd slept there. Fuss punched him twice on his way to bed at lights out. "Sleep tight, Frog," he said.

In the middle of the night Roland went to the toilet, and when he came back, he couldn't find his bed. Moonlight made the beds look white and empty. He froze. The quartermaster, coming in to count heads, found him, and taking him by the collar of his nightgown with the casual care of a mother cat, slung him into his bed. Roland squeezed his left hand to his chest, feeling the blood that ran in the skin between his fingers beat in time with his heart. Then, with his eyes closed, he saw Odile. She was sitting at the kitchen table with the lamp lit, eating and worrying about him. He watched as she rolled radish after radish in salt and bit them off just at the stem.

In the morning, Fuss woke him up by punching him in the head, cheerfully, violently. "Jump, Frog," he said.

After breakfast, the cadets marched in ranks from the mess hall to their classrooms. Roland sat next to Fuss there too, in the front row facing a chalkboard and a huge map. The instructor, Herr Epfig, gave Roland a textbook opened to yet another map, one covered with circles and arrows. "You missed the Punic Wars," he said. "Now we're with Caesar in Gaul."

The arrows were troop movements, the circles troop positions. When Roland had watched armies from Odile's lap, it had seemed part of the natural order, or lack of order, like rain sometimes coming as hail and sometimes as snow. He never imagined that anyone had planned which men would die in the fields beyond Hexwiller.

"Caesar crossed the Rubicon," Herr Epfig said, and Roland, sitting with his text open in front of him, saw water in place of the map.

"The river was deep," Roland said. Herr Epfig took it as a question.

"When and where to ford a river is an important tactical considera- tion," he said. Fuss kicked Roland under the desk and gave him a look so full of love and dislike it reminded Roland of Lena.

It turned out Roland, at seven, was the youngest boy in the school. For the first two days, the Drillmaster did not give him demerits. No one yelled at him. Roland guessed these were the privileges of the youngest. Fuss had been the youngest cadet before he arrived, so Roland could understand why Fuss hadn't been glad to see him. Roland knew he wouldn't stay the youngest cadet either, but when the gates opened on the morning of the third day to let in a new boy, Roland was stunned at the sight of him. He was more than small, he was tiny—tiny and beau- tiful. His name was Louis Dumien.

"A putto," said Herr Epfig. "A marzipan boy."

Roland looked at Dumien, at his curls of gold hair, soft as a spaniel's, the blue eyes, pink cheeks. Roland thought of his own hair, yellow as straw. His eyes the blue of wash water. He stood stiff with the realiza- tion of his ugliness. He *was* a frog, and Fuss next to him, his ears red with humiliation, was as ugly as liver.

"Look at him," Fuss said, as if Roland wasn't looking already. "He's a . . ." Fuss said, his eyes searching Dumien for some imperfection, "a . . ." The drillmaster pointed to the end of the last rank, to a spot half a paving stone to Roland's left, and Dumien, seeing his place in the world for the first time, smiled at Fuss and Roland. "A . . . Butter Boy," Fuss said, loud enough for Dumien to hear.

Roland passed Dumien the bread at supper and earned a poisonous look from Fuss. "Roland?" Dumien asked, taking the basket, "am I made of butter?" That was how Roland discovered that Dumien believed every word he was told. The teachers and masters loved him for it.

If the drillmaster said, "God has chosen the Kaiser," Dumien believed.

If Herr Epfig said, "The gods chose Julius Caesar," Dumien believed.

If the chaplain said, "God chose the Jews for his people," Dumien believed. He was a bottomless kettle of faith.

Roland tested him. He told him one of his dreams. "I saw my grand-mama Odile last night," Roland said as they marched back and forth on the drive between the trees. Dumien nodded. Dumien believed. "She was making daub for the chicken coop. One part mud. One part manure—not chicken, cow. One part straw. And she killed the old white hen. With an ax, not like usual when she swings it over her head. One part blood."

"One part blood," Dumien said, his blue eyes serious.

Roland tried to talk only when they were marching toward the station and Dumien was ahead of him, but Fuss's big ears caught a word or two anyway. "Your granny's the one who's a dead old bird," Fuss said.

"Odile's dead, Roland?" Dumien asked, believing even Fuss.

Roland touched his webbed hand to Dumien's jacket. He felt Fuss smiling at his back, imagining a quick push and Dumien on the ground. But Roland only brushed the rough wool and saw in Dumien a mirrored globe like a Christmas ornament reflecting a thousand faces, all tiny, all smiling. He saw his own face and Fuss's, the chaplain's and the drill-master's. He saw a soldier and Herr Epfig and a woman with a face like Dumien's. Everyone but Dumien. Then Fuss shoved Roland, and the three of them fell in the yellow road. They all got demerits.

The next morning in chapel, they had to stand with stacks of prayer books in their bent arms while the chaplain preached God's love for all sinners. Dumien wept. Fuss stood on Roland's foot. Roland wasn't sure what difference it made that God loved Fuss and Dumien and Drillmaster Erlanger. That made love a big plan, like war. If God loved everyone on earth, it wasn't exactly as though he loved you.

On Sundays after chapel, all the cadets at the school were supposed to write a letter home. Fuss said he did, but Roland never saw him. Dumien certainly didn't. Roland guessed they had no one to write to. In his letters home, Roland sent Lena lists of the battles he'd studied and what he was eating. Lena sent back a week's worth of clippings from a hygiene column that ran in the German paper. Roland gave the clippings to Fuss after he'd read them. He didn't let Dumien see them. He was afraid Dumien would take the advice to chew forty times and sleep with your hands straight at your sides.

Odile couldn't read or write, but she got a neighbor to write a letter for her. She had killed the last goose. There were four chickens left. She was worried about Max.

Since Odile couldn't read, Roland sent her pictures he'd drawn from his dreams, scenes from home that came to him as he slept with his Keppi hand next to his heart. He drew Lena's goat who got loose and ate the robes off Saint Odile in her shrine on the edge of town. "That goat must think he's the Kaiser," Odile said when she saw him, "he's eating up Alsace." Roland printed the words across the top of the picture like a cloud, drew Odile's laughter flying from her like birds. Lena, his mother, had not laughed.

Odile sent a note: *Your mother is too German to have a sense of humor. You should watch out for this in yourself.* Lena sent more clippings. Across the bottom of one she wrote: *Alsace has no culture.*

For his birthday, Lena sent a letter full of her own advice, although it sounded much like the hygiene column's. *You are eight now, a little man, and should begin to act like a gentleman and an officer. Who knows? You might become one.* Perhaps because of his birthday, Lena sent on a secondhand letter from his father. Max wrote he had been promoted to corporal and that he was in charge of a mess wagon. Not bad work, he said, although it was harder to eat the stew when you saw what went in it. Lena had crossed out Max's last lines with a heavy black pencil, but Max's pen had cut deep into the paper, and Roland could still read his father's words to his wife. *At night,* Max wrote to Lena, *I forget the stew and dream I taste your breasts.* Fuss, who was reading over Roland's shoulder, squealed when he saw that. "Breasts!" he said, slapping Roland hard on the back. "That's what babies want—not German men."

Four days after his father's letter, Roland took his place in Herr Epfig's room to find he was facing not a map of ancient Gaul, but one of Germany, Belgium, France. Red arrows poured down from Aachen into Belgium. "The army has moved into Belgium to defend Belgium from France," Herr Epfig said. It was August 1, 1914.

War.

Max. Roland sent the thought up like a reconnaissance balloon. Where was his father?

CHAPTER THREE

G INNY'S TRAIN DELIVERED her into the great arched shelter of the Gare St. Lazare. She stood on the platform holding her overnight case, almost expecting someone to meet her. The concrete vibrated with the engines, the air, with French voices. Yet it was oddly still in the huge train shed. Only a few people moved across the platforms to the arches that appeared to let into the station. Facing her through the right arch, a crowd stood shoulder to shoulder, their faces upturned toward something she couldn't see. The platform shook with the approach of a train, and a murmur went through the crowd. Arms rose to point at something. Then they ran—all at once—old men, women with babies, businessmen with watches still open in their hands. Their feet made the concrete ring. The platform shook the way the old bridge had the day the DeSoto boys crossed it on their way to the Great War, the war her mother had believed would end in Armageddon. Human feet sent shock waves, Dr. Love had told her class, that could make buildings collapse. The train squealed into the station. Ginny began to walk toward the arch. Someone caught her at the elbow. She turned.

"Madame," the lips of a small man in a blue uniform formed the word. A porter. The noise died down as the crowd pushed onto the newly arrived train. The porter held her right elbow, and the overnight case weighed down her left hand.

"Why?" Ginny asked, her first French word squeezing out without thought. She pointed with her chin at the new crowd already forming in the arch.

"Ah," the porter nodded. "They wait for the track number," he said slowly. "A boy writes," the porter mimed large numbers in the air, "writes it on a board."

Ginny nodded. It had started. A new world in a new language. The porter had spoken slowly and still stared at her as if trying to gauge her degree of understanding. Even if he had spoken to her as a foreigner, she had understood. Her French from the academy was there, waiting to be called up.

The porter tugged at her elbow. She looked from his hand to his face. She couldn't see his hair under his cap, but his eyebrows were pale, his face broad and pink. He didn't look French. He looked like one of Papa Ben's patients, like a Florida dirt farmer. But his mouth had a distinctly French pucker—from the vowels. His mouth moved. "Excuse me?" she asked, not quite hearing.

"Madame has," he said, holding tight to her elbow to command her attention, "luggage does she not?"

Ginny nodded. "A trunk."

The porter returned her nod and made a grab for the overnight case in her other hand. "No," Ginny said, holding the case at arm's length. The funeral home had held Paul's body for three days before the cremation—in case of an autopsy. After that, he was hers to put into the only urn Mr. McCue had on hand and from there into her overnight case. The porter spread his fingers out stiff, as if he'd been electrically shocked, to illustrate his offense.

At Grand Central Station in New York, she had only to tell the porter she was booked on the *Île de France*, and her trunk had gotten there almost as quickly as she had in a taxi, but now she didn't know where she was going. She hadn't booked a hotel, and at eleven in the morning, her trunk needed a place to stay worse than she did. "Madame wants her trunk," Ginny took her first step in the French future, "tomorrow." The porter dropped his offended hand and nodded. "This is possible?" she pressed.

"Yes," the porter nodded again, his hand rising again, this time palm open. Ginny wondered if it were true that the revolution in Russia had done away with tipping. It was a constant puzzle, buying minutes of people's time. On the train to New York, she'd asked the Pullman porter what she should tip.

"Well, ma'am," he said, looking at her as if he half suspected her of being a Pullman spy, "you don't have to tip at all. You bought and paid for Pullman service."

"But I want to."

"Fifty cents and no one'll say anything bad about you. Two dollars, and everybody'll remember your name when you ride home."

"I'm not going back to Florida."

"Well, then," he'd looked hard at her. "A dollar, I'd say."

Ginny opened her purse, picked out a one franc coin, and held it up for the porter to see. He hesitated, then with a well-if-Madame-has-only-one-trunk shrug, he took it. He made one last halfhearted grab at her case, then he shrugged again and wrote her name in his notebook. "I'll send for it," she said.

Ginny walked through the arches into the train station. Now, at the end of her trip, she was almost used to train stations, to the air of panic that was all traveling and timetables and not real terror. In Jacksonville, Mrs. Corbet had taken her to the station in Paul's Reo, a *For Sale* sign already in its window. Without Mrs. Corbet she could never have gotten packed up so quickly. It was Mrs. Corbet who had helped her put Paul's house up for sale. After Paul's attorney, Mr. Duggin, told Ginny she was getting fifty thousand dollars, more or less, ten thousand available in cash, it was Mrs. Corbet who helped her decide that she should take five hundred dollars with her and have the rest of the money wired on to Paris. "You'll need cash," Mrs. Corbet said, "if you spot a good business opportunity."

But it was Ginny who insisted on taking time between the lawyer and the bank to shop at Cohn Brothers' for a mourning suit. The saleslady measured Ginny's waist, bust, then brought out a short straight mourning dress. "Widow's weeds for the *It Girl*," Mrs. Corbet said. Ginny shook her head, remembering the sweeping black skirts and hats heavy with veiling the Yankee widows down for the winter had worn in DeSoto.

"It's all we have made up in your size, honey," the saleslady said with a sigh. "In a party dress, an eight like you would be average, ordinary, but most mourning is cut for a body type that's, well," she looked at Mrs. Corbet, a stocky size sixteen, "more mature." Ginny put on the dress and stood as the saleslady tugged at the short skirt, her lips pressed thin, worried that she'd somehow offended her customer.

But Ginny knew her body was average. She knew because she'd never had to hem the dresses her mother bought ready made and because the size of her breasts did not provoke casual comment. She was consciously grateful for her body's invisibility. If only her hair were brown like her mother's instead of red like Papa Ben's, no one would ever stare at her.

The saleslady balanced a black hat with a slight wisp of veiling on Ginny's head. "What positively brilliant hair you have, honey!" she said. Ginny blushed, pulling the veil down until as little as possible of her hair showed. She turned in her new black to face Mrs. Corbet.

"It's not the etiquette," Ginny said thinking about her schoolgirl's uniform at the academy, her student nurse's at Jacksonville Memorial. "It's just that it's easier if what you wear fits who you are." For once, she knew who she was. She was Paul's widow.

"Well," Mrs. Corbet said, shaking her head, "I guess black's about the best protection a woman can pay cash for."

The saleslady had helped Ginny choose a black slip and corselet, a pair each of black kid and cotton gloves, a black coat heavy enough for a winter in Paris.

Now, in Paris, she felt a clear assurance, sharp as glass. She knew what she had to do first. She had to find a cemetery for Paul. She crossed the marble floor to the station newsstand and asked for a map of the city. The agent handed her one the size of a handkerchief. She shook her head. He nodded his and, taking back the first map, handed her a small book almost an inch thick. *Paris: Arrondissement by Arrondissement*. She remembered her French teacher, Madame Duval, explaining that an arrondissement was like a complete town inside the city, a home town. Wherever Paul was buried, that would be her arrondissement, and she would be tied to that neighborhood the way a good dog was bound by love and loyalty to its family's yard. She would learn to know it well enough to see how it changed, season to season, regime to regime.

She would find a school or nursery full of toddling, still round children and volunteer to help. Take up where Fanny had left off in Martinique, teaching them to love color, letting the little girls correct her French like miniature Madame Duvals. As she held the book, Ginny felt a glow starting inside her, a firefly that moved now behind her eyes, now down to touch her ribs. She'd felt the same warmth when Paul had touched her in her hospital bed. It was a warmth that said the past could just disappear and be replaced by the future. Jacksonville had turned DeSoto into history. Now, Paris banished Jacksonville, Dr. Thornton, that mortician, Mrs. Corbet. But not Paul. She carried him with her.

Ginny looked up at the fresh papers hanging from the newsstand.

The agent took a cigarette out of his mouth. "Is the book what you wanted?" She smiled at the agent with a warmth that came from the warmth she felt. She asked him if there were a good cemetery nearby. He took a pencil stub from behind his ear, opened the book and drew a circle. *Cimetière de Montmartre.*

She remembered Montmartre from a song they had learned in French class—it was where Saint Denis had his head cut off, tucked it under his arm and walked with his head still singing all the way to where the great abbey church of Saint Denis would be raised in his honor. A long, dead walk, according to her new map, from the Mount of the Martyrs.

"I go to the cemetery tomorrow," she said. The agent, his face shadowed by newspapers, nodded without surprise.

Actually, she went right after she bought the book. In the back were plans for the underground railways, and it was an easy trip to Montmartre with no changes from one spidery route to another. She got off at the stop called *Abbesses* and climbed a flight of wide stairs to the street above, coming out under a pair of street lights bent like giant grasshoppers. Her fingers were stiff from the weight of Paul's urn, the ten pounds of marble that held his ashes. She shifted the handle to her right hand. It was time to be practical. She would find a hotel, leave Paul in her room, and arrange to send for her trunk before she went to investigate the cemetery.

But was this the sort of neighborhood where there were hotels? Ginny realized she had no idea what kind of neighborhoods were likely to have hotels, in Paris or anywhere. The buildings she could see all looked the same, four or five stories of stone broken here and there by balconies. She stood on the base of one of the street lights, trying to spot a hotel sign. She thought she saw a sign to the left, down a narrow street. Left it is, she decided, then jumped down off the light, thinking suddenly of French policemen.

The sidewalk sloped down toward the sign, and she could feel it in her calves. Florida was so flat, she had never realized it was almost as hard to walk downhill as up. But it felt good to be outside, to be walking. She had been stuck inside her tiny third class cabin during what had turned out to be a rough fall crossing on the *Île de France*. She might as well have had herself packed and shipped for all she'd seen. Now walking made distance real.

The ground floors of the buildings were storefronts, their windows painted with signs. Reading them made Ginny realize all over again where she was. First came what looked like a bar, or rather, she thought, a *café*. There were metal chairs and a table chained to a ring set in the sidewalk, and the air smelled like cigarettes. Then a restaurant called the Gargantua, though it didn't seem large. The specials were posted by the door — one a kind of chicken, the other something with peas. Next was a bakery, doors wide open. The smell made Ginny hungry, but she was already in front of the hotel. It was in a narrow building, barely a room wide, but the sign read, *Le Grand Hôtel de Montmartre*. She was tempted to laugh, but she wasn't sure she knew enough French yet to have a sense of humor in it. The door was open, and a middle-aged woman was sweeping out the dust from the hall to join the dust on the sidewalk.

"Good morning," Ginny called. The woman, wearing a robe and a pair of men's slippers, stepped out onto the stoop. She looked down at Ginny and shrugged her shoulders in a way that made the movement a question. Her hair was the faded red of a very old dachshund, hardly red at all. If she lived long enough, Ginny wondered, would hers fade like that? Ginny wasn't sure she wanted it to. "I'd like a room," Ginny said, remembering what she'd come for. "Your least expensive." She didn't want to spend too much, not before she knew how much it would cost to bury Paul, to live day to day.

The woman shrugged, this time in a resigned way that seemed the opposite of questioning. "You can have it," she said.

"How much?"

"Fifteen francs complete."

"Complete with what?"

"Sheets," the woman said. "Breakfast is extra." Ginny made a quick calculation. At twenty-five francs to the dollar, fifteen francs was only sixty cents a night. Ginny followed the woman inside, took the key with the round brass tag she offered her.

"Room sixteen?" Ginny read off the tag.

"No," the woman shook her head. "Regretfully, it is now room seventeen." She sighed as if at misfortune.

Ginny found the room up one flight of stairs. The door was indeed labeled *17*, though only with a cardboard sign. It was a small room. A narrow bed and a small dresser took up most of the space, but she guessed it had once been larger. One wall seemed to be made of blue flowered wallpaper, and someone was snoring on the other side. Ginny opened the overnight case. Paul's urn lay wedged in by her nightgown. The urn was an unfortunate green, the marble streaked like moldy bread. She touched it with one finger. She didn't feel right about leaving Paul here alone. She closed the case. She would take him with her.

It was then she noticed the can of sulfur powder sitting on the bedside table. Ginny knew what her mother used that for—bedbugs. She pulled back the sheet and searched the mattress carefully, checking around the buttons which fastened the ticking to the cotton batting, but no tiny red spots fled her fingers as she probed the mattress, the pillow.

Downstairs, the woman shrugged. "Ah," she said, "a mere precaution. This arrondissement may be filled with hotels run by Algerians for Algerians, Spaniards for Spaniards, Italians for Italians, but Le Grand Hôtel de Montmartre is a French hotel," she waved a fine thin hand at the lobby, "that just happens to be filled with Algerians, Spaniards, and Italians." She smiled at Ginny for the first time. "I should know—I am Madame Desnos, the proprietor of this, the Grand Hôtel." Ginny gave Madame Desnos the money for the room.

"I'm going to the cemetery," Ginny said.

"You have a husband in the cemetery, madame?"

"Not yet," Ginny said, "but I plan to." Madame Desnos nodded sympathetically. She agreed to send for the trunk. "I'll be back this evening," Ginny said.

But she did not go straight to the cemetery. She climbed up a street lined with fruit markets, followed it until she reached the white pastry domes of Sacré Coeur. Madame Duval had told her students about the lunch pennies she'd given to help build the basilica—a national plea for grace after the Franco-Prussian War. Ginny stood on the marble steps before it, then turned.

For the first time she saw Paris. It was there, hazy and waiting, at the bottom of the hundred stone steps that ran down from her feet. Notre Dame, the Louvre, all the places so famous that even she, even a stranger who'd seen them only in pictures on the walls of her French class, could pick them out from a height. And the miles of stone buildings with lead roofs and terra cotta chimneys. She took the first of the hundred steps down. Only a dozen or so steps below her was a grassy terrace, a landing with two benches where a few people were sitting feeding pigeons and brown sparrows.

One man, his hair a strange yellow in the morning sun, didn't throw crumbs on the ground but held a piece of bread between his fingers. She watched as he changed from a man on a bench into a throbbing cloud of sparrows. She stood on tiptoe, expecting the hundred tiny birds to ascend to heaven with the man's hand still clutched in their feet, their wings pumping furiously. The man would be carried up too, his feet dangling from the storm of sparrows. She waited, a dozen heartbeats, then the birds flew to the earth, not the sky, with their crumbs, and left the yellow-haired man sitting quietly on the bench. She turned away, disappointed, and hurried down the narrow streets that ran toward the cemetery.

The cemetery was larger than it looked on the map. An iron bridge ran over one corner and in its shadow, instead of tombstones like an American cemetery, there were little houses, and past the houses ran cobbled streets. Where one road crossed another, there was a neat green street sign, as if the cemetery paths were avenues, as if the Cimetière de Montmartre were a city, were Paris. She looked through the rusted iron grill of one tomb with the name *SARCY* carved over the door. It looked rather like an elevator inside except for a leaf-clogged altar, a broken stained glass window. On the walls were long rows of names—the Sarcy dead. Husbands and wives and daughters, grandfathers and great grand-fathers, cousins and in-laws. She took a step back. It was too grand. All she needed was something for Paul and, after a while, for herself.

Suddenly Ginny missed Paul, missed him as if she hadn't seen him for a long time, longer than the two weeks he had been dead. She smelled his breath, sweet from a cold Coca-Cola, as he bent over her bed after coming in late from the hospital. She heard again the tired edge in his voice as he told her which patients had lived, which had died. Her heart ached. She held the overnight case tight against her chest. She walked, following the road from the gate deeper into the cemetery, the weight of Paul's urn making him real to her.

The morning of the day she left Jacksonville, Mr. McCue had delivered Paul in his urn to her. When he was gone Ginny had called Aunt Fanny. Fanny had her own cottage at the state hospital in Chatta-hoochee as well as her own nurse, Mrs. Mabes. After all, Fanny'd say to Ginny, I'm not all the way broke or crazy.

Mrs. Mabes had answered the telephone. "Miss Ginny?" she asked. "Are you all right?"

"My husband died, Mrs. Mabes," Ginny said.

"Oh," a sigh from Mrs. Mabes carried over the line, "a telephone never rings for good news does it?"

"Can I talk to my aunt?"

"She's in the hot bath, Miss Ginny, and she can't come out for another half hour. Should I go tell her your husband died?"

"I wanted to tell her that I'm going to Paris."

"Paris? All right, you wait." Ginny heard a door bang.

She sat at the kitchen table, looking past the crates in the living room to her trunk and overnight case by the door—to Paul. The house looked right all packed up, as if it had been waiting to be empty.

A door banged twice. "Ginny? Sweety?" It was Fanny. "Are you all right?"

"I don't know yet, Fanny," Ginny said and felt like she might cry.

She could hear Mrs. Mabes in the background. "You'll catch your death."

"I can't talk long, baby. I'm really not decent. Just remember, when you get discouraged and you want to come home . . ."

"Fanny," Ginny said.

"Don't, you hear? Just don't. I know." The receiver dropped.

"I'll write," Ginny called out.

"Oh, hell," Fanny's voice had come back, "send perfume."

Ginny shook her head. She wished Fanny was here with her in Paris. She would know what sort of monument or tomb was right for Paul, what was merely silly or pretentious.

The road through the cemetery became a circle, straightened out again. Now not all of the tombs Ginny passed were little houses. She passed a marble statue of a soldier saluting. A round pillbox hat was perched on his lifelike head, but he had been cut off at the chest and set on a white pedestal. Ginny hoped that his lack of legs didn't have anything to do with the way he died. Then came another bust, this time a bronze of an artist in smock and beret, brush and palette in one hand. Was it that the dead had no use for legs, for any body part below the waist? She closed her eyes for a moment and tried to imagine a bust of Paul, but all she could see was his name spelled out in her mind, PAUL. Once at the academy she made Mr. Vernon, the art teacher, very unhappy by insisting that when he said *apple,* she did not see a red fruit or taste tart flesh but saw only the letters APPLE in black. Mr. Vernon had been so upset that even now she was a little ashamed of her literalness. All she really wanted was something with Paul's name on it.

She reached the far end of the cemetery and turned right, trailing her fingers along the stone wall. Here were newer graves with simple rectangular stone markers more like the tombstones back home. But rather than standing up, they lay flat like marble mattresses, some black, some white, some rose or purple, the names and dates carved where a pillow should have been. Most had some short sentiment as well—Be At Peace. I Remember. *Paul Gillespie, Beloved Husband.* That might do, Ginny thought.

A few of the tombstones even had photographs, enameled on porcelain, set into their marble. One hand-colored photograph showed a husband and wife, pink-cheeked, blue-eyed, lips red as berry stains. He was holding a flute to his lips, smiling faintly, not playing yet but committed to a tune. The wife was in front of him, staring restlessly beyond the edge of this picture of death.

Ginny stopped in front of one with a black and white porcelain photograph, but no name, no dates. It was the head and shoulders of a young woman, a flapper, wearing only lipstick and long jet beads, a graceful hand poised beneath her chin and her jet, jet eyes. Ginny touched the photograph where it darkened into shadow above the flapper's breasts. How did someone with such passionate eyes die? Perhaps she had gone to a doctor—a doctor like Paul—and something had been found. He would scarcely have looked at her at first, when she came to him still looking like this picture, the object of all other men's desire. But, when her cheeks had thinned, when her eyes became bigger in her drawn face . . .

Ginny started to shake. Paul had come to her at night in the hospital—beloved husband. Held her, stroked her. Running his hands over her fever thin legs, arms, hips until she wanted him so badly she ached. Ginny knew what Paul wanted. Her mother and Papa Ben shared a doctor's matter-of-factness about sex. If it was her parents who had taught her what was biologically natural, it was Paul who made her think she was going to enjoy it. She concentrated on getting well, on getting her body back to being comfortably average. She went at last to live in Paul's house. What had Paul seen then, looking at her? That night he came to her, finally entered her, joined his flesh literally with hers, he held the rungs of the bedstead instead of holding her, imagining someone else, someone with bones as thin as hers had been when she was dying, as bleached clean as those white iron rails. Ginny raised her hand as if to slap the flapper's white face, but she was still holding the case, and she swung it down hard against the marble. Pain shot up her arm. The case sprang open, and the urn hit the ground with a thud.

It wasn't fair. Not fair for Paul to love her only because she was dying, for her mother to love only Jehovah, for Paul to die—go to join the dead he so desired. Damn him. Not fair. She threw the case to the ground beside the urn. She hated Paul. He had refused to love her, abandoned her. Ginny wanted to hit something again. What was she doing here, in this cemetery, in France? They had all tricked her, tricked her into loving them while they gave nothing. Her mother, Paul, . . .

She moaned, then looked around quickly. Some tourists with box cameras turned the corner by the wall. She picked up the urn—still sealed tight, not even scratched—and fled. She went through the gate and up the winding street with its fruit markets. She dug in her heels as she walked, hard enough to make them hurt, but still she wanted to kick someone so badly her legs ached. She threw open the door of the Grand Hôtel.

Madame Desnos looked up, her mouth an O. "Madame's trunk has not . . ." she started. Ginny snatched the key from her so abruptly her fingers snapped.

"Don't talk to me," she warned. Madame Desnos seemed to fold, to disappear out of the corner of her eye as Ginny rushed past, her eyes tight with tears. She made it to her room and shut the door. She was panting. Now she was safe from hurting anyone, from anyone seeing her hurt herself, but her hands shook with the desire to break something. She threw the urn on the bed. It bounced onto the floor. She looked around the room. It seemed to have been designed to frustrate such desires. She swept the lamp off the dresser. It bent where it hit the wall, and the bulb popped, but only softly, almost gently. She threw an empty water carafe against the wall as well. It only thudded dully and landed whole on the carpet. She threw it out the open window. It shattered against the wall of the air shaft, and the pieces rained quietly into the trash below. She lay down on the bed, fists at her sides, eyes shut. She thought about throwing Paul's urn after the carafe. The thought was shocking.

She unclenched her fists, opened her eyes. Above her on the wallpaper was a long, lazy, S-shaped line of bedbugs marching down from their secret home under a loose flap of wallpaper, their trapdoor to her room. She jumped up, grabbed her shoe. Their bodies made tiny red splatters on the blue flowered walls—the blood of the man next door. She brought her shoe against the wall again and again, the heel cutting into her hand where she held it, and soon there was banging from the man in sixteen as well, though whether he was beating the wall for bedbugs or to get her to quit her banging, she didn't try to guess. Finally, she stopped. Then, in one last burst, she threw the open can of sulfur against the wall. Yellow dust splashed over the wallpaper, rose from it in a cloud into the room. She choked, grabbed the pillow from the bed and pressed it to her face for protection—her fingers digging deep into its softness. She sneezed, her head jerked, and the pillow casing gave way in a long rip like a sigh. She watched with amazement as the white feathers floated in the cloud of sulfur, like an angel shot down by a blast from hell.

CHAPTER FOUR

N OW THAT THEY were at war, the drillmaster marched the cadets up and down the drive to the school for three hours each day. When a troop train squealed past, they all jumped. Roland couldn't keep from looking over his shoulder when his back was to the station. The drillmaster slapped him on the back of the head and gave him two demerits, but still Roland looked back, Fuss looked back. It was contagious, this desire to see what was coming. Only Dumien got to the end of the month without demerits.

At night Roland lay in bed thinking of his father. *Max.* Sometimes he felt his call bounce off Odile's. *Max.* He squeezed his webbed hand into a hard fist, feeling the desperate pulse in it, but no dreams of his father came to him.

For a month the map of Belgium and France stayed on Herr Epfig's wall. Battle and victory at Charleroi, at Mons. The army crossed the Marne for Paris. Recrossed the Marne, falling back. Then the map of Gaul reappeared. Caesar was still at war. So, Roland guessed, was the Kaiser, but now the news came from the drillmaster. When he stood before them in the courtyard, he spoke without maps and without detail.

Fuss worried about the lack of news. "I'm German," he said, pulling on one ear. "I deserve to know what's going on."

"A soldier doesn't need to know," Dumien said, parroting the drillmaster. "His officer knows." Roland shook his head, thinking of old Roerich back in Hexwiller and the rabbits he raised for market, what could happen to creatures who trusted too easily those who fed and kept them.

That night after Dumien was asleep, Fuss dangled Dumien's fingers carefully in a bowl of warm water to make him wet his bed. Fuss wanted Dumien to stand extra hours in formation, the usual punishment for anything a cadet did that required an extra set of clean sheets. Dumien opened his eyes. "What are you doing, Fuss?" Dumien asked.

"Trying to get you to piss, Butter Boy."

"Oh," Dumien said, and closing his eyes, fell asleep and soaked the bed.

Fuss was scared that Dumien would tell on him to get out of his punishment. That's what Fuss would have done. So, in the morning before the quartermaster could find Dumien in his wet bed, Fuss went to the infirmary and got the nurse. She came and felt Dumien's forehead. "You are not feeling well?" she asked. She had a peculiar flat way of speaking so that Dumien heard not a question, but a statement of fact. He believed her.

"I am not feeling well," he agreed.

"You are having a pain in the stomach?"

He nodded, and she took him away. During a week in the infirmary, Dumien developed a bewildering array of symptoms. His feet were cold. His head hot. His feet burned. His head was numb. Roland tried to talk him out of it. "Don't listen to Nurse Zimmer," he said. "She's going to get a doctor to cut you open unless you stop listening to her."

"Nurse Zimmer says she knows what's best for sick boys," Dumien said, his eyes as blue as good conduct ribbons. "How can I not believe her?"

"Are you sick?" Roland asked.

"She says I am."

Roland threw up his hands.

Fuss was no help. "He's going to tell. I know it," Fuss said, his ears red as sin. "All they've got to do is ask."

"Tell what?"

"He's going to make it sound like it was all my idea. Damn him. It was his choice—he didn't have to piss."

The first night Dumien was in the infirmary, Fuss, restless with worry, had wandered around until he found a way through a trapdoor at the top of the stairs to the attic and from there up a ladder to the roof. He told Roland he'd picked the lock. "For practice, in case I'm captured." Roland saw that the padlock had been cut a long time before, by other cadets, during some other war.

Roland crawled along the roof with Fuss. They crouched behind the parapet, their backs warmed by a chimney and legs numbed by the cold slate shingles. They kept watch. When the moon came up, they saw the station, its tracks empty, gleaming, waiting. They could see the river, another silver track. A local boy had once been killed listening for a train with his ear to the track. None of the cadets had ever been that stupid, but they were warned time and again about the river. The quartermaster had warned Roland the first time he issued him a new pair of underwear. "Give me that old pair, Cadet Kepper," he said. "I let Cadet Müller keep his, and he snuck down to the river in them," the quartermaster snapped his fingers, "and drowned just like that." Roland had turned his in and fled.

Even when the cadets went on marches with the drillmaster, he kept them well up in the fields where they could only hear the river. "A boy drowned there in '11," the drillmaster shouted over his shoulder to the ranks of boys strung out behind him.

"Cadet Müller?" Roland shouted back.

"What?" The drillmaster turned around, marching backward, to see who had asked. "No," he said. "Müller was the one who drowned in '03." It seemed they always drowned. For centuries the school had taught cadets how to swim in the river. Finally, at the school inspector's insistence, the practice was stopped. Still boys died, snuck down to the river, as if there were no help for it, and drowned.

"I'm going to swim in that river," Fuss said as they watched it from the roof. "I don't believe a word about those stupid cadets." Roland looked down at the silver curves and shook his head. When a war came, it seemed no one could see danger anymore.

Roland tried one more time to make Dumien see. "Nurse Zimmer's gone to the drillmaster for a doctor," he told him. "Please, Dumien," gathering a fistful of his nightshirt, wanting to shake him a little, "believe me instead. Be well." Roland felt Dumien's heart beating and again saw the hundred mirrors in his eyes. This time they reflected only Nurse Zimmer's face and the drillmaster's face. Roland could not see himself at all.

"I must do what I'm told," Dumien said.

That night, Roland finally saw a Keppi in his dreams. Snow was on the ground and snow falling, and a man was falling too. He fell backward, one arm flung up over his head, his breath white in the air, and when he hit the ground, the snow sunk like a pillow. Whoever the man was, he didn't look surprised. He lay perfectly still, his arm over his head, head back, eyes open. Beyond where he lay was a dark line of trees, their branches bent with snow. Roland sat up. He got paper and a pencil. By the light of the moon, he drew the curve of the branches, the curve of the dead man's arm. When the sun came up, he went downstairs and climbed over the gate. The bare trees groaned like boys turning and turning in their beds. At the station he mailed the picture to Odile.

When he got back, Drillmaster Erlanger was standing in the drive. He had his back to Roland, one hand on Dumien's shoulder, talking to him. Roland froze like a rabbit—being off the grounds without permission was good for a lifetime of demerits. "You see, don't you, boy," the drillmaster was saying to Dumien, "why I can't call a doctor out for a cadet—when our brave soldiers might need him more?"

"I see," Dumien said.

"You can be brave?"

"I can be brave."

Out of the corner of his eye, the drillmaster saw Roland. "Kepper?" he said.

"Yes, sir," Roland said, calm in the face of doom.

"Escort our brave Cadet Dumien back to his rank." Roland's arm felt weak as he returned the drillmaster's salute.

"It's a good thing you aren't sick," Roland said when they got inside the gate. "He'd have let you die."

"An officer has to decide who lives and who dies," Dumien said. "It's never easy." They crossed the courtyard.

Roland shook his head. His word was not enough for Dumien. He reached for a higher authority. "I thought it was God who made that kind of decision," he said.

"God?" Dumien asked.

They were walking along the wall of the barracks, and Roland felt a shadow over him, like snow. He looked up and saw a large slate shingle drop out of the sky. It had to be Fuss. He must have seen Dumien talking to the drillmaster. Rat, the slate said. Fink.

The shingle floated through the air. Roland couldn't take his eyes off it. He and Dumien were walking at ease, swaying with each step, Roland this way, Dumien that way. Roland froze.

The slate broke over Roland's head. Roland heard it crack, saw the pieces fly, but he didn't feel a thing. Dumien's mouth dropped open. His eyes were opened so wide they looked lidless, as if he were the one who'd been hit. "Dumien," Roland said, taking him by the shoulders, "talk to me." Dumien only looked at him, his eyes bright with a hundred empty mirrors. Blood stung Roland's eyes, but he could still see Dumien.

Dumien blinked and said, "I should be dead."

"Don't believe it," Roland said and shook him, shook him until Dumien's teeth chattered.

"Shit!" Roland heard someone calling. "Get the nurse!" Roland heard the voice calling again and realized it was Fuss. He looked toward him but couldn't focus. Where the school had been, there were only white spots drifting in front of his eyes like snow. Was this his dream?

Afterward, when he thought about it, Roland remembered sitting in the barber chair in the infirmary while Nurse Zimmer stitched up his head. He remembered seeing Fuss's face in the mirror, watching. But at the time it seemed that he had closed his eyes in the courtyard, and when he opened them again, there was his father sitting on the edge of the bed next to his in the infirmary. He looked like a sad dachshund sitting there, brown eyes, brown hair, soft long nose. He looked like half the men in Hexwiller, like Odile, not much like Roland.

"Papa?" Roland said, speaking to his dream.

Nurse Zimmer appeared. "Ah, good, you are awake. I'll wait outside," she said to Max.

His father was really there. Roland blinked, more surprised by Max's presence than by finding himself alive and awake. He asked his father how long he had been unconscious.

"Three days," Nurse Zimmer said, poised at the door. "But he sat up and ate soup twice," she added to Max, though Roland couldn't remember having done any such thing.

When Nurse Zimmer finally was gone, Max took Roland's drawing out of his pocket, unfolded it on the bed, smoothed it with his hand. He had been in Hexwiller on leave when the letter came for Odile. "What are these?" he asked, pointing to the dark upright lines. Roland looked at the drawing, remembering the details of his dream.

"Fir trees," Roland said. "The edge of a forest."

"And all this?" He touched the blank white paper.

"Snow," Roland said.

Max touched a finger to the tiny man on the page. "Is he dead?"

Roland looked away for a second and then asked, "What did Odile say? Did she see it? Did she know who," he hesitated, looked at the drawing, "who it is?"

"She said forget it." Max held the drawing in one hand. Something about it seemed familiar, something about the angle of the arm, the trees—but not the clean snow. He rode with the mess wagon twice a day up Hartmannswillerkopf to the lines, and there were still fir trees left standing that hadn't been shelled or cut down for huts or fuel. But even the morning after a storm, the snow was always spoiled, turned to mud by wagons, by men stepping into the forest to piss.

Roland didn't like the way his father stared at his drawing. It was like the river, something with its own fascination. If Odile said forget it, then they should forget it. If they did, maybe it wouldn't happen.

Max looked up and saw his son's reflection in the mirror. There was a shaved patch on the top of Roland's head, like a kiss, red with mercurochrome. A bottle of it stood by the mirror. Max refolded the drawing into white squares and put it in his pocket. "Have you heard from your mother?"

"No," Roland said. "Is she all right?"

"I didn't see her," Max said, buttoning his pocket. "She's gone back to Würzburg to live, until we win the war."

"Will that be soon?"

"So they say." Max patted the lump in the covers that was Roland. "So far you're doing a worse job of living through it than me."

Max ate lunch in the mess hall, sitting in the place of honor, at the head of Roland's table where the quartermaster usually sat. "What's your father doing here?" Fuss asked. "Did you write him?"

"He's very handsome," Dumien said.

Watching Max at the other end of the table, brown head nodding, joking with some of the older boys, Roland felt like he was dreaming again. There was this cook, Max was saying, who fell asleep on a mess wagon pulled by a white mule, and the mule just kept going, right through enemy lines. But no one fired a shot because it was dark and the mule looked so much like a ghost none of the gunners wanted to admit they saw it. The boys laughed. It was like seeing Max in his unit, one man among many, pinkly human, perishable. Max waved away the boys' laughter, leaned toward them with one finger raised to make a point. "The best strategy in war is to stay alive." Roland looked at Dumien. He was staring at Max, nodding. For now, Dumien believed.

"Did you tell your father how you got hurt?" Fuss asked. "Did you ask him to get you out of here?"

"Corporal Kepper's come to inspire us," Dumien said.

"Shut up, Butter Boy," Fuss said. "You can't leave, Frog." He squeezed Roland's arm.

Roland thought of the shingle falling through the air toward his head. "I thought you didn't care if I died."

Fuss looked down at the table. "Don't leave me here alone," he said, both ears white.

After lunch, Roland and Dumien walked Max to the drive to catch his train. At the gate, Max shook Roland's hand, Dumien's hand. Roland watched as his father passed between the trees, shrinking, going away. Max raised his arm to wave good-bye, then stopped, recognizing the gesture.

Roland ran. "Papa!"

Max caught him by the shoulders and kissed him hard on each cheek, like a Frenchman, like Odile had done. Roland's head hurt. He was crying. He felt something in his hand, the drawing. The white paper was cold between his fingers, like a snowball instead of just a picture of snow. He felt frozen by it. Max pulled away, and Roland stood unable to move. The branches above ticked like watches. He saw the gray smoke of the train pulling out of the station. Max was gone.

Roland looked back down the road to the school. Dumien was gone. The rest of the cadets were out on an afternoon march. He put the drawing inside his coat. Was death something that could be resisted like sin? At least for a while, like giving up meat at Lent? Roland slipped between the white trunks and into the field beyond. The stubble cracked under his boots. The furrows were lined with ice. He followed them, crossed one field then another, each sloping gently down. He wanted to see the river.

Roland slid down the bank, holding tight to the dried grass. The river wasn't quite frozen. Islands of ice moved on the current, circling the branches in the shallows. He looked into the water beneath the current and ice. The drowned boys were there. They turned slowly over and over in the current, the ice floating over their blond heads like lily pads, like halos. They were all as beautiful as Dumien. Roland put his webbed hand in the water. It burned it was so cold. He spread his fingers. The current pushed at the skin between them, damming up behind his hand. The boys opened their eyes, looked up with slow smiles as if he were their dream. They pushed their streaming hair out of their eyes to see him—curious boys. Their lips trembled, and Roland felt something through his hand, like humming, like breathing. He tried to pull his hand out of the water, but his arm was numb with the cold. The boys reached out to him, their hands opening as slowly as flowers.

Roland stood up taking his arm with him. His hand was blue.

"Left . . . left . . . left, right, left." It was the drillmaster. Roland looked in the water. The drowned boys were almost invisible, curled tight as shells. He crawled up the bank. In the field above the river, the cadets were crunching along behind the drillmaster, lengths of lead pipe slung over their shoulders in place of rifles. Roland saw Fuss, his beret propped up by his ears, wearing a field pack to work off his demerits, but Dumien was missing. Roland waited until they were at the other end of the field, sighting at the horizon with their pipes, and then he ran behind them up the hill.

Dumien wasn't in the courtyard. The door to the infirmary was locked. The toilet empty. "Dumien?" Roland called, his voice rolling over the tightly made beds in the barracks, echoing off the high ceiling.

"Up here!" Dumien called.

The trapdoor was open. Roland climbed onto the roof, blinking in the light of the setting sun. Dumien was standing on the roof looking over the parapet, his hands in his pockets. "What are you doing up here?" Roland asked, taking hold of the waistband of Dumien's trousers.

"I came up looking for you. I thought I heard you calling me," Dumien said, looking down. "Did you go out with the others? Are they back?"

Roland shook his head. "I went to the river."

Dumien looked up, ready to believe. "What river?"

Roland knew he should stop, not tell what he'd seen, not to Dumien, but Dumien's eyes pulled him on, a hundred mirrors in need of truths to reflect. "Over there," Roland said, pointing at the thin silver line at the edge of their world. He opened his mouth, about to tell Dumien about the drowned boys, turning and turning, boys who looked so much like Dumien they could be his brothers, could be him. Roland held his breath. He thought of his drawing. What had he or Max gained from that?

"What did you see?" Dumien asked. The sun's last light fell on them, on the far silver river.

"Nothing but cold, ugly water," Roland said. "It wasn't worth the trip." Down below, the cadets clattered through the gate and into the courtyard.

The next morning, it was Fuss who first noticed Dumien was missing. It was the quartermaster who found him, who dragged him from the river with the hook generations of quartermasters had kept for the purpose. Roland couldn't believe it. It was his fault. Dumien had drowned in his place. And for nothing. Roland remembered his dream again, falling backward into the snow.

"You did it," Fuss said to him, his ears on fire. "You took him down there, didn't you?" They were in the infirmary. Roland thought the quartermaster would take Dumien there, but it was Fuss he found waiting. "You took him yesterday, while we were out marching." Roland tried to back away, out of the room, but Fuss pushed him against the barber chair. "Did he fall in? Or did you push him?"

"No," Roland said. "I don't know." He pulled away from Fuss, and his hand caught the mercurochrome bottle. It exploded on the floor, a red river at Fuss's feet.

"You threw that at me!" Fuss said, astounded.

They both missed Dumien's funeral. Nurse Zimmer locked them in with brushes and a bucket of bleach. They heard the organ start in the chapel. Fuss sat in the barber chair watching Roland. Roland scrubbed hard but the mercurochrome stayed red, an irregular heart spread out on the floor. "You'll have to try harder, Frog," Fuss said. "You wouldn't want me to tell Nurse Zimmer you threw that at me, would you?"

Roland kept scrubbing, the heart wearing away to a kidney, the red to pink. The chapel organ stopped playing, and the cadet drummer started marking time, each beat a heartbeat. The ranks would escort Dumien to the station. The school had no cemetery. It assumed all the boys had someone who would want them dead if not alive. Roland never found out where they sent Dumien. Roland looked over at Fuss. "Go ahead and tell her," Roland said.

Fuss smiled at him, shook his head. "I'd rather punish you myself," he said.

Fuss didn't tell, and Roland felt worse each day. It didn't help that Roland had not done what Fuss accused him of doing. Roland felt guilty—guilty of more things than Fuss knew. He shouldn't have let Dumien see the river. He shouldn't have made the drawing.

Roland stopped being able to sleep. He lay awake trying to remember how to fall asleep. He tried to see Dumien, but Dumien stayed both dead and gone. He tried to see his father, but Max too kept away, as if afraid of the bad luck Roland brought. Night after night he lay awake, not even Odile coming to him. Once, he fell asleep only to dream of Fuss. Fuss was telling the drillmaster that Roland had drowned Dumien, showing how he held him under water. His ears were like flames. Nurse Zimmer and Herr Epfig and the quartermaster and all the long ranks of cadets pointed at Roland. *You're not German,* they shouted in unison. *I confess,* he said, relieved. *I confess I'm not German.*

For the next three years, Roland tried hard not to feel anything at all. Later, when he got drunk for the first time in his life, he recognized the numbness. He grew taller, learned the formula for aiming field artillery. Only in geometry class was he happy. Sitting with his eyes closed, he watched equations turn to pyramids, squares, a kind of dream that hurt no one. At night he lay awake, looking at the drawing, worrying about Max. He stared at it until the pencilled lines stopped making sense. He folded and unfolded the white paper until it was soft as a handkerchief.

One day, he looked down the ranks and was surprised to see that he and Fuss were about halfway between the seven-year-olds in the last rank and the sixteen-year-olds in the first. He was eleven. Fuss was twelve. There were two dozen new cadets whose names he didn't know or couldn't remember.

One of the new boys brought lice, and the quartermaster had the barber chair carried outside and the cadets lined up to have their heads shaved. "This is war," he declared. The mirror wasn't carried outside with the chair, but the first boy he shaved was mirror enough. The cadet hair, red and brown and blond, fell in soft piles on the ground. The hair was raked and burned like leaves. Their berets were washed in lye soap and laid out like land mines to dry in the courtyard.

In spite of these precautions, a fever went through the school that summer. Lungs filled with water, and the boys turned blue as they sat at their lessons, drowning inside their own bodies. A dozen went to the infirmary and didn't come back. Nurse Zimmer thought it was the new influenza—no doctor ever came—and so many died at once that the school got its first cemetery beside the drive under the white trees, close enough for the bootfalls of the drilling cadets to jar the dead. Roland looked to his right and thought, *Fuss. Fuss is still alive.* It didn't make him happy.

Then, one morning during breakfast, the drillmaster came into the mess. "Go to bed," he said. Roland looked down at the bread and hot milk in front of him to make sure he wasn't confused—it was breakfast. "Now!" said the drillmaster.

The cadets lay on their beds in full uniform. About noon, Herr Epfig came to check on them. "What about lunch?" Fuss asked.

"Sleep is the food of the gods," Herr Epfig said. Some of the cadets kicked off their boots, loosened their collars.

"What's going on?" Fuss asked.

"Nothing you can do anything about," Herr Epfig said and left them with that.

Sometime after they weren't fed dinner, Roland fell asleep. All through the long afternoon he'd listened to Fuss's heavy breathing. Then it was quiet, and he was asleep, asleep somewhere dark and as still as ice. Exquisite. Roland wept with relief. Something poked him in his chest, something small and round like the end of a pencil. He shifted, but it didn't go away. He fought to stay asleep, but all he could feel was the pencil, the circle of pressure. *Fuss,* he thought. *It must be Fuss.* He sat up.

It was dark. Fuss was asleep on his bed. Roland still felt the point pressing just under his heart. He touched the spot. There was nothing. He went to the toilet. He started to piss, but the pain became sharper. He held onto the wall. Something had happened.

*   *   *

Max had almost forgotten the drawing. The war had gotten muddier and more treeless, and the death in the drawing seemed unlikely. Then one of the cooks told him a colonel was outside the mess asking for him. A real kraut, the cook called him.

"Corporal Kepper?" the colonel said. "My name is Rettig. Your wife asked me to look you up. I'm an old friend of the family." Max wasn't sure he believed him, but he couldn't think of any other reason a colonel would go out of his way to talk to him. They talked about the weather—cold, damp—and the terrible smell coming out of the mess. A very elderly ram, Max explained. It was hard to get any meat. "Ah," the colonel said, "I know where a farmer has a draft horse. Fat." He showed Max where the farm was on the field map. Maybe he could shoot some rabbits on the way, the colonel suggested. "Auf Wiedersehen," the colonel called out as he left. "Good hunting."

Max went, but he didn't take a gun. Maybe he didn't feel like killing anything. Maybe he realized he wouldn't get a chance. The fields of the farm were white with deep snow. Taking in the pure whiteness of it, Max threw up a hand, as if to ask a question. The bullet went in a little below his heart. As he fell, Max bent his wrist just so—to match Roland's drawing. He saw the fir trees behind him, and then he saw nothing at all.

*   *   *

"Roland?" It was Fuss knocking on the door of the toilet. "Are you in there?" Roland straightened up. It was very dark. Not a light was burning in the school.

"I'm here," he said and opened the door.

Fuss put a hand on his arm. "Let's go up on the roof." Roland hadn't gone on the roof since he had been there with Dumien. He hadn't wanted to, and Fuss hadn't asked. "I want to see what's going on," Fuss said. Roland touched the spot under his heart. Something was still there, a ghost of pain, a warning.

"Why?" Roland asked.

"I think the war's over."

Fuss climbed through the trapdoor and up the ladder onto the roof, and after a moment, Roland followed him. Cold air blew across his face. It was a dark night. There was no moon and even the stars seemed dim. "See anything?" Roland asked. His bare feet slid a little on the slate shingles.

"No," Fuss said. He gave Roland his hand. Fuss's palm was sweaty with fear, old fear. And then Roland saw it—Fuss and Dumien hand in hand, sliding across the frozen field, down the river bank in the dead of night.

"You," Roland said, "you took Dumien to the river. He didn't go by himself. You took him."

Fuss yanked his hand away. Roland lost his balance, fell forward.

Fuss grabbed for him, hesitating only a second, just as he had when Dumien walked into the river, but it was enough. Roland fell over the parapet, headfirst into the night.

"Fuss!" he called, but he had left Fuss behind. He was flying, under the stars. He looked toward the river and saw it, a faint silver line. He saw Dumien and all the drowned singing boys. They waved to him—*Come. You'll be safe here.* He looked further, toward Hexwiller, and saw Odile. She wept she was so happy to see him. *Come home. I'll kill the last chicken.* He knew he could go, fly home, but he wanted to look for his father. Where was Max?

"Frog!" Roland saw Fuss on the roof. He was bent over the parapet looking down, looking for Roland. Roland looked down too, realizing his mistake too late. He saw the ground, and it flew up to meet him. In that second, he knew. Max was dead.

CHAPTER FIVE

W HEN GINNY WOKE up, she lay with her eyes closed, smelling the sulfur that stirred in the breeze from the air shaft, listening to the guest on the other side of the wallpaper turn over and over in his bed like a dog circling to sleep, perhaps hosting the surviving bedbugs. Then she opened her eyes and moved them carefully across the room. The lamp was still broken, Paul's urn on the floor. She had fallen asleep in her clothes.

After a while, she got up. She picked up the urn and put it on the dresser, trying not to look at it. She was afraid of what she might do. How could she have been so wrong? About Paul, about Paris? She brushed the sulfur off her dress with a damp cloth and went out, not bothering to put on her hat. It was afternoon. She had slept around the clock.

"Just remember, when you get discouraged and you want to come home," Fanny had said, "don't, you hear? Just don't. I know." Ginny went back to the cemetery. Where else could she go in her black widow's dress? But this time she did not walk past the tombs or read their inscriptions. She found a small bench in the shade of a staircase that ran from the cemetery to the bridge above and sat down, careful not to sit on the inscription dedicating the bench to someone's beloved someone. If she went home, would she go crazy like Fanny? Crazy with the impossibility of escape, of happiness? Or was she crazy already? Running away to Paris. Listening to Fanny at all.

Looking down at her lap, Ginny noticed how her dress was a shade lighter where she had sponged it off. If she kept washing it, would the fabric fade and fade until it took her out of mourning, until it came out of the water white as a wedding dress? She wished she had someone she could ask for advice. Fanny? She imagined Fanny sitting beside her naked, dripping her bath water on the bench. Crazy Fanny. She felt angry again, betrayed. She turned from Fanny, imagined her mother on the bench beside her. Not her mother as she was now, but a young Claire, wearing a broad-brimmed straw hat, carefully lined to keep out any stray rays of the sun. But Ginny couldn't imagine what this young Claire would say, so she just sat and Ginny just sat. Then her mother cocked her head and said, *Listen.* It seemed Ginny could hear, could feel, the ground shifting in a restless murmur. She remembered that the dead under her, who had lived their lives far from anyone like her mother, who had not seen a single copy of the *Watch Tower*, were eligible to be drawn from the ground to live on the New Earth, to hear the Word at last. The cemetery was a waiting room packed with people eager to rejoin husbands or find new saved ones, to see children again or have new ones born without sin. Her mother nodded, the wide brim of her hat casting a wave of shadow. *The Resurrection of Life*, she said.

Ginny sat up straight. The young Claire was gone, but Ginny saw life. There were cats everywhere, huge orange males, slim calico females. Cats who sat and purred, sheltered under some mossy Madonna's praying hands or a straw ring of dead wreath. How could she have not seen them before? They sat on the tombs over her head and looked down, so round-headed, so small-eared. She remembered Aunt Fanny calling a cat who looked like that a pilgrim cat, telling her this was the oldest sort of cat, the ship cat who'd done his best to eat the rats of the great plague, the black death, until the rats and the cats had both lain down to die.

Then she saw the cat people. A gray-overcoated businessman stopped at the tomb just past her bench and pulled two cans of tuna fish out of his coat pocket. A tall calico mother and three round black kittens came tumbling down, rubbing their faces against the businessman's patent leather shoes. He forked out the tuna, then let the mother cat climb in his lap to knead his overcoat. Ginny turned her head away, embarrassed by this display of affection, but near the gate, a fat henna-haired woman was feeding fish heads to a huge tailless tom and his harem, letting the cats pause between bites to butt at her chin.

All through the afternoon they came, each with his or her own cat tribe or cat family to feed. Then, when the sun was sitting right on the cemetery wall, a huge man with a beret came through the gate carrying two metal buckets. Ginny stood up and was almost knocked down by the cats that came running, all together, strangers and enemies and siblings, their tails stiff with eagerness. The man came forward, set his buckets almost at her feet. They were filled with fresh liver. The man opened his arms, and one giant butterfly tabby leapt into them, butting his head against the man's chest. The man turned to her. "My minions," he said, holding the tabby with one arm and waving the other wide.

Ginny noticed that the rusted doors of the mausoleums nearest her were draped with wool blankets, the floors lined with cut rags—all the solid sanctuary of the dead of Montmartre provisioned for the comfort of cats. She climbed the steps to the bridge above the cemetery, stopped at the top and looked down. The wind from a passing automobile tugged at her skirt. Below her, from the houselike mausoleums, yowls and hisses rose in the cooling air. It seemed to her she was not looking down at a cemetery, at a city of the dead, but at a living city as full of life as the Paris that had lain at her feet when she stood on the steps of Sacré Coeur.

She crossed the bridge and went up the narrow streets until she stood again before the marble domes of Sacré Coeur at the top of the hundred steps. She touched one of the cold pillars behind her and looked down toward the grassy first landing. She saw a glint of yellow in a cloud of wings. The same man was sitting there feeding the birds, long legs folded under him, hand in the air. She blinked, focused her eyes on the back of his head. His yellow hair stood stupidly on end. Probably he was there every day, but Ginny couldn't help feeling that he had been waiting for her, that everything was poised, waiting. She took first one step down and then another until she stood on the landing, close enough to feel on her cheeks the air stirred by the beating wings of a hundred sparrows. The yellow-haired man put his hand down, and the birds flew to the grass with their bread. Ginny sat on the bench beside him, and he offered her his last piece of bread to feed the sparrows. She shook her head. He offered again, then lifted her left hand. He put the bread in her fingertips, placing his palm, his fingers, against hers, a set of praying hands. Then the sparrows came. Never had she dreamed the soft blur of their wings could be so strong. She pressed her palm tighter against his, felt his pulse as well as hers in her wrist. How much blood the sparrows' tiny hearts had to pump to feed the strength of those throbbing wings. She could feel it, the beating of their hearts, their wings. She felt inside her the firefly glow she'd felt when she'd arrived in Paris, but much stronger, as if some great tourniquet had been released. Her whole body felt hot with the pumping of her blood.

The yellow-haired man spread his fingers, and this time the sparrows flew straight up, carrying the crust off to heaven. Ginny watched as the sparrows grew small against the fall sky. They left her behind on the bench, but she was not disappointed. It was enough they had come so close, had touched her.

The birdman stood. She stood. She looked down at the Paris that prowled and purred below her. The birdman started down the steps, his yellow hair glowing in the fading light. He stopped, looked back at her. She took one step down, one more, then another, and as she went, the noise of the city rose up to meet her.

CHAPTER SIX

G ET UP." It was the quartermaster's voice. "Get him up."
Roland opened his eyes and saw Nurse Zimmer's white
breasts. She was bent over him, her arm under his shoulder.
The quartermaster had his feet. He was not on the ground under the
stars. He was in the infirmary, and they were trying to get him out of
bed. Roland could see how injuries had a way of taking days out of a
person's life. He tried to help by sitting up, but his arms were crossed
on his chest and bound with bandages. Something was poking him in
the ribs.

"Concussion, dislocated right shoulder, compound fracture of the
left arm, radius and ulna," Nurse Zimmer said. Was she talking to him
or the quartermaster? Either way it didn't sound like a very impressive
list of injuries for someone who'd fallen off a three-story building. "How
can he expect us to get him up?" She was talking to the quartermaster.

"Because he's a pig," answered the quartermaster, "and we'd better
hurry because I suspect he is a very punctual pig."

They got Roland on his feet and, one on either side, down the stairs
to the courtyard where the cadets stood in formation. They leaned him
up against Fuss. *Fuss.* Roland glanced sideways at him, but Fuss kept his
eyes front and center, for once a model cadet. The staff, including Drillmaster Erlanger, stood in line to the right of the cadets. Nurse Zimmer
and the quartermaster fell in between Herr Epfig and the cook. Facing
them all was a single French officer wearing a breastplate of medals.

"Very good," he said in French, looking down the line from boy to
boy, taking in Roland's bandages, the shaved heads, a few faces still pale
from fever. He shrugged, bringing his shoulders up, holding his palms
out. Roland had never seen anyone so French. "Can you understand

51

me?" he asked, stepping closer. "Who can speak French?" A few hands shot up. Fuss raised his hand. Herr Epfig raised his. Roland's were strapped to his chest. The quartermaster glared at the French officer. "Good," the officer said. "Come here," he motioned to Herr Epfig. Herr Epfig took a step forward, then looked back at the drillmaster. He nodded. Herr Epfig took his place at the French officer's side, translating what he said into German.

"Six days ago, at five in the morning of November eleventh, an armistice was signed between France and Germany. Alsace will soon be joyously and officially reunited with France. Even now our troops are being welcomed in the streets of Mulhouse and Saverne. In a day, they will be in Strassburg. You have been liberated," he said. He waited, but no one made a sound. "I am here to aid in the repatriation of those boys who are German citizens. There is room in France only for those whose hearts and minds are French—no room for separatists, for the chronically unhappy. The school will be reopened, after some changes, but for now all you boys can go home to your anxious parents."

Someone laughed when Herr Epfig got to that part. The French officer frowned. "Quartermaster!" he said, and the quartermaster appeared with a heavy, bound ledger. The Frenchman pulled a notebook from his jacket. "I have made notes from the records. The French boys will fall in here," he pointed to the barracks. "The Germans there," he pointed to the gate. He cleared his throat. "Duval, Georges. Age seven years." Herr Epfig translated. One of the youngest cadets fell out. "Mother in Nancy. Father dead. French."

"Oh," Cadet Duval let out, but Roland couldn't tell which part of the announcement surprised him. The officer went on through the ranks. *French. German. Mother living. Mother dead. Father living. Father dead.* Herr Epfig kept up, but the important words didn't need translating. French. German. They lined up on opposite sides of the courtyard.

"Kepper, Roland. Age twelve years." Finally his turn had come. "Mother living in Würzburg. Father in the German army. German."

The quartermaster stepped forward to help him. "My grandmother . . ." Roland said, but the officer had already gone on.

"Fuss, René. Age thirteen years. Mother dead. Father dead. Orphan of the French State."

"Kepper!" Fuss yelled, his ears pink and scared like a rabbit's. "Don't leave me!" Roland looked at Fuss. He realized how lucky he was Fuss hadn't killed him.

"Left . . . left . . . left, right, left," called the quartermaster, who was going with them to the Fatherland. Roland turned his back on the school and left Fuss alone in the world. At least I'll never see him again, Roland thought.

*　　*　　*

When Lena got the telegram telling her to pick up her son that afternoon at Würzburg Station, she couldn't make up her mind. Should she go? Who knew? She went to the bathroom and turned on the hot water in the tub. She thought about blowing out the pilot light on the water heater, locking the door, and gassing herself. It was an idea she had toyed with for months. So she soaked for a while and thought about what to do. She could stay home. The last thing she needed right now was Max's son. But the authorities, it seemed, knew where she lived, and there might be trouble. She couldn't get in trouble, not now. Lena got out of the water and stood naked in front of the mirror. She was three months pregnant, and she hadn't seen her lover for almost that long. She hadn't seen Max in two years. She didn't know if either of them were coming back, or what would happen if one or both of them did. Instead, she got Roland, coming back like a bad dream.

She went. She wore her best suit. Who could tell who you might see at a train station? On the platform, crowds of women waited for men. Lena, too, searched the faces of the soldiers who got off the train. Who knew? Roland was beside her before she realized it. "Mother?" he said. She stepped back, taking him in. He was as tall as she was, but as thin as bones.

"Lena," she said. "Call me Lena." He was wound up in bandages like a mummy, a jacket balanced on his shoulders, a huge beret squatting like a toad on his bandaged head. "Good God, where do you think you are?" Lena said, pulling the beret from his head and holding it between two fingers. Roland's hair stood up above the bandage around his head. It looked like hay stubble. "God in heaven," she said, rolling her eyes up. A fat red-faced man came up behind Roland.

"Find your mother all right then, Cadet Kepper?" Roland introduced the quartermaster, who tipped his beret.

"You're from the school?" Lena asked. "Good, then take this," and gave him Roland's beret. "Come on," she said to Roland and, taking him by the shoulder, led him out of the station and into the streets of the city.

She put him to soak in the tub, unwrapping him from all his bindings but the cast on his arm. "How old are you now?" she asked, scrubbing his thin legs and back.

"Twelve," Roland told her, wincing as she reached his sore ribs, "twelve and a half." Lena stopped scrubbing.

"What's this?" she asked, poking a finger at what looked like a spot of fresh blood on his chest below his heart. She scrubbed even harder, but the blood stayed there just under the skin. "Damn. What is it? You didn't have a mark like this in Hexwiller. I should know." Roland looked and saw a red star like a birthmark where the pain was. Ever since the train had crossed the Rhine, the pain there had been sharper, more like a knife's point than a pencil's.

Lena left him in the tub and went downstairs to telephone a doctor. Frau Wetzel, the landlady who owned the phone, suggested one. "He's one that'll come," she said, looking hard at Lena. "Not like some. He's very accommodating."

He did come, later that evening. He was not young, not well dressed. He checked Roland's pulse where it came out of the cast on his arm, rubbed the fine skin between the fingers of Roland's left hand. At Lena's request, he poked at the star below Roland's heart, then rewrapped his shoulder. "I'm worried about that cast on his arm," he said. "It may be too tight. Bring him by the office in the morning, Frau Kepper." He smiled. "Then we can take care of that spot, if it bothers you. Don't you worry," he said, touching her arm. He leaned forward, whispering, "Do you want to do something about his hand?"

"You can fix it?"

"Whatever is broken, the doctor can fix," he smiled. Lena was glad she hadn't taken off her good suit or her silk stockings. She might be needing a doctor, a favor. Who knew?

Roland wished his mother had changed her clothes. He hardly recognized her in the suit like a man's suit with a skirt, the hat like a man's hat except for a long feather. She hadn't dressed like that in Hexwiller. It wasn't until the doctor was gone and Lena put on her nightgown that Roland felt he could talk to her. She made him a bed on the couch and sat down beside him. "Lena," he said, "I think Max is dead."

Lena put her hand over her mouth, but that couldn't hold back the rush of emotions. Relief. "Oh," the word escaped from behind her hand as she sat back on the couch. Anger. How could he be dead? She didn't have much money left. How would she live? Max would have forgiven her, gotten a job. Now she couldn't even go back to Odile's house. Guilt. She thought of the soft skin of her lover's neck, a place where she could hide her face, rest. If she was a widow, she could marry again. But was he alive? Who knew? She looked at Roland. One child to support, put in school, soon another. Maybe there would be a government allowance for them, a pension for her. If she wanted to claim the baby as Max's, she would have to move. She couldn't trust Frau Wetzel to keep her mouth shut. If only she could be rid of them both.

"Lena," Roland was reaching for her with his creepy webbed hand, taking her hand from her mouth. She saw his eyes widen.

"Damn," Lena said. He saw her thoughts. He knew she was pregnant. Why was there always a Keppi there to tell her the truth, to never let her escape? "Here," she said, putting his hand on her belly. "Be some good for once. Will it be a little brother or a little sister?"

Roland pulled his hand away, sure of the future for the first time in years. "He's not going to be born," he said.

Lena felt sick. Her son watched her with his blue eyes, only a shade paler than hers. Who knew? He knew. She ran for the bathroom, reached the toilet in time for her dinner to come up. "Lena?" Roland knocked on the door. She had locked it behind her. She could hardly hear him, she was so dizzy, covered in cold sweat. She threw up again, then sat back, wet and shaking. "Lena?"

"Go away!" she yelled back. "Go to bed." She blew out the pilot light on the hot water heater.

Roland beat his fist on the door. "Mother!"

She smelled the gas trickling out. When she turned the hot water on, the gas would pour out into the air, into her. How could Roland know she was thinking about asking Doctor Fix-Anything for an abortion, that she would offer him anything, even money? She was sick again. She turned on the cold water to drown out the sound of her son crying at the door. Who knew? Who knew? When she stopped feeling sick, she would turn on the hot water too. She rested her head on the toilet.

"Lenalenalena," her son begged. She closed her eyes, and there he was. Not Roland, the other one. His wrinkled hands were raised, palms out, like Jesus showing his wounds, or a tiny German parachutist preparing to be dropped from her womb. Then, without moving, she was in the post office, in the line to buy stamps. When she got to the window, the clerk said, "Sorry, only Germans are allowed to buy stamps."

"I am German," Lena said, but the clerk looked past her. The whole line turned around. Two Rolands were standing there. Twins.

"Mama!" they said and ran toward her.

The clerk put a closed sign in the window.

Lena woke up. The white tile was blinding in the morning light, but she was stiff as a shingle, so she knew she was in her bathroom, not heaven. The gas from the pilot light hadn't been enough. She opened the window. The fresh air burned her eyes. She rinsed out her mouth and unlocked the door. Roland was asleep, slumped on the threshold. She bent over him, shook his shoulder. "Get dressed," she said. "We'll be late for the doctor."

The doctor held a square of ice to the star on Roland's chest. He pared away a thin slice with a scalpel, then pressed a piece of gauze to the spot. "Hold still," he said to Roland and took off his gloves. "We'll see in a minute," he said to Lena. He touched his tray of scalpels. "What about the hand?"

"Not today," Lena said. "I have another problem."

Roland lay under the doctor's lamp, the brightest he'd ever seen. The doctor and Lena had gone into another room. He could hear them talking. The pain under his heart was an alarm; the nerves rang like bells. He could hardly breathe.

"Ah," the doctor was back, "let's take a look at that now." He pulled the gauze pad away, swabbed the spot with some alcohol.

"Ouch!" Roland said.

"It's still there," Lena said. Roland looked. A red five-pointed star. "Can you do it again?" she asked. The doctor poked at Roland's chest.

"I can, but it won't do any good. It goes very deep."

"What is it?"

"It's your son . . . part of him anyway." Lena frowned. "Not to worry," the doctor said. "The arm, the hand, the other thing," he looked at Lena, "I can fix."

Lena went back that night, and the doctor gave her a shot of morphine. She lay under the bright lamp, soaking up the light like a lily pad, floating, unthinking. It hurt, but then it was over, and she couldn't remember the pain. "It was nothing, nothing," the doctor said, and she knew it was nothing, a dot of red flesh like you sometimes find in a farm egg you break open for breakfast. Such relief. She sat up feeling wonderful, light.

Lena gave the doctor the bundle of reichsmarks she'd taken from her potato bin. They smelled like wet earth. The doctor shook his head. "I'd rather work on the boy's hand. That interests me." The doctor poured her a brandy. She drank it.

Lena looked at the money, all she had. It was hard to think, her head felt so light. The doctor's offer was tempting. But if Roland's hand was worth that much to the doctor, could it be worth more? Who knew? She remembered the old story about the goose that laid gold eggs. "No," she said, "take the money." The doctor did, still shaking his head. "Watch out," Lena said laughing suddenly. "Money's dirty. You might catch something."

Then she was outside walking home. The icy sidewalk gleamed under her feet. It was snowing, but it didn't seem cold. She crossed the footbridge over the cemetery and, looking down, she saw a thousand candles, red votive lights, burning on the graves below. Like stars, she thought. No, like the reflection of stars in very clear water. She remembered a night on a lake somewhere, stars above and below, the sky with the earth gone away. She leaned on the rail, trying to focus on a single red light. Roland was a star. No matter how deep they cut, that was what he was. The stars were humming, and Lena turned, dancing over the bridge.

Roland sat up, waiting for Lena. Roland took out the drawing. *Max*, he thought tentatively, a small feeler, but there was nothing. He hadn't been able to save Max or Dumien, but it wasn't too late for Lena. He wouldn't let her gas herself. He went to the bathroom and broke a pane out of the window with the heel of Lena's shoe, filling the room with cold sweet oxygen. When he finished, he felt Lena dancing up the street, climbing the stairs.

"Is that you, Frau Kepper?" Frau Wetzel called out.

"It's Lena," Lena said. "Call me Lena."

Roland turned on the radio, opened the door. Lena came through and took him in her arms. They waltzed across the floor, Lena leading, Roland drowned in her arms, until they fell on the couch. "You," Lena said to him, "are made of gold." She closed her eyes. "Or is that silver?"

CHAPTER SEVEN

THE BIRDMAN CAUGHT Ginny's hand at the bottom of the steps. People pushed past them on a sidewalk half-filled by tables of cloth for sale, and the birdman tightened his grip, as if afraid she would be swept away from him. She felt the pushing as a solid thing, something all around her, holding her back, like the dirt packed down on those who heard the call for resurrection. She looked at the birdman. His hand felt safe, familiar, but his mouth smiled at her from the face of a stranger.

She remembered her three wishes from that game she'd played long ago with Fanny: a long voyage, a new name, a mysterious lover. What was she doing here? Maybe she'd been taking a long nap on a hot day in DeSoto, was just waking up from some sticky summer dream. She looked past the strange man's face. Where was she? Long rolls of cloth spilled from the nearest shop door—pink silk, gold crepe, velvet as dark as bruises. Lace hung in great tangles, ribbons in red knots. The birdman shook her hand a little—wake up, wake up.

Ginny gave up pretending she didn't know she was in Paris. The birdman turned away from her, pointing with his free hand at the crowd. "Aren't they beautiful?" he said. Ginny glanced at the backs of two women who passed, arms draped with bright yards of yellow cotton. Then she looked down, afraid they would turn, stare at her. The birdman let go of her hand. "I was going to take a walk," he said. "Would you like to come?" She looked up at him, his yellow head a foot higher than her red one. Behind him were the hundred steps that separated her from the cemetery, from Paul. She ran her fingers through her hair, felt it stand up like the birdman's, full of static electricity. Why not? What did she have to lose?

"Yes," she said, "I would." She gave him her hand.

They started upstream against the shoppers. The birdman stared openly at the people around him as though what he saw were a play and the passersby all actors, but Ginny kept her eyes on the birdman's shoes. She was afraid to look at people for fear they were looking at her too. "Beautiful," the birdman would say, but by the time she looked up, the person he had been watching was just going into a shop, turning around a corner, as if Paris were a vanishing act.

She tried lifting her eyes as far as the passing ankles, but even that was embarrassingly personal. Thick, darned work socks, thin, almost invisible silk stockings, old varicose veins, blue bicyclists' bruises. She looked at the shop windows. The cloth stores gave way to paper shops, and then there was a whole block of upholstery and leather goods. They passed a restaurant called the Fat Ass. Painted on its window was a picture of a donkey trying to take a bite of a great ziggurat-shaped cake while a naked woman pulled on his tail. What kind of neighborhood was this? Anything else like that, she told herself, and I'll turn back. I'm sorry, but I'm afraid I've made a mistake, she practiced saying. I'm sorry but I'm afraid . . .

They passed a used-clothes shop, shoes piled on a table outside the door. An old man with bad skin stuck his head out the door. "Hello, doctor," the birdman said as they passed. The old man shook his head.

Another man, bald, fatly pink, sat two doorsteps down, winding wire around a dark piece of machinery. "You can call me doctor," he said to the birdman. "I'm not proud." Ginny noticed with a shock that the bald man's legs stopped at the knees. She looked away.

"Well, good luck then, doctor. It looks like a delicate operation."

"When it comes to wrapping an armature," the bald man said, "I haven't lost a patient yet."

Ginny looked back over her shoulder at the shrinking domes of Sacré Coeur. Soon they would be out of sight. She knew that she should let go of the birdman's hand, go back alone to the stairs, that this was really crazy, beyond Fanny crazy. But each time she started to speak— *I'm sorry but*—she found herself imagining her hotel room, with no one there but Paul. With no one there. The street they were on emptied into a larger one, then another, like a creek into a river, a river into a bayou. The shop tables were full of new shoes now, hats, sweaters, gloves. There were candy shops and newsstands. The crowds were thick, and she smelled roasting chestnuts. She let her eyes drop again. It was almost dark, and the passing ankles were moving shadows. She kept her eyes on the birdman's thin pair. Then suddenly they were gone, and her hand was empty.

"Up here." His voice came from somewhere to the right and above her. The crowd pushed at her back. Someone elbowed her side. She raised her head to see where she was. The street lights weren't lit yet, but the headlights of the automobiles cast yellow beams into the crowded sidewalk and turned the people ahead of her into grotesque silhouettes. She stopped short, and the people behind ran up on her heels. A hand caught her elbow and pulled her onto the steps that climbed out of the shadows on her right. The street lights came on, and she looked up to see, straight from the print on Madame Duval's wall, the Madeleine, looking even more like a pagan temple in the electric glare than it had in the classroom. The birdman stood two steps above her. He let go of her elbow.

"I'm sorry if I frightened you," he said, his hair brilliant yellow in the light that shone off the white columns of the church. The birdman sat down, patted the marble step beside him. Ginny sat too. "I didn't know you weren't looking." She glanced quickly back down into the crowd. From the vantage of these few steps, the sidewalk below was all ears and hair and hats. She looked away, rubbing her bruised ankles.

"It's not polite to stare," she said and heard her mother's voice behind it—*a lady keeps custody of her eyes*. Even when her mother was standing in some family's parlor, trying to get their lives for Jehovah, she looked down at their carpet, not into their eyes.

The birdman nodded toward the crowd, flowing smoothly now that it was composed of people who were all in a hurry. "Just because you don't look at people, doesn't mean they're not there."

Ginny looked at the people passing below. Four policemen stood facing the street. One turned and pointed—at the Madeleine or at her? She felt warmth rush to her cheeks. Was she the only one afraid to look? Papa Ben had once walked around for a whole day with half his mustache shaved off and neither she nor her mother had noticed. Not even at dinner—those long meals spent examining crumbs she picked off the cornbread, never meeting her mother's eyes. What color were her mother's eyes? She looked at the birdman. His were light blue, like an Eskimo dog. He rubbed a hand through his yellow hair. Ginny stretched her legs down the broad steps. She could cover two if she pointed her toes. The policemen moved on, and Ginny thought she felt the birdman relax beside her. Or was that her imagination? "Where are we going?" she asked.

The birdman stood. "I know a place," he said, "where you can stare at people and they won't notice."

The birdman led Ginny to the Seine, to the Eiffel Tower. From the middle of a bridge over the river, she saw it in the distance as she had always imagined it, a frail pointed skeleton lit up against the dark night clouds, a web tower, all height and no weight at all. It looked just like Madame Duval's desk thermometer copy of it. Then, it exploded with lights. Lightning zig-zagged from the tip of the tower down one leg to the ground. Red flames shot up, turned into arabesques raining gold stars and falling comets. A green crab, a blue fish, a red lion—the signs of the zodiac—danced up into the sky. Then all the bulbs lit up, burning for five long seconds that turned the tower into a flaming torch. She let go of the birdman's hand and held onto the stone railing instead. The lights went out. Green and purple spots floated in their place in front of her eyes. A white flash and the bulbs from the top to the bottom spelled out in fifty-foot letters *C i t r o ë n.*

The advertisement seemed suspended in the sky, the tower invisible behind its light. *1889* read one leg facing her, *1929* the other. The birdman was there beside her, and he lifted her hand from the stone, held it in his. The sign went out. The tower reappeared, its shape outlined only by spotlights. By the time they reached the tower, she had almost gotten used to the electric fireworks. They went off every five minutes.

Then she was under the tower, and it was like nothing she had ever imagined. Its four legs straddled a concrete field larger than the great train shed at St. Lazare, and up each girdered leg ran an elevator the size of a freight car. The birdman released her hand. She looked up into the exposed muscle of the tower. It was too intricate, too powerful for her to stare at long. She got dizzy standing there with her head thrown back, no hand to steady her. She brought her chin down to rest on her chest and aimed her eyes along the platform as if it were only a sidewalk with nothing over it but the night sky. She didn't see the birdman, but she saw what he had brought her on foot across Paris to see. Standing all around her, staring up at Gustave Eiffel's creation that caged them as it rose, were tourists, people she could stare at with impunity, without fear of answering looks. They stood, caught up by the iron overhead as if they were puppets hooked to it by spun wire.

In the light and shadow of the electric fireworks, she looked at the people frozen around her. At first, she saw only some schoolgirls, a woman in a ribboned straw hat. Then a man with red hair near the east leg caught her eye, and suddenly it seemed as if all these hanging puppet tourists were people she knew. Standing there in Papa Ben's shadow, surely that was her French teacher Madame Duval whose hands waved so wildly, so characteristically, and the head of the academy, tiny Dr. Love beside her. There, the tall man touching his finger to the fine arch of his nose, was he some stranger, or was that Paul? A woman near him raised a gloved hand to her broad hat and turned, not toward Papa Ben, but Ginny. Her mother bent toward her, her hat further shading her face. Ginny took a step forward. The birdman caught her hand.

"You see," he whispered to her as if the people around them were asleep, "a good place to practice." Then he led her across the platform, past women with hats and heavyset men, all total strangers. Once out from under the great legs of the tower, she could see the lights of Paris, a city of strangers except for the man who was holding her hand.

They sat on a bench on the edge of the Champs de Mars. Their faces changed colors with the flashing bulbs, their eyes picking up the sparkle of the flying comets, twirling arabesques. She stretched her feet out in front of her and leaned back. She was tired. The muscles in her legs and back ached faintly. It felt good. It felt like she had gotten something done.

The birdman tapped his foot lightly against hers. "If we were sparrows," he said, "we could have been here hours ago, five minutes after we finished our crumbs on Montmartre." The birdman spread his fingers towards the sky. In the clear *Citroën* light she saw that the fingers on the birdman's left hand, the hand she'd held all across Paris, were joined together by a fine webbing of skin. The light streamed through the delicate pink flesh revealing the intricate pattern of veins, a natural model for the iron tracery in front of them. Was it possible to touch a hand, to look at it time after time, and not see such a thing? The birdman took her hand in his again, smiled again. She touched the smooth elastic skin between his fingers.

"Of course, if you were a sparrow," the birdman said, lifting her own fingers to touch the side of her neck just below the curve of her jaw, "and this hand had the strength of a sparrow's wing," with her index finger he traced the great artery down the side of her neck until her finger rested in the fluttering hollow of her throat, "then I would be afraid of you." He tapped her finger lightly on the pulse it held. She felt afraid, aware suddenly of how late if was, how far they were from the other tourists. She'd had enough mystery.

"But I am not a sparrow," she said, feeling the words buzzing in her throat behind her finger. "My name is Ginny Gillespie."

"Genie," the birdman said, turning the *i* to *e* as if she were someone conjured from Aunt Fanny's magic lamp. A breeze caught the birdman's hair and stood it up in the light of the burning tower, electric and more strangely yellow than ever. "My name is Roland Keppi."

CHAPTER EIGHT

THE TELEGRAM ABOUT Max arrived two weeks before Christmas. Lena read it twice, then let Roland read it. It said Corporal Max Kepper had been reported missing on the western front on November 11—the day of the armistice. It said nothing.

Lena had paid Frau Wetzel the rent for December, but after that she didn't know what they would do. She spent a week sitting in offices trying to find out if she could send Roland to Odile. One office said it was impossible because Roland was German and had no French identity papers. Another said he couldn't have German papers because he had been born in Alsace which was, after all, now part of France.

The day before Christmas, Lena was in the kitchen, slicing some cake Frau Wetzel had sent up, when there was a knock at the door. Roland opened it. At first he couldn't see anything. He knew there was a man there, but he saw only a shadow, an emptiness. "Well, who are you?" the shadow said.

"Roland," he said. The shadow stepped into the living room, became a middle-aged man in an officer's uniform, a white bandage across the bridge of his nose.

"Lena!" the man called.

"Odo!" Lena ran from the kitchen. "Odo," she threw open her arms. Odo had two candy-striped packages in his.

"Take these like a good boy, will you?" Odo asked, and Roland took them. They were both very light. Lena hugged Odo, and Odo let himself be hugged. "There, there now," he said, patting her back.

"I didn't know the boy would be here," Odo said to Lena when she let go of him. "I'll go out later and get some candy or oranges."

"Oh, Odo, who knew? I look a mess," Lena pulled off her apron.

"At least I have coffee on. Sit down, sit down." Lena ran back to the kitchen, and Odo sat on the couch.

"Here, boy," Odo said, patting the couch next to him. He shook Roland's hand. "Colonel Odo Rettig. I'm an old friend of the family." Roland put his left hand over his star, expecting a sharp pain, but there was nothing but the usual dull throb, more static than warning.

"What happened to your nose?" Roland asked.

"A horse broke my nose with his nose," Odo said, peeling off the bandage. "He did it twice in one week." He shook his head. "I don't think he liked me."

"Oh, poor Odo," Lena cried when she came in with the coffee and saw how decidedly Odo's nose bent to the left. She reached out to touch him.

"Don't be silly," Odo said, waving her away. "It works fine. The army doctor wanted to break it again, set it straight, but I told the fellow, 'thank you but no thank you.' I'd had quite enough of that."

Later that day, Odo went out and bought a Christmas tree, a goose, a bag of nuts, and a canteen for Roland. Lena got a blouse and some stockings out of the striped packages. Odo kissed Lena's hand and left that night after much whispering. Roland settled down on the couch. The smell of the goose made Roland homesick for Odile, who would have put prunes in it. He concentrated on the prunes. *Odile.* And there she was, pushing prune stuffing down into the cavity, up to her elbow in goose. Roland barely heard the front door open, Lena giggling, but he knew that Odo had come back, and when he heard Lena's bedroom door close, he whispered, "Odile," and his grandmother looked up, cocked her head. *I'll leave the door off the latch,* she said, *a light in the window.*

Odo took a room on the first floor. He kept a few things there. He told Frau Wetzel he didn't need much. "I have a house in Kitzengen," he told her, "but I have business in town, and I'm not a man who likes to hurry." Odo spent the day in the cafe across the street, reading papers, drinking coffee. He came to Lena's apartment each night for dinner. He seemed to think Lena was a good cook and always cleaned his plate. After dinner, he went to the cafe for a brandy and came back upstairs only after Roland was in bed.

Lena bought new clothes, paid January's rent. Roland got his cast off.

"The holidays are almost over, Lena," Odo said one night at dinner, rubbing his finger over the crook in his nose. "You should see about getting the boy in school."

"Well," Lena said, "I thought we might be moving. No sense in enrolling him if we're moving." Lena looked up at Odo, and Roland could see a house in the country in each bright eye.

"Moving?" Odo paused with his fork on its way to his mouth. Lena turned red. "I think you'd better put the boy in school," he said.

But Lena didn't. Each night Odo suggested it, and each day she found some other pressing business. First she took Roland shopping with her, until he knew the inside of all the women's dress shops and department stores in Würzburg by heart. Then she fell back on Nurse Zimmer's tactic and kept Roland in bed sick. One day she would ask him how his arm felt, the next about the pain in his chest. The day she asked about his hand, Roland got off the couch and got dressed. He did not want his hand sacrificed to Lena's war with Odo. He did not really want to be in school, but there were limits to the kind of hostage he was willing to be. He went for a walk, an all-day walk, and that, it turned out, worked as well for Lena's purposes. She couldn't enroll him if he wasn't there. So every morning he went out and climbed up above the Main River to spend the day throwing rocks at the Marienberg Fortress. In the afternoon, coming home, he would stop at the cafe, and Odo would buy him a cup of chocolate, add a touch of his coffee to it, and the two of them would sit like two men, not talking much, until dinner. Roland wished he could have spent as much time with Max.

One afternoon at the fortress, Roland looked up from his search for good rocks to find a girl about his age watching him. She had a pigeon feather stuck in her hair like a red Indian. "I live in Zürich," the girl said, "but I'm American." She crossed her arms over her chest. "We beat you, you know."

Roland nodded.

"This fortress is silly, you know," the girl said. "Quite medieval. It wouldn't stand up to a modern artillery barrage."

"No," Roland agreed politely, although the walls didn't show any wear from the rocks he'd bounced off them. "I don't suppose it would."

"This bluff, though," the American girl waved her arm at Würzburg stretched out like a map two hundred feet below, "is strategic. One good fieldpiece up here and you could . . ." She pointed at the Royal Palace. "Boom!" At Kaufman's department store. "Boom, boom!"

"Joanna!" A woman in a tan overcoat appeared on the walk above them. "Joanna!" The woman said something Roland couldn't understand, and the girl took a step toward her, dragging the feather from her hair. Then she turned, took aim at the old bridge with its eleven saints crossing the Main.

"Boo . . . oom!" The sound echoed, pigeons flew up from the cliff.

"Joanna Marie Ellington!" The girl ran, and the woman chased her. Roland looked down at Würzburg, picking out Frau Wetzel's apartment house, the cafe where Odo sat. He found a good flat stone and threw it as hard as he could out over the Main, toward the cathedral. "Hey!" a soldier yelled down at him from the fortress, waved his arms. "Hey, stop that!"

That night, Roland heard Lena and Odo arguing in her bedroom, Lena's voice rising sharply. He got up and went to the door. Light streamed through the keyhole, and Roland could see Lena and Odo standing naked at the foot of the bed.

"But what's the rush?" Odo asked. "What could happen?"

"Who knows?" Lena said. "I'm not young anymore." Odo held out his arms to her, kissed her on the top of her head. "Not young." But when Odo was on top of Lena, the two of them moving together on the bed, Lena's face looked fiercely young, timeless. It was Odo who looked old, old and tired, his broken nose standing out white as a scar.

Finally, one night in February, Odo stopped Lena as she served dinner. "The boy should be in school," he said to her, putting his hand over his plate. "Do you want him to be a disgrace to his father?"

"You knew my father?" Roland asked.

"Roland," Lena said, "be quiet."

Odo looked at Roland, sadly, seriously. "I met him only once."

"Shut up!" Lena stood, catching the tablecloth, spilling the gravy.

"Where did you meet him?"

"Both of you!" Lena ran from the table, slammed the bathroom door. "Who knew?" came her voice from beyond the door. Odo stood. "This is craziness," he said, shaking his head. "I'm going out."

Roland put his ear to the bathroom door. He heard Lena crying, but no water running. He was making Lena unhappy by being there.

If things kept on like this, she might kill herself. His father was dead. He wanted his mother to live. He rolled a change of clothes in the blanket from the couch, filled the canteen Odo had given him, took bread, a knife, a cheese. Then he stood by the bathroom door. "It's all right, Lena," he said. "I'm going. I'll send Odo back up." The crying stopped.

Lena heard the door close behind Roland. She almost went to the window to call him back. Instead, she sat on the edge of the tub and ran one finger around and around the drain. Odo would marry her now. Maybe he had killed Max for her. She had sent her son away for him, and for what, if not so that they could marry? When he came up, she would wash her face, they would go out. Who knew?

Odo was in the cafe. Roland stuck his bundle behind the door where Odo wouldn't see it, then went and sat next to him. He unfolded the picture of Max in the snow. "Where is this?" he asked.

Odo barely looked at the picture—he was watching the light in Lena's bathroom window. "Near Hartmannswillerkopf," he said. "I didn't mean Max any harm. I only went to see if he was the kind of man Lena said he was. But I liked him. I'd heard about some horses hidden in the mountains. I could have told my own mess officer, but I told Max. He seemed serious about his cooking." Odo shook his head. "I didn't mean to get him killed."

"Do you love Lena?" Roland asked.

"I don't know," said Odo, rubbing a finger over his bent nose. "I don't know much about women."

Roland looked at Odo. He wanted to tell him he would be happier without Lena, that even he, a twelve-year-old boy could see that. But he wanted his mother to be happy, and Lena needed Odo for that. "Max would want Lena taken care of," he said.

"Yes," Odo said, "I know."

Roland put the drawing away. It was done. "You should take Lena dancing," he said. "She likes to dance."

Odo took a bill out of his wallet for the waiter, handed a few more to Roland. "Get the waiter to bring you some dinner. A boy your age shouldn't go to bed hungry." Odo stood. "I am sorry," he said.

"I know," Roland said to Odo, already halfway out the door. "I'll tell Max when I see him."

It took Roland eleven days of walking to reach the border near Freiburg. He hid in the baggage car of a nearly empty train kept running only by the German belief in schedules. No one was going on any visits to France so soon after losing the war, but the trains going east into Germany were packed. From his baggage car, Roland saw long trains waiting on the sidings while guards checked people's papers. The bridges over the Rhine were jammed with horses and people, even a few automobiles. Alsatians like Max, who felt themselves German, or Germans like Lena, who'd counted on a new life in Alsace, were squeezing back into the Fatherland. Roland stayed hidden until his train was safely across the border and into France. He couldn't risk being asked for papers he didn't have. He knew that in the guards' eyes he would be stateless, neither French nor German. What did they do to people like that?

Roland's train was headed west into France, so he got off at the first town. The shops were boarded up, still posted with German signs, but the houses stood open and empty, all their sofas and dining tables and beds sitting out in the middle of the street as if inside and outside had switched places. Except the furniture outside was switched around too—a gramophone on top of an icebox, a chair on top of its table. Roland sat on a piano stool and retied his bundle into a pack he could carry over one shoulder. Near him, a woman in a suit like Lena's opened and shut a dresser drawer once, then again and again. A small girl and a smaller boy chased each other around a bed and a chair, fencing with furled umbrellas. They lashed out at Roland as he passed. The girl threw something round and heavy that landed with a splash in the mud ahead of him.

"Hand grenade!" the boy yelled. It was a brass door knob. Roland picked it up and threw it back, arching it up into the sky, aiming at a big feather bed. It bounced twice.

"Pineapple, spineapple!" the girl screamed and fell back on a velvety sofa.

"No fair!" the boy cried, running to their mother, still opening and shutting her drawer. "It's my turn to die!"

Roland walked south. The road was muddy and full, people going south pushing past people going north. The money Odo had given him was no good in France, so Roland traded what was left for a sausage and a handful of French money from an old man headed to Germany. "Not that you'll find much to buy with it," the old man said, shaking his head. He shook his head harder when Roland told him he was in Alsace looking for his father. "All that way for one body? I heard seventy thousand bodies were never recovered at the Somme. Sucked down in the mud, pounded to dust. Millions dead," the old man kicked the road. "We could be walking on them now."

Roland looked down at the mud. He knew from Odile that the dead were always underfoot. What else was mud? But if you could love one living person out of millions—why should it be different with the dead?

It took Roland three days to learn that Hartmannswillerkopf was a mountain that the French called the Vieil-Armand and to find someone who knew that it overlooked Cernay. He turned west, toward the mountains, and found it hard walking, the road an endless up and down of shell craters. The towns he passed through had also been shelled. Here, inside and outside was one muddy, pockmarked mess. Above Cernay, he climbed into the hills, trusting his feet. No one would be able to tell him where a single corporal had fallen. He ate his last piece of sausage as he walked, but he didn't feel hungry. Having an empty stomach made him feel lighter, made it easier for his legs to carry his body and his pack.

Roland followed a rutted road that snaked up the mountain through dense forest. As he climbed, the trees thinned. Snow dusted the road, lay a few inches thick in the ditches on the side. Soon, blasted stumps outnumbered the leafless trees that remained standing. He heard dogs barking in the distance, though he hadn't passed any farm, seen any people. The barking sounded lonely and hungry. He left the road and climbed through stumps, straight up the mountain. The barking faded. He reached a rocky outcrop and stopped to catch his breath. It was very quiet. The valley stretched out below, mud and ash faded to a hint of green on the horizon near the Rhine. He heard a church bell, far away, lost in the landscape.

On the other side of the rock was a concrete pit half-filled with water, littered with shellcasings. Roland walked along the edge and heard a dozen startled squeals, a rush of feet. A line of thin rats ran from the pit, took their bearings, and disappeared. He tried to go around the pit but ran into a coil of barbed wire. Herr Epfig had told the cadets about this wire, how essential it was to trench warfare, but this was the first Roland had seen. It curled across the ground like an impenetrable rusty bramble. Alongside the wire was a narrow track, and Roland followed it, just as Max had a hundred times in his mess wagon.

70

On the far side of the mountain, the track became less distinct, and soon it disappeared altogether in the snow. After a while the barbed wire stopped too, but Roland kept walking, surrounded by dark pines and deep snow. Halfway across a clearing, he heard dogs again, closer, not barking now but running. He froze as they broke into the open on his right. The first dog, a big black poodle, saw him first and stopped in his tracks. The other dogs tumbled to a stop behind him. Farm dogs, sheep dogs, watch dogs, pets. Hair matted, mouths open. A dozen thoughtful brown eyes looked Roland up and then down. Their breath hung in the air, their tongues warm and wet. Roland eased his pack off his shoulder, got ready to run. Then a twig cracked in the woods behind him, and something flung itself past his legs. Roland jumped.

It was a rabbit, a white winter hare. It ran a crazy zigzag, tiny snowballs racing away from its feet. The poodle barked and took off after it, joyous, silly. The other dogs followed, barking their heads off, snapping at the snow. Roland ran for the trees, hugging his pack. Branches whipped at his face. He ran up and up, breathing harder and harder until he was near the top of the next mountain. Then, through a break in the trees, he saw a meadow with a far line of firs, the same meadow, the same trees as in his drawing.

"Max!" Roland called, "Max!" He scrambled over the snow, thawed and frozen here into ice. "Max!" The sun on the ice was blinding. He slipped and fell, knocking the last wind out of himself. His pack skittered away. He tried to lift himself up, but his hands broke through the crust into the snow. His left hand closed around another hand, its wrist bent just so. Roland dug at the snow like a dog, sending it flying back into the air.

Max. His face was perfectly blue, the hole where the bullet had entered his body a rust-colored star. Roland pulled on the frozen wool of Max's uniform, trying to lift him. "Oh, Papa," Roland said, blinking against the tears that tried to freeze his eyes shut. "How could anyone do such a thing?"

Max's eyes opened, or so it seemed, because at the same time Roland could see a pair of eyes that were shut, as if the corpse were a shadow Max cast. "I guess," Max said, "he didn't know the war was over. I guess I didn't either."

"Odo is marrying Lena," Roland said.

"Is he?" Max brightened for a moment, his skin almost pink. "It seems as if I knew that already. I must have decided it was all right. Otherwise I'd have warned you."

"Warned me?"

Max touched the hole below his heart. "Pain's the best warning," he said. "The body respects it." Max's hand stopped over his head, blue again. A gust of wind blew snow over his face.

"Max!" Roland touched his chest, his own star. He could hardly feel it now, and he wondered if the blood there was drying, turning brown like Max's. "Should I get you out? Take you home, to Hexwiller?"

Max's voice came up through the snow, "No. I don't remember why exactly, but no. Ask Odile. And it's not pronounced *Hex-vil-ler* now, the French look at the signs and say *Ex-vee-yay*. But be careful. The French police can stop anyone and ask for their identity cards—rich Parisians, disabled army veterans, troublesome Alsatians. If they catch you, they'll send you back to the Fatherland, so fast . . ." Max's voice faded to a whisper, then to nothing, as if while he was talking, he had left the room.

"Papa?" Roland said. His father didn't answer. Roland took the drawing from his shirt, and unbuttoning Max's jacket pocket, tucked it into the stiff wool. Then a cloud passed over the sun and Roland shook with the cold, shook so hard he made Max's teeth rattle.

However it was pronounced, the war had not left the lives of the people in Hexwiller untouched. Roland passed house after empty dark house before he found Odile waiting for him outside hers. She kissed him, crossed herself, kissed the iron over the doorway. "You're early," she said. "The chicken's an old bird and won't be done for an hour."

Roland wrapped his arms around Odile, rested his chin on her head. He was taller than his grandmother now. "Why didn't Max want to come home?" he asked.

"This place is bad luck, even for the dead. My grandmother told me. I'm telling you." Odile looked up the street in front of her house, then down. She pushed Roland away from her, into the house. "Wash!" she called after him.

She spat twice over her shoulder. "We should never have stayed," she said, and following him in, Odile latched the door behind her.

CHAPTER NINE

THEY TOOK THE Métro back to Montmartre.

As they entered the white-tiled tunnel, Ginny took Roland's hand and held it fluttering and cold in hers as she bought the tickets. His head turned constantly toward the exit. She felt efficient as a nurse taking a pulse as she led him through the tunnels to their train. It was her turn to lead him by the hand. She pulled him across the gap between the platform and the open doors. "Don't look," she said, and Roland smiled.

She found a seat on the already rocking car, but Roland pulled his hand free, remained standing as close as possible to the door. She noticed how Roland's wrists stuck out a bony three inches from the cuffs of his jacket, how frayed the wool was where the metal buttons pulled at the button holes. In the overhead light of the car, Roland's face took on the color of his egg yolk hair. She felt rich for the first time in her life sitting there with both their thirty-five-centime tickets in her hand. Did it always feel like this when you took care of someone else? Is that what Paul got from taking care of her? Roland stood in front of her looking like a charity, like a person she should avoid. She felt both that she wanted to take his hand in hers and that she wanted to squeeze it tight enough to hurt. She allowed her hands only to hold each other, resting together in her lap.

She watched as Roland peered through the glass doors at the wiring and gray concrete that rushed by inches beyond. He bent his head trying to see a landmark in the maze. She pulled on the hem of his coat and pointed to the map above the door. The lines of the underground railways spread out as delicately as the veins in the webbed hand he pressed against the double doors. He glanced at the map, then looked at her. "May I ask you a question?" he asked, suddenly shy.

"Yes, of course."

"Are you an American?"

"Can't you tell from my French?" Roland shook his head. "But then I'm from Alsace."

"Isn't Alsace part of France?" she asked, trying to remember what Madame Duval had told them about Alsace and which side had ended up with it at the end of the war.

"It is now, but it didn't used to be, and next time," he shrugged, "who knows?"

She stood and lifted Roland's hand from the glass, pulled him to the seat next to her. "I am from America," she said. He blinked, then relaxed, his hand warm in hers. Did it feel like this, she wondered, to have a pet?

"I don't like being underground," Roland said.

She smiled, feeling the certainty and safety of the brightly lit car around her. "I do," she said and kept his hand in her lap until they reached Montmartre.

At the top of the Métro stairs, Roland stopped and looked up at the bright lights that blocked out the stars, then back into the tunnel with the air of a man who has forgotten what he needed at the store. Ginny stopped too, her fingers loosening as Roland's grip tightened. You could pet someone else's cat or a stray and then walk away—go home, go home, don't follow me. What, she thought, turning to Roland, should I do with you? A crowd of people pushed up from the Métro behind them. There was a glitter of diamonds or cut glass, the gleam of a tuxedo shirt. Roland smiled, waved the party-goers onto the street with a broad sweep of his arm as if he were the headwaiter and the street the table they had reserved. A woman laughed, half curtsied. Ginny's fingers curled tight again around Roland's.

The bright light that cancelled the stars came from the red and gold marquees of nightclubs. She had heard of the Moulin Rouge, although its picture was not among the Great Monuments of France that had hung on Madame Duval's classroom walls, but she hadn't realized how close its red lights were to the Grand Hôtel de Montmartre.

She turned her back on the bright lights and walked with Roland up the steep, narrow street to her hotel. Neither led the other now as they found their footing on the uneven stones with the help of the pink aurora the Moulin Rouge cast into the sky. Women in short skirts passed them hurrying down the hill to work the boulevard. Ginny kept her eyes to the ground, afraid to see Roland smile at the women or the women smile at him. Halfway up the hill, the wind caught them, cutting down between the tall houses on its way into the sky over Paris. Roland began to shiver, his hands suddenly icy in hers, as if he were some cold-blooded reptile unable to store more than a few hours of warmth from the sun. She felt, rather than heard, his teeth chattering. She felt the wind on her legs through her stockings, but she was curiously warm, from the steam of the Métro tunnel, from the excitement of the long walk. Her black cotton suit felt luxurious, as thick against her skin as wool, holding in all the heat of her heart. With the birdman beside her, she felt like a rich, kind American.

They turned the corner by the cemetery, and the walls cut off the wind. She heard the cats behind them taking one last turn before settling into their mausoleums for a warm sleep. Roland, she guessed, had no rag nest waiting for him. But then she wasn't sure she had any place to stay either, not after the mess she'd made the night before. "Wait here," she told him, holding out her palm like a crossing guard. She left him leaning against the cemetery wall, and she crossed the street, entered her hotel, trying to think of what to say. Madame Desnos came out of her little room behind the counter yawning. "Ah, Madame," she said. "I had them put your belongings in room one. A much better room." She held out the key, waiting to see if Ginny would take it. "I know you'll be much happier there." You forget a dozen bedbugs, she seemed to be saying, and I'll forgive one torn pillow. "More expensive, of course, but worth every centime." Ginny took the key.

"But tonight I need another room as well, inexpensive but not," Ginny said, "my old room." Madame Desnos shrugged, gave her a large brass key.

"The only room on the sixth floor," she said. "All the way up." Ginny paid for both rooms.

She would give Roland the key as thanks and say good-bye. I'll always remember our walk, she imagined herself saying, your kindness. By the time Roland got up to his room, she'd be safe in her own. The key in her hand, she crossed the street. Roland was not leaning on the wall. She looked both directions. A bright flash caught her eye at the far corner of the cemetery wall. Outlined by the light was a dark panel truck, its doors open, a uniformed man with a camera bent over something on the ground, the smoke from the flash curling over his head. She knew from the movies there would be a chalk-outlined body sprawled on the sidewalk. Roland.

She ran calling his name.

"Yes?" he said, stepping out from the shadow of the wall as she reached the corner. She stopped short, then leaned her forehead against the front of his coat, dizzy from her fear and the sudden sprint. "Look," Roland said, lifting her chin with his fingers. In place of a corpse was a cackling, very alive old woman sitting on a grating with her rag-wrapped legs straight out in front of her. The uniformed man illuminating the scene with his flash wore the blue and red wool of the Salvation Army. The old woman was drinking from a bowl of soup that sent steam in waves over her face. Roland pointed to the panel truck. It wore a red and white banner on its door: *Soup in the Night.*

"Here," a woman's voice came from behind her, and Ginny turned to find a young woman also in the stiff wool of the army. "God blesses you," the woman said and handed Roland and Ginny each a bowl of soup. "He loves you." Roland smiled at Ginny.

Before she could say a word, a flash lit up the ministering angel and her two hungry derelicts. In that hot instant of light, Ginny saw herself not as a genteel tourist widow, but a crazy woman who spent her days in the cemetery, a woman with a wrinkled black dress and a mock halo of unruly red hair. To the eyes of the Salvation Army, to the impartial lens of the camera, she and Roland were twins. She remembered an epitaph from the cemetery in DeSoto:

> Alike in life as peas in a pod
> Now shelled out and gone to God

Then the flash was gone, and she laughed in the sudden darkness. She stared down at her soup with great green and yellow stars floating in front of her eyes as if the ones missing from the Paris sky had tumbled into her bowl. She heard the truck door slam, the engine start. She took a sip from her bowl.

"It's lentil." It was Roland's voice beside her, as nonchalant as if he was talking about a choice he'd made from a menu. She swallowed and felt the soft round lentils slip down to warm her empty stomach.

"Yes," she answered him. The old woman on the grating let out a bark like a dog.

The three of them drank their soup with their backs to the cemetery and laughed out loud together, drunk on the richness of the plain brown lentils. Then she was sleepy, the warmth in her stomach spreading into her blood and making her yawn wider and wider. She gave her empty bowl to the old woman, his room key to Roland, and walked slowly back to the hotel without a word, her mouth full of yawns. She could hear Roland behind her on the street, coming through the hotel door, on the stairs. He passed her as she stood, her key in her hand, on the first floor landing in front of room one. He didn't stop. "Good night," he whispered.

"Good night," she called softly after him. Beyond the door a strange, empty bed waited for her. She could hear Roland going around and around above her on the circular stairs. As she touched the key to the lock, she thought of Paul's urn shining in the moonlight, an almost poisonous green. She imagined walking into that room, turning to ash, falling in a heap on the floor. Not literally perhaps, but she might as well. She would be as good as dead. Roland paused high above her, leaned over the rail.

"Pleasant dreams," he called down and then started the final flight.

She looked up. In the cemetery, the cats were dreaming one great purring dream, asleep in warm heaps. She didn't know what would happen if she followed Roland up, what she would do when she got to the room at the top of the stairs. All she knew was that she didn't want to sleep alone in a cold bed, in a room with a dead man. She wanted to be held. She wanted to hold somebody. After all, she was in Paris where all things were possible. Ginny put the key in her pocket and started the long climb up.

CHAPTER TEN

ROLAND HEARD GINNY on the stairs and held the door open for her. Though each of her footsteps was light, the ground shook. She was more real than the red iron woman in Odile's dreams and she was here. He closed his arms around her.

Ginny felt Roland's arms circle her, and all she could think of was a ring around the sun. She felt like the sun, all warm from the soup in her stomach.

The muscles in her calves shook from the long walk, and Roland shook too. They pulled off their own clothes, tired fingers fighting with hooks and buttons, and piled them on the chair. They undressed like very tired children hardly able to hold their eyes open. Ginny helped Roland unknot his shoes, and then they got into bed, Ginny still in her slip, Roland in his shirt which reached to his knees like a nightgown. Roland pulled the blanket over them, and they lay nestled like spoons, their heads on one pillow, the small lamp by the bed still on. The soup in his stomach rumbled against her curved back, and he tucked his cold feet between her warm legs. She thought of the cats again, all curled together. Roland breathed in and out slowly, his shirt brushing her wing bones. Their tiredness flowed away from them and into the pillow. The room was quiet.

But the warmth that had started in Ginny's stomach spread. First up to her breasts, her nipples rising with the heat, then down, down, until a sweat broke out between her legs. She began moving against Roland as he breathed, and he moved back. Even if she had forgotten, her body remembered what it had wanted from Paul. She rolled over to face Roland, blushing a hot pink, though she tried not to. He touched his lips to her eyelids, cool, soft. He put his arms around her, and she put her arms around him, holding hands with herself behind his back. Their legs clung to each other's, tangling. Her pulse spread from under his lips to her arms, her legs. This, she thought, is really the foreign country—where no one understands the words you learned from books.

She took off his shirt, and he took off her slip. They lay facing each other on the bed, his chin resting on the top of her head. Even lying down he was tall. She felt desirable, sexual, beautiful. Lying there naked, her body looked better than average, and for once in her life, she was glad it did. She rubbed a faint star-shaped spot over Roland's ribs, then she looked down between them.

Roland's eyes followed hers, saw that the hair between her legs was red too. Red and beautiful. He had seen women naked before—Odile, Lena, the girls in the village bathing in the river—but none of them had had red hair there.

"Hello," she said. She put her hand on his penis. His was different from Paul's, uncircumcised, like in her parents' old medical books. Under its hood, his penis was as smooth as the skin between his fingers. She stroked it with her thumb.

Roland reached down to touch what she touched only to wash. He felt her pulse under his fingers. "Hello," he said, and he felt like Max touching Lena, like his grandfather Odilon touching Odile, going back through a hundred pairs of Keppis. It felt better than anything in his life. The perfect joy of it.

When Roland's penis slid inside her, Ginny felt his arms around her, holding her, not like Paul holding the iron bedstead. They moved slowly, together. She lost track of her body. All her blood was trapped between them, beating, swollen. Then it was free, racing to her head. This was the end of the journey she had started with Paul. What the medical books had only hinted was possible. Sensation rolled through her in waves. She jerked back with the suddenness of it, and Roland let her go.

Then she lay still, breathing hard. After a minute, or ten, she rolled over, every muscle in her body relaxed. She lay curled, stomach to back with Roland again, this time with their bare skin touching instead of their clothes, sharing their dampness.

Roland touched the corner of her mouth where it turned down. Looking inside her was like walking across an enormous deserted train station. She was waiting, but far away. He could hear his footsteps on marble. There were other people there, from her past, but she couldn't see them. Her memories were more distant to her than his own dreams.

"I dreamed about you," he said.

"About me?" Ginny couldn't imagine what she would look like in someone else's dream. Maybe like an old photograph, a fuzzy image that could be anyone if it wasn't properly labeled.

"You were up very high," Roland said, "but bending low." He moved his hand through the air as if the dream were in front of them. "Like the Queen of Heaven."

"Oh no," Ginny laughed, relieved his dream was so wrong. It was her mother who wanted to be Queen of Heaven. She yawned so wide her eyes watered. Yawned again. Roland's arm rested on her shoulder, his webbed hand spread on the pillow, pink on the white linen.

Roland held Ginny as her breathing slowed, and again he could see Lena and Max, Odile and Grandfather Keppi, their hearts in their hands, a long line of Keppis bearing gifts, coming toward where he stood, where Ginny stood. He and Ginny would be part of the line, part of the family.

But Ginny slept and didn't know.

CHAPTER ELEVEN

WHEN ROLAND RETURNED from living with Lena in Germany, Odile went to the captain of the local police with four geese, and in the presence of so much dinner, he registered Roland without asking for his papers. Then for ten years everything was quiet in Hexwiller. The market for Odile's geese and ducks and chickens grew every year. When people had money, they ate it up, without saving. "Ten fat years," Odile said, shaking her head, putting her money away, "then ten lean."

Roland finished school, doing well in math, poorly in French history. He'd already learned one such set of lies. He took over Odile's stand at the market, spent his days selling fowl, flirting with the Wolff girl who sold carp. But no girl in Hexwiller, not even Frieda Wolff, was seriously interested in marrying a Keppi. Besides, Roland felt unsettled, unsafe, the way he had marching on the road outside the school during the war. Without proper identity papers, it seemed only a matter of time until there was trouble.

On July 27, 1929, the day Roland turned twenty-three, the captain stopped him on his way to sell Odile's birds in the market. "How is your mother doing?" he asked, as if he didn't know Roland's mother was German.

Roland said he didn't know.

"Ah, well," the captain said, "tell your grandmother I asked."

Odile sent two geese, but still she was worried. She had a dream that she was climbing a hill and at the top stood a monumental and unmoving woman the color of rust, a woman the size of a lighthouse holding a baby as big as a boxcar. To dream large was a good omen, a sign of plenty, but Odile had the odd feeling that the giant red woman was more than a sign, that somewhere she stood waiting, as large and patient as time, waiting for Odile. Odile turned in her sleep and found herself standing before a door in the hem of the woman's great rust red robe. She stepped through it. The folds of the robe rose out of sight above her, and a spiral staircase curled up into the darkness like a spine. She knew she should climb up into the woman's head and see her thoughts, find out where the Keppis really belonged. But she was frightened. She had never climbed so high. She wasn't sure she wanted to leave Hexwiller. She felt the protection of the woman's robe around her like armor. She knew she would not get a second chance, but still she stood frozen, unable to lift her foot onto the first iron step.

The next morning, Odile told Roland about her dream, sent him to buy a map of France. "Where," she asked him, "where if not here?" Roland ran his hand over and over the map, but he felt nothing. She tried her luck and thought she felt a spot of warmth to the south, in the Auvergne.

For the rest of the summer and into the fall, Odile had dreams full of bad omens, dreams she could never remember the next morning. Even if Roland heard her crying, "No, no, no!" and ran to her room and woke her, her dreams betrayed her and took their warning away. She sent another goose to the captain, a pair of ducks to the mayor. "Someone's trying to tell me something," Odile said of her dreams, shaking her head, "but I'm getting old and deaf."

But awake, Odile's hearing grew more sensitive each day. She sat at the kitchen table with her hands over her ears, unable to eat. "They talk and talk," she said of the neighbors. "Even after they're dead, they complain." While she was baking, she heard autonomists plotting, dreaming the old dream of a free Alsace, and she put dough in her ears. Still she heard the people of Hexwiller complaining how unhappy they were. Maybe if there was another war, they would whisper to each other, Alsace would get what she deserved. "Enough!" Odile said. She nailed tight the shutters downstairs, then hung the windows upstairs with quilts.

The captain heard the autonomists as well. He closed the local newspaper. On September first, fourteen men were arrested in Hexwiller by special police. None of them were autonomists, but none were released.

Odile had Roland print a sign: *No Geese for Sale.*

"Why?" he asked.

"We need them for watch geese," she said. So at night while Odile dreamt, calling out in her sleep, twelve geese paced the yard and slept hardly at all.

The second Monday in October, when Roland was at the market doing a brisk business in ducks and chickens, the geese in Odile's yard finally sounded the alarm. All dozen of them, gander to goose, honked for all they were worth. Police were going door to door checking papers, looking for German agents, for anyone with no official right to be in France. "What?" Odile said, cupping a hand to her ear when they came to the door. "I can't hear you."

"Who lives here?" they shouted.

"What?" Odile said. The police went away, but from her bedroom window Odile saw them talking to Emilie Boucher across the alley, looking her way, pointing, nodding. A Boucher had had a Keppi burned for heresy during the Thirty Years' War. She knew what Emilie Boucher was telling the police.

Odile worked hard in the hours left of the day. She dug up her bank from under the chicken house. She wrapped bundles of food and blankets and clothes. She meant to leave with Roland, no matter what he might say. She packed her map. They would find the monumental woman and child. They would go south.

Roland knew about the raids even before Odile. The news went through the stalls of the market like a cold wind, scattering those with a reason to worry. Roland wasn't the first to leave. He lingered, listening for word of Odile. He was afraid for her. Someone was bound to say that she had been sheltering him, a suspicious person with a German mother and no French papers. But they couldn't prove anything if he wasn't there. Roerich, the rabbit breeder, came over holding one of his rabbits by its legs. "I'd be glad," he said, swinging the rabbit absently against the table, "to watch the birds for you. If you need to take a walk."

Roland shook half the money from the sock he used as a bank and put it in his pocket. He gave the rest to Roerich for Odile. "Tell her not to worry," he said. "I'll send for her when I can." He tucked the last duck under his arm, wrapping his webbed fingers around its webbed feet, and left the crate of chickens to the rabbit breeder.

Roland headed down the valley, keeping pace with the dairy wagons and farmers. At Dettwiller, the stationmaster was out in front of the station, checking his watch against the town clock. It was noon. "Hey, son," he called out to Roland, "you selling that duck?" Roland nodded. "You're too late for the market."

"I know," Roland said. The stationmaster put his watch away. "I was hoping to get on a train."

"One's due in two minutes."

"Going south?" Roland remembered Odile's hands passing slowly over her map.

"Not just for you," the stationmaster said. "It's going to Paris, like always." So Roland traded the duck for a ticket and went west, to Paris. It was as easy as falling from a great height.

The train reached Paris after dark. Roland had fallen asleep, and when they pulled into the train shed at the Gare de l'Est, he was still unstuck in time. For a moment he stood on the platform waiting for Lena to meet him. He was almost knocked down by people running. They made more noise than the trains. He thought for a moment something terrible had happened—fire, war. Then he remembered he was in Paris. In Paris. He was twenty-three, had fifty-four francs, ten centimes in his pocket, and he was in Paris. He felt more excited, more alive than he had in a long time in Hexwiller. Right now, being a fugitive didn't seem so bad. No one was waiting for him, but no one seemed to be waiting for anything. The Parisians moved quickly into the street or down stairs that led into the ground.

Roland went outside. The street was noisy too. More cars than he had ever seen buzzed by on the wide pavement, their horns like ganders calling to geese. He followed the crowds from the station across a bridge over the tracks, hundreds of tracks. Who could tell which he had ridden from Alsace? Even the police couldn't follow him here.

People hurried past him, talking very fast, too fast for him to catch more than a word. Everyone seemed excited, as if something was about to happen, as if something was always about to happen. Roland walked with the fingers of his webbed hand spread wide, like a net. People pushed in and out of bakeries, cafes, cheese and wine shops. They hurried home to supper. Roland kept walking.

After a while, the road narrowed and there were fewer people. It was still noisy. Music drifted down from windows, shouts, laughter. People leaned in the shop doors and sat on the steps. The men at the station had all been dressed in suits, and many of the women had worn suits as well, like Lena. Several people had looked hard at his rough wool pants and coat, his collarless shirt. Now, the men seemed to take some care not to look at him at all. They stood with their hands deep in the pockets of baggy pants, wearing oversized cloth caps that reminded Roland of the berets the cadets wore at school. Only the women smiled, nodded their heads, their breasts tugging at their blouses when they moved. The women had short hair with a single dark curl flat on their foreheads. Everyone was smoking, even the women. One blew a smoke ring at Roland as he walked by. He caught it on his finger, and the smoke wrapped around his hand.

The woman laughed. "Want one?" She held out a metal cigarette case. Her eyes were pale green, the color of Frieda Wolff's carp. Roland took a cigarette. He thought he might be expected to pay for it, but the woman only offered him a match. He lit the cigarette, got it going.

Another woman came out of a doorway and took a cigarette from the first woman's case. "You owe me," she said. A scratchy phonograph record started somewhere. Both women's lips were red as goose hearts, drawn like bows. A couple passed on the sidewalk, talking and laughing.

"It's busy here," Roland said, trying to sound as if he had some basis for comparison.

The first woman blew another smoke ring. "It's the fair," she said and pointed. Roland saw lights above the dark roofs, red and white, moving in an arc across the sky, beckoning all to come to the fair.

He finished the cigarette. "I think I will go have a look," he said. He walked through a smoke ring.

"Watch your pockets," the second woman called after him.

The wind carried the smell of burnt sugar and sausages and brought back to him the smell of his own smoky breath. He came out in a traffic circle blocked off at both ends and filled with the street fair. It was as if he had walked into the home of noise. People screamed. Bells rang. *A winner here. Hurry, hurry.* The lights he'd seen from the street belonged to a Ferris wheel several times as high as the one that came once a year to Hexwiller. Above him, a woman screamed. The ground was sour with vomit.

He made his way carefully down the midway. There was a ride with wooden airplanes hanging by chains from a painted sky, a carousel that spun in circles to a song about the cat who went to the moon—it was empty. Roland realized it was late. He asked a sailor what time it was.

"Ten o'clock," the sailor said. In Hexwiller, Odile would be out in the yard with the lamp, making her last rounds with the geese.

Under the next street light, a crowd was forming around a boy with a goat on a tether. The goat was perched on top of a glass jar, moving his feet in a tiny precarious circle. There was scattered applause. The goat jumped down and was led away by a smaller boy. The crowd wavered, feeling the pull of the music, the hawkers. The goat boy smashed a wine bottle on the pavement, then another. The violence pulled the crowd back into a circle. He took off his shirt and lay on his back on the broken glass. The smaller boy stood on his chest. Some women looked away. The smaller boy jumped down and the goat boy stood. The crowd pushed closer. The boy's back was dirty but uncut.

Someone gasped and then there was a round of applause. Roland clapped. The boy brushed the glass and cigarette butts from his back, began passing a hat. People moved off. Roland saw the smaller boy, moving among them, tuck two wallets into his shirt. The woman who gave him the cigarette had also given him good advice. Roland put his hands in his pockets.

Next to the goat boys was a splendid shooting gallery, with more lights on it than anything else at the fair, than anything Roland had ever seen. Its red and gold façade came to a tall point at the top, and the name The Mountain of Gold was outlined in blinking yellow. A man sat watching over the gallery from a booth built on the side like a pulpit. He was draped in a red robe and crowned with a gold turban, but it wasn't until Roland was standing in front of him that he realized how huge he was, as big as the quartermaster and the drillmaster rolled together. His neck was the size of Roland's waist and was hung with yards of gold chain. His arms, big as Roland's legs, were armored with gold bracelets, and his fingers were studded at every joint with bright rings. He was a Mountain of Gold. A gilt sign beneath his booth announced him as *Louis the Mountain.*

Monsieur Mountain smiled at Roland. He waved a gold-tipped cane at his endlessly moving targets. Roland examined them more closely. There was a revolving wedding scene with a suspiciously round-bellied bride. Besides the groom, the priest, and the best man, there was a fat usher who winked at the bride with one large painted eye. "Aren't they beautiful?" Monsieur Mountain said, his voice deep and full of emotion. "So human. In response to a direct hit, the male members of the bridal party drop their pants. The bride, though, disappoints. She drops only her flowers."

Below the wedding was a tropical scene with monkeys and coconut palms chasing a column of soldiers up a pyramid. Although most of the paint had been peppered away, it seemed to Roland that the soldiers wore French uniforms. "In Paris, people pay to shoot their own soldiers?" Roland asked.

"Macht nichts," Monsieur Mountain said, and it took Roland a moment to realize he had spoken in German. "Certainly," this time he spoke in French, "what's more French than a good revolution?"

"Are you German?"

"Me? No," Monsieur Mountain laughed with an audible ringing of chains. "But I was found in a barrel of kraut at Les Halles, or so I was told. At any rate, I have a weakness for Germans. And you?"

"I'm Alsatian," Roland said.

"Ah, neither cat nor dog. Do you want to shoot at my soldiers, nameless Alsatian?"

"Roland," Roland said, touching a finger to one of the guns. He thought of Max, falling backward into his bed of snow. "I think soldiers get shot enough without my help."

"True," Monsieur Mountain said, "they're always popular. Why not shoot for the stars, then? They're harder to hit."

Until then, Roland hadn't noticed the stars and comets raised on rods above the heads of the soldiers, the bride and groom. He picked up one of the rifles. It was heavier than the lead pipe he'd drilled with at school. He sighted down the barrel. It bent to the left. "Try this one." Monsieur Mountain tapped the gun nearest him with his cane.

It was straight. All those years at school, aiming down his length of pipe, sending his thoughts flying toward the target, Roland had always wondered if he could hit anything. He eased the trigger on the rifle. A flying comet disappeared with a small ping. He pulled three times, and three stars fell from the sky.

"Beautiful, Monsieur Roland," Monsieur Mountain said. "Will you shoot another round? A business that looks slow, stays slow. Here." He lifted a doll in a hula skirt off the wall of the stand with his cane. "You've already won this."

Roland knocked down the last three stars and a spinning comet. Bells rang. Lights flashed. A small crowd began to gather. He heard a woman's laugh, a man murmur in reply. Monsieur Mountain put away the hula doll and held up a ukulele. Roland fired another round, taking down a row of coconut palms. Monsieur Mountain turned on some music, something with horns and a rhythm like a train. Roland felt a man at his side. The man gave Monsieur Mountain some francs folded in half. "Ah, beautiful," Monsieur Mountain said and, with a soft grunt, lifted a gold chain from around his neck. He let it dangle from the tip of his cane, a circle of flame in the glare of the electric lights, raising the stakes again. He hung the ukulele back on the wall. "Now we have a contest," he said.

The man who had paid the francs took a rifle, the one with the crooked barrel. He looked over his shoulder at a woman like all the young women Roland had seen so far in Paris—spit curls, red lips. She seemed to have eyes only for the airplane ride, the monoplanes and biplanes, the single silver zeppelin spinning by. The man shot. He missed three times, but the fourth shot he sighted to the right and got the officer leading his men up the sand dune. Roland knocked over two monkeys, a palm tree, and then, since no stars or palms or monkeys remained, he shot the priest. Bells rang.

Monsieur Mountain held out the necklace as if he would give it to Roland, but instead he gave him his hand. "Any ring," Monsieur Mountain said, "for the next win." His fingers sparkled red and gold. The man gave Monsieur Mountain more francs. His young woman was watching now. Her eyes were fixed on Monsieur Mountain's bright hands.

They shot. The man knocked over the bride and three soldiers too worn in service to have the benefit of rank. Roland, hardly aiming now, hit the groom, the best man, the fat usher, and then, closing his eyes, the last poor soldier. But only the first three fell. He looked at Monsieur Mountain, surprised. Monsieur Mountain only smiled. He held out his hand to the young woman. On all his fingers were rings with bright stones, but in his palm he held a plain gold wedding band. "You must choose," Monsieur Mountain said. The woman took a red jeweled ring off Monsieur Mountain's index finger. She led the man off by the arm.

Monsieur Mountain sighed. He held out the gold band to Roland. "This one's real," he said. "Not much to look at, is it?" He tucked the ring under his turban. "Ah, the women are so beautiful. All the people who come to the Mountain are beautiful. How can I begrudge them their gifts?"

"How did you keep that last target from falling?" Roland asked.

"I have a button," Monsieur Mountain said. "Why must a soldier always die when he's shot?" Monsieur Mountain had just raised his shoulders in an elaborate shrug, when Roland heard shouting.

"What do you mean, you shit, letting those girls ride twice for one ticket? Have you a turd for a brain?" A man in a green and brown striped suit was swearing at the boy running the plane ride.

"Him," Monsieur Mountain said, shaking his head and his chains. "Herr Scheiss. He's not beautiful. He turns the air to dung. Hey!" Monsieur Mountain yelled, leaning forward in his booth. "What business is this of yours, anyway? It's not your ride."

The man in the striped suit turned around. "An uncle of mine," he said, "asked me to look after it." He stepped into the glow of the Mountain of Gold. The light caught an ear as red as a fresh scar. Roland couldn't believe it. It was Fuss.

Roland cried "Fuss!" and René Fuss swung around angry, his fist out. When he saw who it was, he kept swinging, catching Roland on the shoulder, a joyous punch like a clapper striking its bell. Fuss looked the same, except his left ear was ragged and torn as if in a cat fight. Half of Roland was happy to see Fuss, a familiar face in the strangeness of Paris. The other half knew better.

Fuss was calling himself René the Foot. "Shit, you're tall," he said looking Roland over with a smile, taking in Roland's muddy shoes, rough jacket. "But you look like a real cheese head."

Monsieur Mountain flicked René the Foot with his cane. "Watch it," he said.

"We were boys together," Fuss was saying. "Frog used to follow me everywhere." He pulled hard on Roland's arm. "Shit, we need to drink."

"Come by in the morning," Monsieur Mountain said to Roland, "and we'll talk about work. I won't believe this Apache hasn't slit your throat until I see you."

Fuss pulled Roland behind the shooting gallery, the rides and hawkers' booths. The night beyond the lights smelled of urine. "I run this girl show here for an uncle," he winked. "It's a good stick." They entered the show tent through a canvas flap at the back. The wooden benches in front of the stage were empty, but the air was still warm with the smell of a crowd. In the dressing room, a blond woman in a robe and black stockings was bent over a bucket washing her face. Her arms were amazingly muscular. Even the back of her neck had muscles as thick as ropes.

"Damn you, René. The least you could do is make sure I get clean water." Fuss shrugged, pulled on his chewed ear. The woman threw the cloth into the bucket and looked up, noticing Roland for the first time. "Oh," she said, pulling her robe closed. Even her breasts had muscles.

"This is my friend, Frog," Fuss said.

"Hello," the woman said.

"Get dressed. We're going to show Frog around."

"I'm Carmen," the woman said to Roland when she was dressed for the street in a black skirt and tight sweater. "Are you working for René?"

"He's in with that old queen at the shoot trap," Fuss explained, "for now." He spat, both ears burning red. "That fat prick has the looks of a La Villette whore. Those butchers like women who heft like a side of beef."

"I wouldn't know," Carmen said. Fuss laughed.

"You're a dancer?" Roland asked her.

"For now. I was an acrobat with my brother, Franz, but I'm dancing for a while, for a living."

"Carmen," Roland said. "Are you Spanish?"

"It's a show name," she said.

"Shit, if you don't like it, Frog," Fuss said, "call her anything you like." Fuss spat into the gutter. Carmen looked like she might hit Fuss, and Roland thought she probably should. "What was your mother's name?" Fuss asked.

"Carmen," Roland said, trying to defuse the situation. "My mother's name was Carmen." Fuss laughed.

Fuss led them away from the fair. The noise and music faded behind them and then picked up again, coming from somewhere ahead. "Why don't we go someplace for dinner?" Carmen asked. "I'm hungry." Fuss stopped in front of a door at the center of the noise. "Why do we have to go here?"

"Because I'm showing my friend a good time."

Fuss pushed the door open. A few notes from an accordion escaped with a rush of smoke. Inside men and women churned on a small dance floor, leaned against a bar sipping drinks through straws. Fuss elbowed a place for them at the bar, yelled something, and moments later handed Roland a glass of creamy yellow liquor. Roland took a sip from the side, keeping the straw out of his eye with a finger. It tasted like licorice. Carmen sipped her drink, which was blue, through her straw. "No bottles," she said into Roland's ear, struggling to be heard over the accordion. She made a motion as if she were striking him over the head with a rolling pin, "fights." She nodded at a row of booths fastened to the wall. "No tables."

Roland nodded. "Fights," he said, and he saw her mouth smile.

"I'm going to get a dance," Fuss said, putting down his empty glass. "Don't let anyone buy Carmen a drink." He headed across the room toward the booths. He put his arm around the waist of a redhead in a plaid blouse with a few buttons popped across her chest and moved her out onto the dance floor. Roland looked at Carmen. He felt sweat roll down his back. She spoke into his ear.

"You can't say no to a dance here."

"To a drink?" His head was beginning to ache.

"If you've got somebody to say no for you." The accordion started again, this time joined by a banjo and a drum set. The musicians sat in a tiny balcony draped with gold coins. They wore red vests and had scarves tied loosely over their heads. "They're not real Gypsies," Carmen said.

"Show Gypsies?"

Carmen smiled. "Those boys at the fair, the ones with the goat, they're real Gypsies."

"I saw the smaller one take a man's wallet."

"That's a real Gypsy for you. Hands like fish hooks," she said, leaning forward. "The two at the fair work for your friend, the Gold Mountain."

The music stopped suddenly, and a man stepped from behind the bar. "Shell out! Shell out!" he yelled. The men on the dance floor reached into their pockets, and coins rang at their feet.

"You pay for each dance," Carmen explained. The accordion breathed out, and the musicians took up where they left off. Roland watched the couples turning, the men's hands low on the women's backs, their shoes sliding over the coins on the floor. Everyone was sweating.

The musicians started the next song. Carmen took his hand, and they moved onto the dance floor. Roland hadn't danced with a woman since he danced with Lena in Würzburg. But he moved his feet to the music, guiding Carmen between the other couples, and found it easy, like driving Odile's geese. When he touched Carmen on the shoulder, she moved right. He pressed her waist, and she stepped back. Once he felt her muscles tense, as if for a moment she might go her own way, then like the geese, she followed his lead. When the call came to shell out, he threw the price of six eggs on the floor.

"Where did your brother Franz go?" Roland shouted into Carmen's ear when the band started up again.

"America," Carmen shouted back. "We're from Nürnberg. There Franz got some parts in movies, climbing and falling. We're both very strong. But Franz climbed into someone else's house. He got away, but the police knew it was him. Then this movie company in America sent him a ticket to New York. They were going to make a movie about these white apes that live on the tops of those tall buildings they have in America, but the police in Nürnberg told the American embassy he was a crook and not to give him a visa. So we came here, and he bought some papers. That was before Christmas. I'm waiting for him to send for me, but now I don't know. He could be in jail. Who knows if the papers were any good? I look at the movie posters, but I haven't seen anything about apes." Carmen shrugged, wiped her hands on her skirt. "So I'm dancing each night and waiting. René—your Fuss—is supposed to watch out for me, but from the start he gives me trouble. One night I hit him," Carmen swung her fist at Roland's head but stopped short, "and that was a mistake. Now, I think, he likes me."

The music stopped. Roland stopped too. His shirt was wet with sweat, his hair stuck to his forehead. The smoke was so thick that he could hardly see Fuss at the bar where he was buying the girl in the plaid blouse a drink. He waved them over.

"Frog," Fuss said, pulling Roland close, "after all these years, you're still too German. You need to loosen up." Fuss threw one arm around Carmen and the other around the plaid girl. "Me," he said, "I'm two hundred percent French." Carmen shrugged off Fuss's arm. The girl giggled. "Shit on that," Fuss said. "Come on," he stumbled toward the door. "We're leaving." Carmen shook her head at his back.

"I'm going home," she said to Roland. "But if René is a friend, you'd better go with him. It's not good to be so drunk, not with money loose in your pockets."

Roland hesitated. Was Fuss his friend? But Carmen turned toward the girl in the plaid blouse, borrowed a cigarette. Roland followed Fuss into the street. He heard him up ahead, ". . . shit place."

Fuss kept them going most of the night, walking miles from one bar to the next, all over Paris. At each place, Fuss knew some girl, bought her drinks. "I'm crazy in love with that girl, Carmen," he told Roland at the third place they stopped, then again at the fourth. "Crazy. Why does she have to act so German?" Fuss put his head on his arms, his good ear on the table, and wept. "I don't know why she can't love me," he would say, pulling and pulling on his ruined ear. "I'm a lovable guy."

Roland was never sure how he got back to the fair, but when he opened his eyes the next morning, he was in the tent of the girl show, stretched out like a corpse on one of the benches, his hands folded across his chest. It was barely dawn, but even the faint light hurt his eyes. He closed them again, groaned.

When he could see the light even with his eyes closed, he washed his face and went out. He found Monsieur Mountain where he had left him the night before. "Ah, what a beautiful morning," he called to Roland. The oldest of the Gypsy boys was shaving the Mountain's neck while the youngest washed his feet. Monsieur Mountain waved them away. "I move," he said, "only when the fair moves, and then it takes two men and a truck, but that's to move two mountains." He nodded at the shooting gallery.

"Where does the fair go?"

"Oh, each one of these traps has a circuit around Paris, a ride that lasts all year. Except each year we have to set up further out. So I suppose it's less a circle than a spiral, out from Paris into oblivion, or the provinces, which is the same thing."

"It's very beautiful in Alsace."

"Ah, well, I'm sure it must be. But then you're here, aren't you?"

Monsieur Mountain put Roland to work cleaning the guns and checking the secret pulleys on the targets. When people started wandering through the fair, the Gypsy boys began discreet hourly runs to Monsieur Mountain, carrying objects the visitors to the fair no longer possessed. They tucked the cameras and watches and purses and wallets under Monsieur Mountain's bulk for safety.

"Aren't they beautiful?" he asked Roland. "I call them Mohammed and Moses. They come to the mountain, so that the mountain does not have to go to them." The boys, Monsieur Mountain explained, had come across the border from Spain, and if they were caught stealing in France they could only be deported. "As near as I can gather, their parents think of me as a sort of finishing school."

Each morning for a week Roland helped the Mountain set up, and in the evenings he worked as his shill, winning just enough to draw a good crowd. Afternoons were his own, and Roland spent them walking across Paris. To him the city seemed like a bigger version of the fair, music mixed with thieves. Still, as long as he saw pickpockets, he knew no police were around. He couldn't afford to be stopped, asked for his papers. At night after the fair closed, he slept on one of the tent show benches.

At the end of the week, Fuss stopped by the shooting gallery to ask Roland to run the airplane ride for him. "Take charge of your future," he said, smiling, smiling. Roland was cleaning the guns' silver barrels.

"No, thanks," Roland said, pausing long enough to watch each plane spin by twice. Did he have a future? At the fair? In Paris? Was there any place he was really safe? "It makes me dizzy."

Fuss hit him hard on the arm. "Someday you'll let me do you a favor, Frog. You wait and see."

The next morning Roland woke up with a start. Someone was shaking him. Carmen. "Get up," she said. "Get out. The police are checking everyone's papers. They've got the Gypsies already. I'm going out the back." Roland sat up, rubbing his eyes, but Carmen was already gone.

He followed her out the back flap of the tent. He couldn't see any police, but he kept behind the booths until he reached the Mountain of Gold. Monsieur Mountain was there, his head bent as if he were sleeping. Roland called to him, staying behind his great bulk. "The noble representatives of the French state have left," Monsieur Mountain answered, not turning his head, "but, to be safe, you'd best stay where you are."

"They took the boys?"

"Yes," he sighed, "and you had better go too." Monsieur Mountain shifted forward and reached under his seat. "Take these," he said, "as a small token." He drew out a cigarette case, two wallets, and with an awkward flourish, a large English umbrella and held them out to Roland. Roland hesitated. "A favor," Monsieur Mountain said. "How would it look if the police found me sitting on this sort of egg?" Roland took the gifts. "Take them to Monsieur Marlotte in Pigalle. Tell him

I sent you. And you'd better take the Métro. You'll be too conspicuous walking with such an ugly umbrella."

Roland followed Monsieur Mountain's directions to the nearest Métro stop. He found the hole in the ground and was preparing to go down it when he heard his name. He turned. It was Carmen, a bundle of clothes in her arms. "Frog," she said, "oh, Frog. I've caused the big trouble." She was crying. They sat on the stairs to the Métro, her spare clothes at their feet. "It was because I was yelling at Fuss that someone called the police. Franz is in jail in Germany and I was blaming René, but now I find out that Franz got in a fight on the ship. Someone was hurt. He never got to New York."

"Why did you think Fuss was to blame?"

"He sold Franz his papers. I thought they were no good."

"Did you tell Fuss that?"

"I shouted that at him. Then I started hitting him. He was crying, begging me not to go home to Germany."

"Did the police pick up Fuss?"

"Not for now. I think he pays plenty for protection, but who knows? He shouldn't go crying like that. People lose their respect." She shook her head. "I've got to worry about Franz. Auf Wiedersehen, Frog," she said and kissed him hard on the cheek. He could feel the blood start to rise in a bruise. She disappeared down the hole.

Roland followed Carmen, and the earth swallowed him. He was alone again, homeless. Thinking about it made him tired and depressed. Even the dark Métro tunnel seemed like a bad sign. Roland found his way to the shop Monsieur Mountain had suggested. The owner, Monsieur Marlotte, looked over the goods Roland laid on the counter and sighed. "How is Monsieur Mountain? This time of year he's usually somewhere near the Gare de l'Est."

"That's where I left him."

"But he sent you all of the way over here to me?" Roland nodded. Monsieur Marlotte began slowly counting out a small pile of francs. "Will you be doing more business with us?"

"No, this is it," Roland said. "Do you know where I might find work around here?"

Monsieur Marlotte sighed again, stopped adding to the pile of bills. "You might try the food stalls on Rue Lepic. They sometimes use day labor." He pushed the money across the counter to Roland.

Roland asked his way to Rue Lepic. As he climbed Montmartre, he asked for work at one place and then another. As one, the shopkeepers shook their heads. He spotted a policeman up ahead, coming out of a bakery with a baguette in his hand. Roland passed him on the far side of the street. As he passed by the bakery, the smell of the bread made Roland's stomach twist with hunger. He counted fifty centimes out of his pocket, crossed the street and went in. A woman about Odile's age was cutting bread for her customers. The warm smell of the yeast made him dizzy. He held onto the counter to steady himself. The old woman looked up at Roland's face and then down at his webbed hand. She came toward him. "You're a Keppi," she said. "I'd know a Keppi anywhere."

The old woman sat him in a corner, brought him some bread and coffee. She started in on the afternoon dough, talking steadily as she kneaded. She had grown up with Odile. Her family had moved to Strassburg in 1873, after the Kaiser took Alsace. Now she was a Clavel, but she'd been born a Woerli. There were still Woerlis, distant cousins, who ran the bakery in Hexwiller. Roland said he knew them. "Of course you know them," Madame Clavel said. "How could you be from Hexwiller and not know them?" She told him about her life, her first marriage in Strassburg, her four in Paris. Then she made him go through all the Hexwiller deaths and births and marriages he could remember, prodding him whenever he slowed. He talked until it was late evening and the last customer had come and gone. Finally she let him stop and told him he could sleep against the oven wall in the bakery. "After all these years, a Keppi," he heard her saying as he made his bed out of flour sacks. "Now what's that a sign of?"

Roland didn't know. Odile would, he thought. Surely. He closed his eyes, and saw not Odile, but Odile's giant red woman with the skirts of rusting iron. She opened her skirts to him, and without moving he was inside. There was a circular staircase, and he climbed it into the giant woman's head. A young woman with hair even redder than rust sat there like the giant woman's soul or maybe her brain. When she saw him, she smiled. Then she stood and led him to two windows, the giant woman's eyes. Through them Roland could see a giant stone man on a far hill. The ground shook. Birds sprang into the air singing. The stone man stepped from his hill. He strode toward the giant woman. The giant red woman shook too, pulling her iron skirts free of the ground. There was all around Roland a fierce bright light as happiness approached.

Roland woke early to the smell of fresh bread and found that Monsieur Clavel had replaced his wife at the ovens. Roland helped him load the great oven and stack bread for the breakfast rush. When it was over, Monsieur Clavel gave him a handshake, three francs, and three long loaves of bread. Roland wandered out into the morning.

He climbed a flight of wide marble steps. Above him he could see a great palace or cathedral, white as an iced cake in the bright sun. The marble steps were steep, and halfway up he sat on a bench to rest. He held up a piece of his bread as an offering, and the birds came like messengers, then flew away with their crumbs, with the news. He waited for the answer. He spent a second night at the bakery, worked the next morning, went back to the bench. Then, at the end of the long afternoon, the woman with the red hair descended the marble steps and Roland took her hand.

CHAPTER TWELVE

I'LL BE AT the bench by noon." Ginny rolled over. The room was still dark, but Roland stood by the bed fully dressed.

He covered her eyes with his hand, kissed her hair. "The bench at noon," he said.

When she woke again, it was light and her stomach was growling. Her dress was on the chair where she'd left it the night before, but her slip, corselet, and underpants were folded neatly on the end of the bed. Roland must have put them there. She thought that should embarrass her, but it didn't. The bench at noon. She sat up, remembering that. She imagined him there, holding up bread for the sparrows. There would be a cloud of them, each free to choose bread or the sky. He would be waiting, but it was her choice whether or not to take what was offered. She flipped the choice in her mind like a coin.

She dressed and went to ask for a bath. Madame Desnos looked up from adding a column in a ledger book when Ginny came down the stairs. "With your new room you get breakfast," she said, waving a thin hand at the end of the counter where a basket with a six-inch piece of bread and a white cup sat on a tray. Madame Desnos took the cup from the counter and returned a moment later with it full of coffee. "Dunk the bread," she advised. "If you had come down five minutes later, I wouldn't give it to you. Even Americans shouldn't be allowed to eat a breakfast baguette for lunch."

"After this, I'd like to have a hot bath," Ginny said. Madame Desnos shrugged.

"If Madame insists."

"I'll be in . . ." *Paul's room*, Ginny caught herself thinking, "room one." She took the tray upstairs. Room one was much larger than her old room or the room at the top of the stairs where she had slept with Roland. It had a wide double bed with a white coverlet and a window on the street. Madame Desnos or someone had put her trunk behind the door, Paul's urn on the mirrored dresser. Ginny sat in the chair by the window with her back to the urn and ate her bread, dunking it in her coffee. Probably she wouldn't go to Sacré Coeur to meet Roland. One night with a birdman, a stranger was one thing—this was Paris. But to go on . . .

"Madame!" Madame Desnos called.

What would Fanny say? Fanny, who had found out everything she'd let herself believe wasn't true. Fanny, who had suffered the kind of heartache they hospitalized you for.

Madame Desnos knocked, and Ginny opened the door. Madame Desnos pointed out the window to the street below. "Your bath."

A tub was walking down the street, a man's legs barely showing under the zinc. "That's not a bath," Ginny said. "It's a turtle."

The man carried the tub on his back up the narrow stairs to her room, squeezing it between the bed and the door. Madame Desnos laid out a pile of extra sheets, a bar of soap. She draped one of the sheets carefully inside the tub. Ginny stood waiting. The tub man reappeared, panting, with a bucket of water, then another. It took ten trips to half-fill the tub. "You can get undressed now," Madame Desnos said.

Ginny felt stupidly American. "I did ask for a hot bath," she said, getting out of her underwear.

"One moment," Madame Desnos said, wrapping a sheet deftly around Ginny, tucking it under one arm. "Here it comes now." The tub man reentered the room with a final bucket of steaming hot water. "Ah, there," Madame Desnos said and led Ginny to her bath.

The water was less than lukewarm, and bathing with one sheet under her and one draped around her certainly felt odd, but that made the bath seem special, almost ceremonial. A French baptism. Ginny let herself sink down underwater, opened her eyes.

"Madame!" Madame Desnos tapped on the tub. Ginny surfaced.

"I'll call when I'm done," Ginny told her. She meant to scrub herself from head to toe. Spring cleaning. She picked up the soap and reached for her feet. She couldn't see her body under the sheet, but her skin felt smooth, seamless. She could almost imagine it the body of a beautiful woman. She scrubbed hard at her stomach, her breasts. She spread her legs, and when she felt between them, she thought of Roland. *Hello, down there, hello.*

Madame Desnos knocked on the door, called to her.

"One minute," Ginny called back, soaping up her hair. Madame Desnos appeared with a bucket, poured cold water down her back. "Whaa!" Ginny yelled, as shocked as a newborn. Madame Desnos took away the wet sheet and wrapped her in a dry one. She wrapped another around her hair. Ginny stepped out of the tub and stood dripping in her sheets while the tub man emptied the water bucket by bucket, then she gave him the three francs he asked. She combed her hair flat and dressed, making herself a widow again. Then she followed the tub man down the stairs.

She took herself out onto the street, not knowing what to do, still thinking, *I won't go.* She wandered down Rue Lepic, and the fruit shops drew her in. The fruit seemed to glow, to be swollen with life. She picked up one perfect orange, then another, feeling the weight of them in her palms. Two oranges. Even they seemed more natural in pairs. Everything around her seemed sexual somehow, as if she had developed a new sense, as if she were hearing music or smelling flowers for the first time, entering a world everyone else had known about for a long time. Red meat and long firm bananas. The way men looked at women as women walked away.

She was aware of her own body, her breasts touching her slip, her legs rubbing together. She bent down to look at some cherries and smelled a rich warmth coming from between her legs, like fresh bread. She wandered from shop to shop and bought wine and cheese. Everything was long or round, male or female. She bought two of everything. She felt breathless. *I won't go.*

But at noon, she did go to Sacré Coeur, descending the steps as slowly as if she were wading into the Gulf of Mexico on a hot summer's day. She didn't let herself look until she was next to Roland. Then there he was. Right there. She didn't look at him as she had looked at him before, at his frayed cuffs, or at least she tried not to. Now she saw him with her whole body, and her body gave out an eager cry that took her by surprise. *My lover,* it said. Roland took the bag with the two of everything, and hand in hand they walked back to the hotel.

Later that afternoon, after they'd made love and were lying sweaty and half-asleep, Ginny said, "I want to tell you something."

Roland touched the damp red hair on the nape of her neck and said, "Yes?"

"I'm a widow, you know." Ginny waited to be asked questions, be forced to find answers, but Roland only nodded.

"Yes," he said. There was a long pause, and Ginny lay listening to her breathing, his breathing. "Tell me a story," Roland said.

A story? Ginny closed her eyes, halfway expecting to see Paul, but instead she saw Fanny rocking on the screen porch of her hospital cabin. "You should meet my Aunt Fanny. She thinks yellow smells like fresh air."

"Who knows?" Roland said, running a hand through his hair.

Ginny looked beyond Roland, thinking about Fanny. Ginny opened her mouth, and out came the story. About how Fanny's senses were all tangled up, how when she looked at a color, she smelled it and tasted it. Ginny tried to imagine all she'd ever heard about Fanny from Fanny's point of view. Fanny had once told her that when she was small she thought everyone was like her. Had thought that when her mother went to bed, overwhelmed by the world, she was feeling what Fanny felt all the time.

It was her first day at Dr. Love's academy that Fanny found out how different she was. Dr. Love himself was teaching her, standing on a stool next to the alphabet chart because he was even shorter than the six-year-olds in the class. Tiny, more than tiny — a perfect dwarf. Fanny couldn't make herself follow Dr. Love's pointer, make herself look at the letters he traced because they were black, the sharpest of colors, and when he let her write her alphabet in crayon, the colors made each letter so delicious it was hard to get past one to the next. Her mother worked hard with her, spending more time with Fanny than with her older sister Claire, who read and wrote and played the piano with ease because none of it mattered to her at all. Finally, in high school, Fanny started to make good grades. She showed a flair for languages. She could get inside them, make them up as she went along without having to spend time over lists of verbs and endings like Claire did. Claire took German — she wanted to be a doctor. Fanny took French — it felt more. It was as red as sweet ripe plums. Red, she would tell Ginny later, as her niece's hair.

"Yes?" Roland said. "And then?"

"And then she graduated, and Madame Duval, her French teacher, recommended her for a teaching job in Martinique." It was Claire who took Fanny to her ship. Their mother was sick again. At first, Fanny wouldn't get on. The gray metal in the sun tasted sour, upset her stomach. Claire laughed at her.

Martinique was better. The colors that bothered her, gray and black, were rare, except in the halls of the school where she taught. The island was green and red and as sweet as the French she spoke all day. Only the blackboard in her classroom made her head ache, her hands shake. She stopped writing on it. Instead she cut out the letters for her lessons from colored paper. A, B, C. Red and green and yellow. She tried not to look at the gray metal of the scissors. The children loved the colored letters. After a month, she moved on to colored numbers: 1, 2, 3. But the principal got complaints from the children's parents. Why didn't the teacher use the school books they had bought? The books were imported from France and expensive and filled with black ink. Even the drawings, apple through zebra, were black. The principal came into her room after school one day and sat at her desk, talking and talking to her. Fanny sat in one of the children's desks and put her head down.

Fanny took a week off after her talk with the principal, spent it painting the walls of her apartment yellow. Ilu, her maid, bought the paint for her and fixed her meals. She had already figured out what Fanny's mother never had, that well-done beef was black, so tasted sharp to Fanny, chicken and bananas were hot in a good way, like the sun. Ilu fed her red beans, never black ones. Ilu's full name was Ilumination. It means all-lit-up, Ilu joked, draining an imaginary bottle and staggering a few steps across the room, but Fanny thought it was beautiful. One day Ilu asked if Fanny would like to visit her village, where the hibiscuses were a deeper red than in the city. When Fanny locked the garden gate behind her apartment, Ilu touched the black painted boards and said, "Ouch, sharp."

"Ouch?" Fanny asked.

"Ouch," Ilu repeated.

At Ilu's village, her children, eleven of them, came running out to see the visitor. They touched the black road. "Ouch," they said. "Sharp. Sharp."

Fanny quit her job at the school, let her apartment go to her replacement. She bought a tent, complete with mosquito netting, and set it up in Ilu's yard. The children followed her to the market. "Hot," they said when she bought a yellow papaya. "Ouch," they said when they touched the black tarpaulin over the stalls.

Fanny slept in the tent, ate at Ilu's table. The neighbors came to visit, brought food and clothes and animals for her to touch. "Is this corn good?" they wanted to know. This pig sick? This cloth lucky for a wedding dress? This beer good for my lover's strength? Fanny started a long poem about life in the village.

Weeks passed before some mail from the States caught up with her. Her mother was still sick. Fanny sent her part of her poem. She signed it *The Poet Laureate of Martinique*. That was a joke. She didn't stop to think that Claire might see the poem and that Claire didn't have a sense of humor. It was her replacement at the school who came out to tell her Claire was on the island looking for her. The new teacher felt she owed Fanny something—the children she'd left her were so wonderful. They drew great red and yellow pictures of fruit and sunsets and sang out their alphabet. They liked school. They liked her. No one else ever had.

Fanny sent the teacher back into town with an arm-load of papayas. Let Claire come. Ilu and her children would prove she wasn't crazy. Here everything she felt and saw and heard was normal. Everyone felt the same things she did. Her last night sleeping in the tent, there was a meteor shower. Ilu came out with some fried bananas for a snack and sat watching the stars fall. Fanny laid out her plans for proving Claire wrong. The children would be brought out one by one. Perhaps they should be blindfolded until the last minute. Fanny didn't want Claire to think it was a trick, to think she was coaching the children. "Do you mean, Mademoiselle Fanny, that all Americans don't see things the way you do?" Ilu asked.

"No, of course not," Fanny said, "but all of you do. That's the point. You're just like me."

Ilu sighed. She rubbed the oil from the bananas on the mosquito netting. "We don't see things the way you do, Mademoiselle Fanny. We were trying to be like the people you were used to, like Americans. We wanted to be polite."

Then Fanny knew it was no use, that she would go back with Claire, that she was crazy anywhere, everywhere. That was why, she told

Ginny and Ginny told Roland, she committed herself to the state mental hospital at Chattahoochee. "And that was why she told me, whatever happened," Ginny said, "not to go home."

"Was this good advice?" Roland asked. Ginny tucked his hand between her breasts.

"So far it has been," she said. So far.

The next morning when Roland dressed again in the dark, she kept her eyes closed, almost afraid to look at him. Maybe it was not too late to change her mind, to put off any chance of disappointment, of loss. But all morning she missed him, his absence an ache in her ribs, as if Montmartre were airless. At noon she went down the hundred steps. She took a deep breath, and when she saw Roland she knew it was already decided.

They climbed Montmartre, walking slowly, hand in hand. "That's where I was this morning," Roland said, as they passed a little bakery on a side street.

"There? Why?" Ginny asked, looking at the front of the Boulangerie Clavel. Through the open door she could see an elderly couple standing behind the counter talking to a customer.

"Working." Roland opened his palm to show three francs. "For our dinner." He led her to a little place a few streets up from the hotel that just said *Claudia* on the door. It smelled of fried fish and onions and had long tables with benches on a flagstone floor. Claudia made a face when she heard Ginny's French, another when she heard Roland's. Still, though the other diners were crowded onto the benches, ten to a side, Claudia seated Ginny and Roland at a small table near the door, a lover's table.

Roland laughed and told Ginny about a teacher he had in Hexwiller after the war who kept him late every day for a year to work on his French. One day, the teacher threw down the chalk, gave up, saying sadly, "It's biology. The German has ruined your lips."

Claudia was tall, over six feet, with perfect posture. Her gray bun brushed the top of the kitchen door when she passed through it. Roland said he'd heard at the bakery that Claudia had been a nun once, or was it an artist's model? The menu, which was written on a blackboard in tiny script, was short—herring or boiled egg with mayonnaise for the first course, stew for the second, a few cheeses, a dessert. A complete dinner with wine was one franc, a franc fifty with cheese and dessert.

Ginny wasn't used to eating in shifts, fish, then stew, vegetables, cheese. She didn't know herring was a fish until she took a bite. "Oh," she said, "it tastes like smoked mullet." She asked Roland if herrings were vegetarians like mullet were. At least that was Papa Ben's explanation for why mullet couldn't be hooked, only netted.

"I don't know," Roland said. "I've never been to the ocean. The only fish we had at home was carp, and people raise those in ponds on stale bread, like chickens." Roland didn't seem to be used to eating in restaurants either. He asked Ginny what a *mayonnaise* was.

"What do you think?" Ginny asked after he'd taken a bite.

"It tastes like egg," Roland said. "Is it supposed to?"

Claudia brought a half bottle of wine with the stew, and Roland poured Ginny a glass. She had never had wine. It smelled like the vinegar rinse her mother made her put on her hair after she washed it. She took a sip. It tasted pretty much the way it smelled. She made a face at Roland, and he added some water to her glass.

After the cheese, Ginny asked for a cup of coffee, but Claudia didn't serve it. "I don't want you sitting here all day," she said. "Go sit in a cafe if you've got time and money to waste. I've got people to feed." Her restaurant, Claudia said, was for the people. She proved her point by pushing a woman in a fur coat out the door. "Go eat at Maxim's," she said. "You can afford it."

On the way back to the hotel, Ginny decided to take Roland to room one, show him Paul's urn. She watched as Roland laid his webbed hand on the cool green marble, turned the urn around on the dresser. "Your husband?" he asked. Ginny nodded. Roland leaned forward. "This is possible?"

"Yes," Ginny said, "quite possible."

Roland shook his head. "So many new things become possible each day."

Ginny touched Roland's hand where it rested on the urn. Suddenly she had a vision of a tall man standing at a door with a ribboned box under one arm. Paul, years before she had met him. How did she know this? That his father was dead, his mother remarried into a lively family full of children and aunts and in-laws more fun than the quiet house he'd grown up in, with more love than he, an only child, could ever provide for her? It was Christmas, and Paul had begged and bribed his way into two days off from the hospital where he was head resident. He walked through the door of his mother's new house without knocking, his gift for her held in front of him, and his mother and her new family all looked up from their presents. Two little girls circling the tree, hand in hand, stopped. His mother stood up, not smiling. "What are you doing here, Paul?" she asked. Ginny felt so sorry for Paul. She wanted to be able to reach him, to comfort him. But Paul was dead.

Ginny told Roland what she'd seen. "How can I know that?" she said. "Paul never told me anything like that."

Roland touched the back of her neck. "How do we know anything?" he said.

Ginny turned from the dresser and Paul. She faced the wide mahogany bed, the covers turned back and ready, a bed Paul didn't need. She thought of the narrow bed upstairs. She should let Madame Desnos rent the room at the top of the stairs to some sleepy stranger. They should sleep here. Her dead husband would be one of the many people from their pasts who watched over them. But she couldn't do it. "Let's go," she said. Roland looked at her, his head tilted to one side as if asking a question, asking her to choose once and for all between Paul and him. But Ginny said nothing. After a long second, Roland took her hand and they went upstairs to bed.

Mornings spent walking Montmartre while Roland worked at the bakery, dinner at Claudia's, nights at the Grand Hôtel. For a week, the days kept that shape. Now when Ginny saw Madame Desnos up late, alone over her books, other women and men alone in the streets, her heart ached. She thought of her mother and Papa Ben, their silent dinner table. What was wrong with the world that so many people went without love? It was as if hatred and loneliness had spread like a desert in a drought, separating men from women. Like up in Alabama where the land had been farmed out, cotton planted year after year right up to the houses until the land was a waste of gullies and dust and the houses were abandoned. Devastation passed down from generation to generation.

She'd heard a man at the Chautauqua say that new ways of farming—new crops, careful rotations, cross plowing—could change all that back, make the land green again. He told his audience he'd need money to set up just one farm, on some land up near Florala, by way of example. Then people driving by would see his fields shining green from miles away like the Garden of Eden and come running up to his house to ask him how to mend their land and their ways. If she and

Roland loved each other, maybe that love would spread. Maybe a new way of living always started out small, as small as a single field or a single family. Ginny thought this and held Roland tight even when she slept.

The bakery was closed Tuesdays, so that morning they went to a secondhand clothes market Madame Desnos told Ginny about. At the first stall, Ginny found a white linen dress with fat red embroidered cherries and tried it on. Roland tried on a blue and white seersucker suit. The label in the jacket was from a shop in Wilkes-Barre, Pennsylvania, and Roland looked almost American. "Let me buy you the dress," Roland said. Ginny looked in the mirror. The linen molded itself to her breasts, her waist, cherries hung in pairs at her hips. She looked young, in love. Her cheeks flushed. She frowned in the mirror, pulled her hair back from her forehead and stuck it behind her ears.

"No," she said, disappearing behind the curtain to put on her black dress again. She felt safer in her black. "But let me buy the suit for you," Ginny said. "You need clothes."

Roland pulled off the jacket, hung it up, and Ginny could tell he was angry. "No," he said.

She opened her mouth, shut it. Afraid of saying something her mother would say to Papa Ben. Something like: *Why should I care what you think?* Once she started, how would she stop? "Look," she said instead, and pointed at a young Negro man passing by with a movie camera mounted on a tripod resting on his shoulder. She hadn't seen a black man since the Pullman porter on the train from Jacksonville to New York. "Maybe they're making a movie." She pulled Roland by the hand, following the camera, the man's head, through the crowd. By the time they caught up with him, he had the camera set up, pointed at a pile of curled Turkish slippers.

Her certainty that this was a fellow Southerner gave her the courage to speak. "Are you making a film about Paris? About shoes?" The cameraman looked up, still turning the crank.

"Hello," he said. As soon as he spoke, Ginny knew from his French that he wasn't American at all. He smiled. What he was doing, he explained, was filming the world. The whole world. Or at least he and the other camera crews who worked for his employer, a rich industrialist and friend of the philosopher Henri Bergson, were. Thousands of feet were filmed every day, he told her, in Paris, in China. The cameraman handed her a card that said *The Archives of the Planet* in square modern type. He gave Roland one too. Roland turned it over in his hand, not really looking at it. "What we're doing will make people see once and for all that the world is really a big village," the cameraman said.

"People have to want to see," Roland said. "There are French and Germans who live close enough to spit on each other, and they do."

"I have to believe change is possible," the cameraman said. "Here am I, an African, in Paris, talking to you." Ginny was nodding.

She could feel the pull of a grand idea. An idea big enough to please even her mother.

"If people could see each other as brothers," she said, "then wars would have to stop." Roland shook his head and Ginny thought, *He's still angry at me.*

"Brothers kill brothers," Roland said. Ginny looked to the African for help, but he had picked up his camera. He made an odd sound with his tongue.

"Click, click," he said. Beyond him, Ginny saw two policemen strolling through an ever-widening gap in the crowd.

Roland took her hand. "Let's walk," he said.

They climbed up to a park called Buttes-Chaumont, up to a high island in the middle of the lake and sat on the steps of the small pavilion. It was cool, the sun just setting. The trees in the park were tall and leafless and not at all like the pines around DeSoto. The park seemed like a forest to Ginny even with the benches made of concrete logs and the lake with its straight sides, and she said so. "In the forests of Alsace," Roland said, teasing, "we have trees taller than Claudia." Ginny laughed, but she felt uneasy, worried by their fight at the market, by Roland's nervousness at the sight of the police. An arc of lights came on beyond the trees, began to spin.

"Oh, look," she said. "A carnival."

But Roland didn't look, he reached out for her with both hands, caught her, as if to keep her from falling. She closed her eyes and saw the police again, gliding like sharks toward Roland.

"Maybe we should leave Paris," she said, suddenly afraid. "I have this feeling something bad is about to happen."

CHAPTER THIRTEEN

MAYBE WE SHOULD LEAVE," Ginny said and sounded just like Odile. Roland touched Ginny and saw her memories forming up in ranks. Her people, his people, they were all there and about to march off into Odile's dream, out of Paris and into the future. Without papers, he could never travel freely. They would go off and leave him. Ginny pointed over his head at the Ferris wheel, frozen against the sky. Then Roland knew what he had to do. He would have to find Fuss.

The next morning, Roland bent over Ginny and told her not to worry, that he might be late. Instead of going to the bakery, he went back to Buttes Chaumont. The crews were taking the fair apart, packing the rides into the trucks. The police were moving them on again. Monsieur Mountain and the Mountain of Gold were already gone. Roland asked for Fuss at the airplane ride. One of the men there swung his hammer as if he might let it fly from his hand in Roland's direction, but the other laughed. "You won't see *him* here sweating his shirt black. The only place he likes to get hot is with the girls at the Black Cat." The Black Cat was the name of one of the bars Fuss had taken Roland to.

Fuss wasn't at the Black Cat, but someone said they'd seen him at the Golden Cock, and at the Golden Cock, at some other bar. It took Roland until noon to track him down to the dance hall where they'd first gone with Carmen. This early, the place was empty. Fuss was sitting at the bar, drawing his drink up its straw. A cigarette was burning in his hand. "Frog, shit!" Fuss said, looking up and seeing him through his cloud of smoke. "I knew you'd turn up. People do, you know? They might mean to leave, leave for good, but still they turn up." He went behind the bar and poured Roland a drink. The bartender was outside, taking a delivery.

"You need this," he said as he handed the yellow glass to Roland.

"What I need," Roland said, looking straight at Fuss, "is a favor. I need papers."

Fuss smiled, pulling on his good ear for a change. "Who told you I did that kind of favor?"

"Carmen."

"That bitch. She'll turn up. Even women turn up. You wait and see."

"How much?" Roland asked. This morning he had counted his money, adding what he'd earned at the bakery to what he had gotten from Monsieur Mountains's pawned goods and what he had brought from Hexwiller. He had one hundred and two francs, forty-three centimes.

"Oh, Frog, you really hurt me. How much? Haven't I been your friend? Do you think I'd let you pay for a favor?" Fuss's ears were purple with alcohol and emotion. He put his hand on Roland's shoulder and squeezed it as hard as he could.

"I can only pay a hundred francs, Fuss," Roland said, wincing.

Fuss shrugged elaborately. "I'll just have to overcharge some other stupid shit. That'll make up the difference. And that'll get you a good set of papers, no toilet wipe."

"How long will it take?" Roland imagined the ground under him shaking the way it had in his dream when the iron woman stepped off her mountain. He knew better than to trust Fuss, but he had to be ready to go when Ginny went.

"If you can go now, we can fix it. If not," he shrugged. "You're a friend, but I'm a busy man."

"I can go."

Fuss took a couple of the bartender's cigarettes as they went out. They took the Métro to Place Denfert Rochereau. Fuss threaded his way through the boulevard's traffic, and Roland followed him, dodging oncoming automobiles. Then Fuss ducked down a narrow street, giving the clear impression of a man who didn't want to be seen, and Roland kept close on his heels. Fuss stopped outside a shop that was closed, an iron grille rolled down over the window. He knocked on the door softly. Roland backed out into the street to read the sign over the door. In red letters it announced, *Destruction of Nuisance Animals*, and in smaller black:

Mice, Moles, Voles,
Rats Our Specialty

Fuss knocked again on the door, three fast raps, three slow. Roland peered through the grille on the window. Curved iron traps large enough for bears hung from chains, and from the traps hung huge rats, their eyes glittering red in the light from the street. Over the rats, a banner read: *42 Sewer Rats Caught in One Night in the Basement of the Paris Opéra.* Looking closer, Roland saw that the rats were stuffed, some rather the worse for wear, bare wires sticking out in place of ears or tails. It had been a while since they had seen any part of the Opéra. The door opened and an old woman stepped out. She smiled when she saw Roland at the window. "Have to keep the grille down," she apologized, out of breath, wheezing a little. "People try to steal them. I can roll it up if you want a better look."

"Don't bother," Fuss said. "We're here to see Henri." The old woman looked expectantly at Roland, ignoring Fuss.

"Some other time perhaps," Roland said. She looked disappointed.

"Henri is in the cellar," she said, not moving from the door. "You know the way." Fuss and Roland squeezed by her. "Never mind, rats," Roland heard her say as they walked away, "the school children will be coming by soon."

Fuss led the way to the back of the shop and started down a long flight of stairs. It was these stairs, Roland guessed, that had left the old woman so winded. They went down, moving quietly. The sound of cards being shuffled drifted up from the musty gloom below. At the bottom of the stairs, Fuss called out, "It's amazing how sound carries. You really should be more careful, Henri."

Roland stepped off the stairs into a damp cellar. He looked around. Under a circle of light from a gas lamp were two small tables. At one, a large man in shirt sleeves was playing patience. At the other, a little balding man sat bent over a stack of wrinkled papers like a bookkeeper. Behind the little man stood a large, black-draped camera and a small printing press. "Oh, Monsieur Foot! What a teaser!" The small man stood up. "You know how much noise the tourists make when they come through. Who would notice us mice?"

"Don't you mean rats, Henri?" Fuss said.

Roland looked beyond Henri. The walls of this cellar were not

111

made of packed dirt or stones, but of bones, human bones, leg bones stacked like firewood with rows of skulls arranged neatly along the top. Every few feet a skull and crossbones were wired to the stacks of fibulae. Roland knew all earth underfoot was full of bones, but it was amazing to see them like this. More dead than even Odile saw in her dreams, more dead than Roland imagined underground even in a city like Paris.

"Impressive, no?" Henri nodded his shiny bald head at the bones. "It goes on for miles. That way," he waved at the darkness on either side of the lantern's light, "and that way. Old quarries—the stone for Notre Dame came from here—filled now with the bones of six million Parisians!" Henri sighed. "I'm told it took seventy years to move them all here, from the old paupers' cemeteries, Innocents and the others. The State wanted to burn them but," he patted the yellow forehead of the skull by his head, "the Church, ah, the one true and Catholic Church, they knew better. They knew that even bones could be made into sacred art." Henri stepped from behind the table and took Roland by the elbow. "Look at this," he said, stopping in front of a four-foot high crucifix made of a double rows of skulls. "Art! Can there be any doubt? Really, though, Zelie should be telling you about this. He's an official guide to the catacombs. Tourists pay him good money to be let down here."

Zelie grunted over his cards. "Better money to be let out," he said.

"I'm a busy man, Henri," Fuss said again, his ears darkening. "My friend can go around to the entrance and pay to tour the catacombs if he wants, but I am here on business."

"A man too busy for death?" Zelie said, looking up from his cards. Fuss stiffened, reached into his jacket.

"Now, now, Zelie," Henri waved a hand as if smoothing the air. "Don't scare the customers." He settled Fuss and Roland in chairs in front of his table then sat down himself. Behind him, Roland heard only breathing and the slippery sound of cards being dealt from a deck. "What can I do for you today, monsieurs?" he asked.

"My friend needs an identity card and a certificate of birth." Henri nodded, taking up his pen. Fuss leaned forward, put his hand on Henri's sleeve. "Henri, when I say *friend* I mean *friend*, and I'm here to see he gets what he pays for—first class paper."

"What nationality is the monsieur?" Henri asked Roland.

"I'm Alsatian," Roland said. Behind him, Roland heard Zelie snort.

"Alsacois," he said and spat. Henri cleared his throat.

"I need you to fill out these forms, Monsieur, and sign these, and then we'll take some photographs. And I promise you, Monsieur Foot, your friend's papers will be better than first class." Henri beamed at Roland, happy in his work. "They'll be works of art."

When he had Roland photographed and measured, his birth date and mother's maiden name all filled in on the proper forms, Henri flipped open a small appointment calendar. He turned to Fuss. "Because you're a good customer, Monsieur Foot, I think I can have your friend's papers ready by midnight with your other orders."

"I'll just stop by in an hour or two to see how you're doing," Fuss said.

"And waste your busy time?" Henri shook his head. "You know you have to get the finished product from Maurice. You wouldn't want to deny him his part in the great journey of life, would you?"

Fuss frowned, his ears a dangerous blood red. "Tell Maurice to be on time. I'm a busy man."

Upstairs, the old woman was waiting to let them out of the shop. She caught Roland's elbow as he passed, nodded toward the window display. "You'll never find a sewer rat by looking for one," she said. "You've got to look into the dark with your eyes unfocused, not thinking about rats, and then zip! You'll see one out of the corner of your eye, then zip! another." She let go of his elbow. "Like shooting stars," she said, and shut the door.

They went back to the dance hall. Roland gave Fuss the money for his papers. "One hundred francs," he said. Fuss wrapped his fingers around Roland's bankroll.

"Feels right," he said. "We can enjoy ourselves until we meet Maurice, the paper man, at midnight, up behind Pigalle."

Roland didn't want to let Fuss out of his sight. He bought him a drink, had one himself, but still felt restless. He stood beside a stool at the bar shifting from foot to foot, tying his straw in knots. He was sure Ginny would be worried by now.

"Go take a shit!" Fuss said. "You're making me nervous." But Roland stayed where he was. Fuss ordered another drink, bought a round for a pair of blond, dark skinned girls.

It was after ten when Fuss finally stood up. One of the blond girls held up her lips, and he pressed his to hers with an audible smack. "That one's crazy for me," he said as Roland followed him out of the dance hall.

Fuss led him down into the Métro, and Roland's throat tightened. They had to wait for a train, then transfer twice. Roland's palms were wet with sweat. He still didn't like being underground.

When they got off at Pigalle, Roland was nervous, but Fuss was humming, his hands in his pockets. Roland thought of Ginny alone in their bed. The hotel wasn't far. He would be with her soon, as soon as he had the papers. The street Fuss turned on ran up a hill lined with tall old houses. The pavement felt slick under Roland's shoes. Up ahead a team of horses was waiting, hitched to a heavy tank car hung with a few lanterns. Roland heard voices and then smelled ammonia. "Shit," Fuss said, and Roland realized he was right. Men were handling long thick hoses, pumping out the cistern of a house in front of them. The smell was unbearable. Fuss threw down his cigarette, and one of the men cursed him.

"It could explode, you bastard," he said. "The shit makes its own gas."

They picked their way over the hoses. Roland looked down. A man was in the pit moving the mouth of the hose back and forth. He wore high rubber boots, but as Roland watched the man lost his footing and fell. Fuss saw it too and grunted, speechless. "Pull him up, you lazy bastards!" one of the men yelled. "Next time it'll be you!"

Roland and Fuss kept their mouths shut and kept going, trying not to breathe. When they reached the top of the street, the wind was in their faces, and they stopped with their hands on their knees, panting, trying to clear their lungs. "This way," Fuss pointed down an alley between two buildings. The alley was darker than the street, but there was light, a strange watery glow like in a swamp, the reflection of the night sky of Paris.

Roland was the first to see the three men. They were standing at the end of the alley. "Maurice?" Fuss called.

"Indeed," Maurice called back, unhooding a lamp. The light caught Fuss in the face, showed up the pink veins in his ears. Fuss and Maurice stood facing each other like dance partners.

"You owe me three sets," Fuss said holding up three fingers. "One set deluxe."

"Only the best for you, Monsieur Foot," Maurice said. Then one of the other men stepped closer, opened his jacket. Roland recognized Zelie, official guide to the catacombs. Then he saw Maurice had a knife.

"Fuss!" Roland said.

"Shit!" Fuss pulled out a knife of his own.

"We hear you've been overcharging your customers, René," Maurice said, circling, "and not passing any of this bonus on to us."

Maurice jumped Fuss, and Fuss's knife flew from his hand. Roland threw himself forward, trying to catch it, but Zelie tackled him. They hit the ground with a thud, Zelie on top. Maurice waved his knife. "You're history, René the Foot," he said, and drove the blade up under Fuss's ribs. Fuss's mouth opened in an O, his eyes wide. He looked like he was blowing bubbles, and from his mouth came a sound like low humming, like the singing of the drowning boys so long ago. He reached out for Roland or maybe for his knife.

Roland made a grab for the knife with his left hand, but the other man stepped hard on his wrist. "Hey, look," he said. Maurice turned away just as Fuss folded into himself and fell to the ground. Maurice brought the lamp over.

"Damn," Maurice said, looking at Roland's left hand, "that's unnatural." The partner put all his weight on Roland's wrist, standing on one foot. Zelie picked himself up off Roland. Maurice leaned down and drew his knife through the skin between Roland's fingers. Roland heard the knife scrape across the pavement four times. A cold numbness spread up his arm, as if he were up to his elbow in a frozen river. *Ginny*, Roland thought, willing himself to think of her, of the warmth of their bed, not the pain. Maurice grunted, and then Roland heard whistles, whistles singing out in the night.

"God damn," Zelie said and kicked Roland hard in the head.

"The sparrows," said a voice, and the police swept down on their bicycles.

CHAPTER FOURTEEN

I MAY BE LATE," Roland said before dawn, before she was awake. "Okay," Ginny said. About an hour later, she woke up. "How late?" There was no one there to answer. She got up. If Roland would be busy working all day, she would have time to go to the bank where her money had been wired, something she shouldn't have put off even this long. The air was cool and clear as she took the steps down from Sacré Coeur. Roland's bench was empty, only a few impatient sparrows picked at the sand.

She went down the street of the cloth merchants, past the women standing, talking with their hands on their hips, like the women in the post office in DeSoto, like women everywhere. She took the Métro, but after a few stops, a conductor stuck his head in the door of the car and told everyone to get off, that the line was closed from the Opéra to the Pont Neuf. Everyone groaned. "I'm not getting off," an old man sitting by the door announced. "Whatever the trouble is, they'll clear the line faster than I can walk to another." The conductor shrugged and went on to the next car. People began to leave.

"I'll bet it's a strike," the woman next to Ginny said, buttoning her coat, her jaw set.

Coming up in the Place de l'Opéra, Ginny became aware of a buzzing in the air, a restlessness, as if a hundred women were gossiping at once. Down one side of the square, a line of people covered the sidewalk for a block. The line ended at a door, and Ginny could see a gold plaque on the wall. She guessed it was some kind of office, but the plaque was too far away to read. "Is this a strike?" she asked a middle-aged woman near the end of the line.

"What are you saying?" the woman said loudly in English. "I don't

116

speak French." She was American. Ginny repeated her question in English. "The bottom's fallen out of the stock market," the woman said. "Everyone's waiting for news."

The stock market. The American stock market. Ginny walked down the block. The door at the far end led into the Western Union office. She hadn't realized there were so many Americans in Paris. Everyone in the line was American — tall, thin, fat, short, all looking at that moment very American, very un-French. A hundred voices hummed, and not one was speaking French. She caught sight of one man, tiny as a child but with a full head of white hair. She raised a hand to shade her eyes, stared at this expatriate copy of her own Dr. Love. The man raised his hand, though he didn't dare leave his place in the line.

It was Dr. Love. He stood on tiptoe, still waving. "Virginia Mac-Kenzie!" he called. "My dear!" As soon as she was close, he took her bare hands in his gloved ones. "We've been looking all over for you," he said. "Your aunt wrote me you were in Paris."

"We?" Ginny asked. Neither the man in front nor the woman behind seemed to be with Dr. Love.

"Mrs. Love. I'm in Paris on my honeymoon." Dr. Love blushed. "Antoinette has captured me at last." His small mouth rolled around Antoinette, his Antoinette.

"Antoinette Duval?" Ginny asked, and Dr. Love nodded. He had married her French teacher, his academy's French teacher. "That's wonderful," Ginny said, though she couldn't quite see Dr. Love, so tiny, so fastidious in his white gloves and white scarf, married to Madame Duval who erased the blackboard with her elbows and stuck extra pieces of chalk in her hair for safekeeping. The Dr. Love she'd known at school had been formal, correct. Now he stood bareheaded, holding both her hands and laughing. Dr. Love stood on tiptoe and looked into her face.

"You look well, Virginia. I was sorry to hear about your husband."

"I hardly knew him," Ginny said. "That's the terrible thing."

"Yes," Dr. Love put his gloved fingertips together and nodded. "I worry about Antoinette and myself. We're not young. She reminds me of the twenty-five years we've already known each other, although not in the same way, of course. Time is precious to us both. That's why we decided to take our wedding trip right away, to return to France together, even though it meant leaving the academy during a school year."

117

"Hey, buddy! Move up!" someone called from behind. The line inched forward with much scuffing of shoes.

"Just why are we in line?" Ginny asked, waving a hand at the door. "What does the stock market drop mean to these people?"

"A few dollars," Dr. Love said, "or everything they have. In the panic of 1907, the market only fell half this much and my father was forced into bankruptcy. Now everyone has stock. This could be the end of America, the fall of Rome, or," Dr. Love smiled, standing on tiptoe, "just the end of me."

The door opened and four men came out of the office, hatless, looking dazed in the sharp October light. A cry went up, *How much? How much?* One of the men turned. "Radio," he said, "is down to thirty dollars." A moan ran down the line.

"Oh, God," said the woman behind them, "I paid one hundred and ten dollars for that."

Ginny heard herself moan. She had no idea what she owned in stocks, what Paul's lawyer had kept or sold, if Mrs. Corbet had sold the house or car yet. Here she was just on the way to the bank. What if her money hadn't arrived? She had a hundred francs on her, three hundred back at the hotel. What if that were all she had in the world?

"They may say it's trading at thirty, but it's probably less," a man in front of them said. "In heavy trading, the wire can't keep up."

First thing that happens in a drought or a panic, Ginny remembered Papa Ben saying, shaking the tube of gold dust he kept in his desk, *is the banks fail.* Her heart twisted painfully in her chest. She wished she had her money right in her hand, in her purse, under her bed, so she'd be responsible for it, not people who didn't even know her. That way if she lost her money, she'd have no one to blame but herself. And she wouldn't lose it, she couldn't.

By noon, Dr. Love and Ginny were only halfway to the front of the line. "It's the telegraph lines," the man in front of them said, passing back what he'd heard. "There was a storm in the Atlantic last night and some of the cables snapped." The door opened and then closed.

"They've locked it," a man up front called. "They're closing for lunch." The line stirred as if there might be a general rush forward, but then it steadied. People set their feet side by side on the pavement, holding their places in the line.

"Maybe we can send a telegram from outside Paris," Ginny said. "Get our own information, get away from these crowds."

"All right," Dr. Love agreed. "Let's try Clichy. I think I remember how to get there."

They took the Métro as far as it went and then a street car. Ginny hadn't been out of the city. Everything in Clichy looked down-at-heels even though many buildings were new. The sight of old farmhouses tucked in between tall apartment buildings surprised her. They had to ask three people before they got directions to the telegraph office. People kept saying they weren't from around there, were new to Clichy. Finally they found it, but the telegraph operator was at lunch.

They found a cafe, and Dr. Love ordered for her. His French sounded just like her French, and both of them sounded like Madame Duval, with a little north Florida thrown in. "Your mother is fine," Dr. Love said. "I see her at the post office now and then."

"I'm glad to hear that," Ginny said, although she could feel herself frowning. Dr. Love cleared his throat.

"You come from an interesting family," he said. "All the women in it have been worth remembering." Then Dr. Love began to talk about ancient weapons. His other love, he called them. Did she think he and Antoinette would like Spain? He had connections with a dealer in Saracen weapons in Grenada. A scimitar would be a great prize to take home. "Providing," Dr. Love said as he paid the waiter for their lunch, "I still have a home." He smiled again as if this were a joke, a mere testing of the waters of impossibility.

"I always knew you would travel," he told Ginny as they made their way back to the telegraph office. "I would look at you in assembly sometimes—so many children—and you were always looking up at the map over my head. When I had the hall redone last spring, I almost had them paint over that map, but I remembered you." He stood on tiptoe to pat Ginny on the shoulder. "I'm glad it's turned out better for you than it did for Fanny. It still makes me sad to think of that."

"If I've lost all Paul's money," Ginny said, "I might have to go home too." She listened to herself, testing the waters. She didn't mean it. She wouldn't go, not and leave Roland. And she couldn't imagine him in DeSoto, walking like some strange tall bird into Perkins' Drugs and ordering a cold dope. Then she couldn't imagine herself, her new French self, drinking a Coke there either.

The telegraph office was open this time, but the man at the front desk didn't have any quotations from the American stock market. He shrugged. Unfortunately, he said, he could send only two telegrams to America. The wires were very busy. Two were all he could handle. Dr. Love gave him a twenty-franc note, and he changed it to three telegrams. Ginny sent one to Mrs. Corbet: STOCKS? HOUSE? ADVISE. Dr. Love sent one to his broker and one to the academy. Replies would be sent to their hotels.

They took the Métro back into Paris. When they reached the Opéra, the line in front of Western Union was still a block long. "I'm going to wait here a while longer for news," Dr. Love said, reaching up to pat her shoulder, "but you must have dinner with us tomorrow. We're at the Hôtel Edouard VII. Antoinette will be overjoyed to see her favorite pupil from the class of '28."

"May I bring a friend?" She imagined Roland towering over Dr. Love, bending down to shake his small hand. Just because she couldn't imagine Roland in DeSoto didn't mean she was ashamed of him. "I'd like you to meet him."

"The more the merrier." Dr. Love gave her hands a last squeeze. "We'll expect you at seven."

Ginny left the square full of Americans and took the Métro for the fourth time that day. She went east, using her map book to find the address listed on her wire receipt as the Bank of France. Away from the line of frantic Americans in the Place de l'Opéra, the city was quiet. At the bank, an officer came out to greet her. Yes, he was happy to be able tell madame her money had arrived. He smiled. He looked happy. But when she asked to withdraw the money in cash, the officer frowned and shook his head as if he, personally, were disappointed in her. He wrote down the account number, then asked her to fill out a form stating her reasons for wanting her money, as if she was getting a loan or was back in the kitchen in Jacksonville with Mr. McCue trying to justify Paul's cremation. He stood with his arms folded, making no attempt to help her.

Ginny looked at the blank lines on the form and thought about writing down a brave promise. *From now on, no one in this world but me is in charge of my future.* Or confessing her fears. *I'm afraid your bank will fail, and I will lose all the money I have in this world.* But finally, she wrote down that part of the truth that seemed most likely to convince the officer to give her back what was rightfully hers. *I plan,* she wrote, *to invest my money in France.* The officer left the room with the form, came back with it signed and stamped in red.

"Your money must be prepared for you," he said and stood to let her out.

"How long will that take?" Ginny asked, rubbing her damp palms on her skirt. She wanted to see her money, touch it. "I'd like to have it as soon as possible."

"The soonest possible will be Friday morning." The officer leaned forward over his desk. "Two hundred and fifty thousand francs is quite a lot of money, madame. Is there someone who can accompany you?" He acted as if he suspected the sight of all she had in the world might make her faint.

"My chauffeur," Ginny heard herself saying and regretted it instantly. She would have to bring Roland, and she didn't want him to be her servant, even as a joke. It would be like denying she knew him.

The bank officer nodded. With Americans you could never tell.

It was six o'clock when Ginny got to the foot of Sacré Coeur, and she was tired. She wanted to talk to Roland, to tell him about Dr. Love. His bench was empty. Then she remembered his whispered message to her that morning. He would be late. Why hadn't she been awake enough to ask why?

Their room at the hotel was empty.

"No, he hasn't been in or sent a note," Madame Desnos said. Ginny went to Claudia's, but without Roland, Claudia didn't seem to recognize her. She pointed toward the door.

"Go eat with all the other Americans," she said. "Only the people eat here."

"Claudia, it's me," Ginny said. "I am people. I eat here every night." She pointed at their table. Another couple was sitting there.

"Madame?" Claudia took a step back, looked at her face.

"Have you seen my friend Roland?" Ginny asked. "Has he been in tonight?" Claudia shook her head.

"Why would he come here without you?" she asked.

Ginny went back to the hotel, but before she was through the door, Madame Desnos shook her head, raised her hands in a grand shrug. Ginny sat in the lobby for a few minutes, then went up alone to their bed. Ten o'clock came and went. Eleven. Where was he? She remembered the afternoon before in the used clothes market. Was it possible Roland was still angry with her? She turned over in the cold bed, turned over again. If he was, would he go off like this? She didn't think so. She closed her eyes. She didn't know.

CHAPTER FIFTEEN

GINNY WOKE WITH a start. The other side of the bed was
empty. No Roland. What if he was hurt? She imagined him
lying at the bottom of Montmartre, bleeding. Then she imagined him on the table of a morgue, the way she had seen Paul. She
dressed in a hurry and went out. The street lights were still on. The image of Roland bleeding floated in front of her in the pink dawn air as
she climbed Montmartre. Would she stand at the top and see him, broken, at the bottom of the hundred steps? In front of Sacré Coeur, the
wind caught her across the face. Her eyes filled with water. She heard
an organ start up in the church behind her. A nun hurried past. Ginny
blinked hard and looked down. The steps were as empty as her bed.

She went down the steps to the landing, but the benches stayed
empty—of Roland, of birds, even of bread crumbs. A policeman came
up behind her, cleared his throat. Ginny jumped. "Has someone been
hurt?" Ginny asked. "I thought I heard an ambulance." The policeman
shrugged.

"I've been here all night," he said. "It's been quiet as a grave."

"I was supposed to meet a friend . . ." she started to ask after
Roland by name, but something about the way the policeman was looking at her, the notebook in his hand, made her stop. She remembered
the police at the market, moving through the crowd two by two. Why
had Roland been afraid? Why was she? "But probably he was delayed
at work," she said. *Work!* She should slap herself. When Roland had told
her he'd be late, he had meant working late. But it was almost light.
How late was late?

She retraced the route she had taken with Roland and found the
bakery on Rue Véron, just three blocks from the hotel. Even though

the bakery was shuttered and closed, she knocked on the door. Two women gave her startled looks as they passed by. Ginny knocked louder. Maybe he had had an accident at work. She imagined a large knife, blood in the flour. A man stopped. "It's not the Clavel's regular closing day," he said. "Something must have happened." A woman stopped.

"How far do I have to walk for bread?" she asked.

"Maybe it's a strike," the man said.

"Don't be absurd," the woman said walking away. "That would be in the papers."

Ginny knocked again, then gave up.

"Maybe," the man said, following after her, "there's going to be a war, and the government has drafted all the bakers."

"Don't be hysterical," the woman's voice drifted back. "Leave that to us women."

Ginny wondered whether she was being hysterical herself. The sun had come up over Paris, and the air was as clear and cool as spring water. It was hard to believe anything bad could happen, could have happened. Ginny imagined Roland asleep in their bed, making up for lost time. The bed would be warm, and she would slip under the covers.

But when she stepped through the door at the Grand Hôtel, Madame Desnos shook her head. Roland had not returned. "Sit down, madame, sit down," Madame Desnos said to her, waving a baguette. "It's still early for men who've been out all night." Madame Desnos, dressed in her leopard-spotted robe, was breaking the baguettes for the guests' breakfasts. Ginny sat on a stool by the counter, one eye on the door.

"You would not believe how far I had to walk to get this bread," Madame Desnos said, shaking her head. "His ankles," she remarked pleasantly, cracking off a chunk. Ginny thought this must be something colloquial and smiled tensely. "His knees," Madame Desnos added breaking off another piece, handing it to Ginny to arrange in its basket. "My husband has sent me a postcard," Madame Desnos paused to choose another loaf, "so he is not dead, and worse still, he says he misses me." She started on a new loaf. "His spine." Ginny dropped an empty basket, and bending to pick it up, she saw Madame Desnos's legs beneath her spotted robe. They were protected only by hose fallen in wrinkled waves around her ankles, and as Ginny stared at their heavy blue veins, she couldn't help thinking of Paul, of his naked blue toes in the morgue, and then Roland, his toes just as blue. She started to cry.

Madame Desnos cried too, taking the scarf off her hair to wipe their tears. Their red heads bobbed together. "No, no, it's not so bad," Madame Desnos said. "I've paid off the loan my husband took out on the place last time he came back." She poked Ginny in the stomach with the last loaf of bread. "Smile," she said. "The mails are slow and people die every day." She broke the bread in two. "His neck."

Ginny ran for the toilet, reached it just in time. She was suddenly, painfully sick. Her eyes burned and her side hurt, felt torn under her ribs. She sank to the floor, pressing her cheek against the cold porcelain edge of the toilet. She thought of Paul's urn in its large, useless room, the narrow bed in the room where she and Roland slept. Why hadn't she made the right choice? Why hadn't she let Roland buy her the white dress? She moaned. Silently she offered Roland the big bed in room one, imagined him in it, sleeping soundly beside her. Madame Desnos knocked on the door.

"Madame?"

Ginny raised her head. "Ah, madame," Madame Desnos pressed a cool hand to Ginny's forehead. After a minute, Ginny got up off the floor and washed her face in the sink. "Feel better?" Madame Desnos asked.

Ginny nodded. "I'm so sorry. I don't know what's wrong with me." Madame Desnos shrugged.

"Nothing's wrong with you. You're just pregnant."

"No," Ginny said, sitting down suddenly on the edge of the toilet. "I didn't know." She didn't know what to say, think. Could she be a mother? She felt stupid, five years old. Claire was the mother, she was just a child.

"The question is," Madame Desnos said, "did your young man know?" Ginny thought of Roland's hand resting quietly against her stomach as she slept. She shook her head.

"He wouldn't run off. He's not like that."

"No," Madame Desnos agreed, although to Ginny's ears it sounded suspiciously like, *no?* Ginny stood up.

"I have to find him. I'm going to go to the police and report him missing. I've wasted too much time already."

"Wasted time? The police are masters of that. You don't know about French police. In America, I'm sure it is different, all your sheriffs and cowboys and Boy Scouts."

"Well," Ginny said, "sheriffs anyway." Even DeSoto County had a sheriff. Madame Desnos nodded.

"Here, the police are not your friends. A few years ago I was robbed. The bankroll for the hotel, which I had hidden under the rug, was taken. I knew who the thief was, a sneaky little Spaniard with those black Gypsy eyes that tell you nothing, but miss nothing. The morning the money is gone, he is too. I know he won't stay in the country. Zip! He'll be in Barcelona, in some bar drinking up my money. So I went straight to the Sûreté. I told them what happened. 'Not an hour ago,' I said. 'You can stop him at the border.' They told me that I had to go back to Montmartre, file an official complaint with the police in my arrondissement. Then the complaint would have to go one place to be signed and another to be stamped before it could be sent on to them.

"I was tempted to go home, forget the money, but I was angry. That Gypsy spending my francs on bad Spanish wine! So I went to the local police, made a statement, signed a complaint. After a week and a half, a man from the Prefecture of Police—not even the Sûreté!—comes to see me. He has decided I have stolen my own money, that there isn't any Spaniard! 'Fifty percent of all crimes,' he tells me, 'are committed by the people who report them. Sixty-five percent of all murders.' " Madame Desnos threw up her hands. "I tell you I was lucky not to go to prison."

Ginny hesitated. She remembered the International Bible Students who'd spent the war in jail just because they were pacifists. "Still," Ginny said, "I have to try. Who else can help me find Roland?" Madame Desnos turned her back on Ginny, fussed with the room keys.

"All right," Madame Desnos said, hurt, "don't believe me. But I'll go with you, and then we'll see who is right."

At the city hall of the 18th Arrondissement, a lone policeman stayed seated behind his desk when they came in. Ginny told him Roland's name, spelled it out, but the policeman made no move to write it down. "Are you a relative of the missing man, madame?"

"He's a friend," Ginny said. The policeman shrugged and blew a puff of air between his lips.

"Only a relative can report someone as missing," he said. Madame Desnos shook her head knowingly. Ginny felt her face turning red. She ran a hand through her hair. She was not going to retreat. She leaned forward over the desk. "Roland Keppi is the father of my child," she said, her voice tight and angry. *Child*, she'd said it out loud. Her child, their child. It was real. She tapped the desk. "Now take his name down." The policeman sighed, but picked up his pen.

"Spell *Keppi* again," he said. She did, and he went off to check the duty book with much more sighing. What if Roland were in serious trouble, the kind that got your name in the paper, got you thrown in jail? If so, why hadn't he told her? Why hadn't she asked? The policeman came back shaking his head. "No Keppis, not yesterday, not last night. No *K*s at all. I shouldn't tell you this," he looked over his shoulder at the empty office, "but your best bet would be to check with the Prefecture of Police. They get all the reports there. Sooner," he paused, "or later."

"See," Ginny said, when they were outside, "we are getting somewhere." Madame Desnos shrugged.

"The Prefecture of Police is over on the Île de la Cité. An even bigger waste of time."

"Well, I'm going," Ginny said, leading the way back to Rue Lepic. A knot of women was standing outside the horse butcher's. One of them stopped Madame Desnos, whispered something in her ear. The woman moved on, stopped someone else. Ginny looked alarmed. Madame Desnos shook her head.

"Neighborhood gossip. Madame Clavel, the baker's wife, has dropped suddenly and unfortunately dead."

"Madame Clavel?" Ginny said, and then she understood. It was all clear to her. If Madame Clavel was dead, then Roland must have spent the night with Monsieur Clavel. The bakery was closed because there were so many arrangements to be made. She could certainly understand that. She saw Roland with the bereaved, despairing baker, afraid to leave him for a moment, even to send word. Relief ran through her, an almost sexual pleasure. She smiled.

"Dead!" she said, and ran off, leaving Madame Desnos to puzzle over the joy in her voice.

The Clavel bakery was still closed, shutters locked, but now there was a wreath trimmed with black ribbon on the door. Ginny knocked. A hand lifted one corner of the shade. The door opened, and a white head peeked out. "I'm very sorry about your wife, Monsieur Clavel, and sorry to bother you now, but I've come about Roland Keppi."

"Come in," Monsieur Clavel said, stepping back, taking in her mourning dress. "Don't tell me Keppi is dead too."

"He isn't with you?"

Monsieur Clavel shook his head. "He didn't come to work yesterday or today." He began to cry. "No one's here with me."

"Oh," Ginny said. Monsieur Clavel sobbed, gulped too much air and hiccupped once, then again. "I think you'd better sit down," Ginny said. She spotted a sink behind the counter and got Monsieur Clavel a glass of water. "Take ten sips holding your breath," she told him. That was Papa Ben's cure.

"Water?" he said, looking quite astonished at what she was asking him to drink.

"Ten sips." Monsieur Clavel held his nose, put the glass to his lips and sipped ten times. Then he hiccupped. "Well," Ginny said, "try drinking from the far side of the glass. That works sometimes." Ginny bent Monsieur Clavel's head down and held the glass for him, just the way her mother had done for her, but the water ran up his nose. "You're not cooperating."

"You'll drown me," he protested, sneezing and hiccupping at the same time.

That left Aunt Fanny's cure. Ginny opened her purse and slapped a franc on the counter. "Hiccup right now, and it's yours," she said. Monsieur Clavel got up, reaching for the money. He opened his mouth. He burped.

Monsieur Clavel handed Ginny her franc with a sigh. He reached under the counter and pulled out a squat bottle. "Brandy?" he asked, pouring a shot for himself.

"No, thank you."

"A roll then?" He offered her a day-old roll from the nearly bare shelves of the bakery. She shook her head.

"No, thank you."

"Please," Monsieur Clavel pressed. "I hate to see bread go to waste." Ginny took the hard roll. Her stomach growled. She tried to bite into it, but her teeth slid off the crust. It was like biting a rock. She slipped the roll into her purse. Monsieur Clavel took a long sip of his brandy, leaned on the counter.

"Tell me what happened," Ginny said. Monsieur Clavel sighed.

"Last night a former customer, a malicious woman, came in and in front of all our best customers accused me of using plaster in my bread." Monsieur Clavel began to weep again, his nose dripping. Ginny gave him her handkerchief. "This woman does this out of avarice, to get a centime or two shaved from the price. I try to take a Christian attitude toward the failings of others. But Henriette didn't share my feelings. 'Business is war, Claude,' she said. I held onto her skirt for all I was worth, I thought she might strangle the woman, let her temper carry her to the guillotine. 'Say a Hail Mary,' I suggested, to delay her. I thought she would knock me out of the way but instead her eyes rolled up in her head. 'I have done what I could,' she said, very faint. Then she slid to the floor. The next thing I knew, the police were taking Henriette," Monsieur Clavel blew his nose, "Henriette's body away." Ginny touched Monsieur Clavel's hand.

"I'll be all right. It's just that we had so little time together. I was her fifth husband, you see. She worked in the kitchen at the Invalides before she came here and had married three of the old soldiers. Not all at once, of course."

"Of course not," Ginny said. "But what about Roland? Is he in some sort of trouble?"

"Not here, no—such a hard worker—but perhaps there were problems where he worked before. It was a shooting stand at one of those street fairs, I think. That's what he told Henriette anyway."

"A fair?" Ginny remembered the look on Roland's face when she'd pointed out the arch of the Ferris wheel against the October sky. As if he'd heard news of an old friend, but bad news. What had he been thinking? Did he have unfinished business at the fair?

"Thank you," she said to Monsieur Clavel. "If there's anything I can do . . ." she stopped, knowing too well that real help was impossible. "Anything," she finished. She shook Monsieur Clavel's hand. He kissed hers. He tried to give her back her handkerchief.

"Please," she said, edging toward the door, "it's yours."

"Thank you," Monsieur Clavel said. "You're too kind. Won't you take another roll?" He pressed two into her hands, his hands warm and soft, the rolls cold as bones. "I just can't believe Henriette is dead. She outlived four husbands. Why not me?"

She took the Métro to Buttes Chaumont. The Ferris wheel couldn't have been more than a few blocks away. She followed the hill down from the park and reached a square called the Place des Fêtes, but except for a pair of overflowing trash cans, it was empty. A woman sat selling fish across from the square. "The police moved them on yesterday," she told Ginny, "but they've set up at La Villette, right by the slaughter-houses. I'm sure it's the same crowd. My son went last night after work and came home with the same worthless junk they were giving out here."

As Ginny rode the Métro to the Porte de La Villette, she steeled herself for what she might find. She had stood one morning with her mother watching two boys and a woman with ankles the size of hams driving a pack of range hogs through a chute into a stock car. The woman was taking Bible study with her mother, and her mother, in re-turn, was paying the freight to New Orleans on the hogs. Ginny hadn't liked watching the hogs, their backs sunburned and peeling, their mouths split by high rising squeals, but she hadn't run away. "I ain't shamed," the fat woman had said to her. "Jesus drove two thousand swine into the sea."

Two prosperous-looking heavyset men in suits sat next to Ginny on the train. They talked of thousands too. "Only one thousand bullocks on a Tuesday!" the smaller man said. "I told him it was inexcusable. I was quite strong with him."

"Pah!" the larger man puffed with disgust. "Communists, every one of them. You're wasting your breath. You should . . ." The train stopped and the men got off. It was La Villette. Ginny reluctantly fol-lowed them. As soon as she stepped on the platform, she could smell the slaughterhouses, the ammonia of the animals' urine, the iron smell of their blood. She wished she had her handkerchief to breathe through. A man pushed by her on the stairs out of the Métro. His shirt was white and clean, but his shoes were caked with hair, his pants dark with blood. She came up into the light and heard the hoarse adolescent cry of a calf going down for veal.

Across the street, huge men wearing bloody aprons leaned on the wall of a slaughterhouse, smoking, eating. An apron, Ginny realized, was the reason the man on the stairs had been able to present such a white front to the world. She started down the sidewalk, her legs feeling numb under her. One of the meat men called after her, "Hey, little gar-lic!" A long whistle followed, but she kept walking. Pastor Russell, the first leader of the Bible Students, had been a vegetarian. Maybe on that at least he'd had the right idea.

Then Ginny saw a Ferris wheel up ahead, frozen against the sky. She couldn't be sure it was the one she had seen before—even the county fair in DeSoto had a Ferris wheel. Ginny had watched it from her window because her mother had forbidden her to go. "Outpost of Babylon," her mother had called the fair. "Drunken with the blood of the saints and the martyrs."

This fair was set up on a small paved triangle beyond the long wall of the slaughterhouse. About a dozen tents, rides, and wooden booths huddled together with their backs to the world. It looked like a shanty town, a dangerous slum. Ginny passed a tent hung with posters of naked women. A man with a ring in his ear stared at her, licked his teeth. If Roland had disappeared at this fair, maybe her mother had been right. *Blood of martyrs.*

The fair didn't seem to have any customers. Most of the booths were shuttered, and none of the rides were moving except a circle of clumsily painted airplanes that swayed and creaked on their chains in the breeze. Two barefoot children, a boy and a girl, stood tossing a bean bag slowly back and forth. They watched her as she approached. Ginny felt numb with irrational fear. The smell of the slaughterhouse seemed even stronger here. Behind her a phonograph began playing a dance that dragged its feet, but she could still hear the lowing of the calves in their pens. "Could you tell me where the shooting gallery is?" she asked the children.

The girl pointed with her chin at the front of a lurid red and gold stand. Ginny's eyes caught a row of guns, a spinning wedding scene with a ludicrously pregnant bride. "Hey Chief, a lady wants to see you," the boy called out.

Ginny turned. A great scarlet woman enthroned in a booth at the end of the stand stretched out her hand. Ginny stepped back. Her years of Bible study came back to her unwilled: *The woman was arrayed in purple and scarlet color and decked with gold and precious stones and pearls. And upon her forehead was a name written, MYSTERY, BABYLON THE GREAT, THE MOTHER OF HARLOTS.*

"Delighted," a deep voice said. The woman was a man. The numbness in Ginny's legs spread upward in a great sandy wave, and she felt herself falling.

"Is she all right?" It was the deep voice, the scarlet man's voice.

"Maybe," a higher voice, the boy. He pulled her arm.

Ginny stood up slowly, holding onto the boy and the corner of the stand. "Good. Beautiful," the deep voice said. A sign on the gallery read

The Mountain of Gold. The fat man in the scarlet robe reached down from his booth, presenting his hand. "I am the Mountain." He folded his hand around hers. The flesh between the jeweled rings was unpleasantly damp.

"I've never fainted in my life," Ginny said. "The smell . . ." She waved weakly toward the slaughterhouse. The Mountain shrugged, the scarlet folds of his gown moving like lava across the slope of his chest.

"La Villette? You get used to it. We're lucky to be here. We almost ended up outside the wall, in Aubervilliers." All his chins shuddered as he said the name of the suburb. "Besides," he said, "whether we are up or down on the food chain," he drew a ring-bound thumb across his neck, "we're all food."

"Please," said Ginny, her knees bending.

"Jesus," the boy said, giving way under her weight.

Ginny steadied herself. "I'm here because I'm looking for . . ." She stopped. Where was her purse? It wasn't on the ground where she'd fallen.

The Mountain let out a bellow, "Beelzebub!" The boy jumped, let go of Ginny's elbow. The barefoot girl peeked around the corner of the booth, chewing a strand of unwashed black hair. The Mountain held out a jeweled hand. The boy pulled Ginny's purse from under his shirt and handed it to her. "See if everything is there," the Mountain said.

Ginny checked. "Yes, it's all here."

The Mountain shook his head. "This pair I call Beelzebub and Bathsheba, because they'd rather rule in hell than serve in heaven." He made a quick stabbing motion at the boy with his ring finger. "Get thee behind me, Satan," he said, "and stay there." The boy grinned and backed away. Ginny started again.

"I'm looking for a friend who may have worked for you—Roland Keppi?"

"Roland," The Mountain sighed. "He had real talent," he said. "Perhaps the police picked him up." Ginny felt cold. *Had* talent. Past tense.

"I've been to the police," she said. "They don't know anything."

"What they know and what they say are two different continents," the Mountain said. "Do you know if Roland was in France legally?"

"But he's French," Ginny said. The Mountain shook his head.

"He's Alsatian, and from the way he acted when the police raided our beautiful fair, I suspect that he didn't have French papers."

132

"Is not having papers serious?"

"To the police, everything is serious," the Mountain said, "but not having papers is very serious. To the police it means you are a criminal. Why else would you be afraid to show your papers? Or you are a foreigner with no passport or visa, perhaps a spy. For the first, they throw you in jail and ask questions later. For the second, they don't ask questions at all. Farewell, France. They deport you. After all, they have good reason to be suspicious of foreigners, especially Germans."

Ginny shook her head. Why hadn't Roland told her? Didn't he trust her? The Mountain stiffened suddenly as if he was in pain and smacked his hand to his forehead. "René the Foot!" he said. "The boy on the carousel told me that Roland came by yesterday morning asking for René the Foot." The Mountain shook. "That excreta! This business reeks of him."

"Who?"

He took both her hands, earnest, intent. "Madame . . . "

"Ginny."

"Madame Ginny, what you should do is go back to the police. You're respectable. The police might tell a nice American girl where a friend of hers has gotten to. And I'll make my own," he paused, waved a swollen hand at the fair, "subtle inquiries. This isn't Alsace or Aubervilliers. In Paris, nothing happens, for better or worse, without someone seeing it."

Ginny looked at the fat man in his woman's dress and wondered what she was doing in this place. "All right, I'll go back to the police," she said. "I'm staying at the Grand Hôtel de Montmartre. Let me know the minute you get news." The Mountain shifted in his booth.

"Good news or bad?" he asked.

"Good or bad," Ginny said. The Mountain nodded.

"Beelzebub will escort you back to the station," the Mountain said loud enough for the two children crouched behind the booth to hear, "and if you don't get there safely there'll be two more unemployed Gypsies in hell." He banged his fist on the side of the booth.

Ginny started back to the Métro with the two Gypsy children. The girl came up beside her and took her hand. "Look, lady," she said, pulling a square of cardboard from her waistband. The cardboard was edged in red and printed with what looked like a poem. Ginny looked closer. It was the Lord's prayer in French. "I'm a good girl," the girl said with a flash of her sharp little teeth. Ginny held tight to the strap of her purse.

At the station, the boy unhooked his sister's hand from Ginny's. "Basta!" he said and waved the girl away. He offered a last word of advice, looking very serious. "Don't hold your purse like that by the strap," he said. "That won't do no good if I got a knife. Hold it close, like this." He cradled an imaginary purse between his ribs and the curve of his arm.

"Like this?" Ginny held her purse like a football player about to run with the ball. The boy nodded.

"Don't forget. People who take care of what they got, keep what they got." He nodded again, agreeing with his own advice, then left Ginny at the head of the stairs. She got out her map, had just opened it to plot her way home, when she heard a shout behind her.

"Get away!" A stout man in a suit, a twin for one of the men she'd overheard on the Métro coming out to La Villette, was pinned against the wall by the boy who was making the sign of the cross in his face.

"Please, Monsieur, you got to pray for our poor mother," the boy was yelling.

His sister was weeping and praying in Spanish, "¡Jesús, María, San José y todos los santos!" She waved the card with the Lord's prayer in front of her like a fan.

"My God," the man said. "Somebody help me!"

"Help yourself," the girl said and pushed the card into the man's face. A knife flashed, and Ginny saw the man's pocket fall open, a white triangle of underwear laid bare.

"My wallet!" he cried out, astonished. Some meat workers near the stairs stretched out their arms, but they were used to catching penned cattle, slow and confused. The children ran like cats, low and fast. "Thieving Gypsies!" the stocky man yelled, but they were gone. Ginny held her purse close to her body as she stepped onto her train.

She took the Mountain's advice, remembering also the advice of the policeman in Montmartre, and went to the Prefecture of Police. Inside, there were lines of people, halls full of the same buzzing she'd heard yesterday in front of Western Union, but here the people were all French, and their problems were with various French systems, not American ones. "I want to find out if the police are holding a friend of mine," Ginny told the sergeant at the front desk. "Which office is that?"

"Well," the sergeant pulled on his chin, "there's the Sûreté, the Municipal Police, the Frontier Police, Judicial Police, Public Hygiene and Security Inspectors, the Gambling Police, not to mention all the branches of military police, and any one of them might have arrested your friend." The sergeant shrugged. "But you can start with Captain Barjou," he pointed at a door across the courtyard. A sign on it read *Lost Property*.

"Thank you," Ginny said. "You've been a great help." The sergeant shook his head.

"I doubt it," he said.

Behind the door was another sergeant. "May I speak to Captain Barjou?" Ginny asked. An officer came in with a manacled prisoner, borrowed a match from the sergeant, and lit the prisoner a cigarette.

The sergeant nodded his head at the officer who was now pouring the prisoner a cup of wine. The officer was tall with a beak of a nose and a neatly pressed uniform. "Captain Barjou is occupied," the sergeant said.

"I've come from the 18th Arrondissement." Ginny raised her voice loud enough for the captain to hear. "The policeman there told me I should come here. He said you would get any reports that had been filed." The captain gave no sign that he heard. "I'm looking for a friend who's missing, a man named Roland Keppi."

"We do get all the reports," the sergeant said. "After they progress up the chain of command. When did your friend go missing?"

"Yesterday." The sergeant shook his head.

"Come back in a week." He crossed his arms across his chest, sat looking up at her.

She brought out the name the Mountain had given her. "Well then," she said, "do you or Captain Barjou know where I might find a man called René the Foot?"

"René the Foot?" The sergeant signaled Captain Barjou to step over. "Is he in jail here? May I see him?" Ginny persisted.

The sergeant looked up at his captain, then grinned. "Sure," he said, "you can see René the Foot any time you want."

Captain Barjou coughed, straightened his collar. "René Fuss is in the morgue, madame. I'm afraid he is quite dead." The prisoner let out a laugh, choked on his wine. The sergeant snorted. Ginny felt her cheeks burning, but refused to give up.

"When did he die?" she asked. "Was anyone with him?" Captain Barjou looked at the sergeant.

"Stabbed, last night," the sergeant said.

"Now, what was the name of that fellow you were looking for?" The sergeant was interested now. "Did he know René too?" The sergeant grinned at her. Did they think Roland had stabbed this René the Foot? Could Roland? No. She shook her head. No.

Captain Barjou waved the sergeant back. "If René Fuss was a friend of yours, madame," he said, shaking a fatherly finger, "then I advise you to cultivate a higher class of acquaintances." The prisoner laughed again, the cigarette bobbing on his lip. The sergeant laughed.

Ginny slammed the door of the office behind her. She pulled her fingers through her hair. She wanted to take one of the cannons in the courtyard and turn it on the Lost Property Office. It was like going to see Miss Anderson, the dean of women at Dr. Love's academy, a balding woman who smacked girls on the back of the knees with a yardstick if their skirts were too short. Miss A's favorites were the bad girls, the smokers, the ones who were always in trouble. They were the insiders. The only other people who stood a chance with her were those giants and strangers to school life, parents. Ginny needed someone now with that kind of clout.

Dr. Love. She had forgotten Dr. Love. He would know what to do. He was used to commanding respect—despite his height. What time was it? Ginny heard the click of the Lost Property Office being locked behind her. She asked the sergeant at the front desk for the time. "Five o'clock," he said. She was due for dinner at the Edouard VII at seven.

A doorman threw back the great gold door of the Hôtel Edouard VII. Ginny almost turned her ankle, the white carpet was so thick. It was like walking on an angel food cake. It amazed her that the word *hotel* could be applied to two places as different as the Grand Hôtel de Montmartre and the Edouard VII. She stepped carefully across the virgin carpet to the front desk, a block of marble as white as the carpet.

"Doctor and Madame Love, madame?" the clerk said, his accent humbling hers. "I regret to tell madame that the Loves are no longer with us. However," he bowed slightly from the waist, "they did leave a note for madame, with their profound regrets." Ginny slit the heavy white envelope with the silver letter opener the clerk handed her. She recognized Madame Duval's—Madame Love's—loopy handwriting and florid style:

My dear Virginia,

    I regret deeply not having the chance to walk Paris for at least a few days in your company, but the telegraph wire brings my dear Love news of reverses, and we must leave without delay.

    Until we meet again in more certain times,

Your friend,
Antoinette Love

More certain times. Ginny wasn't sure she could imagine them. Whom could she, an American alone in Paris, turn to now? Madame Desnos had been more than kind and loyal, but standing here in the blinding white splendor of the Edouard VII, Ginny could see clearly that she did not have the weight to move the immovable, to open whichever bureaucrat's locked files had the secret of Roland's disappearance, to open whatever cell door held Roland. She turned the note absently in her hands, rubbing a finger across the hotel's gold seal.

"I must send a note," Ginny said to the clerk, trying to sound determined, American, and rich.

"Madame?"

"Stationery, please," she said, holding out a black-gloved hand, "and a pen." The clerk paused for a moment, then gave a slight nod.

"Certainly, madame. Will one sheet be sufficient?"

She wrote her note at a desk in the lobby, handed it sealed to the clerk. "Would you please," she said, slipping a fifty franc tip into his palm, "see that this is delivered to the American Embassy? It's urgent." The clerk slid his hand into his pocket.

"Without delay, madame," he said.

CHAPTER SIXTEEN

GINNY SLEPT IN room one, but without Roland beside her, the big bed was cold. Madame Desnos woke her the next morning with a cup of warm milk and a toasted heel of bread. "Milk won't come up if you vomit."

"And toast?" Ginny asked, sitting up carefully.

"That's meant to come up. You don't want the dry heaves." Ginny touched her tongue to the milk, took a bite of toast.

"I think I'm okay," she said.

"Stand up," Madame Desnos said. Ginny put her bare feet on the floor and slid out of bed. She put one hand on her stomach. Nothing happened.

"I don't think I'm going to be sick."

Madame Desnos tapped Ginny's belly lightly with her index finger. "Lift up your nightgown." Ginny blushed but raised her gown to her chin. "Look." She pointed to Ginny's reflection in the mirror on the dresser. Ginny saw two breasts larger than her own, their nipples darker than she remembered. Her body, hidden under her clothes, had changed while she wasn't watching. "When was the last time you fell off the roof?" Madame Desnos said.

"What?" Ginny was still staring at the strange body in the mirror.

"Had a visitor," Madame Desnos went on, "followed the moon."

"You mean menstruated?"

"Bled."

"I don't know. I've always been light and irregular. I . . ."

Madame Desnos shook her head. "Didn't your mother teach you anything?"

"Yes," Ginny said, letting her gown drop down to cover her, "but I guess knowing didn't help, did it?" Her breasts bobbed. Madame Desnos patted her back.

"What you need," she said, "is a good brassiere. Get dressed, and we'll go shopping."

"Not this morning. I have things to do." Madame Desnos raised her eyebrows and frowned, trying to show both surprise and hurt.

"Later," Ginny said, touching Madame Desnos's shoulder lightly. Still Madame Desnos lingered, adjusting the dresser scarf under Paul's urn.

"This is a nice vase."

"It's an urn," Ginny said. Should she tell Madame Desnos the truth? Even to her, it now sounded bizarre. Madame Desnos looked at her, eyebrows raised. "I had my husband cremated," Ginny said, "and that's what holds his ashes." Madame Desnos let one eyebrow drop. The other stayed arched.

"Well," she said, "it's still a nice vase."

When Madame Desnos left, Ginny lifted her gown again and looked closely at the body in the mirror. She traced a wide circle on her stomach with one hand. What was inside her right now? What would be there next week? In a month? She knew so little. She'd seen the four-color charts, tadpole to fetus, seen the healthy babies in the nursery and the others floating lonely in their glass jars, but really she knew nothing. She shivered, cupped her hands over her stomach. Whatever was in there, it was hers to protect. For the first time, she let herself consider the possibility that Roland, like Paul, had abandoned her. What evidence did she have that he hadn't? Madame Desnos thought so. She closed her eyes and imagined her mother nodding, agreeing. And Fanny? Even Fanny shook her head, looking sad. Ginny wrapped her arms around herself, hugging her stomach and her fear.

She went back to the Edouard VII. This time the clerk behind the ice desk smiled when he saw her crossing the snowdrift carpet. A letter from the embassy had come not an hour before. Ginny took the letter to a small table in the lobby, away from the clerk's quick eyes.

It wasn't from the ambassador, but from the ambassador's first secretary, a Mr. A. Eugene Atwood, who, in a rather stiff, angular hand, wrote that regretfully, there was not an ambassador currently in residence, although President Hoover would no doubt be appointing one shortly. He himself was currently quite busy helping to organize the International Conference on the Treatment of Foreigners to be held at the embassy. However, if he could be of help to her, he would be pleased to receive her in his office at ten.

Ginny put the note back in its envelope. She couldn't wait for Herbert Hoover to make up his mind. Mr. Atwood would have to do. If he was in charge of an international conference, he had to be an important man. It might not be easy to make someone with such Yankee handwriting, so much like Paul's, understand her situation. She hoped Mr. Atwood was both important and easily moved, if not to sympathy at least to action. She hoped Mr. Atwood was a lot like Papa Ben.

The marine on guard at the embassy door showed her down a narrow hall to the first secretary's office. A thin boy, who looked younger than she was, announced her and then said she could go in. Ginny stood for a moment outside A. Eugene Atwood's door and imagined herself able to control his heart and mind, his entire central nervous system. Then she went in. The office was spacious and well lit, with a maroon carpet almost as deep as the one at the Edouard VII. A. Eugene Atwood stood and held out his hand. The light from a large window behind the desk streamed past him and ran in ribbons down his outstretched arm. He was palely blond and tall and young. She blinked in the sunlight.

"Miz Gillespie," he said, his voice soft as butter. Ginny let him take her hand. He gave it the gentlest of reassuring squeezes. He wasn't a Yankee, but a fellow Southerner. "Here, let's draw those drapes. The sun gets so low this time a year, it shines right in all afternoon," he said, and smothered the light with maroon velvet. He clicked on a desk lamp. Ginny sat down in a plush chair and looked at Mr. Atwood more closely. Her first impression had been wrong. He wasn't young, his hair was white not blond, his eyes an almost colorless blue, and his shoulders had a bureaucrat's stoop. "Where are you from, Miz Gillespie?" he asked, using *from* in the Southern sense, meaning where your folks were buried, where everyone would instantly recognize your mother's maiden name.

"From north Florida, the panhandle," Ginny said. "A little town about half-way between Jacksonville and Pensacola called DeSoto."

"I'm from Georgia myself . . . Macon. Although," he sighed, "I can't say I've been back there any too recently."

"Would you want to go back?" Ginny asked. "Permanently?" Mr. Atwood smiled.

"Now you got me. No, I don't suppose I would. Still, from this distance I can hazard a certain nostalgia."

"Are you really in charge of a conference on the treatment of foreigners?"

"Pardon?" Mr. Atwood was still drifting on a warm Southern breeze. He reached in his pocket and fastened a pair of pince-nez on his nose, like President Wilson had worn. They brought his pale blue eyes into focus. He flipped open the calendar on his desk. "Oh, yes, that's this month. Last month was the Conference for the Revision of the International Classification of the Causes of Death. Grim topic, but it went quite well, all things considered. The month before that was the First International Conference on Sanitary Aviation." Now his voice was clipped, professional, with no trace of a drawl.

"You don't specialize in the treatment of foreigners?"

"This month I do," Mr. Atwood said, "at least until tomorrow when the conference begins. Then the experts we're bringing in take over, give their papers, et cetera. And I'll get busy with the next conference on the agenda."

"Oh," Ginny said. "But you answered my note about Roland Keppi. I thought you could help."

"The embassy would like to help." Mr. Atwood looked at her through his glasses, his eyes cool windows of blue. "But according to official embassy policy, what we can do in this case may be limited."

"Limited to what?"

"Actually, to this conversation, Mrs. Gillespie."

Ginny leaned back in her chair. She had to find some way to move him, to shame him, to turn him into the kind of Southern man too vain to say no to a lady. Otherwise, she was lost, Roland was lost. Perhaps she should cry. "Mr. Atwood, I know I can confide in you." Ginny reached across his desk to rest her gloved hand on his. "I am with child."

Mr. Atwood nodded stiffly, but didn't move his hand from under hers. "Your husband . . ."

"Has been dead longer than I have been . . ." Ginny paused, "pregnant."

Mr. Atwood's eyes looked more worried than shocked. "I do see your problem."

"Mr. Atwood, forgive me for saying this, but if you do not help me find Roland Keppi before his . . . our child is born, I do not think your people back home in Macon would be correct in calling you a gentleman." Mr. Atwood stiffened, then sighed.

"Perhaps not." He took off the pince-nez and rubbed his eyes. "Ah, Miz Gillespie, it is hard to do good in this world."

"It is hard," Ginny said, "but we have to believe it is possible." She held her breath, imagining Papa Ben with her ticket to Jacksonville in his hand.

Mr. Atwood's eyes were almost wet. Then he blinked, put his glasses back on. His eyes hardened once more. "All right, Mrs. Gillespie. I suppose I could have someone look into the facts of the case."

"Thank you," Ginny said, her voice breaking. She was surprised to find herself in tears, unplanned and uncontrollable. Her cheeks were wet, her chin dripped. Salt tears stung her lips. "We've been so worried," she said, and as soon as she said it, it struck her. *We.* She put one hand to her stomach and saw her baby, its face as wet as hers, fists in its eyes.

She returned to the hotel full of her news, but she found Madame Desnos with an envelope in her hand. "No one wastes money on a telegram full of good news," she said as she handed it to Ginny, her thumb leaving a damp oval on the envelope. Her hands were sweaty with fear. Ginny slit open the telegram. It was from Mrs. Corbet. She sat down. She had forgotten her fear of losing her stocks, her money. It seemed unimportant compared to losing Roland.

DUGGIN SHOT. 662 SOLD. WILL SEND NEWS ASAP. YOURS CORBET.

Exactly ten words. Duggin was Paul's lawyer, 662 Ponce De Leon Way, the address of Paul's house. ASAP was shorthand for *as soon as possible.* She had seen Papa Ben write it on the bottom of past due bills. She reread the telegram. Duggin shot. That was bad news. No lawyer would get shot or shoot himself over nothing. Ginny imagined a grainy newspaper photograph of Duggin slumped forward at his desk, bleeding black blood over her white stocks like a bad guy shot holding up a bank. But the sale of the house was good news. At least in Mrs. Corbet she had someone looking after her interests, someone with a more personal interest in them than the late Duggin or the Bank of France. "Damn," Ginny said, suddenly remembering the officer at the bank, her promise to bring Roland with her when she came to get all the money she had in the world, money that would be ready for her to pick up today. What was she going to do with all those bundles of francs?

"Is it terrible news?" Madame Desnos asked. "Is it a death? Worse, loss of money?"

"Do you have a suitcase I could borrow?"

"A suitcase? Are you going somewhere?"

"Just across town," Ginny said, afraid Madame Desnos wouldn't be able to sleep if she told her she intended to keep two hundred fifty thousand francs in her room, "to get something that belongs to me."

"I think I do have an old suitcase my husband left the last time he was here." Madame Desnos dug in the maid's closet and came up with a dusty cardboard and leatherette suitcase.

"I just need it for a little while," Ginny said. "Then you can have it back."

"Keep it. If it was worth anything, I'd have pawned it."

She took Monsieur Desnos's suitcase with her to the bank. The sight of it did not reassure the bank officer. "Are you sure you wish to do this, madame?" he asked as a teller packed the bundles of fifty-franc notes into the bag. He was actually wringing his hands, twisting one hand in the other until both were bright red and sweat dampened his cuffs. Ginny was not sure, but what else could she do? Besides, who would guess what she had in Monsieur Desnos's poor suitcase? "I feel I must remind you," the officer said, "that the bank cannot guarantee your safety if you persist in this matter."

"It's not your worry any more," Ginny said, closing the suitcase, giving it an experimental heft to check its weight. It didn't feel heavy. Ten thousand dollars in francs weighed less than Paul's marble urn. "Besides, my bodyguard is waiting for me outside."

She carried the suitcase back on the Métro and no one looked twice at it, carried it with her up Montmartre toward the hotel. She felt almost invisible. Even Madame Desnos did not look up when she came in, went up the stairs. In her room, she added the few hundred francs she had left from what she'd brought over to what was in the suitcase. Then she sat on the bed next to the suitcase, looking at the money. Suppose she lived another fifty years—that seemed reasonable. Fifty divided into what was in the suitcase meant she had just five thousand francs, two hundred dollars, a year to live on. Mrs. Corbet would send the money from the sale of the house but that wouldn't add much. Ginny took the wrapper off a bundle of bills and counted out nine hundred francs, enough for a month at the Grand Hôtel. At that rate, she'd spend the five thousand francs in six months just on her room, before her baby was even born.

Ginny stood up, paced to the far corner of the room and back. Every franc she spent meant one less for the future, hers, Roland's, the child's. She would have to find some way to make as well as spend money. Perhaps she could buy a shop, something that she and Roland could run? It would be daring but at least she would be risking her capital herself. She suspected that Paul's lawyer, late and perhaps unlamented, had lost more money than that for her without her having any say.

Ginny stopped pacing, looked around. Two hundred fifty thousand francs might not be much to live on for fifty years, but it was a lot to hide. Where did people hide money? In the dresser or under the mattress seemed too obvious, the first place a thief would look. Her mother had always kept her money in a copy of the *Watch Tower*. She'd known how unlikely it was that Papa Ben would pick up that magazine to read.

Ginny opened her trunk, pulled out her winter coat. The bottom tray of the trunk lifted out. She could hide the bundles of bills under that, but what if someone stole the whole trunk? It looked worth stealing, much more than Monsieur Desnos's old suitcase did. Ginny closed the suitcase with the money still in it and took it downstairs with her. Madame Desnos was busy making coffee. "I'm putting the suitcase you lent me back in the closet," Ginny said.

"Shove it all the way back," Madame Desnos called from the kitchen. "I don't want to trip over it every time I need a broom."

Ginny pushed the suitcase behind the buckets and stiff mops and bald brooms. When she came out, Madame Desnos had a cup of coffee waiting for her. "Don't throw that suitcase out," Ginny said, trying to keep her voice casual. "I might need it again. It's much more practical than my trunk."

"If I could make myself get rid of anything," Madame Desnos said, "I wouldn't still have this hotel."

Ginny tried to give Madame Desnos the money she'd counted out for her room, but Madame Desnos waved it away. "No, no, you don't owe me anything."

"I haven't paid in two days." Madame Desnos blushed.

"You don't owe me," she said. "I usually just get fifteen francs for your room. I've never had an American guest before. I was overcharging you."

"Oh," Ginny said.

"But I intend to make up the difference." Madame Desnos waved her long index finger. "I wouldn't want to leave you with the wrong impression of the French businesswoman."

"Well," Ginny said, "when I've caught up, let me know. I don't want to take advantage of you."

"Madame?" The door to the hotel had opened and shut without their having heard it. Beelzebub stood there.

"What business do you have here?" Madame Desnos said, shooing the Gypsy boy with both hands.

The boy ignored her, held out a piece of paper. Ginny took it. It was from the Mountain. "Here," she said, and gave the boy a franc. He waited for a moment, hoping for more. Then he was gone in the blink of an eye.

"They're faster than rats," Madame Desnos said. Ginny opened the note.

Madame G.,

It is a sad tale I pass on to you. Here it is, in brief: René the Foot was stabbed and killed Wednesday night. The police apprehended four men—Maurice Petit, Robert Zelie, Bernard Dottin, and Roland Keppi. Yesterday, Zelie gave evidence. Last night, Petit and Dottin were charged with murder and Roland was deported to Germany.

I continue my inquiries, madame, but I have not, as yet, been able to ascertain where, or if, R. is being held in that alien land.

Yours ever, the M.

Ginny let her finger rest on the word *deported*. Last night while she slept alone in the big bed, Roland had been moving away from her at the speed of a train. She imagined him passing handcuffed over the border into Germany, cold, alone. Did he know, did he believe, she was searching for him? Ginny handed the note to Madame Desnos.

"Germans," Madame Desnos said, shaking her head, "that's never good news."

CHAPTER SEVENTEEN

GINNY TELEPHONED THE embassy. It was late, but with luck
Mr. Atwood would be there, would know what to do. Madame Desnos put the call through for her, holding the telephone at arm's length as she shouted the number at the operator. Then
she handed the telephone to Ginny.

"Hello, hello," Ginny said, talking on a French telephone for the first
time, hoping she had the right piece pressed to her ear.

"Hello . . . oo," Mr. Atwood's voice echoed up from the bottom
of a deep well. Ginny raised her voice, told Mr. Atwood the news.

"I was just on my way out, Mrs. Gillespie. I'll have someone telephone the German Embassy. Telephone you . . . ou."

"Do you hear an echo?" Ginny asked, but the line had gone dead.
Ginny handed the telephone to Madame Desnos. "I didn't even know
you had a phone."

"*I* don't have a telephone," Madame Desnos said. "That would be
unjustifiable. But a grand hotel has to have one, or at least my husband
thought so." Ginny sat down to wait.

It was past nine when the telephone finally rang. Ginny had fallen
asleep on the couch in the lobby, but the bell woke her. Madame
Desnos, who was still up, going over her accounts, got to the phone first.
"Hello! Le Grand Hôtel de Montmartre," she shouted. "Hello, hello!"
She handed the earpiece and then the mouthpiece to Ginny. "It is some-
one for you."

"Hello?" The voice wasn't Mr. Atwood's. It was very young, very
Yankee. "Mrs. Gillespie?"

"Yes?"

"This is Harold Bottoms, First Secretary Atwood's secretary."

"Yes?"

"Mr. Atwood has gone to the reception for the conference on the treatment of foreigners, but he wonders if you would be kind enough to come to his office tomorrow at one?"

"One?" Ginny said. "In the afternoon?" What might happen to Roland while Mr. Atwood breakfasted, sat at his desk over coffee, ate a good hot lunch?

"Mrs. Gillespie," Mr. Bottoms said very seriously, "do you want me to repeat that message?"

"What?" Ginny said, not understanding. "No, thank you, Mr. Bottoms. There was a terrible echo earlier today, but I can hear you quite well."

"All the embassy's lines," Mr. Bottoms lowered his voice, "go through a switchboard at the Prefecture of Police."

"You mean the police listen in?"

"I thought a person in your position would want to know."

"What position?" Ginny asked, losing his logic.

"Sorry. Shouldn't have mentioned it." Mr. Bottoms lowered his voice again, until he was whispering. "I'm new to all this. I've never spoken to an agent before. Good night, Mrs. Gillespie," he said, his voice faint.

"I can't hear you, Mr. Bottoms," Ginny said. "Are you there, Mr. Bottoms?" Mr. Bottoms was gone, but Ginny heard breathing, as if someone were listening silently on some other extension. "Stop it!" She slammed the receiver down.

"Who was that?" Madame Desnos asked, alarmed. Ginny's heart slowed. What she had heard was probably just another echo, the sound of her own breathing bouncing back.

"Someone from the embassy," she said. "I think."

*　　*　　*

"By one o'clock Mr. Atwood hopes to have the whole matter settled," Ginny said the next morning as they drank their coffee, aware that she said it for her benefit as well as Madame Desnos's. Ginny poured herself another cup of coffee. She needed it. After talking to Bottoms, she hadn't slept.

"One o'clock?" Madame Desnos said. "Then we have time for shopping." Ginny opened her mouth to say no, but Madame Desnos cut her off. "Do you want breasts that bump, bump, bump on your knees?" Ginny hesitated. She wanted to go to the embassy, but what good would sitting outside Mr. Atwood's closed door do? He must have had a good reason for not wanting her there until one. She couldn't afford to make him angry. Who knew who he had to see about a case like Roland's, how sensitive such inquiries were? Besides, she felt clearly that she owed Madame Desnos something, though she wasn't quite sure what. With a nod she gave in.

They went to a store called Monoprix. A red and white banner over the door declared: *Everything from 0.50 to 10 francs.* "I've been wanting to come here," Madame Desnos said, pulling her scarf off her faded red hair. "They claim everything they sell has the price marked right on it and that everyone gets the same price, no bargaining." Madame Desnos shook her head. "We'll see about that." The inside of the store was as open as a barn, lit by rows of overhead lights. There were wooden bins overflowing with socks and hand towels, shelves stacked high with teetering dishes, glass cases protecting glittering ranks of watches and rings. Everything in the store was symmetrically arranged. Even the waxed floor was divided into perfect black and white squares. It looked like the Woolworths in DeSoto where her mother had gone twice a year to pick out Ginny's clothes. It looked like any five and dime store. What it didn't look like were the tiny stores on Rue Lepic with their displays of two hats, a pair of gloves.

Ginny caught sight of herself in a three-way mirror, Madame Desnos behind her, her hair a fainter reflection of Ginny's. "This kind of store is new here?" Ginny asked.

Madame Desnos nodded, heading straight for a formidable tower of black brassieres, stacked cup to cup. "Ah," she said, "here we go." She held one up to Ginny's chest. To Ginny the cups looked huge, like something made to fit the stone women dancing on the facade of the Paris Opéra. Madame Desnos held up a second, even larger brassiere. "These may look big to you now, but you have to plan ahead. You won't believe how big your breasts will be by your ninth month . . . " Madame Desnos cupped her hands and held them a foot from her chest. "Mine were like African melons."

"Yours?" Ginny asked. Madame Desnos turned over the white price tag pinned to the largest brassiere. "I didn't know you had children." Madame Desnos checked the price on the smaller one. Ginny waited for Madame Desnos to go on.

"They're both seven francs," Madame Desnos said, putting the two brassieres back in the bin. "That makes the biggest one a better buy." She looked at Ginny. "I don't have any children," she said. "I had a son once . . . for a little while. For as long as a bird sits on a window sill, a streetcar waits at a stop." Madame Desnos snapped her fingers. "That long."

Ginny didn't know what to say. She put her hand on Madame Desnos's shoulder. A bird sits, a streetcar waits, no time at all. Less time than she had had Roland, Fanny happiness, Paul life.

"He woke up one morning with a fever that couldn't be brought down." Madame Desnos's shoulders shook slightly, as if remembering the crying she'd done. "His brain cooked like an egg. 'Believe me,' the doctor said. 'I'm as upset about it as you are,' he said." Madame Desnos shook her head, "I told him I didn't believe him."

"I'm sorry," Ginny said, her hand moving in circles on Madame Desnos's shoulder, around and around until the shaking grew faint and then stopped. "Were you alone? Was your husband there with you?" Madame Desnos let go of the breath she'd taken, snorted like a horse.

"He was where he always is—somewhere else, with someone else. He never even saw his own son." She shook her head. "That's his punishment. But you won't have to be alone when your baby comes," she straightened her back and Ginny removed her supporting hand. "Not if I am breathing air." They stood face to face, their cheeks flushed to match their hair.

"And I'll have Roland," Ginny said.

"Touch iron," Madame Desnos tapped the metal column next to her with one finger. "Now . . ." Madame Desnos said with a fierce shake of her head, "about these brassieres." She caught the elbow of a salesgirl who was trying to squeeze past them in the aisle with a stack of men's hats. "All these brassieres are seven francs?" Madame Desnos asked pointing at the bin.

"Yes, madame," the girl said, rocking back on her heels to balance her hats.

Madame Desnos picked up one of the brassieres and snapped a strap. "What's wrong with them?" she demanded.

"Wrong?" the girl asked. "Why, nothing, madame. They are per-

fectly fine brassieres. I'm wearing one now. I bought one for my mama."
Ginny couldn't imagine buying her mother underwear.

"Then why," Madame Desnos dropped the brassiere she was holding
into the bin, "why at such a price, do you still have so many?" The girl
was stumped.

"I don't know. Maybe we just got them in." Madame Desnos shook
her head, standing her ground. "Let me get the manageress," the girl said
and fled, her hats leading the way down the aisle.

"No liver, that girl," remarked Madame Desnos, turning back to the
brassieres.

"They seem fine to me," Ginny said, picking one up. "Do you really
think there's something wrong with them?"

"There's always something wrong if you look hard enough."

The manageress appeared, a thin woman with lacquered fingernails
and a breast pocket full of red pencils. "May I be of some little as-
sistance?" she asked.

"Why is this brassiere," Madame Desnos held one up, "which is
smaller and cost less to make, being sold for the same price as the larger
brassieres?"

"The difference in the amount of fabric is not enough to affect the
price," the manageress said. "The real cost is in the labor." She ran a nail
down one carefully stitched seam. Madame Desnos beamed. The bargaining had begun.

"Then this one," Madame Desnos pulled another brassiere from the
bin, "should be marked down. The seamstress was incompetent." Madame Desnos handed the brassiere to Ginny. Holding it up to the light,
Ginny could see where one of the tiny stitches that zigzagged from cotton to elastic had missed its mark, reaching only from cotton to cotton.
Ginny handed the brassiere in question to the manageress.

"A minor flaw," the manageress said, shaking her head, "but we don't
sell seconds. I'll send it back to the manufacturer." Madame Desnos nodded in sympathy.

"So much trouble for you," Madame Desnos said. "Wrapping. Addressing. Postage. Forget I showed it to you. It was the one my little
friend wanted, but we'll find another like it I'm sure—somewhere else."

"No, don't go." The manageress reached for the bin. "I'm sure if
you'd look you will find another that would suit . . ." Madame Desnos
shook her head. Ginny shook hers. The manageress sighed and, taking

a red pencil out of her pocket, she wrote a new number over the printed price on the flawed brassiere's tag. "Six francs," she said, handing Ginny the brassiere, "but don't tell anyone."

"You're too good," Madame Desnos said, smiling. The manageress retreated with the compliment, shaking her head. Ginny started for the cash register, but Madame Desnos caught her arm, took the brassiere. "You don't want that one," she said. She picked up a seven-franc brassiere and started to switch tags. Ginny took the brassiere back. She didn't want to get arrested, turned in by the manageress over a franc, not with her appointment with Mr. Atwood getting closer with each tick of the clock.

"This one's fine," she said. "Thanks for your help."

Madame Desnos frowned. "Americans," she said, "they're too innocent to be safe on the streets." But at the cash register, her good humor returned. The cashier handed Ginny her receipt, and Madame Desnos allowed herself a satisfied snort. "One price," she said, "indeed."

But Ginny had something else on her mind. She whispered to Madame Desnos, "I have to go to the bathroom. I don't think I can wait."

"You don't have to keep it a secret. It's something all women do," Madame Desnos said loudly. "Wait a few months—you'll have to pee every time you swallow."

"There's a public toilet across the street," the cashier said sympathetically. "When I was pregnant if I didn't go every hour, my hands would swell so badly I couldn't make change."

The toilet was underground, down a flight of stairs lined with pink tiles decorated with lilies. At the bottom, Ginny turned in a complete circle, taking in the pink and white stained-glass lilies set in the stall doors, the hand-painted murals of lily-languid pink girls.

"Philomène!" the attendant cried out, coming down off a ladder where she had been fixing one of the toilet tanks.

"Marie-Louise!" Madame Desnos threw open her arms. "I haven't seen you in . . . I thought you were still in Le Puy."

"No, no, I've been in Paris for twenty-five years. First, at a toilet over by the Eiffel Tower and then here—a promotion."

"Indeed," Madame Desnos said, waving her long, fine-fingered hand at the splendid toilet.

"I'm Ginny Gillespie," Ginny said, holding out her hand to Marie-Louise.

"But of course," Marie-Louise said. "Your daughter, Philomène?"

"Regrettably, no," Madame Desnos said. "But a friend." She patted Ginny's hand. "No daughter for me. And you?"

"I might as well have become a nun like everyone else in our class. My husband died in the war. Since then . . ." She looked around her. "Only women come down here."

"You've known each other a long time?" Ginny asked. She tried to imagine Madame Desnos as a child, but saw a only a half-sized adult shrugging, her hands on her hips.

Marie-Louise smiled. "We were baptized on the same day. My mother always said the priest dropped Philomène on her head."

Madame Desnos blew a breath out between her lips. "The sot."

"Look over here." Marie-Louise waved Ginny to a beveled glass case behind the attendant's desk. It was filled with the sort of mementos former pupils sent to the teachers at the academy. There was a stuffed baby alligator next to a set of Eiffel Tower salt and pepper shakers. A photograph of Marie-Louise smiled out at Ginny. "Tokens from clients," Marie-Louise said, dismissing the accumulation with a wave. "But this," she took a small hand-tinted postcard from the case, "this is Le Puy."

Ginny took the postcard, held it up to catch the light. It was an amazing scene, as strange as a town on Mars. A red-tiled town stood surrounded by pillars of rock, like stalagmites hundreds of feet high. At the top of one stood a chapel, on two others what looked like giant statues.

"Volcanic lava forced up through cracks in the earth formed the pillars," Madame Desnos said, "at least that's what Sister Benoît told us in school. The soil around them washed away, but there they still are. Just to climb up to St. Michel's," she touched the chapel perched one of the rocks, "used to take me thirty minutes, and that was when I was young." Ginny looked at the postcard again. It still looked strange.

"Where is Le Puy? Is it near here?" Ginny asked.

"Le Puy near Paris?" Madame Desnos arched her eyebrows. "Never."

"It's not close to anything," Marie-Louise said. "But still, my sister Zoé—you remember her?" Madame Desnos rolled her eyes. "She's back in Le Puy now, and I'm thinking that in a few years I might give all this up," Marie-Louise pointed up at the Paris they could hear dimly roaring overhead, "give it up and retire to Le Puy."

"And live on air," Madame Desnos said.

Marie-Louise put the card back in the case. "Like birds of the air," she said.

"Who reap not and neither do they sow," Ginny added. Even Madame Desnos nodded in acknowledgement of the power of the thought. The three of them stood silently, facing each other. The toilet around them as pink as a womb. The world seemed much more than a flight of stairs away.

"May I use one of the stalls?" Ginny asked, hating to be the one to break the silence, but in real pain now.

"But of course," Marie-Louise said, "the third from the end has the most comfortable seat." Ginny closed the wooden door after her and sat down on the toilet. Marie-Louise laughed at something Madame Desnos said. Madame Desnos laughed. Ginny sighed as the hot stream flowed out of her, her bladder deflating like a balloon. How was it possible to have kidneys and stomach and liver *and* have room for a baby? She rubbed a hand over her stomach, tight as an inner tube, feeling the answer.

When Ginny was finished, Marie-Louise waved away her money. "What is joy, if not happiness in service?"

"You sound like Sister Benoît," Madame Desnos said, washing her hands. As they left, Marie-Louise kissed Madame Desnos on both cheeks. She kissed Ginny too.

"Any friend of Philomène is a friend of mine," she said to Ginny.

"Feel better?" Madame Desnos asked.

"Ask me after I talk to Mr. Atwood," Ginny said. How could she feel better until she knew where Roland was, how he was?

When Ginny arrived outside Mr. Atwood's office at five minutes to one, the tall thin boy who had let her in before leapt to his feet.

"Mr. Bottoms?" Ginny offered him her hand.

"Mrs. Gillespie," he said, smiling conspiratorially at her. "I'm honored to meet you." He opened the door to Mr. Atwood's office for her, shut it behind her.

"Mrs. Gillespie," Mr. Atwood said. He was drinking a cup of coffee. "Let me have Bottoms bring you some coffee." He pushed a buzzer and the secretary stuck his head in. "Would you care for cream?" Mr. Atwood asked. Ginny nodded, shifting impatiently in her chair. "Cream." Mr. Bottoms disappeared.

"I thank you for having Mr. Bottoms call last night," Ginny said. She chose a neutral tone. "Has he been with you long?"

"Long? He's been out of Harvard about five minutes. Why?"

"I think he thinks I'm a spy." Ginny waited to see what Mr. Atwood would do. He took off his pince-nez and blinked his blue eyes. He coughed.

"The United States of America doesn't have spies in Paris," he said. "The French are, after all, our allies." Ginny tapped the telephone on Mr. Atwood's desk with her finger. The door opened—Mr. Bottoms with her coffee. He saw her hand on the telephone and made a small gulping noise. "Set that coffee down before you drop it, Harold," Mr. Atwood said and waved his secretary out. "I'll talk to him."

"Good," Ginny said, trying to sound emphatic. "I don't want any trouble with the French authorities." She wasn't sure Mr. Atwood, good American and diplomat that he was, understood how irrational the French police could be, how dangerous.

"Now," Mr. Atwood set his coffee cup to one side, put on his pince-nez, "concerning your inquiry about," he glanced at a paper on his desk, "Mr. Keppi. Mr. Bottoms has been in contact with a clerk at the German Embassy. Really, Mrs. Gillespie," he looked at her over his glasses, "we're indebted to the German practice of excellent and detailed record keeping." Ginny took a deep breath, held it.

"Where is he?"

"In a German detention center, the location of which the clerk was not authorized to disclose."

Ginny let go of the breath she'd been holding. "A detention center?" she asked. "Do you mean a jail?"

"A detention center," Mr. Atwood said, "is a place where people are held pending a hearing on the charges against them. Since this is a routine matter, the United States Government is willing to enter a statement as to the facts in the case and ask for Mr. Keppi to be released to your custody." Ginny sat up straight.

"How soon?" she asked. Mr. Atwood coughed.

"As I said, there must be a hearing."

"When?" Ginny felt herself slipping in her chair. Mr. Atwood coughed.

"In May," he said.

"May!" She counted forward. "That's six months!" She couldn't imagine it. Roland had been gone only three days and it was almost more than she could stand. "Why?"

"I'm afraid," Mr. Atwood sighed, "that the current economic and political situation in Germany has put a strain on their judicial system. It is unfortunate."

Ginny leaned back in her chair. How could she wait for months? And what if it turned out to be more than six months, eight, nine? The baby would be born and . . .

"But surely," Ginny said, "I can visit him?"

"That," Mr. Atwood cleared his throat, "would require permission from the German ambassador and *that* would require an exchange of protocols on the ambassadorial level." He sat back, his face studiously neutral, waiting for Ginny to remember there was no American ambassador. Ginny looked into Mr. Atwood's blue eyes. She couldn't read them. Maybe she should forget Mr. Atwood, go to Germany right now, get on a train. But how would she find the detention center? She shut her eyes and thought of Germany, imagining it laid out in front of her like a map. She could almost see Roland. He *was* there, somewhere. About that at least, Mr. Atwood was right. About the rest, she would just have to trust him. She opened her eyes.

"Can I write?"

"Indeed," Mr. Atwood said. "That is covered by international convention. Bottoms can forward your letters to the office in Berlin in charge of such mail. But I'm afraid I cannot guarantee Mr. Keppi will be allowed to reply."

"Why not?" Ginny asked. She wanted to say, *Why the hell not?*

"It will be up to the German authorities. If they refuse, an appeal for exemption would have to be signed by the ambassador and . . ." Mr. Atwood shrugged.

"I know," Ginny said, "I know." Mr. Atwood gathered up the papers on his desk, checking his watch as if to tell her he was already late for a meeting. But Ginny had shut out all thoughts of Mr. Atwood. Soon Roland would have a letter from her, and after a little while longer, another. Maybe the months would go quickly that way. A test, but one they would pass.

"All right, Mr. Atwood," Ginny said. "We'll try it your way."

CHAPTER EIGHTEEN

ROLAND WOKE UP sweating and thirsty. He was lying on his back on a thin mattress. He seemed to have on nothing but a pair of hiking shorts and an open-necked cotton shirt. He had kicked off his blanket. He sat up and looked around. He was in a round stone room about thirty feet across with a floor made of wide, well-worn boards. One small window hung with blue and white checked curtains was set far up the wall just under a high, vaulted ceiling. On the opposite side was a heavy wooden door under an arch. There were a dozen or so mattresses scattered around his with men asleep on them. It was just after dawn, or so it seemed from the pale light that leaked through the curtains. Roland lay back down and closed his eyes. He had no idea where he was.

Then he remembered a fight. He had been in a fight with some men. Fuss had been there too. He could remember Fuss's eyes opening wide, his jaw dropping. Fuss slumped to the ground. Dead? What would death be like for Fuss? An endless drill, slow marching up and down the road outside the school with a full pack. Fuss had been knifed, then . . . what? Roland thought he remembered a train ride, the lights of houses passing, an empty station floating in fog. Roland felt himself drifting, thoughts piling up. He tried to concentrate on the fight, the sound of the police whistles, but his head hurt. He sat up again, and what had been a dull ache in the back of his head shot forward and stabbed his left temple.

He remembered someone—Zelie?—kicking him in the head, someone else standing over him with a knife. He felt his head with his hands but the skin didn't seem broken or even bruised. He looked down at his left hand. The skin between his fingers hung loose like an old rooster's comb, the fingers standing alone and unconnected. His hands were mottled with brown a shade duller than dried blood, and the edges of the cut were healed, pink but not sore. He hugged his hand to his chest. Ginny. Where was Ginny?

He had no sense of her. Even with his eyes closed tight, he couldn't see her or feel her. Where was she? He was cut off, as high and dry as a fish thrown up on the bank. It was as if the walls around him blocked out even the memory of the world and his people in it. Roland squeezed his hand until the bones ached.

The man on the mattress next to Roland stretched, yawning. Roland let go of his hand, and the blood rushed back in, tingling. "Excuse me," Roland said. "What day is this?"

"I don't speak French," the man said in German, and Roland felt a twinge in the spot on his chest that had appeared the day Max was shot, a spot that for years had been as faint as a freckle. Roland repeated his question in German.

"It's Monday," his neighbor said, with a weariness in his voice that made Roland think he had been asked the question often. His neighbor sat up. Roland saw that his right arm below the elbow was missing. The man scratched his stump.

"How many days have I been here?" Roland asked.

"Days? It's April third," the one-armed man said, shaking his head. "You've been here five months."

"Months!" Roland said. "Five months?" How could that be? Five months. Ginny would think he had abandoned her. What if she had ignored her aunt's advice and gone home, back to America? Surely she wouldn't.

"Hey, you haven't gotten upset before. Maybe that's a good sign." The man held out his left, and only, hand for Roland to shake. "Willy," he said, "Willy Nachtman."

"Roland Keppi."

"Keppi," Willy repeated. "You've been saying your name was Louis Dumien." *Dumien?* Roland didn't know what to say. He had a quick flash of himself following orders, never angry, a saintly zombie.

"It is Roland Keppi."

"Yeah," Willy said, "that's what the guard said."

"Guard?"

"I should have said *guide*. That's what we have here, guides."

157

"Is this a prison?"

"Very good," Willy said. "You're asking new questions."

"Well, is it?"

"I might say yes. Then again, if I said no, you couldn't say I was lying." Willy shrugged.

"A prison in Germany?"

"Of course we're in Germany. Where else would two Germans be?"

The other dozen men in the room were waking up, a groan here, a cough there. Roland heard a bolt slide, and the wooden door opened to reveal a young man wearing a neatly pressed tan shirt, leather shorts with a large ring of keys hanging from them, and a pair of hiking boots. He crossed the room, stepping over the still prone men, and using a thin pole that leaned against the wall, slid open the blue and white curtains. Light poured down into the room through iron bars. There were more groans. "The bright sun is up," the man in the leather shorts sang out, kicking at the men still flat on their mattresses. "The dark night is dead. Good morning! Good morning! the little bird said." He clapped his hands. "Downstairs! In five—count 'em on your fingers—minutes!" Then he went out, leaving the door open behind him.

"Five minutes," Willy said, getting up off his mattress with a grunt and reaching for a pair of brown shoes. All but one of the men got up too, with a chorus of complaints, and began putting on their shoes. Roland saw they were all dressed like he was—tan shorts, white shirts, brown shoes, like two dozen sons with the same mother. Then the last man got up, and Roland looked twice. He was very tall, a head taller than Roland, with a heavy dark beard, and he had on some sort of hooded robe that reached just past his knees, made of the same brown wool as the blankets. He stretched and then walked gracefully out the door in his bare feet. "Why?" Roland started. Willy shook his head.

"When they gave him shorts, I hear he scissored them up into scrap. Come on." Willy showed Roland how to roll up and store his mattress. Roland followed him down a steep flight of stone stairs into a larger, but equally round room.

If they were in prison, it was not like any prison Roland had ever imagined. This room had four windows, all placed high up in the high wall and hung with the same blue and white checked material that was on the window upstairs. A half-finished mural of young boys hiking was painted all around the room. Next to an open cupboard, the man in the brown robe was counting out plates. The other men who'd been asleep upstairs were taking down benches stacked on a large table near two closed doors. Roland took one end of a bench, and Willy took the other with his one hand. A blond man with thick muscles lifted a long wooden table too heavy for five men and carried it effortlessly to the middle of the room. "They won't bring breakfast until we've set the table," Willy explained. "They're very big on manners."

When the plates, silverware, and glasses of water had been distributed, the men sat down with their hands folded in their laps while the robed man at the head of the table, his hooded head bent, said a blessing. Then one of the doors opened and a cook in a white apron walked into the room carrying a big steaming bowl of potatoes. "Breakfast!" he announced. Roland took two. Everybody else took one, although there were plenty. When Roland tasted his, he knew why. The potatoes had been boiled unpeeled, cooked without salt or butter or onions. They tasted faintly of hot water and dirt.

Willy bit into his and sighed. "I must've lost thirty pounds. When my hearing comes up, they'll have to look hard to find me."

"Hearing? I still don't understand," Roland said. "Am I in prison?"

"You are in . . ." Willy waved up at the bars showing between the checked curtains, "detention."

The blond strongman who had carried the table looked at Roland, then leaned toward Willy and said, "He's talking a lot. Finally he's okay in the head?"

"Seems so," Willy said.

A thin man with glasses so thick they were almost opaque broke in. "We," he said, "are being held in a temporary detention center pending a fair and impartial hearing to decide the dispensation of our cases."

"Yeah," the strongman grunted, "and then they send you to prison," he stole a glance at the man in the robe, "or to the nut house." The robed man smiled down the length of the table at Roland.

"Richter has covered the basic possibilities," Willy said, nodding at the strongman, "but it doesn't pay to be too sure who's going to end up where." Willy went on. As far as he could see, he said, it defied logic. He, Willy, was a deserter of eleven years standing, yet so far they had questioned him most about a rash of sheep thefts near where he'd been picked up. And he'd been seen by the doctor a half dozen times.

"Doctor Digestion," Richter the strongman spat on the floor. "I never want to see another potato."

"I hear he's due in this afternoon," Willy said. "So at least maybe we're in for a change of menu." The cook came out again and took away the half-full bowl of potatoes. He shook his head and sighed. Richter lifted the table with one hand, carried it back to its corner.

"Is that all we get for breakfast?" Roland asked. Willy shook his head like the cook.

"Now you're Mr. Hundred Questions," he said. "Ask the doctor when he comes. He'll be glad to tell you what you get to eat and why. Come on, we've got work to do."

"We do?" Roland asked. Willy rolled his eyes.

"It's like training a dog," Willy said to no one in particular. He held his thumb and forefinger an inch apart. "That much memory." He took Roland by the hand and led him to the wall. "The mural," he said. "I'm in charge of the mural." He waved at the round-faced boys, some mere outlines, who hiked around the room. He stepped back. "I call it *March to the Future*. Although, actually," he turned in a circle to take in the whole sweep of the mural, "the poor lads end up back where they started. Before I lost my arm, I used to be more particular about what I painted. Then I did nothing but nudes." He patted the stump of his right arm. "But what can I say? I got over being so finicky."

"How did you lose your arm, Willy?" Roland asked. "In the war?"

"Let's just say I stuck it once where it didn't belong." He gave Roland a brush and some medium brown paint that Roland recognized as the same not-quite-dried-blood color that stained his hands. "Start filling these in," Willy said pointing to the hills that swelled rhythmically behind the boys' blond heads. Roland looked closely at the brown already applied to the wall, less in brush strokes than smears.

"Who did this?" he asked. "It's a mess."

"Don't be so hard on yourself," Willy said, rubbing his fingers through the hair on his chin. "That took you months." Roland pressed his hand to his head. He wondered if it were possible to lose so many chunks of time from your life that when you woke up you were dead.

Willy assigned the man with thick glasses to work on the light green grass under the boys' boots, but as soon as Willy's back was turned, the man dipped his brush in Roland's brown paint and dotted a few crawling beetles below where Roland was working. "You don't remember me, do you?" he said. Roland shook his head. "I'm Johann Schmidt. Not a distinctive name," he said, sneaking in a worm, "but then, who am I?" He flung out his hands, paint flying off his brush. "Who would call me a man of distinction?" Roland's head ached.

"I still don't really understand where we are," he said.

"Do you mean physically?" Schmidt peered up at him through his thick lenses. Roland nodded. "Well, that's not a very difficult question. We're in a country town called Hinkelsbach, in a castle a rich Englishman built, or I really should say rebuilt, before the war. Now it's going to be a hostel, a place of physical and spiritual rest for Germanic youth. But first we have the privilege, and I do mean privilege, of preparing said castle for its young visitors." Schmidt mixed a little of Roland's brown with his green and added a grasshopper to the bottom of the mural.

"The privilege of shoveling out bat shit, you mean," Willy called from the far side of the room where he was sketching in more youthful German heads with his left hand. "Because that's what you'll be doing, Schmidt, if you don't knock off with the bugs and get going on that grass. And you, Keppi, over here." Willy waved him across the room.

Roland brought his brush and brown paint with him. The boys on this side of the room strode bravely through uncharted space. "You want me to add hills?" he asked Willy.

"No, I want you to . . . ." Willy turned a key in an imaginary lock in front of his mouth. Roland looked hurt. "Around Schmidt, no word's a good word," Willy whispered, not moving his lips.

Roland looked over his shoulder at Schmidt who was hiding an anthill among the long blades of grass. He remembered a lecture Drillmaster Erlanger once had given the cadets about what to do in the event of capture by the enemy. They should be careful about talking to any prisoners they didn't know, he'd said. Especially anybody who seemed too interested in things like how many men were in their unit and what caliber guns they had. "The price of that new buddy," the drillmaster had said, glaring down at them all, "could be the blood of your comrades in arms."

"Watch him at lunch," Willy said.

Roland went back to his hills. "Say," Schmidt said, squinting at Roland's handiwork, "that's very much in the classic tradition of realism. Not that I pretend to any knowledge of higher artistic criticism, but you have quite a precise and accurate eye. I knew a truly great forger once . . ."

Roland picked up his pot of paint and moved to a set of hills between the doors. He had filled in the arch of one hill, his head aching from so much looking up, and was starting another, when the man in leather shorts that Willy had called the guide tapped him on the shoulder. "Housefather Huhn wants to see you, boy," he said. Roland looked over his shoulder at Willy who made a shooing motion with his one hand.

The guide unlocked the door to the right of the one the cook had come through, and when they were in the hall on the other side, locked it behind them. This part of the building looked newer. They walked down a hall lined with shelves of athletic equipment — bows and arrows, soccer balls, Indian clubs — and stopped in front of a door labeled *HOUSEFATHER*. The guide knocked, then opened it and waved Roland inside. The housefather, a tanned man with short graying hair, stood up from behind a desk as Roland entered. Like the guide, he was wearing leather shorts, but his were held up by fancy red and green felt suspenders. The guide saluted, said, "Keppi, sir," and then left. Housefather Huhn sat down, flipped open a file.

"Ah, yes, Keppi. I'm glad to hear you are more alert today, Keppi. I'm sure Doctor Krebs will be happy to hear this news too. Do you feel more like yourself?"

"I'm not sure," Roland said truthfully, looking down at his file. A series of dates had been written after his name, scratched out so only the last one showed. "What is that date after my name?"

"May fifteenth," the housefather said, "is the current date scheduled for your hearing." Roland felt another stab in the star on his chest. "We have you boys only for a few short months."

Roland was confused again, "But I'm not a boy." Housefather Huhn sighed.

"Believe me, I know," he said. "But we're not jailers here. We're trained youth workers. We volunteered especially to staff the Hinkelsbach hostel. This current situation is, I admit, a bit odd for us. But, as I say to the staff, showing young boys the right path in life isn't completely different from working with detainees, people who have, well, gone astray from that path. And, to avoid confusion, we do try to follow the same rules and regulations now as we will when the hostel is officially open."

"I'm not feeling well," Roland said, looking for a chair, his head pounding. "May I sit down?" The housefather shook his head.

"I'm afraid that's against the rules. Sitting in the staff's quarters would encourage the boys to think of themselves as equal to those in authority. I myself am generous to a fault, so," he waved at the office, empty of any furniture but his own chair and desk, "I had the temptation removed."

Roland felt his knees go soft, then fold. A rush of black spots, like Schmidt's ants, swarmed up over his vision. He fell on his side. His legs were moving, but he couldn't get up.

"Oh, dear," Housefather Huhn said, bending over him. "You're not well. The doctor will be so unhappy."

"May I borrow a sheet of paper for a letter?" Roland asked from the floor. He had to reach Ginny, tell her he loved her, tell her to wait . . .

"You may borrow all the paper you'd like, but I'm afraid you aren't allowed to mail letters. The hosteling experience is designed to encourage independence in boys. Besides, we've been warned very strictly against letting detainees contact persons who might themselves be potential witnesses or who might seek to influence the judgment of the cases." The black dots swarmed over the housefather's shoes and cut them off from Roland's sight.

Roland woke up as the guide was dragging him into the main room. Seeing the robed man counting out the plates, Richter carrying the table, the cook bringing in the boiled potatoes, he thought he'd slipped back in time to breakfast, was getting further from, not closer to, May fifteenth, to his love, his red-headed Ginny. Then the cook announced, "Lunch!"

Willy helped Roland off the floor and onto a bench, and Roland, gripping the edge of the table with both hands, managed to stay upright. Willy kicked him under the table, rolled his eyes in Schmidt's direction. "Watch him," Willy mouthed. The guide came in as the cook left.

"You're wanted, boy," the guide said to Schmidt who nodded meekly and followed him out. Willy kicked Roland again. He leaned close.

"Smell his breath when he comes back," he whispered, his own breath tickling Roland's ear. Richter the strongman grunted in agreement, then spat.

Roland helped himself to a potato. This time it tasted only like water. As he was finishing, the door opened, and Schmidt returned. He sat down, helped himself to a potato, and mashed it around his plate with his fork. Roland leaned across to get the water pitcher and caught a whiff of Schmidt's real lunch. Salt pork, onions and cabbage, dark bread, cheese, and beer. "Whew!" Roland said, caught off guard. Schmidt blushed, pushed up his glasses, took a bite of potato.

Richter glared at Schmidt and ground his teeth as if he were chewing bone. The guide came back in. "Party's over!" he said, motioning for them to clear the tables. "The doctor's here." He tapped Roland. "Upstairs and take off your shirt." Roland went up the stairs to the room where he'd spent the night. He took off his shirt, pulled out a mattress, and sat down. Then he noticed the man in the brown robe sitting on a pile of mattresses, hemming curtains with a slow even stitch. The light from the small window fell across the blue and white fabric, reflected blue on the man's face. Roland blushed and crossed his arms over his chest. The robed man smiled at him, then went back to his sewing.

"The dining room," a voice echoed up the stairwell, "is the great execution chamber of German civilization." A bony man, dressed in a loose-fitting white suit, appeared at the doorway, Housefather Huhn at his side. Like the man in the robe, this new man was abnormally tall and had to bend to fit through the door. "I must tell you," he went on, "last week a dear friend of mine since childhood died of acute indigestion."

"Your friend didn't follow your diet, Herr Doctor?"

The man waved a long bony hand, refusing to be sidetracked. "And the week before that, three prominent men died in Nürnberg, two on the same evening, all of acute indigestion. In the past year, according to my calculations, the greatest percentage of any one cause of mortality in Bavaria was in the one malady, acute indigestion." He shook a long finger in the housefather's face. "Don't think that you are safe, my friend. Not one man in a thousand has a stomach in normal health. And who is to blame?" He looked around him, but neither Roland, the housefather, nor the man in the brown robe volunteered an answer.

"The wives! Oh!" he raised his hands over his head, his fingers straining toward the ceiling high above, "there is nothing that will so irritate the mind and the nerves as indigestion. The husband is cross. The wife cries. What is the cause? She served a fine dinner of stewed pork and cabbage—all manner of foods cooked up with fats and served together. There was one woman of my acquaintance from Bamberg who, when

I told her that her husband had died of acute indigestion, grew so angry, she ordered me out of the house. But when her second husband died in terrible pain and another male acquaintance fell dead at her table, then she came to me! She begged me to save her five boys, all blue-faced from the fat choking their blood." The man in the white suit looked around him.

"And no wonder!" he said. "Can one man in a hundred name the Four Simple and Cardinal Dietetic Rules?" The robed man smiled, the housefather looked away, Roland shook his head. The man in white counted the points on his fingers, "*One*—No fats! *Two*—No baking sodas, yeasts, or other gaseous poisons! *Three*—No spices or desiccating salts! *Four*—Each food cooked and served by itself! I ask you, how do the cows eat in nature? They eat grass, pure grass—not bread, bacon, butter, and grass. Nature, sir," he struck the housefather on the back, "must be our model." He wheeled and stuck his hand out to Roland. "You don't remember me, do you?" Roland shook his head no for the second time. The man grabbed Roland's damaged left hand. "I am Doctor Krebs," he said. "I cured you." He wiggled the ends of Roland's fingers.

"Thank you," Roland said, pulling his hand away. The touch reminded him of Lena's doctor's interest in his hand. "I am feeling better."

"What's this?" Doctor Krebs asked, poking at the red star risen anew on Roland's chest.

"It's nothing. An old scar."

"Hah!" the doctor said. "Don't deceive yourself. It's the poisons in your system rising to the surface. That's what's been giving you those headaches and fainting spells, but soon your system will be clean as a whistle, and then," he slapped Roland on the back, "you'll be strong as a cow. Never seen a cow faint, have you?" The doctor nodded at House-father Huhn and moved on to the man in the brown robe. The guide came in leading the other detainees and lined them up along the wall.

"So, Sister Eugenia, how are you feeling? Doesn't that hood start to itch when you don't shave?" Sister Eugenia held one finger to his lips, then went back to his sewing.

"He calls that hood a wimple," the guide said, shaking his head, "but he won't talk after lunch."

"Ah," Doctor Krebs said. "Silent meditation. Very good for the digestion. That's an excellent sign."

Housefather Huhn coughed. "You know I hate to interfere, regulations put matters of health and sanitation clearly in your purview," the housefather strained to keep his voice low, "but this sort of thing, well, it sets a very bad example for the other boys, I mean, detainees. Couldn't we just get him out of that . . ." he choked at the word *habit*, "those clothes and into something more appropriate for a boy—man—of his sex."

"Change comes from the inside!" Doctor Krebs said and poked the housefather in the stomach. "From your guts! From properly fed guts. Do you cut off a thief's hand to stop him from stealing?" He waved a long arm in Willy's direction, and Willy frowned, his eyes narrowing. "Won't he learn to steal with one hand, with his toes, if the urge is strong enough? On a proper diet, all the irritations of the system that lead to crime are eliminated. In mere weeks, with proper diet, this poor man will voluntarily surrender the delusion that he is a nun. Why, after some months, even the bars on these windows won't be necessary."

"We'll be too weak to move," Roland heard someone in the lineup mutter. Dr. Krebs ignored the remark, raising his hands in rhetorical questioning.

"Do cows," he said, "wander from a green, fertile pasture?"

"Yes." It was the guide. Both the doctor and Housefather Huhn turned to stare at him. "My dad's did," he said. "I chased them all over." The doctor waved his hand.

"Properly fed cows," he said, "would have spared you the exertion." He walked down the line of detainees, poking a stomach here, a tongue there. He took Schmidt's pulse, removed his glasses, and peered at the whites of his eyes. "Very good. Coming along nicely. The pressure of the blood is definitely lower thanks to a proper diet." Willy rolled his eyes. The housefather coughed.

"Shall we go down?" The housefather waved a hand at the door.

"I need to talk to the cook," the doctor said, following him out. "I think carrots . . ."

"O Lord," Willy said. "Last time he had us on carrots my piss turned bright orange." He pointed at Roland's hand. "And your fingernails." Roland looked down. It was true, at the end of each nail, just growing out, was a half moon of yellowish orange.

"I have decided," Richter said, the muscles in his arms standing out like great tree roots. He spat. "I am leaving." Willy laughed.

"That's a good one," Willy said, thumping Richter's thick back as if he had told a great joke. Roland looked at Richter's frowning face. He didn't look like a man who was kidding.

Schmidt pushed his glasses up, cleared his throat. "Carrots contain pro-vitamin A, an excellent aid to night vision," he said, glancing sideways at Willy. "Proper nutrition for us thieves, wouldn't you say?" Willy slapped him hard on the back, knocking him to his knees.

"I wouldn't say," Willy said, not laughing, "and if you were smart you wouldn't either."

At dinner they had carrots, boiled whole. The cook served them with his usual sigh. Doctor Krebs stayed long enough to taste one, rolling an inch of the root around on his tongue. "Onion!" he said to the cook. "I definitely taste onion." He spat out the offending bite.

"Perhaps one of the pots . . ." the cook said.

"*Perhaps* will not do," the doctor said. "Scrub them with borax before you cook breakfast."

Everyone ate their fill of carrots, glad, for now, of the change. The cook came out to get the empty bowl. "I'll need some help with those pots," he said to the guide.

The guide tapped Roland on the shoulder. "I guess you'll have to do."

Roland went to the kitchen. The cook was dumping a sack of carrots into a sink full of water. "You can help wash these," he said. "Those pots don't need scrubbing anyway." Roland scrubbed the carrots one by one and handed them to the cook to have their tops cut off. "Look at this," the cook said, waving a ferny carrot top under Roland's nose. "This is the way things grow in nature. Mixed up. Greens and roots. Doctor, schmocter." He cut the top off another carrot with a vicious whack of his cleaver. "I'm a good cook," he said, throwing the knife down. "No one knows how hard this is on me."

"You do the best you can," Roland said, sorry for the cook who was almost as much of a prisoner as he was. "We all understand that. Tonight the carrots were boiled very nicely." The cook wiped his nose on his apron.

"Thank you," he said. "I appreciate your telling me that."

After helping in the kitchen, Roland climbed the dark stairs to the first floor, ready to roll out his mattress, but he found nothing but an empty room. He felt his way back down to the kitchen, but the door was locked, as was the door to the staff's quarters. He went back up to the first floor. Standing in the center of the empty room, he could hear distant snores above him. He hadn't known there was another floor. Outside the door, he felt around and found a flight of stairs going up. When he had climbed to the second floor, he could tell that the stairs continued to climb after the landing to yet another floor. He opened the door and found the detainees stretched out on their mattresses just like before, only closer together because the second floor of the tower was smaller than the first in the same proportion that the first was smaller than the ground floor.

Roland found his mattress already unrolled for him, a blanket folded at the end. He lay down. The floor was damp and smelled like bleach. Willy's voice came out of the dark. "Richter just finished scrubbing it down before dinner. Huhn wants to store cots for the boy hikers on the first floor. And surprise, surprise, my hearing's been moved again. May twenty-fifth," he said.

"But mine's May fifteenth. Weren't you here first?" Roland heard Willy scratch his stump.

"I didn't want to tell you," Willy said. "And besides, I figured what difference did it make when you couldn't remember your name from one day to the next? Since I've been here, eight months now, there hasn't been a hearing. Oh, always there's some good excuse. The hearing officer is sick, then his mother dies. If you ask me, these are the sort of excuses you use to fool boys—at least the kind Huhn would use. Me, I figure I'm not getting out until this whole damn tower is one long mural from bottom to top." Willy sighed, then patted the blanket over Roland's legs. "Go to sleep," he said. "Have some good dreams." He rolled over.

Roland lay back on his mattress, stunned. He had to get out. Ginny would be waiting. Odile. He fell asleep trying to picture their faces, see what they were doing. In the middle of the night, he heard a telephone ring. He sat up, rubbed his eyes. The telephone was right beside him, between his mattress and Willy's, sitting upright on the floor. It went on ringing and ringing, but Willy didn't wake up, no one moved. Roland picked up the receiver, his hand shaking. He had never spoken into a telephone before. "Hello," he said.

"Roland!" It was Ginny.

"Ginny," Roland said, relief pouring through his body. He almost dropped the telephone.

"Roland, where are you?" Ginny was crying. "You promised to meet me. I don't know what to do. Roland, you promised. Where are you?"

Roland tried to talk into the telephone, answer her questions. "Where are you, Ginny?" he asked, but the telephone didn't seem equipped to carry his voice, only Ginny's. She sobbed on the other end.

"You said you'd be here. It's dark."

"Tell me where you are!" he screamed into the black mouthpiece. "How can I come to you if I don't know where you are?"

Roland woke up in a sweat, shaking. The telephone operator—she would know where Ginny had called from. He felt the floor beside his mattress, but there was no telephone. No telephone. What was he going to do?

CHAPTER NINETEEN

THE BANGING woke Odile. The booms were joined by the sound of her heart pounding, the cannon fire she heard in her dreams. Downstairs, the geese set up a terrible racket. Someone was beating on the front door. Odile sat up slowly. She put her feet on the floor, stood up. After three weeks in bed, it wasn't easy. She'd gone to bed the day Roland left and stayed there. She'd told herself it was to save her strength until Roland sent for her, but actually life just seemed like too much work all of a sudden. The last thing she'd done was bring the geese inside, into the kitchen, so she wouldn't have to go down every morning and night to feed them. In the kitchen, they fed themselves from open sacks of grain, growing fatter as she grew thinner. Now, the honking from down below doubled and redoubled in intensity, the geese straining themselves with the effort. Odile felt herself getting angry. She yanked back the thick blanket she had hung over the bedroom window and leaned out. The morning light was blinding.

"What fuck is this?" she yelled out the window in her bluntest Alsatian. "An old woman can't die in peace?" A man stepped back from the door, the light glinting off his bald head and glasses. It was Guillaume Scholly, a boy she'd grown up with who was now the town's priest—or was he the protestant minister? In Hexwiller the two churches, Catholic and Protestant, were mirror twins, with a matched pair of towers, bells, graveyards. Over the centuries, the Keppis had gone to first one, then the other, and now Odile had trouble telling which was the true church of God and which only the calm but false reflection.

"There you are," he said. "I thought you were dead."

"Well," Odile said, "I thought you'd been dead for years." The bald head shook an emphatic no.

"Open the door," Scholly said. It was Odile's turn to shake her head. "I can't," she said. "Not without your help at least. It's stuck."

It took four tries to get the door open, the hinges screaming at each attempt. "Good Lord, Odile," Scholly said when his eyes had adjusted enough to see the dozen geese scattered throughout the kitchen, the nests on the unlit stove.

"I'm sure the Lord is good," said Odile, shooing a goose off a chair and sitting down. "But what about you?"

"I'm very well, thank you," Scholly said. "And how are you?"

"Terrible," Odile said, holding out one thin yellow arm. "Don't I look it?"

"Are you in pain?" Scholly took her wrist but couldn't decide what to do with it. "Have you seen a good doctor?"

"Who is the good doctor these days?"

"Dr. Stoeffler sees to my needs," he said, handing her wrist back to her.

"Stoeffler," she said, "sounds Alsatian." She shook her head sadly. "No Alsatian can cure me. They're what's killing me, the whole unlucky lot of them. You should try to sleep in my bed." Scholly blushed. "The screams!" she said. "They'd stand your hair on end!" Scholly rubbed a hand across his bare scalp.

"Well," he said, politely changing the subject, "I've come this morning because I have a letter for you."

"From Roland? From my grandson?"

"What? No, from Henriette Woerli. Do you remember? Daughter of Walther Woerli, the Woerli who moved to Strassburg? We were all in catechism together."

Catechism. So Scholly was a priest then. "Henriette Woerli? Of course I remember her. Nice girl, always had flour in her hair."

"Flowers? I don't remember . . ." Scholly shook his head, getting back to the matter at hand. "When I got the note last week, it seemed to me I remembered hearing that you'd died and been buried in the other church. But then I happened to see Dr. Pogue—he's the head heretic there now—and I asked him about you, but your name didn't ring any bells. So . . ."

"You came to deliver my mail," Odile cut him short. He nodded and held out a piece of white paper, slightly wrinkled and folded in half. "Well," Odile said, crossing her arms, "you'll have to read it to me."

Scholly took off his glasses and wiped them on his sleeve, then tore open the note.

My friend—

It was in French, and Odile, her French rusted away by Alsatian and German, could barely follow its meaning. "Lord," Scholly said, "what abominable handwriting."

My friend—
    Is H-willer still a dump? I hear your son got Xed in the War. Mine too. Your grandson told me this and that you were not Xed. He is working at my husband (5th) bakery. He is a good boy. Not handsome but good. When I saw him I said to myself—A Keppi. What does this mean? Then I thought—if anyone knows, it is you.
    The bakery address is on the back of this paper.

Fondest affections,
Henriette

Odile took the letter from Scholly, turned it over. "Is this the address?" She pointed to a square patch of writing in the corner.

"Rue Véron, Paris," Scholly read. "I'd say so."

"Well, well," Odile said.

"That's a deep thought." Scholly laughed at his own joke.

"You can let yourself out," Odile said, and Scholly did, still laughing.

Rue Véron. Paris. Roland had said he would send for her. But how? He would be afraid to send anything in writing, and he couldn't come back for her. It wouldn't be safe. She waded through the geese to the church calendar on the wall. It was still on October. Above the dates and lists of saints' days a crippled pilgrim wept at Lourdes. As she flipped the month to November, the new picture caught her attention. It was a Madonna and Child, red as rust, as dried blood. Even without the tiny people who stood, the size of beans, at the Mother of God's feet, Odile knew this was a Madonna the size of a lighthouse, the giant iron woman of her dreams. Odile clasped her hands over her heart. A sign! Surely, a sign. She tore the page from the wall, stuffed it between her breasts.

She went up the stairs to her bedroom. Under the bed was her money bag and the bundle of clothes she'd wrapped around her map the day Roland had left without her. She'd put the bundle under the bed and then gotten under the covers to wait for Roland to send for her. Now she couldn't wait any longer. She was weak from not eating enough, from staying in bed. Just climbing the stairs had left her out of breath. If she went back to bed, she would be buried here in Hexwiller by that idiot Scholly, and in the bloody earth of Alsace she would never find peace. Eternity would be one more sleepless night, noisy with the complaints of her fellow dead, the cries of the dying, the endless moans and sighs of the living. She would leave Alsace, leave her house. She would go to Paris and find Roland.

Odile put the bundle on top of the bed and beat the dust balls off it with a pillow. A few clothes and francs seemed little to show for a lifetime, for a dozen Keppi lifetimes. She looked around the room at the carved cupboards and benches, the paintings on glass of saints' lives and family miracles. It was easy to think of a house and its furnishings as permanent, as a world in themselves. But they were wood and, like her own body, would rot and soon turn to dust. It was going to be hard enough to get her own flesh and bones to Paris. But she did take from under the covers the brick bed-warmer her husband had given her and set it next to the bundle. *Madmoisel Odile*—her husband had painted in yellow on one side and *1880* on the other, copying her name and the date from their wedding contract.

Poor Odilon! Her grandmother had warned her daughters against naming both their children, born only a week apart, after St. Odile. "God could get confused," she'd said, "and send only one soul." And when Odilon asked his cousin Odile to marry him, their grandmother had even stronger warnings. "If you live in one house," she'd said, "one of you won't live for long." Odile had known her grandmother was right, but how could she say no to Odilon? Since their joint baptism, Odilon had always been there, close enough to touch, far enough away to focus her eyes on, like her own toes. When he asked her to marry him, she couldn't refuse him any more than she could say *no thanks* to her next breath of air. She couldn't make herself see him as a separate person, as someone who could be denied what he wanted. He *was* her.

Now she had trouble remembering what he looked like. When they had been married six months, he woke up one morning covered with red raised spots, like flocked wallpaper. "My, don't I look silly?" he said. Twelve hours later, he was dead. At the time, Odile was six months pregnant, and her mother was scared to death the baby would come out

173

pockmarked, but Max had been born without a spot on him. It was as if Odilon had had nothing to do with the creation of his son, as if he had passed through the world leaving behind only a single brick bed-warmer.

Odile tucked the bed-warmer into her bundle, put on the wool vest embroidered with tulips and goslings she always wore to weddings and funerals, and went downstairs. She took out her money bag, stuffed fat with single franc notes, and bound it with a strip of cloth around her stomach. She added what food she had to the bundle, some old dried apples and hard cheese. She tied a rope around the bundle and slung it over one shoulder, draped an extra blanket across her back. Then she took a double handful of grain and backed out of the kitchen into the yard, calling to her geese.

They got slowly to their feet and made their fat, slow way into the yard. They looked up curiously at the sky as if they'd forgotten the sun in their weeks in the kitchen, let it pass into goose myth, something only half believed in. Odile opened the gate to the yard. Robed in her blanket, she crossed the narrow courtyard in front of her house followed by twelve geese as serious as Christ's disciples. She banged on Madame Boucher's door until curiosity got the better of Madame Boucher's stubborn nature, and she stuck her head out. The twelfth goose stepped forward out of the line of geese, a martyr, a feathered saint, and offered herself to Madame Boucher. "For you, Emilie. Rain falleth on the just and unjust alike." It was the oldest curse—forgiveness. Madame Boucher stood her ground. She spat at Odile's feet, kicked the goose back into the yard and slammed the door. "God bless you, in spite of yourself," Odile called after her. The goose began walking around Madame Boucher's house.

The line of eleven geese trailed after Odile on her last walk through the town of her birth. One by one, she gave them away. To the Schollys, who raised sons into crooked grocers and absentminded priests; to the Blancks, whose beautiful daughters all became nuns; to the Liehns, whose ugly daughters were all staunch Protestants; to the Wolffs, who helped sack the town under Clovis, King of the Franks, and then baptized everyone still alive; to the Ohls, who burned the town in the Peasant War and turned the survivors back into good Catholics; to the Laprades, a family who'd spied for the Kaiser and Napoleon the Third with scrupulous impartiality; to the Bolles, autonomists and members of the League for Home Rule; to the Lahrs, hardworking coal miners; and to the Woerlis, baking cousins of Henriette the Messenger. Odile gave away ten of her twelve geese. Geese fell on just and unjust alike, and Odile was careful to warn everyone—everyone but Madame Boucher—not to eat their gift. "A watch goose is worth its keep," she said, but she knew some would look to tomorrow and some would not. Most not. That was what made Hexwiller such an unlucky place to live.

In front of the little shrine of St. Odile, she met Roerich, gentle breeder of children and rabbits. It was dusk when he saw Odile coming toward him, wrapped in her blanket, followed by two geese. "I've stayed too long already," she said to him. "Time to go."

"Where?" Roerich asked.

"Away. Here," she said, giving Roerich the next to last goose. "Keep him until Easter." He took it, nodding with great seriousness. Then Odile turned her back on Hexwiller, and the last goose followed, shaking the dust of the place from her webbed feet.

Odile caught the last train of the day where it stopped to take on water at the foot of the hills. She gave the twelfth goose to the conductor, and he gave her a seat in second class. She was exhausted, almost too tired to breathe. She dozed, but she was so light that the train's vibrations kept sliding her across the hard bench. Several times she woke up just short of hitting the floor. She used her blanket to lash herself to the armrest. Then she leaned her head on the thick glass of the window. She sighed, her eyelids fluttering down and then up. The night drifted by outside, mountains and stars. The lights of towns came and went, and soon she slept deeply.

"Are you ill, madame?" Someone was speaking to her in French. She opened her eyes and saw a man holding her left wrist, trying not to stare too obviously at her webbed hand. For a moment, she thought she was back in her house with Guillaume Scholly, but this man was younger, though not young, and wore a tie, not a clerical collar. "I'm a doctor," he said. "The conductor was worried about you."

"Oh," Odile said, "are you Dr. Stoeffler?"

"Alas no, madame. My name is Gadet." He was timing her pulse with a great gold pocket watch. Odile let her head rest on the window again.

"How quiet it is," she said, though the engine hooted and boiled up ahead. "We're not in Alsace, are we?"

175

"No," the doctor said, trying to remember his school geography. "We've already crossed the Vosges, I think."

"I don't hear a single complaint, not a groan, not a shriek. These must be happy people here."

"Happy as most, I imagine," he said.

"Good." Odile slid down on the seat. She closed her eyes. "So quiet," she said. "Blessedly quiet."

"Please, madame." Dr. Gadet squeezed her shoulder. "I think you should stay awake. The conductor is bringing some coffee and bread. I'm afraid you have let yourself become," Odile opened her eyes to see him shaking his head like a worried dog, "seriously undernourished. I fear your vital system itself may be weakened." Odile floated along on the concerned sound of his words, not quite following what they meant. She patted his hand. The conductor arrived with her coffee and a long plank of buttered bread from his own lunch. They both watched her chew and then swallow with the greatest concern.

"What do you think?" the conductor asked Dr. Gadet. The doctor gave a barely perceptible shake of his head and frowned—not good, not good. But Odile felt wonderful. The coffee was hot, the butter sweet, the bread more delicious than any she could remember tasting. She could feel the train stretching, reaching toward Paris as if the track were a muscle in her own body.

"You have family in Paris, madame?" It was the conductor. Odile smiled, nodded.

"Is someone meeting you at the station?" asked the doctor. Odile frowned, shook her head. She dug under her blanket, into her vest pocket, and handed Henriette Woerli's letter to Dr. Gadet.

"There," she said, pointing to the address, "my grandson."

The doctor and the conductor exchanged glances. "I'll take her," the doctor said at last with a sigh. "If I take a taxicab, it isn't too far out of my way."

Odile kissed the back of Dr. Gadet's hand, then held up her cup for more coffee.

CHAPTER TWENTY

EMILIE BOUCHER SAT in her kitchen in Hexwiller, stewing in anger. Odile Keppi had mocked her for the last time. She got out a bottle of sweet wine and poured herself a glass. "Like she was Christ!" she said out loud and felt better. "She doesn't even go to church. If she went to mass, the bells would split open." Emilie's glass was empty, and she poured herself another. She remembered her mother telling her that when they baptized a Keppi, the water turned black. "If a Keppi fell in the Rhine and drowned," her grandmother had said once, "there'd be dead fish all the way to Holland." Emilie Boucher laughed.

She remembered late one night, hearing her father laugh. "The Keppi women do it with geese," he'd whispered to a cousin from Mulhouse. "Those hands . . ." his voice had sunk down too low to hear.

"It's a wonder," the cousin had said, not whispering, "they don't end up laying eggs."

When she finished her third sticky glass, Emilie Boucher threw open her door and nearly tripped over the damn goose Odile had given her. It ran off honking down the hill. Emilie stepped carefully into the courtyard between the two houses. The sky was dark with high clouds hiding the stars and the moon. She heard the distant honking of other geese, then a few shouted *good nights* as men left the tavern down the lane for home. Emilie Boucher stood shivering in the courtyard, watching Odile's bedroom window for a sign of light. She knew Odile was inside, the dark heart of the dark house.

"Odile Keppi!" she yelled up at the window. "I know you can hear me!" She picked up a piece of kindling and threw it at the window. There was a soft tinkling of glass breaking and then . . . *laughter*. She could swear she'd heard laughter, but she couldn't see anything, not the

177

broken pane in the window, not Odile's face peeking, peering out. She went back in her house and got a lantern.

"Odile Keppi! I know you're there," she said. She shone the lantern up at the window. The broken pane showed jagged and dark, and inside . . . *a white flash of teeth.* Someone smiling. She raised the lantern higher, stepped closer to the house. An old broom got caught between her legs, and she almost fell, the lantern swinging. She caught hold of a carved downspout, an open mouthed fool, the last red paint peeling off its cracking forehead. A pagan prophylactic. A hideous thing carved to appease not God, but gods. She put the lantern down, snatched up the broom, and swept a small heap of straw together, piling it against the house under the rain spout. She took a handful and twisted it, lit it from her lantern. "Keppi?" she said, softly now, as if she were calling a cat. Now she saw the humor in it all. She could laugh a little herself. She dropped the burning twist onto the pile of straw. "Let there be light!"

The fire leapt up in the night as if the mouth of the painted face breathed it in. It swept up the downspout and onto the roof. The wooden shingles blazed as if they were paper. The house burned like a dream, like a fever. Emilie Boucher stood there until she felt a warm rush past her ankles. All the straw in the yard was on fire. Her house was on fire. She screamed and ran, her shoes burning, and she heard geese all around her in the night. Honking, honking, they sounded the alarm.

Schmitthiessler, the shift captain at the mine and Hexwiller's fire chief, heard the geese, but he didn't put down his hand of cards until he heard the church bells and saw a red glow through the window of the mine office. "Of all the luck," his opponent, a young miner named Kling, said, although his hand was not a particularly good one.

"Get the pumps ready," Schmitthiessler said, setting off the alarm that called the men in the mine shaft to the surface. There were only two men down, a pair of engineers working on one of the coal screws, but he would need all the hands he could get to man the pumps. By the time he and Kling had rolled the two hand pumps out of the shed, the engineers were there as well as four townsmen who had come running to help haul the pumps up the hill. Only four, not the dozen who turned up to train each summer on the solstice, pumping water over each other and drinking free beer.

"Damn," said Kling, sweating already. "Where is everybody?"

Schmitthiessler wasn't surprised. That was the difference between townspeople and their paid fire chief. For Schmitthiessler, it wasn't anything personal. It was hard for a family man to tell his wife and kids and cows to save themselves while he helped Schmitthiessler pump water onto somebody else's house. But still, he couldn't afford to let anyone foolish enough to volunteer get away. He counted eight men. It would take eight men, four to a pump, to haul the two wheeled carriages up the steep hill into town, then the same eight, two to man each pump, a pair directing each hose, to wash down the flames. At least he had Kling, who was from a flatlands town near the Rhine and unmarried to boot. Schmitthiessler put him in charge of one pump and took command of the other. "Head out," he said and then, "Watch your feet!" as a steel rimmed wheel rolled over the toe of one of the engineer's boots.

The heat hit them halfway up the hill, and then Schmitthiessler knew how bad this fire was going to be. The houses in the heart of Hexwiller were already gone, the top of the hill was a tight ball of flame, and the houses in circles around it were going up—boom!—like bombs as the heat hit them. The ground underneath hummed with the sheer energy being released. Schmitthiessler shook his head. He and Kling might just as well go back and finish their card game for all the good the two hand pumps were going to do. Or better still, get the hell out, over the next mountain.

"Over there! Use that well!" Schmitthiessler yelled at Kling. The fire was like a great deafness, sucking up all other sound. Schmitthiessler got his pump hooked up and yelled to the two men at the handles to wait for him to take the hose farther up the hill before they started pumping. Then Kling was there, alone. "What the hell!" Schmitthiessler said. "Where's your pump?" Kling shrugged.

"It's broken, the seals. No pressure." Schmitthiessler glared at him, then shrugged himself. Kling was probably telling the truth, otherwise he would have run off like the three men he'd sent with him. Schmitthiessler motioned to Kling to help him with the hose. Some more men from the town were there and were now starting, God help them, a bucket brigade. With Kling's help, Schmitthiessler got the hose halfway up the main street, to the foot of the Protestant church, and back at the well the men started pumping. The water came out in casual spurts.

Schmitthiessler had Kling point the hose at the walls of the house next to them. It was old and half-timbered, hopeless. By the light of the fire, Schmitthiessler could see an inscription carved above the lintel, outlined in red:

This House Rests in the Father's Hand
Who Wards Off Fire in the Fatherland

Schmitthiessler heard a goose honking. Then the door opened, and out came an old man in a nightgown. He had his granddaughter under one arm, a white goose under the other. Schmitthiessler recognized him as an old miner, Gummpa Lahr. "Good night! Sleep tight!" called the girl back to her house, but her Gummpa shook his head.

"It's God's judgment," Lahr said, heading down the street without looking back. "Next time by fire!"

Schmitthiessler stepped back, looking up the hill. The base of the church tower was burning, the bells clanging in the updraft, high pitched enough to cut through the dull roar of the fire. The old man was right. The people were gone. The houses were going. It was like the end of the world. Of course, all fires are the end of somebody's world. Schmitthiessler shrugged, about to turn back to Kling, take his place at the hose, but then, up where the street was awash in flame, he saw a few people moving, dark, slightly cool silhouettes in the red heart of the fire. They moved slowly, not running, then stopped, looking down at him. Their faces mirrored his amazement. They waved.

"Do you see that, Kling?" he asked, pointing up the hill at the shadows. "Kling?" The hose lay on the ground. The water pumping from it ran uselessly in the gutter, steaming in the heat. Kling was gone. "Kling!" Schmitthiessler put all the air in his lungs into it. "Kling!" He heard someone laughing above him. It was Kling leaning out of the upper window of Lahr's house.

"Look," Kling said, pointing up the hill. "Look." Schmitthiessler looked, and he saw that the shadow people had swollen into a crowd, moving—no, dancing—in the street. Inside the burning houses, their sides opened by flame, people were hugging each other and crying, as if they were welcoming pilgrims and long lost daughters, as if they hadn't seen one another in years, in lifetimes. They sat at great tables piled with food and began singing, passing babies hand to hand for the blessing. "Look," Kling said again, and this time he was pointing beyond the burning church tower, to the Protestant cemetery sprawling up the hill. The gate was on fire, and the rose bushes were burning. Beyond the cemetery, the vines in the vineyards, leafless with winter, burned on their trellises, row after row of low flaming crosses. The very cracks in the rocks seemed to be on fire. "Look," Kling said, and the hill heaved with a great explosion. The ground lurched out from under Schmitthiessler's feet, and he fell face down on the hot pavement.

The mine had exploded. The coal seams under the town were on fire. Schmitthiessler couldn't breathe. He couldn't hear. He was out of a job. Blood started from his nose and his ears. Kling was beside him, helping him up, his lips working and working, mouthing the word: *LOOK!*

People were pouring out of the cemetery, hundreds of people, helping one another through the broken wall, the blasted gate, as if they were stepping off a train. Handsome young men. Beautiful women. They hugged each other and wept bright fiery tears. A young girl turned toward Kling, waved to him. *Come, come.* Schmitthiessler grabbed Kling's arms, but the girl opened hers.

"Don't look," Schmitthiessler said, but Kling struggled with him, knocked him down. Kling's clothes burst into flames as he ran up the hill. Waving his arms, he ran burning into the wall of flame. Schmitthiessler shut his eyes, waiting for the scream, but he heard nothing but the roar of fire. He was afraid to look. Afraid to see either reality, the dancing risen dead or Kling's burnt corpse. He turned on his side and began to roll over and over, down the hill. He followed the trail of water from Kling's hose, and when he reached the bottom, cool human hands picked him up.

CHAPTER TWENTY-ONE

A WEEK AFTER her appointment with Mr. Atwood, Ginny came downstairs and found Madame Desnos sitting at the counter with her head in her hands, the contents of a large envelope strewn in front of her.

"My husband," she said, "was hit by a streetcar." Ginny stood poised, unsure how to react to the news. Madame Desnos held up a sheet of paper in one hand, ran the other through her faded red hair. "This is a copy of the official notice of death. It appears he was both drunk and in Marseille." She picked up a second sheet. "This is an affidavit from an attending physician who says," Madame Desnos blew a breath out through her lips, "that Monsieur Desnos died instantly and, it seems, without any awareness of pain." Madame Desnos tugged viciously at her hair. "Would that I was so lucky! This," she held up a sheet of lined paper, "is a preliminary bill from some mortician for embalming what was left of my husband, with an escalation clause for each day the body is held prior to burial. And this," she waved a sheet of heavy, cream-colored paper, "is a letter from a law firm in Marseille claiming the Grand Hôtel de Montmartre in payment for my husband's debts, including loans taken out with the hotel as collateral. The assistant head of the firm informs me that a representative will be on the premises this afternoon and I am to have the books of the Grand Hôtel de Montmartre open and ready for his inspection. He thanks me for my cooperation and asks me to be prepared to vacate said hotel." Madame Desnos held the sheets of paper above her head, then let them drop. They rained over her shoulders, floated to the floor. "I say shit on cooperation." She brushed past Ginny. "I'm going to pack."

Ginny picked up the cream-colored letter, tried to decipher its lawyerly French. Madame Desnos had until 2:00 P.M. to ready the hotel for its new management, that much was clear. She put the letter back in its envelope and went to the closet—her heart raced as she opened the door—but the late Monsieur Desnos's suitcase was just where she'd put it. If Madame Desnos was leaving, so was she. She took the suitcase upstairs. There was room in it for what she would need. She wrapped Paul in her nightgown, packing him with his francs for safekeeping. Even after all that had happened, he was still her responsibility. Then she put on her coat and took one last look at her trunk abandoned in the corner. She picked up the suitcase. With the money and Paul, it wasn't light. She leaned as she carried it down the stairs.

"One moment!" Madame Desnos called from behind the counter. Ginny set her bag down with a thump beside the one Madame Desnos had packed. Madame Desnos cut the telephone cord with a pair of scissors. She handed the telephone to Ginny. "Put it in my suitcase," she said. Ginny cleared her throat.

"What are you going to do about your husband's body?"

Madame Desnos paused for a moment, one hand in midair, then she smiled. She dug around under the counter until she came up with a sheet of writing paper. She wrote a quick note, sealed it in an envelope, and copied the Marseille mortician's address onto the front. "Don't worry," she said to Ginny, putting the letter into a net shopping bag. "This will take care of him." Ginny watched as Madame Desnos took the long brass room keys and dropped them into the bag with the letter. They carried their suitcases into the street, and Madame Desnos locked the door of the Grand Hôtel de Montmartre behind them, putting that key too in her net bag.

"We don't have anywhere to go, do we?" Ginny asked as they started down the street, their suitcases heavy in their hands.

"You put that question so well," Madame Desnos said, "it answers itself."

Ginny started up Rue Lepic. Madame Desnos took a few steps then stopped. "I won't permit this," she said.

"Permit what?" Ginny asked as she turned around. Madame Desnos set down her suitcase.

"For you to leave the hotel, become homeless, because of me. Not with the baby."

Ginny shrugged, moving her shoulders up and then down like she'd seen Madame Desnos do a hundred times. "No one gets to live in a grand hotel forever," she said, trying to sound more like Madame Desnos than Madame Desnos. She kept climbing up the steep hill. It worked. Madame Desnos followed, sighing.

"Ooof," she said, "why did I want that telephone?"

"Maybe we should take the Métro to the Gare St. Lazare," Ginny said. "At least we can check these bags for the day while we decide what to do." Ginny looked down at her suitcase. Did she dare check it? Would it be safe? Madame Desnos gave a small shrug of agreement.

"Oh, all right," Madame Desnos said. "If we get on at Abbesses, we won't have to change lines." They walked in silence, Madame Desnos shifting her suitcase from hand to hand, cutting east toward the Place des Abbesses.

"Madame!" a voice called after them. "Madame!" Ginny turned to see Monsieur Clavel run out of his bakery toward them. He looked thinner, as if in his grief he was forgetting to eat his own bread. "I saw you and your friend go by and thought, *How can she pass by my bakery without stopping in?*" He looked at their luggage. "And then I saw your suitcase. Are you late for your train? I brought you something for your trip." He wheezed, out of breath, and held out a pair of freshly baked rolls.

"You're too kind," Ginny said, and meant it. She kissed him on the cheek and he blushed. She took the rolls.

"Do you need more? I baked plenty." He was still panting a little.

"Thank you, no," Ginny said, then paused. Surely Monsieur Clavel was as honest as the porters at the Gare St. Lazare. And how safe would her money be on the Métro? She remembered the helpless protests of the man the Gypsy children had robbed. "Well, actually," she said, "we have errands to run. Would it be too much trouble if we left our luggage in your shop for a few hours?"

"Of course not," Monsieur Clavel said and led the way back to the bakery.

Inside, a young woman with a floury coil of black hair on the top of her head was kneading dough. She moved the white mass back and forth on a board effortlessly, the well-developed muscles in her forearms barely tensing. "This is Agnès, my Henriette's daughter. She's come from Strassburg to help in the bakery." The young woman smiled, her lips white with flour, and dipped a little as if she might curtsey. "She's been a great comfort," Monsieur Clavel said, wiping his forehead with the end of his apron. "When a spouse dies," his voice cracked, "it's hard to go on."

"Indeed," Madame Desnos said. Ginny shot her a quick warning look.

"What if we put our suitcases over there," Ginny asked, pointing past Agnès to the back of the shop, "out of the way?"

"Any place is fine," Monsieur Clavel said, "so long as you don't mind a little clean flour." Madame Desnos let Ginny take her suitcase but kept her net shopping bag hung over one arm. Ginny struggled with the two suitcases, carrying them to a far corner behind a wall of unopened flour barrels. When she set her suitcase down, she had to make herself let go of the handle, turn casually away. A sudden rush of customers filled the front of the bakery.

"We'll be back before you close," Ginny said.

"What?" Monsieur Clavel called out, busy with three orders at once.

"We'll be back," she repeated.

"Won't you take a few more rolls?" he called after them. "They're really very light."

Madame Desnos walked toward Sacré Coeur without talking, and it was Ginny's turn to follow. They went down the long steps, retracing more or less, Ginny realized, her first walk across Paris with Roland. Ginny ate Monsieur Clavel's rolls one at a time as they walked. Madame Desnos stopped to mail the note she'd written to the mortician. Finally, when they could see Notre Dame, Madame Desnos sighed and slowed down. "I've been in Paris a long time," she said, "but I've never liked that church—too many points, too new." Ginny wasn't sure she'd heard her correctly.

"Notre Dame, new?" Madame Desnos nodded.

"In Le Puy, the town where I was born, the cathedral is so old it has a statue of Isis."

"The Egyptian goddess?"

"Ah, well," Madame Desnos waved her hand, "so a teacher at the state school told me. The church calls it the Black Madonna." Madame Desnos shook her head. They crossed to the middle of the Seine and stood on the bridge, looked back at the city. "In Le Puy there is a woman who sits every day in the market and sells vegetables that the other vendors have thrown down as too old or too rotten. Believe it or not, even the mayor waits his turn in line each day and pays for the privilege of her weighing him out rotten parsnips." Madame Desnos untied her shopping bag and pulled out one of the keys. "I think you would have to live in Le Puy a very long time to know why this is so."

"Perhaps you should go back there," Ginny said. She felt a chill, as if Madame Desnos were already far away, and she was alone.

Madame Desnos held the brass key between her fingers and let it drop into the Seine. Ginny watched as one by one the keys fell, golden beads on a rosary, raising a tiny glinting splash apiece. When they were gone, Madame Desnos wiped her hands on her skirt. "My great aunt has a shop in Le Puy. Lace—that's the big trade there—postcards, religious bric-à-brac. She wrote to me over a year ago asking me to come take over the shop. She said there was more business than she could handle at her age. But then, of course, she is ninety-two."

"Will you go?" Ginny asked.

Madame Desnos shook her head. "I promised you wouldn't be alone when your time came." Ginny looked back at the city. In the cool afternoon light, it looked gray and unfriendly. The baby wouldn't be born for eight more months. Where would they stay? Another hotel? She imagined money leaking from her suitcase, every day finding it lighter. Monsieur Desnos and Paul were beyond all such worries, but the living needed a way to live.

"I've been thinking of buying a business," Ginny said, "something Roland and I could run together."

"Not a hotel," Madame Desnos said, frowning. "That is my advice."

"Do you think in Le Puy? . . ." Ginny let the question trail away, imagining a town where all the shops were lit in the warm pink light of the underground toilet.

"You could join me in the lace trade," she said. "Handle the orders from England and America." She looked cheerful for the first time all day. "I can tell you have a good head for business. Most women do."

"Do you really think your aunt might take me on as a partner?" Ginny said, still looking at Paris. Madame Desnos raised a shoulder.

"We shall see. At least," Madame Desnos said, "at my aunt's, we will not have to pay night after night for our beds." Ginny thought again about her suitcase. She wasn't sure she had a good head for business, but she did have money to invest.

"I'll have to tell Mr. Atwood."

"Good," Madame Desnos said. "It is settled."

Ginny telephoned the embassy from a post office. Mr. Bottoms answered. Mr. Atwood had already left for the day. Ginny hesitated. Should she wait until tomorrow, ask Mr. Atwood for his advice? No. He might throw up his hands, write her off as professionally hopeless, too much trouble to help. And then where would Roland be? They had agreed what was to be done and a new address wouldn't change that. She handed the receiver to Madame Desnos, listened as she gave Mr. Bottoms her aunt's address.

"Le Puy," he said to Ginny when she took back the telephone. "Aren't you lucky! The Auvergne has some wonderful climbing. I love rocks!" Madame Desnos pulled on Ginny's arm.

"What is he saying?"

Ginny translated. Madame Desnos shook her head doubtfully. "A man who loves rocks?" she said.

They went back to Montmartre. "We have to get to Monsieur Clavel's before he closes, or we won't get our bags," Ginny said, trying not to sound unusually worried. She imagined her suitcase, her money, in the dark, empty bakery. Did thieves break into bakeries at night looking for money? Day old rolls?

The door to the bakery was closed when they got there, but Ginny knocked and it flew open. A distraught Monsieur Clavel popped out. "Oh, madame, please help! I could not stand for another woman to die in my bakery." He twisted his floury hands in his apron.

"What are you talking about?" Madame Desnos asked. Monsieur Clavel stepped back from the doorway, and Ginny could see an old woman's back, skinny as a cat's, under a black woolen vest. She was sitting on the floor with her legs out in front of her, wooden shoes lolling on her feet. Agnès knelt beside her, feeding her pieces of roll, speaking what sounded like German a mile a minute. The old woman's mouth was full of bread, and so she only nodded in reply. She swallowed and took another roll from a pile in Agnès's apron. Ginny stepped through the door. The old woman turned around, her mouth open, her hand wrapped around a roll. A web of skin between her fingers shone as yellow as an onion's skin against the crust of Monsieur Clavel's bread. Ginny went down on her knees beside the old woman who took hold of her arm, yellow fingers wrapping around her wrist. The old woman's eyes opened wide.

"Little mother," she said. She kissed Ginny's red hair, began to cry. "Little mother." In Ginny's stomach the baby, that tiniest embryo, leapt like a fish.

"Who," Madame Desnos asked, standing in the doorway with her arms crossed, "is she?" Ginny looked at Agnès.

Agnès stood up, brushing off her knees. She held out a letter. "She's Roland Keppi's grandmother, Odile Keppi," she said. "She has a letter from my mother telling her that her grandson was working here. But," Agnès touched her apron to the corner of her eye, "as I have told her, Mamma has passed on, and her grandson . . ." Agnès shrugged and held her palms outward and empty.

"Her grandson," Madame Desnos said, "is in a German prison." Agnès translated this into Alsatian.

"Oh!" Odile shouted and fell backward like an overbalanced chair.

"She's dead!" Monsieur Clavel said. "O Henriette, if you can hear me, help!" Ginny felt for Odile's pulse.

"She isn't dead," she said, lifting Odile off the floor by one elbow, signalling Madame Desnos to take the other. "But she's very emaciated. She needs some hot liquids in her stomach. We'll take her to Claudia's." Agnès hung Odile's bundle over Ginny's shoulder.

"Wait, madame!" Monsieur Clavel called from behind them. Ginny turned and saw he had the suitcases. She couldn't believe she had almost forgotten them, after all her worry. Monsieur Clavel put her suitcase in her free hand.

"Thank you!" she said. Madame Desnos took her bag with a grunt. Monsieur Clavel kissed them both.

"Claudia's!" Madame Desnos said when they were outside, Odile between them. "That den of iniquity! It brings all the wrong sort of people into the neighborhood."

"Really?" Ginny nodded toward the hotel two streets away. "That's what Claudia said about your hotel."

"My hotel!" Madame Desnos moaned. "I could cry."

"If we don't hurry," Ginny said, shifting Odile's weight to balance the suitcase, "I'm going to fall down."

But when they got there, Claudia's was dark, the windows shuttered. Ginny leaned Odile on Madame Desnos and banged on the door.

"Max?" said Odile, "Roland?"

Ginny knocked again.

"All right, all right. Who do you think you are, the police?" Claudia threw open the door. "The restaurant is closed. I've sold it. Go away." She started to shut the door, but Odile, smelling food and acting on instinct, stuck one wooden shoe in the door. Madame Desnos pushed forward.

"Have a sense of propriety," she said. "We've come for a call." Claudia looked at Odile's face, as yellow as a gourd in the light from the door.

"She's fainted," Ginny said. "Couldn't you sell us a bowl of soup?"

"My God," Claudia said, letting them in, "I've never seen such a pathetic crew." She took a bench down off one of the tables and told them to sit. Ginny piled their luggage in a heap at one end. "Soup!" Claudia said, peering at Odile. "She looks like she needs the last rites." She brought back a bowl of broth and a spoon. Odile stirred it suspiciously, tasted it.

"Thin," she said. Claudia shrugged but took Odile's bowl back to the kitchen and stirred up the pot. When she came back, she had four bowls and four spoons.

"I've had soup boiling in that pot day and night for twenty years, but we might as well finish it off now. I doubt those American Bible salesmen will be interested in observing my little traditions." Ginny looked up from her bowl.

"What men?"

Claudia handed her a pamphlet. On the front was a lurid picture of a woman dressed like a dancer from the Folies Bergère riding a dog with six alligator heads. The number *666* was printed in red underneath. It could have been a cover for the latest issue of the *Watch Tower*, but across the top it read, *Texas Baptist Men's Fellowship*. "Baptists," Ginny said, unsure what the mainline American faiths believed. "I guess they're in favor of Armageddon too. Maybe all Americans are."

"They bought my restaurant this morning. Paid much too much for it, I'm happy to say. They intend to turn it into a mission, to preach the end of the world."

"What will you do?" Ginny asked.

"Retire for a while and then . . ." Claudia waved a vague hand at Paris outside, "if the world does not end, maybe the Baptist men of

Texas will be happy to let me buy back my old restaurant at, say, half the price."

Madame Desnos cleared her throat. "As of today, I too have retired from business," she said.

"Well, then," Claudia said, standing up, "I think this calls for a bottle of wine." She opened a door at the back of the room and disappeared down some stairs. Odile finished her soup, and Ginny got her another bowl and some bread from the kitchen. She had just started on that, when Claudia emerged from the cellar with a dusty bottle of wine and four glasses. "It was a gift," she said. "A gift shouldn't be allowed to turn to vinegar." She opened the bottle and poured an inch in each glass. "Now we need a toast."

"To new lives?" Ginny suggested, one hand on her stomach, thinking of Roland.

"To new lives," Claudia echoed. They all drank except Odile, still busy with her soup. Madame Desnos drained her glass, and Claudia refilled it.

"To love," Ginny said, finishing her inch of wine.

"To love indeed!" Claudia said.

"If you say so," Madame Desnos said. Claudia refilled all their glasses, smiled at them over the top of hers.

"To the end of the world!" Claudia said and held her glass high over her head, as if offering the toast as a temptation to God. Odile looked hard at her, then reached up, plucked the glass from her hand, and threw it over her shoulder like salt pinched for luck. The glass hit the stone floor with a delicate pop, dissolved into needle-sized slivers. Ginny froze.

Claudia laughed. "That settles that," she said.

"We should drink to Le Puy," Madame Desnos said, a little sulkily. "If we're still going."

"To Le Puy," Ginny drank.

"To Le Where?" Claudia asked, taking Odile's glass.

Odile stood up and began searching through her bundle. She pulled out Odilon's brick, shook her head, put it back. She searched the pockets of her vest, then the pockets of her skirt. Madame Desnos raised her eyebrows. Finally, Odile found what she was looking for between her breasts. She spread a wrinkled piece of paper on the table, flattening it with her palm. "To the mother," she said. They all leaned forward to see. It was a picture of the Madonna and Child, but judging from the size of the humans who stood at her feet, the Madonna was the size of a church steeple.

"That," Madame Desnos said, pointing stiffly, "is Notre Dame de France, the iron statue that stands over Le Puy."

Odile beamed at them, took back her glass. "Le Puy," she said, drinking. "Le Puy."

CHAPTER TWENTY-TWO

W
HEN THEY WERE settled in their compartment on the train
to Le Puy, Madame Desnos sniffed the air, then looked suspiciously at Odile. "That old woman," she whispered to
Ginny, "smells." Odile lashed herself to a seat and sat eating one of Monsieur Clavel's rolls, crumbs scattered over her chin. She looked weak and
old. "And she has the hand of a reptile." Ginny shrugged, busied herself
finding just the right place for the suitcase full of francs. Across her lap?
No, under her feet.

Then the train was underway, and Madame Desnos had something
else to occupy her mind. "Oomph," she said, holding her stomach with
both hands. "It's been so long, I'd forgotten. I get sick riding on trains."
Odile sat up, offered her a roll. Madame Desnos looked at the bread as
if it were a poisonous mushroom. "Excuse me," she said, pressing one
hand to her lips, and ran from the compartment. Odile gave the roll to
Ginny, started on another herself. Ginny watched her. Roland's grandmother shared his webbed hand. Did she share his intuition?

"I think I have arranged everything," Ginny said to Odile, pronounc-
ing each word of French carefully, giving it time to sink in. "For Roland
to go free, to meet us in Le Puy." Odile listened silently as Ginny explained about the hearing, about Mr. Atwood. She felt an odd buzzing
in her chest as she spoke, as if the baby were echoing her words. "I think
I have arranged everything," she repeated. "Have I?" Odile spread her
hands, palms up. A Keppi's fate was never easy to read. She offered
Ginny half her roll.

Madame Desnos threw open the compartment door, flopped down
on the seat. "Ooof," she said. "I shouldn't have had that wine." A minute
later she said, "Oooh, I shouldn't have had that soup," and left them

again. Odile slid down in her seat and closed her eyes. When Madame Desnos reappeared, she lay down on the seat next to Odile, throwing one arm over her eyes. "I haven't felt this bad since my honeymoon." Odile began to snore.

By dawn, Madame Desnos and Odile were piled on top of one another on the bench like firewood, snoring high and low in turns. Ginny alone was awake. She got a pad of paper out of her suitcase and wrote Roland a long letter, telling him about Odile's sudden appearance and the decision to go to Le Puy. She didn't tell him that she was scared. She was warm and cheerful and not quite herself. Without knowing it, she followed the unwritten rule of all women whose lovers were in prison, at war, at sea. Avoid speaking of what you fear or it will come true.

She gave the letter to the conductor to mail. An hour after dawn, the train pulled into St. Etienne. "Feeling better?" Ginny asked, rubbing Madame Desnos's shoulders.

"No. I'm just too weak to moan."

The stationmaster told Ginny that since it was a Sunday they would have to take the motor omnibus to get to Le Puy. When Madame Desnos heard that, she broke down. "Please," she waved desperately at the tall, narrow houses of St. Etienne. "This is a nice town. Couldn't we just live here?" Ginny shook her head. Everything was arranged.

"You'll live to thank me," Ginny said, hoping she was right.

Ginny found the bus shelter in front of the station and settled Odile and Madame Desnos on one of the benches with the luggage between them, draping one of Madame Desnos's limp arms over the suitcase with the money. The air was cold and clear as water. "Watch her," she told Odile who was momentarily awake. Rubbing her hands together against the chill, Ginny turned her attention to the schedules and ticket books hanging on the walls. The destinations on the schedules, the buses, and the ticket books were all numbered, but as far as she could tell, none of the numbers matched. "What do you think?" Ginny asked. Madame Desnos shrugged weakly. Odile shook her head. Ginny shivered, shifting from foot to foot, and tried to decipher the timetables.

"Oh no," Madame Desnos said, lifting her head, pulling the luggage closer to her. A crowd of women pushed into the bus shelter, each with at least one bent oak rug beater in her hand. Were rug beaters a specialty of St. Etienne, Ginny asked a woman who had two. The woman shook her head.

"The Gypsies were selling them at the market," she said. "A real steal." The women all attacked one of the hanging books, ripping off tickets. The woman with the two beaters tore a ticket from the same book.

"How do I get to Le Puy?" Ginny asked her.

"You take a ticket," she said, pointing with one rug beater at the book, "and pay the driver. When the tickets are gone, so are all the seats." Ginny looked at the book. There were only two tickets left.

"If I don't have a ticket, I can't get on?"

The woman tapped her rug beater at a faded sign painted on the shelter wall: *EVERYONE MUST HAVE A TICKET!* Ginny frowned. What should they do? Wait for the next bus? She looked back at Madame Desnos and Odile on the bench. She felt the energy that had carried her this far draining out with each cold breath. They had to go on. Delay would only weaken them all.

"Leave me," Madame Desnos pleaded. "I promise I'll get on the next bus." Ginny read the small print on the sign:

With the Exception of:
Disabled Veterans, Amputees, the Civil Blind,
Pregnant Women, and Women with Babes in Arms.

Ginny tore off the last two tickets. The bus drove up, stopping with a squeal that made Ginny's teeth ache. "Good-bye," Madame Desnos said. "Write when you get work." Ginny took her by the arm.

"We're getting on that bus," Ginny said, pulling her up, "now." The crowd of women surged forward and pushed Ginny and Odile and Madame Desnos and their luggage into the bus. Ginny gave the driver the two tickets, paid for the three of them. "I don't have a ticket," she said, "but I'm pregnant." She wondered how she would prove it, she wasn't even showing yet, but the driver gave her change without looking up.

"All the women who get on this bus without tickets say that," he said. Ginny wrapped one hand around her suitcase, the other around the back of the driver's seat. Would he try to put her off? The driver shrugged. "Better get a seat while you can," he said. Ginny managed to squeeze herself, Madame Desnos, and their two suitcases next to an ancient troll-like woman with four rug beaters. She didn't seem to have

194

any teeth. Odile made room for herself and her bundle beside two men on the seat behind them. No sooner were they seated, when there was a last minute rush of women, all without tickets. The driver let them on, though some of them were as old as Sarah when God spoke to her in her tent. The extra women stood in the aisle as the bus started off with a rattle of corrugated metal.

"Eat, little mother," Odile handed Ginny a piece of cheese one of the men had given her.

"Thank you," Ginny said. She sucked out the soft, creamy center and then nibbled away at the harder, moldy edge. Next to her, Madame Desnos closed her eyes, just the sight of the cheese making her sick. "Sorry," Ginny said, licking her fingers, then she put her arm around Madame Desnos. "Try to sleep."

"Yes, little mother," Madame Desnos said, only a little sarcastically. The ancient woman next to Ginny sighed and snuggled closer, as if she too wanted nothing more than to call someone mother again.

The bus rolled up hill and down, the seats first straining forward, almost shaking free of their bolts, then backward, almost tipping over. It stopped in villages, at inns, at crossroads, and goat paths. At each stop, some of the women got off and were greeted by children and friends who admired their rug beaters.

As the afternoon wore on, the bus emptied out. The men sitting with Odile got off, waving to her as the bus drove away. In the next village, six women got on with feather dusters. Red and purple dyed feathers strayed here and there, floated in the air. "Gypsies?" Ginny asked. They nodded. More people got on at the next stop and more at the stop after that. Soon the bus was crowded again. The driver stopped in front of a church and a man who'd waved him down tried to squeeze on.

"Oh, no," one of the women standing on the steps by the door said, holding him at bay with her duster. "Not without a ticket." The driver bent down and tied one of his shoes.

"I'm a disabled veteran!" the man said, trying to push her aside. The women in the doorway looked him over, counted his limbs. "I'm an invalid!" He got one foot in the door.

"Yeah, an invalid," one of the women said, touching her temple, "an invalid in the head!" The woman closest to the door thrust her duster at him. The man jumped clear as the bus began to roll.

"I've got a schedule to keep!" the driver called to him as he closed the door. "Can't wait all day!"

At the next stop, the old woman beside Ginny got off along with most of the women with feather dusters. Madame Desnos sat up straight. "You know. I feel better." She looked out the window. The bus groaned up another hill. "We're getting close now," she said. Odile sat up, yawning, and looked out the window. The bus reached the top of the hill, and Ginny looked out over a wide river valley. The red-tiled roofs of the town below clung to the sides of a massive stone outcropping. It looked just like Marie-Louise's postcard. Le Puy.

Above the town rose a rough pillar of rock, and on the very top stood the huge Madonna, Notre Dame de France. She was big and she was red, a rusty iron red somewhere in color between Madame Desnos's hair and Ginny's. She stood with her giant red arm wrapped snugly around her big baby Jesus, her other hand supporting his iron bottom. Jesus raised his smaller red hand in a two-fingered blessing. Ginny squeezed Madame Desnos's hand. The bus started down the hill, and the sun sank lower and lower, until it sat on the rim of the valley.

"Look," Odile said, pointing, and Ginny saw other rock pillars, one with a chapel on top, another with a white marble statue of a man holding a second oversized baby.

"Joseph and Jesus?" Ginny guessed.

"The stepfather of God," Madame Desnos affirmed dryly. Then the bus descended into the valley, and Le Puy rose up in front of Ginny.

Madame Desnos had the driver let them off at the foot of the town, at the bottom of a street so steep the sidewalk was a set of stairs. Ginny took a deep breath, then let it out. "My great-aunt's shop is this way,' Madame Desnos pointed up.

Ginny hesitated, her foot on the first step. "Maybe we should have sent a telegram, let her know we were coming."

"Nonsense," Madame Desnos said. "I'm her closest family." They picked up their bags and climbed. A bright stream of water rushed in a channel down one side of the street, and the houses that leaned out over it looked older than anything Ginny had seen in Paris, older than anything in Florida but the sand.

Madame Desnos turned off the street and into a narrow, covered alley that ran up and up. All three of them were breathing hard from the climb when the alley ended at a small courtyard open to the sky.

"Look," Odile said, pointing up. The giant iron woman was right above them, even redder in the light of the setting sun. The base of the rock she stood on formed the end of the courtyard, a long wall closed in the right side, but on the left were three old houses, five stories tall. The first was painted light purple, the second, yellow, and the last was a deep china blue. The ground floor of each had three tall windows and a door. In the purple one was a small grocery, a bin of purple and white turnips on display in one window. The yellow one had a sign painted in green over the door, *Auberge du Soleil*, but its door and windows were shuttered. The windows of the deep blue house were hung with framed squares of white lace, and a sign painted in neat white script stretched across its façade: *Mme. Alix — LACE*. Next to the door, a hand-printed plaque hung on a nail:

MUSEUM OF HAPPINESS
Smile and come in

A tabby cat was bathing himself in the open door.

"Here we are," Madame Desnos said, "home." As one, the three women started forward. The cat ran inside. A tiny woman appeared in the door, leaning on an ebony cane. She was dressed in a plain black dress with a modest lace collar, but set on her head at a rakish angle was a small cloche hat covered with gold bird of paradise feathers.

"Welcome, dears," she said. "Come in, come in." She kissed first Madame Desnos, then Odile, then Ginny as they passed through the door. Inside the shop, lace was everywhere, slithering out of boxes piled to the ceiling, in heaps across what might be a counter. *Lace*, Ginny thought. *My future.* The woman in black leaned on her cane and trod a narrow line, like a path shoveled in snow, through the lace. They followed her, a single-file parade, into the back of the shop, through a curtain of lace, and into a tiny blue kitchen. She sat them down at a little round table, the size of one in a pastry shop, and poured them hot cocoa from a pot on a one-burner stove. She sat down, beaming at them. The wrinkles in her face formed an intricate web, like the lace in the window and just as white. "Now, dears," she said. "Who did you say you were?"

Madame Desnos frowned. "I'm your grandniece Philomène," she said. "Remember, Auntie?" Then she introduced Ginny and Odile.

"You must all call me Calixte," the aunt said.

"Why?" Odile asked.

"Because that's my name," the aunt said. "Calixte Alix."

Aunt Calixte lit a lantern from the stove, took Ginny's elbow for support, and led them up the narrow stairs of the house. Madame Desnos and Odile bumped after them with the suitcases. Calixte climbed past the first floor without stopping. On the second floor, she opened the door to the left and the door to the right and shone the lantern into each in turn, revealing two small rooms as full of boxes of lace as the shop below. She tried the third floor with the same result, but on the fourth floor was one large bedroom overlooking the street. She opened the windows, unlatched the shutters, and the last light of the day shone off her gold-feathered hat. Except for the curtains, the room was empty of lace.

"This was my mother's room," she said, turning to Ginny. Ginny looked longingly at the wide white bed and its two cloud-sized pillows. Sleep welled up in her like the warm tide in the Gulf. Calixte squeezed her arm gently, smiled. "Why don't you take this room? I think it suits you. I'll take Philomène and—Odile, was it?—over to the Auberge du Soleil. Monsieur Liotard, dear man, left me the inn, or at least the key to it, in his will." Ginny nodded, yawned, her eyes watering. She stretched out on the white sheets and closed her eyes, imagining Roland beside her on the wide bed. First Madame Desnos, then Odile, kissed her good night.

"Sweet dreams, little mother," Odile said, but Ginny was already asleep.

CHAPTER TWENTY-THREE

GINNY WOKE THE next morning to the sound of something below her window clicking rhythmically, musically. More clicks joined in a complex, shifting pattern. Yet the sound was too faint to be music, at least any music she'd heard. She imagined that inside her, the baby began to hum. Ginny listened with her palms pressed to her stomach and hummed back. The room around her felt more transparent than glass, like a membrane with light, air, and sound moving freely through the walls to her. Voices drifted up, a short laugh. She went to the window and pushed back the lace curtains. Three women were sitting in the courtyard with what looked like brocade pillows in their laps. Above the pillows, their hands hovered like Roland's sparrows, fingers moving too fast to see. Ginny turned from the window and stretched.

Besides the bed, she saw there was a tall walnut dresser and an equally tall armoire, both too large to have fit up the narrow stairs. Had they been built in the room? She started to wash her face in a basin of fresh water someone had left on the dresser, then froze. Where was her suitcase? She got down on her knees and looked under the bed. Then she saw the suitcase sitting just inside the door. She set the suitcase on the bed and opened it. All her money was there, but one of the bundles of bills had come undone, and Paul's urn was buried in worn franc notes. She brushed the loose francs from Paul's urn, held up one bill. In the morning light, the money looked as useless as old newsprint. Ginny shook her head. She had been wrong to think it was her whole future, to be so worried about it. The money was nothing, nothing compared to having Roland back with her. And when Roland came, she would be able to decide what to do with Paul's ashes and her money once and for all. She closed the case and, after a moment's indecision, put it in the armoire.

She went downstairs and found Madame Desnos, the tabby cat wrapped around her ankles, watching the women from the door of the shop. "They're making lace," Madame Desnos said, pushing the cat away with one foot.

"More lace?"

"More lace and that's not the half of it. They're making it for Aunt Calixte, for us—if you are still interested in this crazy business."

Madame Desnos led Ginny next door to the Auberge du Soleil. As soon as she stepped through the door, Ginny heard Odile singing, a little weakly and out of key, and smelled something with garlic and onions boiling away on the stove. Odile had taken over the kitchen of the inn. "Bacon," Madame Desnos said, nodding toward the kitchen with pursed lips, "in large quantities, seems to have revived her."

"A miracle," Calixte said. She was sitting at one of the inn's five wooden tables, drinking coffee. She had on the same plain black dress or one just like it, but on her head she wore a straw bonnet covered with red lacquered cherries. She smiled at Ginny, patted the seat beside her.

"Two hundred and ninety-six, two hundred and ninety-seven." A woman Ginny had not seen before was standing by the window. She was wearing a pink satin bathrobe and kicking her leg up over her head. "Two hundred and ninety-eight." Her pink slipper touched the low ceiling of the inn. Her knee touched her nose. Odile brought out two more cups of coffee and a basket of bread.

"Eat, little mother," she said, her own mouth full of something. "Eat, eat." Ginny tried to catch Odile's hand, but she disappeared back into the kitchen.

"Two hundred and ninety-nine."

"Your coffee is getting cold, dear," Calixte said to the woman.

"Three hundred!" The woman stopped, panting, and Ginny saw she was fifty or so, Madame Desnos's age. The woman came across the room with her hand out.

"This," Madame Desnos said, "is Zoé Saby. She runs the grocery next door. You met her sister, Marie-Louise, in Paris—remember?"

"Mademoiselle Saby, of course," Ginny said, remembering Marie-Louise's face bathed in the pink light of her underground toilet.

"Zoé," the woman said. "Everyone calls me Zoé." Her eyebrows had been shaved off, new ones drawn in like black accent marks. She shook Ginny's hand, kissed Madame Desnos, Calixte, and sat down with a sigh. "I'm a professional dancer." She took a sip of her coffee, making a face. "Cold." Odile came out of the kitchen with rolls and butter for Ginny and Madame Desnos and took the offending cup away. She brought out a hot cup and set it down in front of Zoé with a clatter. "I do a thousand leg kicks a day, don't I, Calixte?" Zoé said, adding three lumps of sugar to her coffee.

"Every day," Calixte said, smiling.

"Since she was a child," Madame Desnos said, not smiling.

"You remember, Philomène? How touching." Zoé sipped from her cup. "I didn't know you knew I was alive. How I envied you older girls then." Madame Desnos choked. Aunt Calixte raised one finger from her coffee cup.

"Now Zoé," she said. Zoé sighed.

"Calixte thinks I'm bad on purpose, to upset her. She has theories about mental hygiene."

"I think, dear child," Calixte said, smiling at Zoé sympathetically, "you are less careful of what comes out of your mouth than you are about what you put in it. But that hurts you more than me and hurts the rest of the world not half as much as you hope."

"I apologize," Zoé sighed. "I'm just feeling blue today." She leaned close to Ginny and whispered, "sexual tension." Then out loud, "I'd better go back to the store and finish my leg kicks. That will help." Calixte smiled absently.

"Do, dear," she said, waving a hand. "I have to talk to Madame Gillespie and my niece." When Zoé had gone, Aunt Calixte said, "Please don't be hard on Zoé. She has a great love of life."

"Love of men, you mean," Madame Desnos said, sulking. Aunt Calixte smiled at her.

"Well, Philomène, half of all life on the planet is male, isn't it?" Madame Desnos frowned. Aunt Calixte stood up, took Madame Desnos's arm. "Perhaps we'd better go to the shop. Do you want to come too, dear?" she called to Odile.

"No," Odile said. She stood with her arms folded in the doorway to the kitchen like a pillar, like a woman who knew who held up the house. "I'm going to cook a goose." She wiped her hands.

Outside, the women were still making lace. Ginny could see now that they were sitting on low stools and that the pillows they held in their laps were special ones. Each had a cylinder set in its middle like an Edison phonograph. Around the cylinder was a complicated pattern for the particular piece of lace they were making, and the patterns were porcupined with glass-headed pins. The clicking sound was made by wooden bobbins, each wrapped with silk thread, that the women made fly through the air, around and between the glass-headed pins. Some of the pillows were bigger than others, with more pins, more bobbins, and the result was a lace, a silk webbing, more intricate than any spider could make.

"Good morning, madames," the lace makers sang out to Ginny and Madame Desnos. "Good morning, Mademoiselle Alix. What a beautiful hat." The bobbins clicked. "Good morning, Mademoiselle Saby." Zoé stood in the grocery door, changed in a remarkably short time into a tight pink and white dress, striped round and round like a peppermint stick. She waved at Ginny, motioning for her to come over. Ginny touched her chest. *Me?* Zoé nodded. Aunt Calixte had gone over to talk to one of the lace makers. Ginny could see the wooden cherries on her hat bobbing in agreement with something the woman said. Madame Desnos stood beside her aunt, arms crossed, tapping her foot. Ginny went to see what Zoé wanted.

"I hope you're enjoying the tour," she said, waving a pink-nailed hand at Aunt Calixte. "Calixte always cheers me up. She is never blue. I owe her my whole life, really. Thirty-five years ago, she came in and lay down on our couch one day, and when she got up, she said to my mother, with me right there, 'Irène, if it makes her happy, you should let Zoé dance.' "

"Did you?" Ginny asked.

"Did I what?"

"Dance?"

Zoé ran her hand from her hip to her thigh. "At the Folies Bergère," she said, arching her back and thrusting out her breasts.

"That must have been interesting," Ginny said, trying to imagine what working in that nightclub she and Roland had hurried past on their way to Montmartre would be like. Zoé looked at Ginny, sensing doubt.

"Anyone will tell you," Zoé said. "Even Philomène."

"Ginny!" Madame Desnos was calling her. "Are you coming?" She stood waiting in the door of the shop. Aunt Calixte was already inside.

"Yes," Ginny called back. Zoé touched a bright nail to Ginny's hand. "The stories I could tell." She used her thumb and forefinger to zip her lips shut.

"Why," Madame Desnos asked, when they were inside the shop standing in the narrow aisle, "why are they making more lace when this house is stuffed to bursting with it?"

"They're making lace," Aunt Calixte said, scratching the tabby cat's back with her cane, "because I buy it from them. I've always bought their lace. My father bought their lace. They have to live. It's not their fault I decided to stop selling it after he died."

"Decided to stop? Do you mean you could sell all this lace, if you wanted to?" Madame Desnos asked.

"Of course, dear. Handmade lace is a rarity, like kindness from strangers, like love. The demand always exceeds the supply. Wait till you see the letters I receive, from Paris, London, even Japan."

Madame Desnos crossed her arms on her chest. She moved her gaze slowly from one end of the shop to the other, silently pacing off acres of lace. The cat mewed and ran into the kitchen, as if it heard distant thunder. "Then can you tell me, Auntie," she said, her face a mask of false patience, "why it is you don't want any of this lace sold?" Calixte smiled with real patience.

"Do you know, Philomène, that even when you were a child, you reminded me of my father. He was quite the businessman." Madame Desnos raised one eyebrow, not quite certain she was being praised. Calixte gently touched her niece's arm. "It's not that I don't want the lace sold." She stroked Madame Desnos's arm as if it were the jumpy cat. "I just don't want to sell it myself. You're welcome to sell all the lace in the shop. I think you'd be quite good at it. That's why I wrote to you, asked you to come. You'll find the box with the letters from the buyers, the ledger with the old accounts and addresses on the desk in the corner." She pointed at a heap of lace. "At least I think it's that corner." Madame Desnos went to the corner, picked up a piece of lace and handed it to Ginny, picked up another and hung it over her own arm, then another and another.

Ginny held up the lace in the light from the windows. The pattern was incredibly complex, more complicated than Papa Ben's charts of the nerves in the human body, than the calculus Dr. Love had tried to teach her. It was beautiful but, it seemed to her, a little inhuman. "I don't understand," Ginny said. "This is a lace shop. Why did you decide to stop selling lace?"

"The museum takes up all of my time, dear."

"The museum?" Ginny asked. Aunt Calixte held one finger to her lips, her face hidden by the shadow of her cherry bonnet. She nodded at Madame Desnos still digging for the ledgers, crooked her finger. Ginny set the lace down and followed Calixte's slow climb up the narrow stairs to the first floor. On the left hand door a small sign read:

The Shrine of Faces
please wipe your feet

The door on the right had a larger sign:

Are you ready for?
The Museum of Happiness

Ginny wasn't sure she was. "What's in the shrine of faces?" she asked. Calixte smiled and opened the door. Ginny could see the room was white, cobwebbed with lace. "Oh, more lace," Ginny said, trying not to sound disappointed.

"Look closer, dear," Calixte said, drawing her into the room. Ginny looked at a large piece hanging on the wall in a heavy, gilt frame like a portrait. It *was* a portrait. An old-fashioned gentleman with a great scimitar of a nose stared out of the lace. Underneath his extravagant cravat were the words, *Order and Progress*. "That's the president of the republic," Calixte said. "I did it for the Universal Exposition of 1899."

"You did it?" Ginny looked from the portrait to Calixte and back again. She tried to remember some of the names for lace from the descriptions of brides' gowns in the DeSoto paper. Without realizing, she had absorbed Claire's contempt for all such useless and beautiful things.

"I made it on that." Calixte pointed to a lace maker's pillow twice the size of those Ginny had seen on the street, with an uncountable profusion of bobbins hanging down from the cylinder in the middle. "Then I did this one." She pointed at a companion framed piece. Two naked women held a banner raised high between them. It proclaimed, *Work Is Liberty*. The lace was very fine, the crossing and recrossing of the thread almost microscopic, but it varied in texture. The faces were smooth, the hair wavy. Calixte silently read the motto on the banner, shrugged. "I did that one for my father. I had wanted to do a portrait, but I couldn't get him to sit still long enough."

Ginny looked at the lace in the next frame. It was a tall man with wild hair. A bird sat perched on his extended hand. Roland?

"St. Francis," Calixte said. Ginny read the motto at the saint's feet. *Consider the birds in the sky. They do not sow or reap or gather in barns.* A change from Calixte's father's work-is-liberty motto. "I did that one," Calixte went on, "because I wanted to be a Poor Clare, a female Franciscan. Their convent is just behind the wall on the other side of the courtyard. But my father, poor dear, was afraid I'd have too much time to think and might become melancholy like my dear mother. My father was afraid of thinking. He believed a smile was proof against all trouble, and he raised me to smile and keep busy. Thus," she nodded at the lace, "the handiwork." Calixte shook her head, peering closely at the tiny exquisite knots in the lace portraits. "Then one day, soon after he died, I was folding some ordinary lace, some shawls that Madame Sabatier— the mother of the oldest lace maker outside—had made, and I held one up to the light." Calixte led Ginny to the window, pulled a piece of lace at random from a box. "What do you see?" she asked, holding it up.

"Silk threads," Ginny said. Calixte shook the lace and it shimmered in the sunlight. She pointed at the upper corner.

"The Virgin Mary as a young girl," she said, tracing an outline with her finger. Then she ran her finger down one edge of the lace. "The water that sprang from the rock at Moses's command." She tapped the far corner. "A Siamese cat." She laughed, and Ginny did too, although she didn't see any of the things Calixte saw.

"Our eyes put together shapes we can recognize," she said. Calixte put down the piece of lace and picked up a smaller one done with gold thread. She shook her head.

"Look at this one," she said, touching the gold lace with a finger. "And see my mother's bare head, the afternoon sun shining in her hair."

Ginny looked, preparing herself to pretend again. First there was nothing, but then she saw a sad face gazing out at her from the gold lace. She blinked hard. Calixte sighed.

"She does look sad, doesn't she?" she said. "She died when I was only five. My father told me she died because she went out in the rain without a hat. A silly thing to say to a child, but I believed him. Actually, dear," Calixte put one hand on Ginny's arm, the gold lace forgotten in the other, "I rather suspect she killed herself." Ginny took Calixte's hand in hers. "What a poor liar my father made!" Calixte nodded to herself. "It was true, though, that my mother never wore a hat. She had beautiful hair and was quite vain about it.

"At any rate, I made up my mind not to let the rain kill me, and so I wore a hat all day every day, indoors and out. I wasn't going to go off and leave my papa." Calixte touched the wooden cherries on her hat. "Thus the hats. To this day, when a woman in Le Puy tires of a hat, she knows where to send it. People can be very generous with things they don't need." Ginny nodded her head in agreement.

"If you don't believe what your father told you, why do you still wear a hat?" Calixte put the gold lace back in the box by the window.

"There's another portrait of my mother in the museum," she said, changing the subject, it seemed to Ginny, quite deliberately, "and a matching one of my father. Done in oils on canvas, in case you've had enough lace." Calixte gave Ginny her arm and led her across the hall to the door of the Museum of Happiness. Ginny heard someone cough at the bottom of the stairs.

"Auntie," Madame Desnos called in a tightly controlled voice. "Could you spare a moment?"

"You go in, dear," Calixte said to Ginny. "I'll be right back." Ginny waited until Calixte had started down the stairs, then pushed the door open and stepped inside. She didn't know what to expect. The room was darker than the Shrine of Faces. At first she couldn't see anything, but after a minute, her eyes adjusted enough to make out a tall empty bookcase, a bare wooden floor. The Museum of Happiness seemed to be empty. Ginny blinked. Was it all a joke? Then she saw the glowing outline of a window. She felt her way across the room and pulled back the heavy curtain. Light splashed into the room, spilled across the dusty floor and onto a stack of women's hats that almost touched the ceiling. More hats were scattered across the bottom shelf of the bookcase. Green-feathered and black-beaded and blooming with fat pink cabbage roses. A harvest, a plenitude. Calixte's hats.

Ginny looked up and saw the portrait of Calixte's mother hanging alone above the bookcase. In the light from the window, her hair was so black it looked almost blue, and she wore a deep purple dress that matched the shadows under her eyes, the bruised color of her lips. She looked dramatically, purposefully sad, as if she had held one dark memory throughout the sitting. She reminded Ginny instantly of her own mother. She felt a stab of pain at the thought of Claire, so fresh it caught her by surprise. What did Calixte's sad mother, her mother, have to do with happiness? Where was the portrait of Calixte's father?

"Unfortunately," Calixte was standing at the door, "the wire holding my father's portrait broke." She raised her hands palm up in a fateful shrug. "He fell behind that bookcase, which is much too heavy for me to move. But if you look carefully between the bookcase and the wall, you can still get a glimpse of him."

Ginny leaned on the bookcase, put her cheek to the wall. She could just make out the edge of the portrait wedged in between the wood of the bookcase and the cracking plaster of the wall, could just make out a corner of a smile, a single laugh line, a red slice of cheek. From the parts she could imagine the whole, the smiling busy face of a smiling busy man. Oddly enough, he also reminded her of her mother, of that part of her mother that specialized in keeping too busy to think. Handing out *Watch Towers* every minute of the day she didn't spend reading one, not leaving a second for an unguarded thought. But he also reminded Ginny of Fanny, always joking. *I'm not all the way broke or crazy.* Always secretly sad. Was that happiness? She eased herself upright using both hands. She thought she felt the baby shift.

Ginny heard Calixte shut the door. Calixte sat down on a narrow cot that had been hidden behind the door and looked up at her mother's portrait. "Sit down," she said, patting a spot beside her. Ginny sat next to Calixte and saw that the bed was made up with fresh sheets. Ginny realized that Calixte slept in the museum.

"Once I discovered that even the most ordinary lace was full of faces, I gave up my own lace making. Why should I go to all the trouble, when the patterns were everywhere? After my father died, I gave up selling lace too. I saw too many faces in the lace I bought to be able to bear parting with it. But I didn't see my mother at first, everything but her. Then one afternoon I was looking at a black silk shawl that a woman on a farm outside of town had sent in especially for me to see, and there she was."

Calixte stood up, spreading her arms in the air. "She was carrying this stylish little cream derby on a platter like St. Agnes carrying her poor severed breast, and Jesus stood behind her with a flock of very white sheep, whiter than they ever are in the fields, believe me. *Poor*

Mamma, I thought, *martyred for want of a hat,* and for the first time in my life, I began to cry." Calixte dropped her hands to her sides. "Then I realized that I was wearing a cream derby just like the one on the platter, and I cried harder. I hadn't forgiven my mother for dying, for leaving me. I was punishing her, over and over, each time I put on a hat. And what was worse, she hadn't noticed. She didn't want me to forgive her. I tore off the derby, and she just stood there with Jesus, not even looking at me. I cried and cried. I cried myself sick. Finally, I sat up and put away the shawl and said to myself, 'What now?'" Ginny nodded. She knew that question.

"I used to go over to the grocery in the afternoon to watch Zoé practice. Her mother disapproved of her dancing. So I went over there and lay down on the sofa to think. Zoé, dear girl, was practicing splits. And as I lay there, I had a vision." She paused, checking to make sure she had Ginny's attention. Ginny nodded. "I saw my mother again, but this time she was sitting at a table in heaven with my father, laughing. They were laughing and playing with this."

Calixte took a box from the bookcase, opened its hinged lid, and handed it to Ginny. Inside was a metal wheel, like a cake pan, mounted so it spun freely, like a miniature carousel. Its hub was a smaller circle of mirrors. "Look through here." Calixte pointed at a hole in the lid and gave the wheel a spin.

Through the hole, Ginny saw a pink baby toss a small blue ball into the air. He caught it and laughed, tossed it up and laughed, caught it and laughed, over and over. His joy was contagious, undiluted. Each time the ball flew up was a triumph over gravity. Each time he reached for the ball, it returned to him out of love. Ginny laughed. Calixte laughed. Ginny imagined she heard her mother laughing, Fanny laughing, a whole chorus of surprised, delighted laughter. Then the baby slowed. The ball froze in midair. Calixte pointed to the inside of the wheel, and Ginny saw not one, but a dozen pink babies drawn in every stage of the ball toss. "It's called a praxinoscope," Calixte said. "The man who invented it lived in Le Puy. They were very popular for a while, moving pictures that came before what they call moving pictures now."

Calixte closed the box, smiled. "I know for a fact that my mother never saw one when she was alive, so it was a vision, not just a memory. A vision to remind me of all the times I've been happy in this life. We have all been happy, sometime, somewhere, but we tend to forget happiness, just as adults, we forget we were ever babies." Calixte tapped the lid of the praxinoscope. "So then I forgave myself and my hats, which are my own harmless form of vanity. And I started this museum as a reminder. It has sorrow," she waved a hand at the portraits, the hats, "because I have felt pain and grief. My father was wrong in pretending he hadn't. Haven't we all? Haven't you?"

"Yes," Ginny said and felt tears hot in her eyes. She thought of her mother and Fanny in separate prisons of their own making, Paul as cold in life as in the morgue, Roland so far from her. Calixte took Ginny by both hands. Her smile was brilliant.

"But in spite of that," she said, her eyes as blue and round as the laughing baby's ball, "my life is joy!" Ginny felt Calixte's hands warm on hers. She wanted to take her in her arms, hold her like a baby, protect her. "Not everyone's life is in this museum, only mine, but this is what I say to you." Calixte whispered, "Everyone has their own museum of happiness. Up here," she kissed Ginny on the forehead, "where no one can touch it. Can you see it?"

"Yes," Ginny said, in love with Roland, her baby, everyone. She felt Le Puy around her like a pink light, like a dawn. It was something she had never felt before, something like joy. "Yes, I can."

"I'm so glad, dear," Calixte squeezed her hands. "I'm afraid it's a skill you're going to need."

CHAPTER TWENTY-FOUR

The morning of Doctor Krebs's next monthly visit, House-father Huhn woke the detainees himself. He went over to Sister Eugenia, who was on his knees beneath the window.

"Doctor Krebs is a very patient man," the housefather said. "However, if this morning he finds you are unexpectedly and completely cured, I'm sure he will be delighted. Shall we," he signalled the guide, "surprise him?" The guide in his leather shorts stepped forward and set a neat stack of clothes at Sister Eugenia's feet—tan shorts, white shirt, brown knee socks, and a pair of brown men's shoes. "If you would be so kind, Sister," the housefather gestured at the clothes. Sister Eugenia lowered his head. "And I'm afraid I'll have to ask you for the scissors out of your sewing kit," the housefather continued. "There will be no more dismembering of uniforms."

"All right, boys, nothing to see you haven't seen before," the guide said, waving them toward the stairs and breakfast.

After a few minutes, the housefather came down smiling broadly, the brown robe and hood of Sister Eugenia's habit limp over one arm. He went into his office. "I find this a fascinating psychological experiment," Schmidt said, shoving his glasses up on his nose. The cook appeared with the carrots, but no one took any. They all watched the stairs. The guide came down.

"Why aren't you eating?" he asked.

"The blessing," Willy said, rubbing his stump contemplatively. "Sister Eugenia always asks the blessing." The guide smiled.

"You, Keppi," he said. "Go up and get him."

Roland found Sister Eugenia sitting beneath the window, sewing as usual. His head was bare of its hood, his face above his beard was a pale oval surrounded by skin even whiter, as white as an egg. But more than his head was bare. Except for the blue and white curtain in his lap, he was naked, his chest hairy and luminous. The clothes the guide had given him were torn into small squares and arranged by color in neat tan, white, and brown stacks on the floor.

"It's amazing," Willy said, coming up behind Roland. He picked up one of the patches. It was leather. "It's a miracle. Even the shoes. And in five minutes, tops." All the detainees piled into the room. Schmidt ran downstairs for the guide, who sent him for the housefather.

"Downstairs, boys. Now!" the guide said, and they scrambled for the stairs, were back at their breakfast when the housefather passed through, led by a shaken Schmidt, caught in the role of the bearer of bad tidings. Housefather Huhn frowned at them, then went upstairs.

They heard one short shriek, then the housefather was back with the guide and Schmidt right behind him. "Give him back his . . ." he choked again on *habit*, "own clothes."

"And the scissors too? There are all those curtains to hem . . ." the guide started.

"The whole damn sewing kit!" the housefather said. Schmidt took a tentative step toward his place at the table, but the housefather caught him by the back of his neck. "Oh no you don't," he said, intent on punishing at least the messenger. He pushed Schmidt toward the stairs. "Clean up that mess! I don't want one scrap of it left. And consider your hearing postponed. Indefinitely!" The housefather slammed the door to the staff's quarters behind him. The guide disappeared after him, came back with Sister Eugenia's habit, the scissors. He handed them to Roland.

"Here," he said, "take this upstairs." Then he turned to the others. "Remember our friends the bees—busy makes happy. Get to work!" On the stairs, Roland passed Schmidt coming down with a broom and a bundle of scraps. Schmidt's eyes were bright with tears behind his thick glasses.

"Postponed," he said, his voice trailing away down the stairs. "Indefinitely."

Roland handed Sister Eugenia his habit, turned his back. When he turned again, Sister Eugenia was back in his habit, a bride of Christ. Roland gave him the scissors. The nun beamed at Roland, closed one hand around Roland's wrist, a finger raised to his lips. He pulled

211

Roland's torn, webbed hand toward him. Roland made a fist, tried to pull his hand away.

Sister Eugenia shook his head, smiling gently, as if at a child. He lifted the sewing kit from his lap and opened it to Roland like a book. The light from the window shone like mercury across the tiny blades of the scissors, the needle gleamed silver above a bright tail of blue thread. Sister Eugenia raised his eyebrows, questioning.

Roland went down on his knees. Sister Eugenia was a quick tailor. The scissors cut open the edge of Roland's loose webbing, drops of blood springing up in the wake of the sharp blades, bright drops that fell one by one onto the blue and white checked curtain in Sister Eugenia's lap. Then Sister Eugenia picked up his needle, and zig-zagging threads made their own web, fitting the skin between Roland's fingers back together. When he was done, Sister Eugenia knotted the thread and bit it off. He wrapped a strip of blue and white curtain around Roland's hand.

Roland stood. "Keppi!" It was Willy. "Are you going to take all day?"

Roland walked toward the stairs, the floor floating under him. The whole tower seemed unreal as glass. Downstairs, he looked over Willy's head at the mural, barely focusing. What he saw was not a line of marching boys, but a long line of Keppis, strung out over the hills, marching south: Odile and Odilon, Lena and Max, Ginny swollen with child. The blood rushed to Roland's cheeks. *Child.* Ginny was seven months pregnant with his child. And he alone was missing from the line. Why? Because he was locked away in detention. But it wasn't too late. Not if he could get out.

Ginny! He called to her. She turned toward him, set her feet firmly on the brown earth and reached out to him, ready to pull him through all time and space to be with her. He strained to catch her hand, stretching, stretching, the tips of their fingers brushed. "Jesus, what do you think you're doing?" It was Willy's voice. Ginny disappeared. Roland spun around, angry.

But Willy wasn't yelling at Roland. Schmidt was hunched over the big bowl of cold carrots left over from breakfast, shoveling them into his mouth. He had carrot in his hair, on his glasses.

"Stop that before you make yourself sick," Willy said, but Schmidt only ate more rapidly, stuffing carrot after carrot in his mouth faster than he could chew. "Hey," Willy said. "I think he's trying to kill himself." He stood looking on. Schmidt started to choke. It was Roland who moved, knocked the bowl of carrots to the floor. But even the carrots Schmidt had eaten were too much for him. Roland took off Schmidt's glasses. He looked up without seeing, the whites of his eyes a carroty yellow. Roland and Willy carried him upstairs, laid him out on his mattress. Sister Eugenia knelt beside him, held his head.

"Toss those carrots, Schmidt," Willy demanded. "No vegetable is worth a human life." Schmidt shook his head. His breathing was quick and shallow. His lips were sealed.

"The doc's here!" It was the guide. "You, Keppi, get the others." He jerked his thumb up to show they were on the floors above. "Lucky for you the doctor's here, Schmidt," Roland heard the guide say as he left. Roland climbed the stairs and found some of the detainees scrubbing the walls on the next floor. "House call," he said, heard them groan, kept climbing. The rest were on the top floor of the tower. Here the rafters and roof twenty feet above formed the only ceiling, and where some of the tiles were missing, rectangles of blue sky and white clouds took their place. Most of the detainees were shoveling pigeon and bat droppings off the floor, but Richter the strongman was high up in the rafters, poking at nests with a broom.

As Richter's muscles rippled and tensed, Roland had the feeling he knew this man, his movements suddenly familiar. Was this something else he had forgotten? A dead bat fluttered down. "Hey!" someone yelled.

"The doctor's here!" Roland called to them. Richter hung from a beam, listening, then slid down a rope twenty feet to the floor, landing on his feet with a thud like a great ape. The others started down the stairs to the room where they slept, and Roland followed the jostling unhappy line.

Doctor Krebs was already there, standing with the housefather. Roland held his newly bandaged hand behind his back, but the doctor ignored Roland and Schmidt prone on his mattress, turning a smile instead toward Sister Eugenia on her knees at Schmidt's head. "I want to share with you, Sister Eugenia, some thoughts I've had recently," he bent over low, almost whispered, "about the Last Supper." The doctor straightened up, spread his arms. "Have you ever stopped," he said, "stopped to consider exactly what Our Lord ate before he was crucified? Partially raw fatty lamb, bitter uncooked herbs, salt in great quantities, the fermented vinegar we dress up with the name wine." Sister Eugenia smiled. Schmidt moaned, trying to attract the doctor's attention. "I ask you, Sister," the doctor went on, waving his long arms, "did not his suffering truly begin then? What are a few nails compared to the scourge of acute indigestion?" Sister Eugenia beamed at the doctor, letting go of Schmidt's head.

"Then we should eat meat too, doctor," Sister Eugenia said, his voice hoarse from disuse, "that we might share in Christ's suffering." The doctor frowned.

"Oooooo!" Schmidt moaned. Dr. Krebs turned toward him.

"And what, pray tell," he leaned over Schmidt, "is the matter with you?" He poked his index finger into Schmidt's stomach. Schmidt opened his mouth and ejected a continuous, powerful stream of pureed carrots, playing first up and then down the length of the doctor's white linen suit. Carrot bits and carrot juice flew through the air. The housefather jumped back, but carrot splattered his legs, his leather shorts. "I take this as a sign," Doctor Krebs said, not moving, holding his hands carefully away from his clothes. "Time to change back to potatoes."

At these words, Sister Eugenia rose in a single swift motion, his arms spread like the wings of some giant, brown mother bird. He scooped up Dr. Krebs, suspended his long body by the collar of his coat and the seat of his white linen pants, walked with him to the open door, and tossed him casually down the stairs. The housefather stood frozen by surprise and his dislike for the doctor. No one moved as they listened to the doctor bump down to the floor below, his bones crackling like green kindling in a hot fire. He hit the bottom with a thud. "Damn," the housefather said, as he walked, not ran, to the stairs. A curse from Dr. Krebs echoed through the tower. He wasn't dead.

It was at that moment that Roland noticed Richter wasn't in the room. A thought hit Roland like a bullet knocking over one of the Mountain's tin soldiers. Franz Richter, the strongman, the man who had said he was going to leave and meant it, was Carmen's brother. He was the man who had been offered the part of an albino gorilla in the movies because there wasn't any wall he couldn't climb up or down. Roland pulled Willy's good arm. "Come on," he said, and Willy followed him, uncomprehending, up the stairs.

"What?" But when Willy saw the hole in the roof, a now man-sized rectangle of sky, Richter's bare legs dangling half in and half out, he knew what was up. Roland heard Richter grunt. Roland grabbed the rope, started up. A pain shot up his arm from his stitched fingers, but the strength of the long line of Keppis was his now. Then he looked down and saw Willy, one armed Willy.

"I'll pull you up," Roland said, "when I get to the top. All you'll have to do is hang on." But Willy cradled the stump of his arm like a man who had once taken such a chance and lived to regret it. Richter, already on the roof, started to pull up his escape rope and Roland with it. "Willy?"

"No," Willy said. "It's already May. My hearing's in just two weeks, I can't . . ." He turned away, facing the same direction, the same future, as the boys in his mural.

"God in Hell," Richter pulled Roland onto the roof and looked with dismay at his unexpected catch. Roland sprawled on his back at Richter's bare feet, slapped his palms down on the tile roof to keep from sliding feet first into space. A warm breeze blew up his bare legs, on his face. It was the first time he had been outside in more than six months. He looked up and saw a sky as blue as the one in Willy's mural. Richter stood over him, balancing himself with his toes. He took a step forward, ready to throw Roland back through the hole. Roland held up one hand—*wait.*

"Where's Carmen?" he asked. Richter put his foot on Roland's chest, ready to shove.

"Who?" He spat.

"Your sister."

"You know Lisel? How?"

"Where is she?" Roland felt himself slip, his heels sliding an inch.

"On the other side of the river," Richter pointed out into space. Roland raised his head high enough to look. Below him stretched Hinkelsbach, the houses looking strangely square and sharp-sided to Roland after the round walls of the tower. Roland raised his head higher. The farthest thing he could make out on the miniature skyline was a section of town wall. The river Richter was talking about had to be on the other side of that.

"Hey!" Someone was shouting in the courtyard below. Roland sat up, digging his heels into the loose tile roof. A car had pulled up and men were piling out.

"Police!" Richter said. "How did they . . ." Roland guessed the police were for Sister Eugenia, but this was no time for talking. Richter was holding the rope, looking down longingly at the courtyard, so unexpectedly full.

"Not that way," Roland said. He moved sideways like a crab across the roof of the tower, circled it, looking down. He spotted the roof of the housefather's office. He took the coiled rope from Richter. "Come on," he said, and slid off the roof in a shower of loose tiles, bumping hard against the wall of the tower. He felt Richter's shadow fall across him, his weight jerk the rope, but Roland kept his eyes on the roof below.

"Hey!" Now someone in the tower was yelling, an arm appeared at a window, swung out like a hook to catch the rope. Roland let go and fell.

He hit the roof hard, off balance, and fell to his side. Instinct kept him rolling, and so Richter's feet missed his face. Richter stood up, silhouetted against the blue sky. But Roland kept moving, sliding down the roof of the housefather's office until he caught the gutter. Then he swung down off the roof and landed in a narrow alley, his shoes sinking up to his socks in the muck. Over the sound of his own panting, he heard Richter jump from the housefather's roof and land with a thud on the next roof, finding his own way to the river. Roland looked up at the tower. A blue and white curtain fluttered at a window. Otherwise, the gray tower looked uninhabited. More shouts came from the courtyard. Roland followed the alley, keeping close to the wall. He heard a car start.

The alley got wider, more public. He spotted a brochure from the Hinkelsbach tourist office next to a used condom. He picked up the brochure, and when the alley joined an almost equally narrow street, he made himself walk ahead with his bandaged hand in his pocket, glancing from time to time at "Hinkelsbach, Walled Town on the Main." In his shorts and knee socks, he hoped he looked like any young hiker, like one of the young Germans in Willy's mural. He made himself hum. He kept walking, trying to look like he was wandering. He made himself pause to look up at the fine seventeenth-century town hall, following the brochure's injunction to admire the gables ornamented with scrollwork. But what he saw was Richter, a bent shape against the sky, arms hugging the crown of a roof. They were both almost to the town wall, to the river where Carmen was waiting.

Roland reached the wall first, climbed the wide stairs to what looked like a ten-foot-wide sidewalk in the air. Down below, the brown river flowed quickly, so swollen with the spring rains that the wall was its bank, whatever path or road that usually separated them completely underwater. Richter came over the roof of the nearest house, jumped to the wall, afraid to let his feet touch Hinkelsbach ground even for a second. He was panting.

"Across the bridge," he pointed up river. Roland groaned. Even before he turned, he knew what he would see. Their side of the bridge was under water. A black car, Carmen's car, stood on the other side, but how to get there?

A stone chip flew from the parapet. Another. Roland heard the third shot, the shout, "Up there!" Richter stood paralyzed by the sight of the drowned bridge, a large target black against the sky.

"Jesus," Roland said, grabbing the front of Richter's shirt. He pulled Richter with him over the parapet, held him the long second it took them to fall and hit the water. Roland heard Richter grunt, then the brown river closed over their heads.

CHAPTER TWENTY-FIVE

As WAS HER HABIT, Claire MacKenzie was up at dawn sitting in the kitchen reading. It was the new booklet for young people that the printing house and headquarters in Brooklyn had sent her.

> God's limit of time to the Gentiles as nations expired in 1914, as we have already seen. We should, therefore, expect shortly to see the awakening of Abel, Enoch, Noah, Abraham, Isaac, Jacob, Melchizedek, Job, Moses, Samuel, David, Isaiah, Jeremiah, Ezekiel, Daniel, John the Baptist, and other ancient worthies mentioned in the eleventh chapter of Hebrews.
>
> These princes will form a nucleus of the new kingdom on earth. If Jerusalem is to be the capital of this new kingdom, it should be able to get in touch with every locality. Christ's kingdom is to undo in one thousand years all the evil brought about in the previous six thousand years. *Old-fashioned methods will not suffice.* Already we see great changes coming in. The wireless and radio can carry messages halfway around the world now, and by the time the princes are brought forth, these inventions will be perfected to reach all the way around.

Did this mean she should buy a radio? Claire wondered. She had always resisted them as wasters of both time and money. She read on.

> The princes can easily radio their instructions to any part of the world. Think of Prince Abraham having some general instructions to give, calling "Attention" and all people everywhere

listening and hearing every word he speaks, as easily as though he were addressing them from the platform of a public hall!

Everybody in the world will be *in one room*, so to speak. The room will be a little larger than we may have been accustomed to hold meetings in, but what of that! Now when we read Isaiah 2:3 and Zechariah 14:16–17, we see how easy it will be for all the people to go "up to Jerusalem."

Of course, if the princes should desire to make a personal inspection of some public work, aeroplanes will soon be so perfected that it will be a matter of but a few hours ride to any part of the earth to or from Jerusalem.

No doubt many boys and girls who read this book will live to see Abraham, Isaac, Jacob, Daniel, and those other faithful men of old come forth in the glory of their "better resurrections," perfect in mind and body. What a privilege to be living just at this time and to see the ending of the old and the coming in of the new! Of all the times in earth's history, today is the most wonderful!

Claire looked up from the booklet. She wasn't sure to whom she was going to give the two dozen copies of *Princes in All the Earth*. A Jewish child would be first choice, but the only Jews in DeSoto, the Goulds who owned the underwear factory outside town, were childless. She supposed the next choice would be the children of the women she'd already visited, who'd taken *Golden Ages* from her. Some of their offspring were wild, made their mothers despair of the world. She closed *Princes* and her eyes, rested her head on the kitchen table. In another hour, she would go out. This was her day to take the Word door to door. She set high standards of perseverance for herself. Mansion or shack, owned by white or Negro, she could knock on the door until the house shook, until someone inside gave in and came running to open the door, to be surprised at the sight of Sister Claire, a mere woman of the faith in white gloves and a hat. When she knocked on a door, she imagined herself as the iron rod of justice. For the wicked shall be cut off. The transgressors altogether destroyed. *Boom, boom*, the mighty brought low.

Claire opened her eyes. Someone was knocking hard on the kitchen door. "Dr. Ben?" A man was calling. "Open up, it's an emergency." Claire opened the door. It was Jack Harlin, the postmaster. "Miz Mac," he nodded, peering around her into the kitchen.

Claire was alone in the house. She hadn't seen Ben in days. "He's not here, Jack," she said. "I think he went off hunting, and I don't know when he'll be back." Someone was in danger of dying, she could tell that from Jack's face. He took it all so hard, as if it mattered, as if this life were all there was. Even when it was some ancient Yankee who died, like the old woman who'd moved into the Carter place and got pneumonia one winter because she was too crazy to buy oil, Jack wept, gave out the mail all day with a fool's tears running down his face.

"It's Miz Combs," Jack said. "She's gone and rat poisoned her grandson."

Mrs. Combs had taken several issues of the *Watch Tower* from Claire, had talked in her loose and lazy way about starting home Bible study. "I guess I'd better go over," Claire said, thinking, *Rat poison—strychnine. That boy is gone.* If he did die, that would be one less child to give a copy of *Princes in all the Earth.* "You keep looking for Ben though. He'll have to sign the death certificate."

She found Ben's spare bag in his office, put in a lavage hose and a bottle of tannic acid, the antidote for strychnine. If the convulsions hadn't started, she'd try to wash the boy out with tannic acid and water. The Combs's place was just across the back alley, a low white house with a neat lawn. Mrs. Combs worked as a clerk in the Woolworth's. But Mrs. Combs's daughter—whose name escaped Claire—was a stupid-looking girl who had gotten herself pregnant and then run off, leaving her mother in charge of her bastard son.

Claire had learned to be dispassionate about the troubles in other people's lives. People without faith were bound to be tried. That's why the false churches went on and on about hell. Compared to the hell the preachers cooked up, people's troubles in this life seemed puny. But as she explained over and over in the homes she visited, the wages of sin is death, not hellfire. Pastor Russell had proved that. The choice was Earthly Paradise or dust.

Claire opened the Combs's door without knocking. Any noise could set off a convulsion in a strychnine case. The poison stripped away the insulation between the nerves, made the body into a badly wired house where any current in one nerve ran through all of them. Nora Combs was sitting on the flowered sofa with her hands in her lap. On the table in front of her, mixed in with *Saturday Evening Posts* and *Ladies Home Journals*, were *Watch Towers* Claire had left.

"He's in the back bedroom," Nora Combs said. She shook her head, looked up at Claire. "I caught him in the backyard playing with matches." She shook her head again, looked back down at her lap.

"When did you give him the poison?" Claire asked.

"What time is it now?"

Claire looked at her watch. "Eight-thirty."

"I went down to the post office at eight. It was eight wasn't it?" Nora Combs nodded at the front door, and Claire realized Jack had followed her over.

"Right about," Jack said. Nora nodded again, her head a little loose on her neck.

"I dosed him right before that."

"How much did you give him?" Claire asked.

"A couple spoonfuls. I mixed it with his cod liver oil so he'd swallow it quick. I thought he'd die right off."

Claire headed for the bedroom, opened the door without expectation. A half an hour was long enough with strychnine. She remembered the poisoned rats she'd seen as a girl, smiling in the face of death, rictus of the facial muscles. But the boy on the big bed was breathing, lying quietly. Claire moved forward as noiselessly as possible. The boy's mouth opened, but Claire held her finger to her lips. "Shush, now." She drew the blinds, darkened the room as much as she could. She sat beside him. Now she recognized him as the boy she saw riding his bicycle up and down the alley, back and forth, only to the edge, she imagined, of his grandmother's property. A little prisoner. She'd also seen him out in his yard once, trying to set a fledgling robin on fire with a magnifying glass.

What a strange world it was that went on around her. She hardly noticed it most of the time. But now, here was this boy. His eyes were dilated, his respiration advanced, his fingers twitched. She watched him for two full minutes. No convulsion.

She would try lavage, though it might set one off. There was a sink in the far corner of the room. She stepped to the door and motioned to Jack. "Get me a bucket of water and a wash pan from the kitchen," she said. "And then give me a hand."

She found some of Nora Combs's black stockings in the big dresser drawer. She rolled the boy on his side. His eyes were wide now. His mind would be racing, all his thoughts coming at once, and he would be afraid. That was one of the symptoms—increasing fear—along with a sensation of falling. She tied his hands to the bed posts, took the lavage tube out of the bag and oiled the end of it. Using the tube as a measure, she estimated the distance down to his stomach and kinked the tube around the fingers of her left hand to mark the stopping point. She put the free end between his lips. "Open up, this is medicine," Claire said. It struck her that his grandmother probably had used just about the same words, *Swallow this, it's good for you.* At any rate, the boy didn't seem to be listening. His face was flushed, and his breathing was quick and shallow. Claire eased the tube forward, and he began to swallow. Jack came in and filled the bucket at the sink. She fed the tube slowly down the boy's throat an inch at a time until it was played out up to the mark.

"Hold his feet," she told Jack. She put the wash pan under the boy's chin, hung the bucket from the bed post, and poured tannic acid in the water. Then she started the siphon in the hose. The boy tried to sit up, pull away, as the cold water flowed out of the hose into his stomach. He got one foot free and kicked Jack. Claire pinched off the tube with one hand, shutting off the water. Then she held the end, open, over the pan. She kept the boy's head down with the other and felt his pulse racing under his fine blond hair. Milky colored water poured back up the tube, splashing into the pan.

Claire reversed the flow and started a second lavage. This time the boy's breakfast came up, some sort of cereal and raisins, swollen fat little raisins each one carrying three times its weight in strychnine, little plump pillows of rat poison. Claire ran the lavage twelve times. Water and tannic acid in, poison out, until what came out was clear. She ran some charcoal water down the tube, then pulled it free. She untied the boy's hands, and he rolled onto his back. His respiration was still fast, but his heart rate was down.

"No opisthotonos?" It was Ben standing behind her. She shook her head. He could see for himself that the boy's muscles were relaxed, not rigid.

They both stood there watching the boy breathe. It was the first thing they'd done together in years. Then, out in the living room, a woman screamed, and Claire knew somehow that it was the boy's mother, Nora's stray lamb of a daughter, whose name, it now came to her, was Laureen. The screams rose higher. Claire caught the name *Bobby*, which she guessed was the boy's name. "Go shut her up, Jack," Ben said, but it was too late. She was already in the room.

"Bob-bob-bob-bobby . . ." She was a big woman, and Claire saw with amazement that she was actually tearing her hair from her head.

Bobby started to sit up, then his head arched back, his mouth opening in a smile so wide his face seemed split. "Damn," said Ben. Jack pushed the mother out of the room. Claire could hear the sound of her fists on his wide, soft chest. The boy rose off the bed, his arms crossed over his chest like a mummy's, until only his head and heels touched the sheets. He stopped breathing. His eyes stood out, full of this fear that was all fears. The veins stood out across his neck, as if they were trying to escape. They shone blue, and the blue spread through his face. For two minutes he didn't breathe. His body arched, impossibly balanced. Claire was conscious of all the oxygen she and Ben were drawing out of the room. In, out, in, out. She took twenty breaths before the boy slumped to the bed.

The boy looked into Claire's eyes, and she saw in his what they both knew—that he was as good as dead. She didn't dare speak or touch him, his nervous system so sensitive now that anything could set off a convulsion. She couldn't stand it. She took one of the old *Golden Ages* from the bedside table and tried to explain it to him with only her eyes. In the end, it would all be all right. He looked at her. He was falling, so frightened.

AUTOMOBILES FORETOLD IN THE BIBLE!
> The chariots rage in the streets
> They rush to and fro through the square
> They gleam like torches
> They dart like lightning

Claire had learned that the old world was just about to go. All the new inventions were evidence of the Lord's presence on earth, signs of his secret return. She found the list in the *Golden Age* and read through it to herself:

Automobiles, adding machines, aeroplanes, aluminum, antiseptic surgery, artificial dyes, automatic couplers, barbed wire, bicycles, carborundum, cash registers, celluloid, correspondence schools, cream separators, Darkest Africa, disk plows, Divine Plan of the Ages, dynamite, electric railways, electric welding, escalators . . .

The boy arched back, all his muscles extravagantly flaunting their strength, the stronger partner of any set winning, his arms wrestled over his chest. He smiled at the ceiling as no one had ever smiled in that room.

. . . fireless cookers, gas engines, harvesting machines, illuminating gas, induction motors, linotypes, match machines, monotypes, motion pictures, North Pole, Panama Canal, pasteurization, radium, railway signals, Roentgen rays, shoe-sewing machines, skyscrapers, smokeless powder, South Pole, submarines, subways, talking machines, telephones, typewriters, vacuum cleaners, and wireless telegraphy . . .

It took two more hours. Ten convulsions. After the tenth, when his muscles finally let go, he didn't start breathing again. His skin stayed blue.

"God himself will be with them," Claire said, throwing back her head, almost shouting. "He will wipe away every tear from their eyes, and death shall be no more, neither shall there be any mourning nor crying nor pain any more, for the former things have passed away."

"Damn it, Claire," Ben said, slapping the magazine from her hands. "God damn it all." She stared at him as if he wasn't speaking English, as if she didn't understand a word that he said. "I better go talk to the sheriff," he said. "He'll probably want an autopsy." He put the lavage tube in his bag.

Claire brushed a hand over the stack of *Golden Ages*, backed past him out of the room. She hadn't done enough for this family. Magazines weren't enough. If she had made Bobby get down off his bike and come inside when she and his grandmother were going over the Bible, if she had gotten the new children's booklets a month, a week earlier . . . then none of this would matter. Bobby would be safe—would still have died, but only to live again.

"You don't know what it's like to have a daughter go bad on you." It was Nora Combs. She was standing waving her arms at Sheriff Buxton, at her daughter Laureen who was lying on the couch. Nora had a red welt on the side of her face, and Laureen was looking at her as if she were a cockroach, something filthy beyond human understanding. "She knows," Nora Combs said, pointing at Claire, "she knows what it's like to have a daughter go bad."

Claire flinched. Virginia bad? Like slovenly Laureen, like poor dead Bobby? Not like that. Ginny had been better than that, good but willful, inclined to the sin of pride.

"She told me she wanted her daughter to die," Nora Combs went on, "that she'd be better off dead and safe in heaven."

Claire felt weak. She leaned one hand on the wall. Had she really told Nora Combs something so personal? Perhaps. She'd been so upset at Ginny's desertion. But, at any rate, Claire knew the truth when she heard it. It was true. She had wished Ginny off this trouble-filled earth.

Ben came out of the bedroom, drying his hands on a towel. Nora Combs was getting hysterical now, her breath coming in sharp hiccups. "I'll give her something," Ben said to the sheriff. To Claire he said, "Why don't you go on home now? I'll be over as soon as I clear this up."

Claire straightened up and nodded. She made it through the door and into the hot mid-day sun. But she didn't go in the house to wait for Ben. She got in her Ford. She had to know where her daughter was, and she had a pretty good idea who could tell her.

*　*　*

It took her two hours to drive to Chattahoochee. The March sun was unseasonably hot. The green lawns around the white buildings were empty. In Florida, even crazy white people didn't go out in the sun. Fanny's cabin was down a long drive from the main buildings, set back in some pines. Claire was glad she didn't have to go into the public wards. She hadn't been there since she was a medical student, but she remembered the doctor giving them the tour, pointing out a poor woman, skin leprous with pellagra, who said God spoke to her from her suitcase and told her to throw herself down the stairs. Later, she met a young doctor who'd gone on the tour years after she had. He too had been shown an inmate whose suitcase had suggested a jump off a third floor landing. That time, though, the patient was a man, as if insanity were nothing but a theatrical stock company, with certain roles always good for a long run.

Claire drove past one of the wards. A few men moved jerkily across the lawn in front of it, their stop-and-go locomotion the telltale sign of tertiary syphilis. They were wind-up toy men whose wiring was as wrong in its own slow way as Bobby Combs's had been.

Mrs. Mabes was sitting in a chair on the porch dozing over a glass of tea. Claire knocked on the screen door. The metal mesh buzzed softly in the thick air. Mrs. Mabes put on her glasses, unlatched the door. She frowned at Claire. "Oh, it's you Miz MacKenzie," she said. Claire knew Mrs. Mabes disapproved of her, a woman who would keep her own sister under lock and key. But Claire had never wanted Fanny to be here, in the state hospital. It had been Fanny's idea, Fanny's revenge.

Fanny was sitting in a rocking chair inside the cabin. It was just as hot and close inside as out, but the darkness gave an illusion of coolness. "Sister Claire," Fanny said, her voice empty of irony. Claire *was* her sister. Claire sat down on the bed.

"Fanny," she said, "tell me where Ginny is." Fanny creaked back and forth in her rocker, looking at nothing in particular. For a long minute, Claire wasn't sure if Fanny had heard her. Then Fanny focused her eyes on Claire.

"Why do you want to know?" she asked, and the question made Claire ashamed. Fanny was protecting Ginny from her, from her own mother.

"I want to write to her, that's all," Claire said. "I don't approve of what she's done, but she is still my daughter." Fanny leaned forward in the rocker, put her hand on Claire's knee.

"You won't hurt her, will you, Claire?" Claire blushed.

"I only want to write her, Fanny," she said, "and have her write back." Fanny looked up at the ceiling, then out the door, her rocking stilled.

"I find it hard," Fanny said, "to be sure of what's good in this world." Claire opened her mouth, a Bible verse poised on her lips. Then she looked at Fanny and shut it. Her answers were not answers to Fanny, and Fanny knew where Ginny was. Claire leaned back against the bed's headboard, prepared to be patient. "Love," Fanny went on, "now love should be a positive good." She began rocking again. "I love you, sister, and you love me—I've never doubted—but it's done neither one of us much good. Has it?"

"No. I don't suppose it has," Claire said and thought of how heartbroken their own mother, dead all these years, would have been to hear her say that. From the first seconds of Fanny's life, her mother had loved her and had wanted Claire to love her too. Claire remembered her mother pulling back the pink blanket to show her Fanny's unbelievably tiny head, all squashed and red.

". . . remember the *Morte D'Arthur?* From Miss Beggs's class?" Claire realized Fanny was still talking to her. "In honor of Miss Beggs, I think I'm going to send you on a quest, sister. A quest, a test, a scavenger hunt. If you want to know where Ginny is, ask Dr. Love. If you care enough to go there and ask him where your daughter is, he'll tell you." Claire sat up straight.

Dr. Love. Claire had never, ever, liked that tiny man, not even when he was their teacher—openly encouraging Fanny in her eccentricities. When she had brought Pastor Russell back to speak in DeSoto in 1915, Dr. Love had come, and for a moment, she'd had hopes for him. Perhaps he was a sheep, not a goat. Dr. Love had gone up after the lecture and argued with Pastor Russell, the true and faithful servant. The little man said the European war would end within the year. Pastor Russell predicted a longer war leading up to Armageddon in 1918. Pastor Russell was right, of course. The war continued just as he said it would, and Armageddon had been delayed only to lengthen the Harvest Time.

"If Dr. Love knows where Ginny is, you know too," Claire said. But Fanny crossed her arms and closed her eyes and refused to be moved.

So Claire left, started the long drive back to DeSoto. She stopped at a gas station in Chipley and on an impulse bought a bag of boiled peanuts and a Coca-Cola. She hadn't eaten all day, and the Coke was cold, the peanuts deliciously salty. She ate them as she drove. She hadn't had a boiled peanut in years, not since the days when she and Ben were first married, when they'd ride out together on horseback to see to the medical needs of turpentine crews and logging camps. Then they'd always stopped at the tiny stands with their illiterate hand-lettered signs, *Bolled P-nuts*. She wondered if Ben still stopped, ate a bag by himself. Maybe, she thought, he would be waiting when she got home. Maybe she should go there instead of Dr. Love's, stop somewhere and pick up another bag of peanuts, take them to Ben. Maybe. But she kept driving.

She drove through the outskirts of DeSoto, past the lake, her house, and onto the grounds of the academy. Then she was standing outside Dr. Love's tall brick house, under a ridiculous pair of crossed battle-axes that had been rigged up as an arch over the front gate. She rang the bell. It crossed her mind that it was still not too late. She had a copy of the *Watch Tower* in her bag. She could give it to Dr. Love, say to him, "Did you know, sir, that millions now living will never die?" The door opened.

"Do come in, Mrs. MacKenzie," Dr. Love said. "Your sister called."

CHAPTER TWENTY-SIX

THE RIVER CLOSED over them, the current even stronger than Richter's muscles. They hit the bottom, tumbled over and over in the mud. Roland opened his eyes underwater and saw an orange peel float by in the brown murky water, a turd. He saw Richter, bug-eyed, in front of him, saw his own hand still holding Richter's shirt. Then he looked beyond Richter and saw they weren't alone. In the brown light of the river swam drowned boys. Roland tried to count them, but gave up. There were hundreds lining the bottom of the river like carp. This time they did not look pretty or young. Brown mud filled the wrinkles on their white faces, made them look like ugly old men. One—Dumien?—opened his eyes and wet bubbles rose from his lips to the surface. *Hurry*, each bubble said as it burst. Was this a message from his own child swimming inside Ginny?

Above him, Roland sensed, without being able to see, Carmen racing in the heavy black car along the road by the river. *Hurry*. The drowned boys hovered in front of Roland, watching him, their faces a glowing dead white in the muddy water. Then one by one, they joined hands until they formed a wall, until their very number blocked the current. Roland felt himself moving sideways through the water, swept toward the bank. He looked back for Dumien but the boys were gone, swept away. *Hurry*.

Carmen found them, coughing, stretched out on the muddy bank next to a large dead carp. She pounded Roland on the back, hard enough to hurt, and water streamed out his nose. "Stupid men," she said, shaking her head. She didn't seem surprised to see Roland. She had a box of clothes in the car, gave them each a pair of pants, a shirt. The pants were way too large for Roland, too big even for Richter after months of carrots, but Carmen dug in her box and came up with two belts. While Roland was changing in the back of the car, his hair dripping on the upholstery, Carmen told him her plan. She had new false papers for Franz. They would sail for America from Marseille, a town where a blind eye could be had for a reasonable price. They had six days to make their ship. Roland should come. Shake the dirt of Europe, unloving, unlovable continent, from his feet. But he would have to get papers. Roland coughed. Brown water rolled in his lungs. He thought of Fuss and the last time he'd tried to get papers.

"Where are we?" he asked. Carmen looked at a map.

"Outside Kitzengen," she said. "So Frog, are you in or out?" Roland shook his head. *Kitzengen.*

"I have business of my own."

Carmen signalled her brother who had been changing behind the trunk. Richter spat, then got in, taking Roland's place in the back, crouching down to hide.

Roland watched as the black car drove off. "Meet us in Marseille," Carmen's voice drifted back.

Roland asked a woman selling flowers if she knew where he could find Odo Rettig, Lena's Odo. Had Odo brought Lena home to Kitzengen? Even if he had, what help did Roland have any right to expect after ten years? The woman stared at Roland, taking in his comically large pants, dirty bandaged hand. "Herr Statebankingminister Rettig?" she asked. Roland nodded. She pointed to a half-timbered building topped with a large gold clock. It was nearly noon.

"Do you think he'll be in?"

"I don't see what difference it makes," the woman said, nodding at his wet shoes. "His secretary isn't going to let you set foot on his carpet."

Roland paused in front of Odo's office door, his hand raised, reaching for the bell. He knew the woman was right, that no secretary worth his annual salary was going to let him in. He went outside and around the building, found a door that was unlocked. Roland hesitated, his hand on the knob, then went in. He found himself in a paneled hall lined with portraits in gold frames. Other Rettigs? Other banking ministers? The light was too dim to tell.

"Hans, is that you?" A door in the paneling swung open like a trap. A man in a dark banker's suit stood framed in the doorway. He had white hair, a round open face, and a nose as badly broken as any boxer's.

"My boy," Odo said, reaching out for Roland, looking him up and down, taking in his long legs, the baggy pants. He took Roland by the hand. "How you have grown!" Odo gripped Roland's hand as if unwilling to let him go for an instant.

"We'd better go into your office," Roland said, glancing over his shoulder, down the hall.

Odo made Roland sit in the leather chair at his desk. Odo perched on the edge of a couch. Roland stared at the papers scattered across the desk. They were heavy with seals, spread like a winning hand of cards across the mahogany surface. He read the signatures. There were letters addressed to Odo from the chairman of the Center Catholic Party, from the archbishop of Würzburg, from the representative for Kitzengen in the Reichstag. All were friends of Odo Rettig, Bavarian Banking Minister. A rich man, an important man, a man with connections. Odo.

"Your mother," Odo said, with a slow blush, "is the kind of woman who likes a man to make the most of himself."

Odo listened to Roland's account of his time in the Hinkelsbach hostel. When Roland finished, Odo shook his head. "First, you need papers." Odo picked up the phone on his desk. "Hans!" he shouted into it. A second later, a door popped open and a small gray-suited man appeared. His thin eyebrows shot up with surprise when he saw Roland at Odo's desk. He cleared his throat. "Yes, Herr Minister?"

Odo stood. "No lunch, Hans. We have work." Roland stood too. "Rest," Odo waved him toward the couch. "You're safe here." Odo turned to Hans. "The mayor first," he said as he and Hans left the room. Roland stretched out on the fragrant leather couch, rubbed his eyes. The blue and white bandage Sister Eugenia had wrapped around his hand was filthy, stained with what could only be his own blood. Roland unwound the bandage and held his hand to the light. There was some dried blood on the stitches, but they had held. They showed dark against the white skin of his webbing. Where was Ginny at this moment, this instant? He closed his eyes.

He woke to the sound of Odo shouting into the telephone. "This is Bavaria," Odo said, "not Russia, not France, Huhn." *Huhn.* Odo was talking to the housefather. Roland sat up. "I've arranged for a hearing officer to be there tomorrow, and there had better not be any irregularities." Odo hung up.

"I have a friend there, a good man, Willy Nachtman," Roland said. "A veteran," he added, hoping Odo remembered Max, the war.

Odo looked at Roland, lost for a moment in some remembrance, then nodded. "I'll speak to the hearing officer," he said. "He's an old friend." Odo shook his head. "Youth hostels! Germany is a republic now, the Kaiser is gone for good, and we don't need to rebuild castles for our boys to sleep in like princes. Your mother wouldn't agree with me though. She is a great believer in the youth movement." The phone rang, and Odo answered, "Good, Hans. See to it."

"You'll have papers," Odo said after he hung up, "and until then you will be safe with me." He looked at Roland's hand. "Here," he said and gave Roland his clean white handkerchief. Roland tied it around his hand. Odo looked into his eyes. The whites were a carroty yellow. "What you need is the iron in a good German beer." He hooked his arm through Roland's and led him out of the office and down the street to an inn.

"Lena speaks of you often," Odo said when they were seated, each with a liter of dark brown beer and a slab of black bread spread with lard and rock salt.

Roland looked at Odo. "What does she say?" The beer went down his throat and straight to his head. He felt dizzy. He bit into the bread, rich as flesh. Odo took a great bite of his, washed it down.

"Your mother has a past," Odo swallowed, struggled to find the right words, "of her own making, but then," he sighed heavily, "don't we all, a little? Very German, I think." He wiped his hands, took a photograph out of his pocket and laid it on the table. It was Lena, crowned with a blond helmet of hair, surrounded by six very blond girls. "Your half-sisters. No boys."

Roland bent over the photograph. Lena had filled out. She had two chins, and her bust was enormous, straining the buttons on the uniform blouse she wore. The girls were dressed just like her, stiff blouses, kerchiefs, armbands. Two sat beside Lena on a couch while the other four posed cross-legged on the floor at her feet. Lena looked straight at the camera, but the girls were looking off this way and that, their eyes squirming though their bodies were still, as if, in the second after the shutter closed, they had been up and running, leaving Lena alone in the room. Yet Roland doubted they had gone far. With her bowl haircut and double chins, Lena floated in the picture like a big bubble. Her daughters were smaller bubbles, trapped by some strict but natural law.

Odo touched the front of Lena's uniform. "She is impatient with our Weimar politics," he said. "She always was one for action." Odo put the photograph away. "Will you stay? Your mother is at a rally in Munich, but she'll be home tomorrow night." He drained his glass of beer. "She would be happy to see you." Roland took a deep drink, then shook his head.

"No," Roland said. He had said goodbye to his mother when he left for school and when he had left Würzburg. Three times seemed too much. "I have business in France." First he would go to Hexwiller, get Odile. He knew she was worried. Then on to Paris as quickly as he could, to Ginny, his Ginny. She must be more than worried, desperate, frantic. Did she think he had abandoned her? Roland thought of his child, who would be born in two months. He looked at Odo, sure that Lena had never told him about her abortion, his one unborn son.

The owner of the inn came up to the table with a brown package. "Delivered for you, Herr Minister Rettig," he said, his head bobbing. Odo gave the package to Roland. He tore off the wrapper. A passport for Roland Rettig, naturalized German citizen. Max's star gave a final ghostly twinge.

"It is for the best," Odo said. "I do not mean your father any disrespect, but no one throws a Rettig in jail." Roland wasn't so sure. He knew, like any Alsatian, that no one was safe forever. Odo got out his wallet, paid for their beers. "Here, this time take enough to go by train." Odo folded some bills and handed them to Roland.

Odo walked with Roland to the train station. Roland tried to buy a ticket to Hexwiller, but the stationmaster couldn't find it in his fare book, so he gave him a ticket to Dettwiller, the larger town nearby. Odo stood with Roland until the train came, which, since it was a German train, was exactly on time. They shook hands. "I'll tell your mother you're well," Odo called as the train pulled out.

Roland spent the night on the train. The customs police only glanced at his passport as he crossed the border into France, into Alsace. Nobody was looking for Roland Rettig. In the morning at Dettwiller, Roland asked for a ticket to Hexwiller. The woman in the ticket booth looked at him with alarm. "You can't go to Hexwiller," she said. "No one can go to Hexwiller. It isn't there." Roland protested.

"But my grandmother is in Hexwiller."

"Not if she's alive, she's not. No one has lived there for six months. Some of the survivors are still camped down by the canal." She pointed out the front door of the station, and Roland saw the luminous black and yellow stripes of a large tent, borrowed, perhaps, from some unprosperous fair. Roland walked to the camp, a dozen surplus army tents arranged in a circle around the striped big top. The tents were empty, but geese called out as he walked by, Odile's geese. Children ran around him laughing, playing keep-away with an apple. The children had faces he knew, blue-eyed Ohls, thin-faced Bolles, Laprades, Blancks, Liehns, Wolffs, Lahrs. He found the adults in line in front of the big top. Father Scholly grabbed both his hands, shaking and weeping, squeezing the bandaged one too hard.

"My dear boy," he said, forgetting Roland hadn't been in Hexwiller when it burned, "thank God, you're alive!" Roland pulled free. Old Frau Wolff, standing behind Father Scholly, touched a finger to her temple, rolled her eyes. "Now, don't tell me," the priest said, his eyes clouding over, "what was your name?" Frau Wolff kissed Roland on the cheek.

"Don't you want to wait in line for government bread?" she asked. Roland shook his head.

"I need to find my grandmother. Have you seen her?"

"Odile Keppi?" Frau Wolff pulled her lip, thinking hard. "Not since the night of the fire," she said. "She gave my daughter Frieda a big white gander. Maybe she knows something." Frau Wolff pointed to the far side of the big top. "She's over at the market. She sells carp she catches in the canal." Roland circled the tent and found the market, Frieda with her carp, and Roerich with a brace of young rabbits. Roerich hugged him, but Frieda seemed to have forgotten their flirting. She blushed, shy as a stranger.

"She gave us all a goose," Frieda said. "All of the families that are here, that is. Mine honked like mad when the fire broke out, but still, it spread so fast, I only had time to grab the goose and Mama." Roerich nodded, sadly.

"I ran out of my house with my children, the goose under one arm and a pregnant doe I'd been watching in the other, and then, boom, up it went. They say it was a fire in the mine. They're holding the captain of the mine crew for suspected negligence, but no inspector has been able to go near the mines." Roerich shook his head. "The whole mountain is on fire. I do not think it will ever cool down, not for years."

"I hope not ever," Frieda said. She looked at Roland, expecting him to be shocked. "Everyone is saying it. Everything I had in the world is burnt up, and I have never felt better." She went on, talking faster, spitting with the effort to get out what she had to say. Wolffs weren't talkers. "A cousin in America saw the fire on the newsreels," she said, "and he said the same thing, said watching the old place burn made him happier than Christmas, and he sent us money for a ticket to Milwaukee, Wisconsin." Roerich put his hand on Frieda's arm to calm her. She took a breath, then went on, "Good-bye to bad luck, that is what I say. That's what a lot of us say." She folded her arms, nodded twice, done.

Roerich looked into the distance, toward Hexwiller, and Roland turned and looked too. He thought he saw a faint plume of smoke.

"Odile?" Roland started. Roerich shook off his thoughts.

"She left before the fire began. Someone said they saw her get on the Paris train. Come on." He put his hand on Roland's shoulder. "Let's take a rabbit or two and have a good hot meal together before you go." He took Frieda's arm. "Before everyone goes."

They sat down to lunch on tables inside the big top, a wood stove blazing away in the center ring. Frau Wolff fried Frieda's carp, and there was toasted bread, stewed rabbit. As Frieda had said, everyone seemed happier than Roland could remember. People who hadn't spoken to each other in years, generations, sat together and broke bread. It had taken some months for them to understand that they were never going back, but now everyone was full of plans. The Ohls were going to Lorraine, the Woerlis to Paris. Roland gave Frau Wolff the rest of Odo's money. She and Frieda were going farther than he was.

When the meal was over, Roerich walked out with Roland, stopping by his rabbits. "Here, take this one," he said, and he swung one of the young bucks out the cage and handed it to Roland. Roland protested.

"Take it," Roerich said. "I don't need it. Two rabbits is the same as a hundred, or it is soon enough."

The 2:00 P.M. express train to Paris arrived at the Dettwiller station at 2:14 P.M. Roland gave Roerich's rabbit to the brakeman who let him on board. But a rabbit was not a duck or a goose, and Roland had to ride to Paris in the baggage car. He lay down on the mail. Soon he would be with Ginny. He would walk through the door of Ginny's hotel and she would turn, see him. He imagined her hands flying up in surprise, the smile starting on her face. They would go to eat at Claudia's, have at least two bottles of wine. He imagined himself in the warmth of their bed and let the train rock him to sleep.

It was dark when the train finally pulled, hissing, into the Gare de l'Est. Paris was damp and cooler than it had been in Alsace, cold for May. When he reached the hotel, a wagon piled high with furniture was standing in front. A driver, sitting on the back with his arms crossed, whistled tunelessly. Roland opened the door of the hotel and looked in. All the lights were on in the lobby, but the couch and counter were missing. "Gang way!" the wagon driver yelled as two men appeared in the lobby at either end of a mattress. They pushed out the door, and Roland jumped back. Two painters, their overalls splashed with fresh white, followed the mattress, and behind them came a bald man in a suit with a pencil behind each ear. The painters headed off down the street, knocking off work for the night, but the bald man began to argue with the two men carrying the mattress, waving one of his pencils for emphasis. The driver jumped down to join in.

The door to the hotel stood open and empty, the light from inside spilling onto the street. Roland took a step through the door. "Looking for something?" the bald man laid a hand on his shoulder, pulled him back.

"For someone," Roland said. "I'm here to see Madame Ginny Gillespie." The bald man looked at him suspiciously.

"That name sounds familiar," he said, scratching an ear with his pencil. "Is she one of the ex-tenants who signed a complaint? Because if she is, let me tell you—let me tell her—that the only one liable for damages is the former management and . . ."

"I don't know what you're talking about," Roland said. "Is Madame Gillespie in?"

"Gillespie?" The bald man pushed his pencil back over his ear. "Now, I remember. Wait right here," he said and disappeared into the hotel. The two moving men followed him in. *He's gone to get Ginny*, Roland thought, but when the bald man came out a moment later, he was alone. He held out a thick letter. "I couldn't bring myself to send this all the way back to America," he said. "So, since this Gillespie is a friend of yours . . ." He handed the letter to Roland with a waiterly flourish,

236

glad to be rid of it. Roland read the name written in a tight neat script on the envelope: *Virginia MacKenzie Gillespie*. Then the two moving men reappeared, staggering under a carved mahogany dresser that Roland remembered from Ginny's room. The driver ran to help. Roland put the letter in his pants pocket and tried again.

"Is Madame Desnos in?"

"Oh, don't even mention that name," the bald man said, stabbing at the air with his pencil. "If I could get hold of her. After what she's done—locking out all the tenants, running off with the keys, the accounts, the money. And when she had her husband's corpse, ten days dead, delivered here, three thousand francs freight due . . ." He stopped, words failing him, then pointed up at the sign over the hotel, now draped in a white sheet. "As a lawyer I can assure you, once we change the name of the hotel, we will no longer be legally liable." He turned from Roland to the driver who was roping the dresser on the back of his wagon. "Don't you go running off," the bald man said in a loud voice. "By the terms of your contract . . ."

Roland gave up. He would try Monsieur Clavel. But as he approached the bakery, he saw that sign was draped in white too. The door was open, but people were passing in with loaves and out with empty hands. Roland's heart sank. At that moment standing in the cold damp of the Rue Véron, it seemed his whole world, not just Hexwiller, had disappeared while he lingered in Housefather Huhn's tower.

"I don't care what you say," a young woman coming out was saying to the man with her. "It's disgraceful. Henriette Clavel has only been dead seven months. And marrying her daughter!"

"Now, Annette," the man said, "someone had to take care of the old screw and he didn't father her, some earlier husband did that. They marry like this all the time in the Bible." Annette was not appeased.

"And that music!" she started, but just then a big woman in an embroidered vest like the one Odile wore on special occasions hooked Roland's arm through hers and dragged him out of hearing, toward the bakery.

"Madame Clavel is dead?" Roland asked her.

"Yes, more's the pity," the woman said as they squeezed through the door. "But look at the good living she's left to her daughter."

There was barely room for them. The place was packed to the walls. At the first chord squeezed out by an accordion player near the window, a line of women began dancing, stomping their wooden shoes. The women moved faster and faster as the man played a song Roland hadn't heard since before the war, since he was a baby. Men lined all four walls, whistling and shouting as their women danced by. Monsieur Clavel sat above it all in a chair trimmed with white ribbons perched on the counter where the cash box usually sat. Next to him, in another beribboned chair, sat a dark-haired young woman, her muscular arms straining the sleeves of a white satin blouse. Flowers and loaves of bread shaped like fishes were strewn along the counter under her feet. She looked like a Woerli.

"Keppi! Is that you?" Monsieur Clavel stood, his chair teetering precariously. The big woman with the embroidered vest lifted him down. "What a blessing!" Monsieur Clavel shouted over the accordion, kissing Roland once, then twice on each cheek. He waved a hand at the dark-haired young woman, smiling down from her chair. "Let me introduce you to Agnès," he said, pulling Roland across the room. "Tonight is our wedding night." Agnès bent low and kissed Roland on the cheek.

The line of women broke up, and the men chose partners for a more modern dance. "Dance with her," Monsieur Clavel said, pushing Roland toward Agnès. "It's good luck for the bride to dance as long as she can." Agnès jumped down and spun Roland around so hard it took his breath away. The woman in the embroidered vest spun Monsieur Clavel.

"My aunt, Françoise," Agnès said, nodding toward the woman dancing with Monsieur Clavel. "My whole family came from Strassburg to dance at my wedding." Roland spun Agnès, and she whirled back to front like a top, but in the split second she faced him, she asked, "Did your grandmother find you?"

"Odile was here?"

"You didn't know?" Agnès stopped spinning, breathing hard.

"Six or seven months ago, she came in asking for you, and then your wife came," Roland blushed, "and this woman, who used to come in here sometimes to buy bread, always very . . ." Agnès squeezed her thumb and forefinger together, "tight with her money. They took your grandmother . . ." A big man with a drooping moustache grabbed Agnès and spun her laughing.

"Not so much talking, little girl," he said. "That's for wives, not brides."

"Took her where?" Roland raised his voice above the accordion.

"To . . ." Agnès panted, spinning madly, "to see a woman named Claudia," she said and was gone, swept away on a wave of spinning Woerli brothers and uncles.

Claudia's. Roland squeezed toward the door, two aunts and a grand-father kissing him on the way out. The accordion music followed him as he ran toward Rue Lepic. But when he got there, he saw that Claudia's sign was missing altogether. A tall man in an apron was mopping the front step. He looked up when he saw Roland coming. He had a long, hungry face that reminded Roland of Lena's ill-fated goat. The restau-rant behind him looked closed. "Is Claudia here?" Roland asked.

"She might be, son." The man spoke slowly, as if savoring each word. He had a strange accent. "Why don't we go inside and talk about it." He smiled, showing a large, even set of white teeth.

"Why? Is Claudia there?"

"Actually," the man said, "no. I'm the only one here." Roland felt tired and hopeless. What now? "Are you hungry, son?" the man asked him, smiling. Roland thought of the Clavel's matrimonial loaves, fresh from Woerli ovens. His mouth watered. "We serve our free meal at lunch, but I cooked today, so there is lots left." The man opened the door to the restaurant and a dark peppery smell drifted out. Roland swallowed hard. He was hungry.

The man showed his teeth again and waved him inside, closing the door firmly behind them. Roland took Ginny's seat at their old table, and the man disappeared into the kitchen, then reappeared almost as quickly carrying a steaming bowl and a baguette of bread. He put both in front of Roland and sat next to him. Roland dipped his spoon into the bowl. It was full of some kind of stew, bits of meat floating in a bril-liant red grease. He took a bite, and tears sprang to his eyes, his ears rang. His mouth was on fire.

"You like it, don't you, son?" the man asked, staring at him. "I'll be hurt if you don't. It's what we eat back home in Texas." He leaned close to Roland, his eyes wide open, as if he might cry. Roland took another spoonful. His lips burned, but his tongue had gone numb. It was amaz-ing food. Two spoonfuls and his stomach felt full to the bursting.

"It's very filling," Roland said, taking a big bite of bread.

"I'm so glad you like it," the man said, smiling again. "Of course, it should really be served with, with," his French seemed to fail him, "thin flat bread." Roland looked up from his stew, sweating. Claudia's looked the same except that a map of the world hung in place of the blackboard menu. Fat red arrows cut across the map toward Jerusalem.

"Is that a plan for a war?" Roland asked. The man looked at the map.

"The Last War, son," he said. "Let me get my Bible, and I'll tell you all about it."

"I can't stay," Roland said, holding his breath as he swallowed another spoonful of the stew, but the man was already on his feet. He smiled down at Roland. "I have to go," Roland said.

"I won't be a minute," the man said. He picked up Roland's bowl. "I'll bring you seconds while I'm up." He disappeared again into the kitchen.

Roland went straight to the door, afraid for a moment it would be locked, but it wasn't. "I have to go," he called, then let himself out. In the street, he found his heart was pounding. His stomach glowed like an oven. He wandered through Montmartre, hoping his feet might lead him somewhere, that he might suddenly pass under some window where Madame Desnos or Claudia was sitting, and they would see him, run calling his name, waving a message from Ginny. It began to rain.

Finally he gave up and returned to the bakery. The lights were still on, but most of the guests had gone home. The bride and groom had retired upstairs. Aunt Françoise was still dancing, spinning around the room with a fish-shaped loaf for a partner, but the accordion player was packing up to leave. Roland found a spot near the oven and stretched out on some flour sacks, closed his eyes.

Ginny. Odile. Madame Desnos. Where had everybody gone?

CHAPTER TWENTY-SEVEN

A FTER A MONTH in Le Puy, Ginny's stomach ballooned out, as if the baby were eating as much as Odile was cooking. Madame Desnos brought Sister Luc, the maternity matron at the hospital, to see Ginny in her room at the top of the house. "Sister Luc," Madame Desnos said, handling the introductions, "let me present Madame Gillespie." Ginny shook the tall nun's hand, trying not to stare at the metal crucifix around her neck. She had never met a nun before.

Sister Luc listened to Ginny's stomach with a stethoscope, and Ginny wondered how she could hear anything with the white cloth of her coif between her ears and the earpieces. "A good set of heartbeats, yours and the fetus's," the nun said, straightening up. "From what you've told me and my examination, I would say the baby is due in July. So it's perfectly normal for you to be putting on so much weight now. By May, your baby will weigh two or three kilos, almost as much as when it's born."

"Then what does it do for the two last months?" Madame Desnos asked. Sister Luc shook her head.

"Rest and get wrinkled, I guess," she said. Ginny looked down at her stomach, at the baby that had to get out the way it went in.

They walked Sister Luc down the stairs and to the door of the shop. They stood in the courtyard. "I would feel better if she'd had a child herself," Madame Desnos said after the nun had disappeared down the tunnel-like alley. "Or Calixte or Zoé . . ." she waved a hand at the blank wall of the Poor Clares' convent, "or anyone in this whole virgin town except for me!" Ginny remembered Madame Desnos's dead son. What if . . .

"She has one," Odile said, coming up behind them, a basket of

241

mushrooms under her arm. She was pointing up at the giant iron woman. Madame Desnos shook her head, unconvinced.

They kept busy. Odile opened the other rooms in the inn and soon had a few paying guests—two pilgrims, a traveling salesman—to help eat the feasts, each one large enough for any homecoming, she spent her days preparing. Madame Desnos wrestled the books into order. Ginny sent off a barrage of letters to American and English lace dealers. Her stomach kept growing. Her mourning dress split at the seams, and Calixte sewed her a white waiting gown trimmed with lace. Zoé did her best to keep them all entertained.

Each morning, Ginny worked answering Calixte's backlog of letters from lace buyers. Each afternoon, she wrote Roland, telling him about Le Puy, but sometimes as she did she felt a sense of hopelessness. In Paris she'd imagined each word she put to the page flying to Roland, reaching him before the paper it was written on. Now the words sat on the page. She wrote to Mr. Atwood and got back a note admitting that it appeared Mr. Keppi was not currently allowed the privilege of writing letters. But Mr. Bottoms enclosed a dozen little white slips, official German postal receipts for her letters, so at least she knew some of them were getting through.

She began writing Roland twice a day. In the morning letter, she told him her dreams. How one night she had woken up sure she heard geese honking. How one night she had seen him underwater, curled like the baby she carried inside her. In the afternoon, she wrote about how the business was doing, new orders and money starting to come in, or about how much like a whale she felt. If she stood for long, her legs and feet swelled, so she sat in the door to lace shop with her feet propped up on a chair, sorting lace and listening to the lace makers softly gossiping. She told Roland that the sounds comforted her, that the courtyard rose around her like a cradle, the iron woman looking down on her like a mother of mothers. She didn't tell him how, in the same courtyard, she felt trapped, as if she had grown too large to fit through the tunnel that led to the outside.

She tried to keep busy learning the things she and Roland would need to know to make a living. In Le Puy, a living was lace. She spent January sorting through the piles of it that covered the counters of the shop. She enlisted the help of Madame Sabatier, the oldest lace maker who passed back and forth through the shop with bricks she heated on the kitchen's small stove to warm the lace makers' feet. Ginny would hold up a piece of lace, and Madame Sabatier would rate it. Good. Better. Best. Madame Sabatier was proud of her long association with the lace shop. "General Pershing's wife bought lace from Mademoiselle Alix," Madame Sabatier volunteered on one trip through to the kitchen. "She arrived here," Madame Sabatier paused dramatically, "in an automobile."

Slowly, Ginny began to see the differences in the lace herself. One newer box of lace, though, surprised her. As far as she could tell, every piece in it was identical. She asked Madame Sabatier about it. "Same pattern, same lace," she said, passing through to the kitchen without stopping, a cold brick in each hand. Calixte came in looking dashing in a straw gondolier's hat with a trailing red ribbon.

"No mystery really, dear," Calixte said, picking up the cat and petting him. "There's bound to be repetition like that when there's no one to make new patterns."

"No new patterns? Why not?" Ginny asked.

"It's a talent, a gift," Calixte said, "usually a male one, although I knew one great woman pattern maker."

"You made patterns for your lace, didn't you?"

"Yes, but portraits are different. To make a design like this," she put down the cat and picked up a shawl whose threads swirled in tight arabesques, variations within variations, "you have to be able to hold complex patterns in your head."

"How complex?" Ginny asked.

"Close your eyes," Madame Sabatier said, coming out of the kitchen with two hot bricks wrapped in rags. "Now imagine a brick wall. How may bricks can you see at one time?" Ginny closed her eyes, concentrated.

"Five or six, I think."

"Good," Madame Sabatier said, "average. A dozen and you could make a simple pattern, like for a child. But for that shawl, you need to be able to see a hundred bricks and remember where a thousand others are and how you laid them."

"That's like memorizing the Bible, Genesis to Revelation," Ginny said.

"Actually," Calixte said, "it's more like writing it."

By Easter, Ginny had organized all the lace. Each long lace drawer was labeled and each piece of lace that lay neatly inside was separated from the next by white tissue. In the process, Ginny uncovered things Calixte said she recognized but had been missing for years. One was a revolving rack of black and white postcards. Ginny set the display on top of the counter and was just starting to dust it when one of Odile's pilgrims wandered in and picked out a card. "The Black Madonna in the cathedral," he said, showing it to her. It was a picture of a doll-sized statue wearing an embroidered robe that covered her like a Mexican's poncho. Out of a hole cut in the front of the robe, baby Jesus peeked as uncertainly as a baby kangaroo. Ginny touched the Madonna's round middle. Mary. Isis. Always the mother and baby. Where were all the fathers? Where was Roland? "It's very old," the pilgrim said. Ginny nodded, unsure if he was talking about the statue or the postcard.

"I don't doubt it," she said. Madame Sabatier stopped on her way to the stove and looked at the postcards. "My God!" she said, holding out a faded photograph of a young, very pretty lace maker at work. "That's me!" Ginny offered her the card, but Madame Sabatier shook her head, put it back on the rack. "Let someone pay cold hard cash to get me for a change."

Ginny looked through the rest of the cards as she dusted. There was one of the cathedral and one of a hospital. The hospital—the one where Sister Luc worked?—was an ordinary three story white building with one windowless wall where the names of donors were engraved next to the amounts they had given. But the cathedral was like nothing Ginny had seen. The front was flat, decorated with a geometric pattern that looked almost Arabian, and wide steps led up to a dark covered porch. It looked old, older than anything.

Ginny showed Madame Desnos what she'd found. There were postcards of the lace shop itself, of the Auberge du Soleil, but there were none of the iron woman, Notre Dame de France. "Maybe it wasn't finished when these were taken," Madame Desnos said. "It's made of cannons we captured at Sebastopol from the Russians. They were melted down."

"Like in Isaiah," Ginny said, using her knowledge of the Bible deliberately, playfully, like a pianist running through a scale. "And they shall beat their swords into plowshares, and their spears into pruning hooks."

"Beat them into tourist attractions, you mean." It was a traveling salesman who was stopping over at the inn. He walked to the counter, gave the postcard rack a spin. "I mean, look at this town. First, they build the cathedral, in what, 1100? I'm sure it was a big expense at the time, but look how it pays off over the years. You should see this place on the Feast of the Assumption, packed to the attics. Then, when the pilgrimage business slows down a bit after the revolution, they mix religion with a little patriotism and what do you get? Our Lady of French Military Success. The iron maiden. See the view and feel holy. I tell you, I like this town." Madame Desnos smiled at the salesman.

"And what, Monsieur, do you sell?"

"Souvenirs," he said. "China plates, cups, salt shakers, and thermometers. All custom painted to your design." He drew his hand through the air as if unrolling a banner. "Le Puy: City of Saints. Le Puy: City of Lace. Le Puy: City of Beautiful Women." He checked Madame Desnos's face for a reaction, found it studiously blank.

"Perhaps we could use a few items," Madame Desnos said, putting her arm through his, "but we'd have to talk price. Let us talk over some coffee. Do you have any samples?"

"Price, sure, that's important," the salesman said, letting himself be drawn out of the shop, "but vision is what you need. That's what built this town. And you're not in the game by yourself, you know. Carcassonne is just down the road, and it's the most up-to-date medieval city in France."

An hour later, Madame Desnos returned to the shop beaming, alone. She had two blue plates in her hands. She set them on the counter. "Free samples," she winked at Ginny.

"See," Ginny said, teasing her. "Men are good for some things." Madame Desnos made her most elaborate shrug.

At the end of April, Ginny got a short note from Mr. Bottoms. Mr. Keppi's hearing was scheduled for May fifteenth. Mr. Bottoms had prepared the deposition and had obtained a purchase order for Mr. Keppi's train ticket. Mr. Atwood, he wrote, sent fond regards.

Ginny wrote Roland one last letter, allowing it time to make its way to Germany. Then she settled in to wait. She strained to hear any unusual sounds in the courtyard, Roland's footsteps, his voice. She was too restless to sit in her chair. She prowled the courtyard in her white waiting gown with her coat thrown over her shoulders. Where was Roland? Was he on his way? The baby seemed to sit right on her stomach, and for the first time since she'd been pregnant, Ginny lost her appetite. But Odile cooked more than ever, one feast for lunch and another for dinner.

"Ugh," Zoé said, one night after her third helping of dumplings. She thumped her stomach. "If the prodigal son doesn't come home soon," she said to Ginny, "I'm going to have to buy a whole new wardrobe."

Odile's cooking drew more and more paying guests to the inn. One afternoon, a widowed farmer who raised ducks outside of town showed up with a freshly killed drake tucked under one arm and asked Odile to fix it for his dinner. Odile put the duck in the oven, sat down, closed her eyes, and lost track of time. The duck burned a deep leathery brown. "Just the way I like my duck," the old farmer said, chewing on a wing. He poured Odile a glass of red wine. "To your cooking," he toasted. The wine's ruby color shone through the webbing between Odile's fingers. Seeing that, the farmer felt his heart rise without knowing why. All he knew was that he liked his ducks, and he liked Odile. He wasn't the sort of man to see the connection. He raised his glass. "To the cook," he said. After that, he came to the inn every night for dinner.

On the morning of Roland's hearing, May fifteenth, Sister Luc came to inspect the bedroom at the top of the house. Even though the birth was still two months away, she wanted the required bandages and towels in a carpet bag by the door. Ginny stayed in the courtyard, waiting for Roland. "How lovely Our Lady looks from this angle," Sister Luc said to Ginny when she came out. Sister Luc was looking up at the red face of the Notre Dame de France. "But if you climb up inside, what a view!" She threw open her arms. "You can see halfway to Paris."

Then Ginny knew where she had to go. She knew instinctively, the way a sea turtle knows where to find its beach of white sand. She had waited long enough. Everyone was busy: Madame Desnos in the lace shop with Madame Sabatier, Zoé in the grocery, Odile in the inn, Calixte upstairs in the museum. Ginny left the courtyard, waddled more than walked up a street until she found the iron gate at the bottom of the path to the statue, and squeezed herself through. She started up the stone steps that snaked back and forth up the rock, taking her time with each one. The baby was heavy but quiet, as if it were trying to be as good as it could. Ginny climbed slowly, but still she found herself panting like a dog, her mouth open with the effort of the climb. She rested on the benches supplied at each turn.

Finally, after an hour, Ginny reached the top of the rock. She rested, sweating, at the statue's base, her head even with its smooth toes. The folds of Mary's robes rose seamless above her, a sleek iron skin. Ginny leaned over the railing, looked down at the blue front of the lace shop far below. She saw a tiny foreshortened Madame Desnos cross from the shop to the inn, a white sheaf of papers in her hand. Odile came out and began sweeping the courtyard. Neither looked up. Not even Odile seemed to have any idea that Ginny was watching her. Ginny wondered if God didn't feel a bit like she did in that moment—all knowing, lonely.

Then she turned her back on the world and, pulling open the door at the base, entered the iron statue of the Mother of God. Ginny paused inside and waited for her eyes to adjust to the sudden dimness. When they did, she saw that inside the statue was not smooth like the outside, but made of rough metal plates bolted together, like a ship or a bridge. But in the gray metallic light, the joints looked more like ribs, vertebrae. A spiral staircase rose in front of her like a dinosaur-sized spine, and Ginny climbed up it, balancing herself carefully, trying not to look down. Stage by stage she went up, past Mary's knees, arms, chest, the hollow alcove that was baby Jesus, until she stood in Mary's head. There, everywhere a human hand could reach, the iron plates were covered with writing. But it wasn't the sort of graffiti Ginny remembered from the girls' bathroom at the academy—*Vagina is a province of China*. She knelt to read.

They were prayers to the Mother of God. For my daughter, for my neighbor, for my husband. For health, for fertility, for a good job. Her mother's religion didn't admit the possibility of answers to personal prayer, but here was a place where this oldest of human desires was acknowledged, made manifest. Ginny saw a stub of a pencil on the floor. She picked it up and wrote. *Please Mother, protect and care for your children: Claire MacKenzie, Papa Ben MacKenzie.* Ginny paused, then began writing again, listing Fanny, Mrs. Corbet, Dr. Thornton. She tried to remember everyone, even people whose names she didn't know. She wrote down one iron plate to the floor, continued on the next one. Madame Desnos, Monsieur Clavel, Marie-Louise Saby. Her hand ached, the baby shifted uncomfortably against her bladder. Sister Luc, Madame Sabatier, the widower who was so smitten with Odile. Then she listed the dead people. Paul, Madame Desnos's husband, their baby son. She wanted to be selfless, to do good deeds and so be deserving of good fortune. She wrote until her head was empty of all names except one. Roland Keppi, she wrote on Mary's iron skin. *Roland. Roland. Roland.* She dropped the pencil and stood up, steadying herself with one hand. She felt like she'd cast a net, a spell.

She opened a hinged porthole in Mary's forehead, looked out at Le Puy and the valley beyond. She saw the giant stone Joseph gazing longingly across the valley at his wife. The first time Ginny had tried to sing Christmas carols at the academy with the rest of the students, Dr. Love had told her, since her mother didn't believe in celebrating Christ's birth, it would be better if she just sat and listened to the songs the other children sang about Jesus and Joseph and Mary. Afterward, Maude Abbot had appointed herself to explain Christmas to Ginny. Maude said that God had been Mary's first husband, Jesus's real father, but he had died and gone to heaven. God had been her family's choice, but, Maude had whispered to Ginny, when Mary wed Joseph, she married for love. Ginny had laughed at Maude then, but she liked Maude's story better than the one in the Bible. Why, she wondered, shutting the porthole, didn't Mary and Joseph stand together on the same mountain?

Ginny opened a porthole in the back of Mary's head and looked out over the road from Paris. She saw a car, heading for Le Puy, no bigger than a raisin from up there. It threw up a long cloud of dust. She stuck her head out the porthole. It was a large black car, a limousine, one an ambassador or his first secretary might drive or be driven in. *Was it possible that Mr. Atwood had come himself? That Roland had gotten here so quickly? Who else could it be?*

Ginny hurried down the iron staircase in the statue and the stone stairs on the rock, her arms wrapped around the baby. Still, somehow the car beat her to the lace shop. She found it parked on the street, cooling motor ticking softly, just outside the courtyard. She ran, still holding her stomach. Calixte was standing in front of the grocery. "Don't hurt yourself, dear," she said. "The young man can wait." Ginny smiled at Calixte and slowed to a brisk walk. When she entered the lace shop, she saw a man's back bent over the lace on the counter. Then he turned, a package in his hand.

"Mrs. Gillespie." It was Harold Bottoms. Ginny pushed past him, looked in the kitchen. No one else was there.

"Where's Roland?"

"I'm afraid there's been a bit of a mix-up," Mr. Bottoms said, blushing furiously. "I've had word from the detention center in Germany that Mr. Keppi has escaped. Mr. Atwood is out of the country so I felt it my duty to . . ."

"Roland is free?" Ginny leaned back on the counter, her legs weak with exertion, relief.

"Yes, but . . ." Mr. Bottoms held out his hand, and Ginny saw he was offering her his package, a folder tied with red cord. "The man in charge of the detention center, a Mr. Huhn, forwarded this in care of my desk." Ginny took the folder, tore at the knot in the cord. "Here," Mr. Bottoms said, taking a Boy Scout knife out of his pocket, "let me help you." He cut the cord, and a shower of blue envelopes fell from the folder to the floor at Ginny's feet. She looked down, her mouth open. Her letters to Roland. All of them. Unopened. He was lost to her. He would never find her, never know how hard she had searched for him. A pain started in her back, and she imagined the baby throwing up its hands in disgust at the mess she had made of it all.

"Oh," she said. She dropped the empty folder, her hand frozen in midair. A pain ran down her thighs.

"Mrs. Gillespie?" Mr. Bottoms took her hand, chafed it between his, afraid she was going to faint. Ginny felt something give inside her, like a line parting when she'd gone fishing with Papa Ben and caught her hook on a gator or a log. She squeezed Mr. Bottoms' hand.

"Damn," she said, doubling over. She felt a warm rush of water between her legs, heard it splash on the floor at her feet like a wave breaking.

"Help!" Mr. Bottoms said. "Somebody!"

CHAPTER TWENTY-EIGHT

WHEN ROLAND WOKE the next morning, the oven in the Clavel's bakery was cold. He guessed the newlyweds were taking a day off from bread. He let himself out, taking one of the day-old loaves in the shape of a fish with him. Outside, the sky was low and gray, and the weather was still unseasonably cool. As he tucked the bread into his pants pocket, he felt the crackle of paper. Ginny's letter. He turned it over, read the return address. *Sister Claire MacKenzie, P.O. Box 4, DeSoto, Florida, USA.* Ginny had a sister?

Then it hit Roland. *America.* Ginny had returned to America. As he looked at the envelope, he became more and more sure of it. Gone to America. And Odile? She had gone too, gone with Ginny. She wouldn't let a Keppi baby be born without her. He climbed up Montmartre until he stood in front of Sacré Coeur looking down at his old bench. *America.* He would have to go after her. If he could reach Marseille in three days, he could sail with Carmen and Richter to America, to—he looked again at the letter—Florida.

Roland looked down at the tangle of streets. He didn't have money for a train. He would have to walk to the edge of the city, try to find a ride. He went down the steps. When he reached his old bench, the sparrows rose up. He took the stale fish loaf and crushed it under his heel, spreading the symbol of Monsieur Clavel's good luck and hoped for fertility across the white stone. The sparrows came hovering down, the wind from their wings sweeping the crumbs into the air.

It took him the rest of the day to cross Paris on foot, north to south. At twilight he reached the Place d'Italie and over the sound of cars, he thought he heard, faint as faint, familiar unmusical music. "Is there a fair set up near here?" he asked a woman rolling down the shutters on her shop.

"Do I look like a woman who has time and money to waste?" she said.

He asked a man selling newspapers on the corner. "Well," the man said, "there's a sort of one, over behind that school." He pointed his chin at a building across the road. Beyond the school wall, Roland saw the lights of the Ferris wheel wink on.

It was a sadly diminished fair, no tent full of dancing girls, no airplane ride, no carousel. Then Roland saw the Mountain of Gold, bright in the spring night. The stand was busy. He watched from the edge of the gold circle of light as a crowd of young sailors jostled each other to get at the guns. One sailor shot off a round, taking down the pregnant bride, the old priest. Another got the groom, two wedding guests. Monsieur Mountain offered the winner a buxom hula doll, lifting her skirt a little to show off her charms, but the sailor, his eyes on the rings glittering on Monsieur Mountain's fingers, put down money for another round, going for gold. Monsieur Mountain pointed at the monkeys flying by, the palm trees, the stars. The sailor waited for the soldiers, then shot off his rounds. None fell.

"Hey, wait a minute," he said, but his buddies, anxious for their turn at the game, pushed him to one side and took his place. Monsieur Mountain looked up, his eyes heavy and hooded, barely showing in his wide white face. Then he saw Roland. "My beautiful boy!" he said. "You look terrible." Roland stepped forward, grasped Monsieur Mountain's outstretched hands. They were cold as fish, and the rings on his fingers turned freely.

"You've lost weight," Roland said.

The Mountain lifted his great shoulders, let them drop. "Did your woman find you?" the Mountain asked. "Is she here?"

"Ginny?" Roland said. "Here? You met her?" The Mountain nodded, waved his hand.

"Yes, but not here. She came to the fair months ago when we were up north, near La Villette. That would make it November. She brought news that you'd disappeared," the Mountain looked hard at Roland as if to make sure he was really there. "Poof! Like a franc note." Roland leaned on the stand. He imagined Ginny alone, frightened, looking for him. But she had been looking. She had wanted to find him.

"Do you know where she is?" Roland asked.

"It's a hotel, some place in Montmartre. I have the address somewhere." Roland shook his head.

"I went to the hotel last night. She's not there. I think she went back to America."

"The sad truth is that most people in this world end up back where they started," Monsieur Mountain said shaking his head.

"Hey!" One of the sailors banged on the counter of the shooting gallery. "What does a guy have to do to shoot his gun around here?" Monsieur Mountain turned to the sailor.

"Pay," he said. "It's simple, and that's the beauty of it. You pay and you play." The sailor gave Monsieur Mountain a wad of francs. "You play and you win!" the Mountain said, swinging into his spiel. "Every player's a winner at the Mountain of Gold because winning, gentleman, is a beautiful thing." He pointed a ringed finger at the comic wedding. "Fire when ready." As the first gun banged, the Mountain turned back to Roland, with a wave offered him one of the guns.

A Gypsy girl squatted in front of the Ferris wheel, lifted her skirt, and sent a long stream of urine across the pavement. It ran under the booth. "I have to leave," Roland started. The Mountain held up a glittering hand.

"I've been in this business long enough to know what prize it is that you're after," he said. He held out his other hand, opened it. In the center of his palm was the gold wedding ring no mark was ever smart enough to take. He put the ring in Roland's bandaged palm. Roland closed his hand around it. It seemed a good sign.

"Thank you," Roland said.

"It's nothing," the Mountain said.

*   *   *

Roland walked all night, heading south. At first there was a confusion of roads crisscrossing his road, trying to lead him off west or east, but by daybreak the highway stretched out before him as clear as a railroad track. He passed a stone mile marker: *Fontainebleau — 4 Kilometers*. An automobile came up behind him, honking. Roland held up his bandaged hand in the pink dawn, and the car skidded to a halt. He had a ride. He got in. The driver let the clutch out with a bang, and they shot off down the hill.

"Thank you," Roland said.

"You are most welcome," the driver said. He was a young man with a thin moustache and a hat covered with fish hooks and feathers. "Excuse my French, please. I'm from Padua. I'm Italian. My car," he waved a proud hand at the leather seats, polished chrome, "is Italian." Outside, the sun came up yellow, the sky shone a clear blue. They hit the bottom of the hill and started up the next one in a whirlwind of gravel. In the back seat, long poles hung with line swayed with each curve. Wicker baskets slid back and forth, whatever was in them jingling like bells. "I am the captain of the Italian fly fishing team." He made a casting motion. "Do you know this sport, fly fishing?" He nodded his head toward the back seat.

"I'm not sure," Roland said, taking a closer look at the poles, unsure whether the Italian fished for flies or with flies.

"These flies," the Italian touched the feathers on his hat, "are retired champions." He paused, looked at Roland, the car swerved toward a ditch. "The Pope fly fishes," he said, straightening the wheel. "The King of England, of Sweden. The Czar of Bulgaria. King Victor Emmanuel III of Italy. I know that for sure because I teach him." Roland looked closer at the bright little bunches of feathers.

"Do you catch many fish?" The Italian dismissed the question with a wave of his hand.

"Is not important," he said. "At the big tournaments, we cast at a circle drawn on the floor. It's the eye, the hand," he touched his hand to his eye, "the skill. That's what counts. But for hobby, I still like to get out and fish the stream."

"Is there good fishing around Padua?" Roland asked.

"Padua? No." The Italian shrugged. "That's why I'm here. These hills are full of water that's got to get down somehow, over rock, under trees. To me, that says *fish*." They tore up another hill, gave a long, throaty honk when they passed a farm wagon. Roland could feel the distance being eaten by the Italian's big tires. Marseille and Ginny were getting closer with each hill they rolled up, flew down. The sun rose higher and higher in the sky, until it was out of sight above the car's windows.

Finally the Italian slowed down. "I go west here," he said, pointing to the left side of a fork in the road, "to Dijon. You?" Roland shook his head.

"America," he said. The Italian laughed and stopped the car. Roland got out, shut the door. The Italian's tires spun, caught, and he was gone.

The road was quiet. A few trucks passed Roland without stopping, then some farm wagons, but no cars. He walked up hill and down. The sun on his back felt hot. Finally at the top of the tallest hill yet, he stopped for a rest in a tiny village with only three houses. The woman whose fence he was leaning against kept peeking out through her curtains to see if he had gone, but Roland stayed put, waiting to try his luck on the next car. If he missed Carmen and Richter in Marseille, he might never get to America. You couldn't stop a ship to catch a ride for free.

Finally, the woman came out of her house with a bucket. Roland was afraid she was going to throw water on him, but instead she offered him a drink. "You'll never get a ride here," she said. "All trucks." A heavy truck struggled up the hill, went by in a cloud of noise. "And truck drivers," the woman shouted to make herself heard, "are all communists." Roland took the dipper she held out and drained it, the icy water stinging his throat, the stitches in his hand. Behind him he heard the growl of an engine, two engines, climbing the hill. He gave her back the dipper, ran into the road. "All communists," he heard her say.

"Stop!" Roland said, holding up a dripping hand. A small van rolled by in low gear without pausing. "Stop!" A large truck crested the hill. Roland stepped into the road, both hands held high, closed his eyes. Brakes squealed.

"God!" He heard a door open, someone jump out. He opened his eyes and saw a bald man with large waxed moustache. "I guess you do need a ride," he said. Roland heard the van that had passed him backing up. He turned around.

A man jumped out of the van. "What is going on here? Why did you stop?" he said, his tone superior.

"Don't get so excited, Doc," the bald man said. "We're not going to put him in the van with your wonder machine. But we need someone in the back to keep all those canisters from coming down on our necks. Ballast," he patted Roland's arm.

"Well, all right then, Harris," the Doc said. "But let's get going, shall we?" Harris gave Roland a hand up into the cab of the truck. As soon as he saw the young African sitting behind the wheel, Roland knew who they were. Harris helped him over the front seat into the back of the truck, and he saw the canisters, piled like loose pot lids, each with a label stenciled in black, *ARCHIVES OF THE PLANET: Flammable Film.*

"Where are you taking all this?" Roland asked.

"Dr. Reynaud," Harris said, waving a hand at the van on the road ahead of them, "is leading us to his hometown where our employer has a warehouse. Our employer, or rather our ex-employer, has gone bust, broke, entered a state of financial embarrassment along with, it would seem, half the other rich, philanthropically-minded men in the world. So all this gloriously vain human experience, all this filmed and documented life is going into storage to emerge on some future brighter and better day, I hope. But for now, the cameras of the Archives will roll no more. One cameraman up the Yangtze and, I believe, another somewhere on the Nile are the only two on the project who remain blissfully unaware, as yet, of their unemployment."

The African shook his head. "After this," he said, "I'm going back to Liberia, to my mother's house in Monrovia and eat until I put on ten pounds. I've seen enough of this Old World for a while."

"Nonsense, Michael, you're going with me to the New World," Harris said, "where top-drawer cameramen such as ourselves will be wel come in Hollywood."

"My grandfather came from America," Michael said, shifting gears "He didn't care for the place much."

"America?" Roland asked. "You're going to America?"

"Right now we're agreed as far as Marseille," Harris said. Michael snorted. "No final decisions until we see what's at the docks. We have to get rid of this film first, though."

Roland stretched out on the canisters. The truck was slow, but if they were going on to Marseille, it was the perfect ride. He closed his eyes, felt the truck struggle up a hill and then another before he lost count of them in sleep.

A cramp in Roland's stomach woke him up. He doubled over, hardly breathing until slowly, slowly it passed off. Then he sat up, still holding his stomach, afraid the pain would come back. It was getting dark and a damp patch of fog drifted into the truck, brushed his cheeks. Michael had turned on the headlights. Roland looked over the back of the front seat and out through the windshield. A ewe appeared in the road, disappeared. "Where are we?" he asked. He saw the brake light of the van in front of them flash red then go off.

"In the middle of nowhere," Michael said, waving a hand at the patches of fog beyond the windshield. The fog grew thicker and thicker until the van disappeared altogether. The truck barely seemed to move through the fog, even the sound of the engine was muffled in the damp gray air. Harris rolled down his window and stuck his head out. Roland leaned over the front seat, and all three of them strained to keep their eyes on the road, one minute there, the next gone. Was he getting closer to Marseille? To Ginny? Or were they turned around, heading back toward Paris? It was impossible to tell.

"The headlights just shine right back in my eyes," Michael said, reaching out to turn them off. Suddenly the fog parted, and Roland saw the rear of the van stopped ahead.

"Stop!" he said.

Michael stood both feet on the brake pedal, threw his arm out trying to catch Harris, who hit the windshield a second before Roland did. Metal canisters flew through the air, slammed into Roland's back. The truck skidded sideways, and the front tires gave way with two long whooshes. The truck stopped, all three of them tangled in the front seat, covered with yards of motion picture film.

"Are you all right in there?" Doc poked his head in Michael's window.

"Maybe, Dr. Reynaud," Michael said, holding the back of his neck. A thin line of blood ran from his scalp down his cheek.

Harris looked dully at Roland and the mess of film and metal canisters. Then his eyes widened. "Good God," he said. "All that film." He threw open his door and jumped from the truck. "Get out!" he yelled. Roland rolled across the seat and out the door. Michael followed him tangled in film.

"I have two punctured tires," the doctor said. "I was waiting for you." Harris ran past him and tumbled into the ditch. Michael was right behind him, still trailing a few yards of film. The doctor put his hands on his hips, stayed put. Roland stood looking at the rubber shreds that were all that remained of the front tires. They weren't going to take anyone to Marseille. What if Carmen and Richter sailed without him? What if . . .

For a minute, no one moved. Then the doctor lost his temper, turned toward the ditch. "If that film didn't explode on impact, it's not going to go up now," he said. "Get up here and do something about these tires!" Harris appeared out of the fog and walked slowly up to them, wiping his head with a handkerchief. Michael walked around the van, came back shaking his head. "We shot two, you shot two," he ticked them off on his fingers. "That's four flats, and you're the only one carrying a spare."

"Well, then," the doctor said. "You will have to find three more tires." Harris put his hand on his brow and made a show of peering into the fog. The doctor glared at him. Harris shrugged.

"So I guess I'll take a look around," Harris said. "See if I can find some semblance of civilization." He disappeared into the fog. The doctor gave Michael his handkerchief.

"Clean your face," he said. Michael came over to Roland, still standing in front of the ruined tires.

"You all right?" Michael asked. Roland held his stomach with his bandaged hand. The pain was starting again, a deep slow cramp. *Hurry,* it said. *Hurry.*

"I have to go," Roland said, turning from Michael, starting away.

"Whoa ho," Michael said, grabbing his arm. "Did you bang your head even harder than I banged mine? Where you going to go in this fog? Off a cliff and down a snake hole, most likely. You think that they're going to be any more trucks swimming along in this soup? You stick with us." Roland looked from Michael to the tires. The pain pushed in his stomach hard, like a fist, then it was gone, leaving his legs weak with relief. He had to get to Ginny.

"I have to go," he said, moving his feet without getting anywhere. Michael hung onto Roland's arm with both hands.

"Good luck for good people!" It was Harris, back already. "Not twenty yards down this road I found a rich and benevolent farmer who owns a veritable mother lode of used tires. He's assured me he can find tires or at least inner tubes to get us on our way come morning, and," Harris made a low bow, "he's agreed to take in payment for said rubber, something we happen to have in abundance, I might even say, in surfeit." The doctor caughed impatiently.

"What?" he asked.

"He wants to see moving pictures."

"See?" Michael said to Roland. "What did I tell you? In the morning, the fog'll rise up like bread, and we'll be on our way." Roland opened his mouth to argue, but the pain started again, and he shut it, biting his lip. Michael loaded Roland down with film canisters, kept a careful eye on him as he and Harris carried the projector. The doctor brought up the rear with a gasoline-powered dynamo he unloaded from the back of the van. The fog was so thick Roland couldn't see the ground under his feet. Each step felt like falling. Somewhere between one step and the next, the pain faded away.

"Over here." It was the farmer's wife with a lantern. She led the way to a stone barn, threw open one of the wooden doors. The cows had been moved out of their stalls, and there were a few men and women and children sitting scattered in the straw. The farmer was busy drawing mugs of homemade wine from a barrel, and it gave off a sweet fruity smell that mixed with the smell of hay, cows, and humans to drive the cold of the fog from the barn. More men came in, a priest.

Michael set the projector on some crates near the door while Harris and the farmer's wife hung a white sheet on the barn wall to use as a screen. The doctor ran electric lines from the projector to the dynamo outside. There were extra crates, and Harris set them up like seats, then helped himself to a mug of wine, and settled down on one. More women arrived, whispering to each other. Michael took the film canisters from Roland, and the farmer pushed a mug into Roland's hand, sat him down on a crate next to Harris. Michael took a reel of film out of one canister, and Roland watched as he worked it through the projector like thread through a sewing machine. Children were chasing each other through the loft, sending down dusty showers of hay. Somewhere in the barn, a baby cried. The pain gripped Roland below his navel, a cramp that moved up slowly, until his stomach was twisted in a fierce knot. The mug fell from his hand, splashed wine on his leg, and landed unbroken on the straw-covered floor.

Roland heard the dynamo start up with a bark outside. The light in the projector came on. Roland panted, tried to breathe, then the pain dug in and took his breath away. The doctor came back in. Roland bent double, felt his face wet with sweat. Michael started the film moving through the projector. The pain eased for a second. Roland looked up at the screen. He saw the Eiffel Tower, heard an appreciative murmur of ooohs and aaahs from the other occupants of the barn. In quick flashes the screen showed grapes being harvested along the Rhine, Strassburg cathedral and the moving figure of Death in its astrological clock. Then Roland saw a cathedral unlike any in Alsace. Its stone front was flat, slashed with a crisscross pattern, but then the cramp seized him again. He blinked and the lines snaked, turned into the veins in his eyes. On the screen, the cathedral disappeared and was replaced by a picture of a tall tower of rock. The camera climbed up and up a flight of stone stairs, bumping along in Michael's or Harris's or some other camera-man's arms. Then there she was, the giant red woman, the iron woman from Odile's dream, his dream, her skirts rising into the sky. Roland grabbed Harris's arm.

"Where is that place?"

"What? Oh, that's Le Puy," Harris said. "Dr. Reynaud's hometown.

Roland gasped for breath. The giant woman was in Le Puy. Ginny was in Le Puy. The pain hit him again so hard, he felt like someone had kicked him in the balls. He fell off the crate, followed his mug into the straw. He twisted in the hay, bent his head back to see the screen. The camera traveled down now, looking over the edge of the rock the iron woman stood on, followed her gaze down into the town below. Roland saw a tall house, a window where the darkness pressed against lace curtains. He heard Ginny cry out. He bit his hand, tasted blood. Ginny needed him, and he wasn't there.

"Are you all right?" Harris's voice came from somewhere in the darkness above. The camera floated down from the rock, crossed a court-yard, moved with the wind through the open door of the house, up four flights of narrow dark stairs.

"That's a great shot, Harris," Roland heard Michael say. "How in the world did you get that?" At the top of the stairs, a door opened, the light from the projector poured into a room.

"Who is it?" It was Odile, standing in the doorway squinting, and beyond her Roland could see Ginny's legs, but a nun was bent over her, hiding her face and body. He heard Ginny cry out again. Odile raised a hand to shade her eyes, looked straight into the light of the projector. She stretched her hands out to him, hands as red with blood as they had been the day she lifted him, dreaming, from between his mother's legs. Roland reached for Odile, and her warm, strong hands closed over his. She pulled him forward, the surface of the screen breaking around him like thin ice. From behind him, he heard Harris's voice, tinny and faint. "I must be getting old," Harris said. "I don't remember shooting any of this."

CHAPTER TWENTY-NINE

AROLD BOTTOMS AND Madame Desnos half carried, half walked Ginny up the four flights of narrow stairs to her bedroom. On the first landing, the pain doubled her over, then eased off. When they got her to the bed, she lay down and closed her eyes, panting. The pain came again, stronger than before. She screamed.

"Get, Sister Luc," Madame Desnos yelled out the window to Calixte and the lace makers below. "Hurry." Odile came running up the stairs.

"Out," Odile ordered Mr. Bottoms. Ginny kept her eyes closed, but she could imagine how brightly he was blushing. Odile lifted the bedraggled lace hem of Ginny's gown. "Spread your legs, little mother," she said to her. Ginny let her knees fall away from each other, and a pain arched up her cervix as if she were about to split in two. "Don't push," Odile said, rubbing Ginny's stomach with one hand, reaching into her vagina with a careful finger.

"What do you see?" Madame Desnos asked. Ginny felt Odile's hands leave her, the pain ease, and she opened her eyes. Odile and Madame Desnos were standing together at the end of the bed.

"One foot," Odile said. "That's what I see."

A foot. Ginny tried to remember what the procedures were for a breach birth, but the pain came back full force, and she couldn't think. If one foot was sticking out, then the crucial question was, where was the other one? The baby had to get two feet out to be born. She thought she felt the wandering foot like a boot in her spine. Maybe, she thought, dizzy from panting, this baby doesn't want to be born. *Please*, Ginny thought, holding her stomach with both hands. *Pretty please.*

The next pain hit hard, and she closed her eyes and let out a yell. It went on and on. Then she heard Sister Luc's voice. "Don't bear down.

Try to relax." She felt fingers inside her again, colder than Odile's. Ginny thought she heard Sister Luc's thoughts. *Hail Mary, full of grace, blessed art thou among women and blessed is the fruit of thy womb . . . where is that other foot? There? No. I can't get it.* Sister Luc pulled her hand free. Ginny knew that she was in trouble. The pain eased, and she opened her eyes to see Odile holding her hand, Madame Desnos standing white-faced by the door.

"Breathe," Odile said.

"I am," Ginny said, taking a gulp of air, staring up at the cracks in the ceiling.

"I'm going to give you something to relax you, Madame Gillespie," Sister Luc said, holding a mask over Ginny's nose. Ginny smelled ether, and it reminded her of Papa Ben when she was little. He never used ether any more. Then pain came again. It filled up her body until there was not room for her and the pain both. She drew in a deep breath, heavy with ether, and slipped out of her body, like a scuppernong grape out of its skin. She bobbed near the ceiling, saw her body still lying wet and straining on the bed beneath her. From above, she watched her lips move, heard a horrible sound come out of them, saw Odile squeeze her hand hard, competing with the pain.

Ginny could feel herself sinking back toward the bed like a leaking hot air balloon. She took another deep breath of the ether. This time she shot up through one of the cracks in the ceiling, out above the roof of the house. She floated in the cool air. She looked down and saw Calixte and Mr. Bottoms and Zoé and all the Sabatiers standing in a huddle in the courtyard, looking up now and then at the windows at the top of the house. She started to sink again, the ether ebbing, and her feet brushed the cold tile of the roof. She breathed in and was up again, so high she could see the white walls of the hospital. On one of them was a long list of people who'd donated money to the hospital. She read off some of the names: Bergougnhoux, Eyroud, De Jax, Clapier, even an Alix. The list made her think of Paul. He would have liked to be on such a list. If he couldn't be in a hospital, his name, at least, could be on one. Then the wind caught her gown and blew her up and away from Le Puy. "Help," she said.

"Don't talk," Sister Luc's voice came to her, unbelievably faint. "Save your . . ."

She was somewhere out at sea. The waves were taller than the ships she saw, tossing like bath toys, down below. She was high enough to see the curve of the earth. Even the Graf Zeppelin, crossing the ocean on its trip around the world, was a slow shadow below her. The sun rose in front of her, the stars trailed behind her feet. She sank a little, then caught a warm updraft above the Gulf Stream and turned south. Below her, looking like a half sunken log, shining swamp green, was Florida. She swooped low over the pines and palmettoes.

She saw the window of her mother's room in DeSoto, saw her mother bent laboring over a letter, love passing from her to the page, to her daughter, like a hard birth, like this birth. The wind caught Ginny again, and down below she saw Papa Ben's yellow Marmon snaking its way home through the pines on a sandy road. Then DeSoto was gone. The breeze didn't take her far this time, and as soon as she looked down, she knew where she was. Fanny was dancing on her screened porch to a slow-playing phonograph record. *I faw down and go boom! Boom!* Fanny shook her hips and laughed. It was a little party, for her new doctor, a few friends of Mrs. Mabes. *Faw down and go boom.* One of the visitors was smiling at Fanny, his hat in his lap. He was the farm agent, and he had come to talk to the doctor about planting the new thin-shelled pecans on the doc's land. But now, all he could think of was Fanny. She smiled at him and started the record over again. *I faw down and . . .* She took him by the hands and pulled him out of his seat to dance. *I faw . . .* She was the most beautiful woman he'd ever seen, her eyes the color of hybrid blueberries. "Boy howdy," he said.

Ginny felt something tugging at her. She looked down and saw a thin tube curving from her body into the distance and over the horizon, an umbilical cord. She was still tied to her baby. She touched the cord, heard Odile's voice humming through it as if it were a telephone wire. "Sister Luc," Odile said, "that foot is blue."

The baby couldn't breathe. Ginny felt it pushing desperately against the flesh she'd left behind, the flesh that was suffocating it. Ginny tugged on the umbilical cord and shot back over the ocean. She pulled herself back, hand over hand. She thought about the baby, how strange it would be not to have it moving inside her any more, how alone she would be. It was cold up so high, and the wind cut through her wet gown. Her arms grew tired. She warmed herself over the memory of Roland like a stove. She kept going. Calixte had been right, memories did have power. She pulled on the cord and imagined Roland reeling her in at the other end.

Finally, she saw Le Puy down below. The moon was up and a dense fog was rolling in. She saw the iron woman reaching out for her stone man. The ground shook as Joseph pulled first one stone foot, then the other, free from his rock. "I've got the other foot." Ginny heard Sister Luc's voice, surprisingly close. "Thank God." Then she was falling down, down through the clouds, toward the roof. The air around her shook as Joseph moved toward Mary with great stiff-legged strides.

"Who is it?" Ginny heard Odile calling to someone. "Roland? Is that you?" Joseph closed his stone arms around Mary. Thunder shook the sky.

"Push, Madame Gillespie, push!" Sister Luc yelled, lifting the ether mask. Ginny fell through the roof, hit the bed hard, and felt the baby squirt from her body like a watermelon seed. She heard the baby cry.

Roland looked down at his hands in Odile's, too shocked to ask how she'd gotten him to Le Puy. But then he saw Ginny, almost flat against the sheets, and he knew why Odile had done it. He threw himself on the bed beside Ginny, held onto her.

When Ginny hit the bed, she didn't stop. She kept falling, down floor after floor like a bathtub in a burning hotel. She fell through piles of lace, through the Museum of Happiness, past the postcard display in the shop. She hit the ground, and the cold earth closed over her head like dark water.

Roland wrapped his arms around Ginny, warming her with his body. He saw Sister Luc lay the baby on Ginny's breast, press a bandage between Ginny's legs, trying to get the bleeding to stop.

God, it's cold. This far down, Ginny thought, the sun never has a chance to warm the earth. The baby began to suck on her breast, pulling on her nipple with a warm, wet mouth, but Ginny felt as if the baby were giving, not getting warm milk. Heat spread out from her breast through her body. She felt Roland's breath warm on her neck. "Ginny!" She heard Roland's voice. He was shaking her gently, as he had that first day at the bottom of Sacré Coeur. "Wake up!" She opened her eyes and was surprised to see light. She blinked.

Roland kissed her lips. Odile lifted the baby from Ginny's breast so Sister Luc could tie the umbilical cord. Then she held it up for Ginny to see. The baby thrashed its arms and legs, trying out the air. It had

had no extra two months in the womb to rest and get wrinkled. Its skin was pink and smooth. Ginny held Roland's hand. It was their beautiful baby and, Ginny saw, every one of its fingers and toes was delicately, perfectly webbed. The baby's tiny penis unfolded and sent a golden arc of urine through the air. It fell like dew.

"Boy howdy," Ginny whispered, her voice hoarse.

"You're right," Odile said. "It is a boy."

Madame Desnos opened the window and shouted down to the courtyard, "It's a boy!"

"A boy!" Calixte shouted back, but Ginny could have sworn she said, *What joy!*

CHAPTER THIRTY

GINNY AND ROLAND and the baby spent the next three days in bed. Odile kept everyone else out. She brought up a tray with a plate of roast pork for Roland and a bowl of beef marrow soup for Ginny. "Good for the blood," she said to her, but when she saw how painfully thin Roland was, she marched back downstairs and got him a bowl too. Only the baby didn't have to have his food sent up. He ate whenever he felt like it, around the clock.

The first day Ginny slept, and Roland sat holding the baby, reading all of her letters to him – about Ginny's mother, Dr. Love, Mr. Atwood. The second, they lay side by side with the baby between them and watched him, hour by hour. His moods were contagious, like the happiness of the baby tossing the ball in the praxinoscope, and Ginny found herself feeling sleepy or hungry, awake or full when he did. When he rubbed his fists in his eyes, she rubbed her eyes. She noticed how much her movements were like the baby's, a little clumsy, a little uncertain, human. When Ginny combed her hair in the mirror, she was struck by how much her face looked like the baby's, how much Roland looked like the baby. Unless, Ginny thought, caught by logic, the baby looked like them.

The third day, they sat in bed taking turns holding the baby in their laps. They told each other their stories, told them so well that later it would seem like they hadn't been apart at all. In the years to come, Ginny would catch herself comparing someone to Housefather Huhn or she would overhear Roland telling their son about the army of women who rode the buses with feather dusters. She told him about Le Puy, the lace business, her hopes for a life together here. "I'm slow," she said, "but I'm learning."

"Then I'll learn too," Roland said. He gave her his hand and she unwrapped the bandage. The webbing was healing, the stitches almost ready to come out. But there would always be four ugly white scars, proof that they had been separated, that bad things had happened. Odile interrupted them to bring up an envelope that Mr. Bottoms had left. Inside were Roland's French passport and identity card. Roland showed Ginny and Odile the German papers Odo had gotten him. "When it rains," Odile said, leaving them to their story telling, "it rains hard."

By the morning of the fourth day, Ginny had finished her account, but Roland was just beginning to tell her about climbing into the back of the Archives of the Planet truck when Calixte came in. Ginny and Roland pulled the covers over their bare chests. "Archives, dears?" she asked, overhearing Roland. "There are two trucks full of archivists here. A bald man called Harris has offered to take Zoé to Hollywood, which is, I believe, one of the United States. And Philomène is off discussing business with Dr. Reynaud. It was his cousin Emile, you know, dear," Calixte said to Ginny, "who invented the praxinoscope. May I hold the baby now?"

Roland lifted the baby from his lap. Calixte held the baby's face to hers, kissed each cheek. The baby gazed up at Calixte, gurgling to her as if she were another baby.

"Dear little dear."

"Where's Odile?" Ginny asked. The baby began to fuss hungrily.

"Gone to see a farmer about a duck," Calixte winked. "If you know what I mean." Ginny took the baby and held him to her breast. He sucked hard. Maybe love wasn't contagious, she thought, but desire seemed to be. Calixte changed the subject.

"Have you named the dear yet?" Calixte said, playing with the baby's webbed toes. Roland looked at his son.

"Claire," he said. Ginny was startled by the sound of her mother's name. "Children give a second chance," he said, "even to names."

"Claire," Ginny repeated, trying the name out. She lifted the baby from her breast. "Claire?" Ginny returned the baby to her breast, and he began sucking more fiercely than ever. Roland kissed Ginny, and Ginny kissed him back, cupping the back of his head in one palm and Claire's in the other. Calixte looked politely away.

"Doctor Reynaud is giving a demonstration, free and open to the public, at the Auberge du Soleil tomorrow night," Calixte said.

"Is he going to show a moving picture?" Roland asked.

"No, dear," Calixte said. "It's something new and, I'm afraid, too complicated for me to explain. I'm sure the doctor will make it all clear with his demonstration. All I know is Zoé is going to be part of it, and she is going to make history." Ginny raised her eyebrows. "I'm glad I saved the letters she sent me from Paris," Calixte added, "since she is going to be famous."

"Letter!" Roland jumped out of bed. He wasn't wearing pants. Calixte covered her eyes. He dug through the pockets of his trousers, pulled out a thick letter and handed it to Ginny. Even before she saw the address, Ginny knew who the letter was from. Her vision of her mother's pained effort came back to her. Calixte saw the look on her face and turned to leave.

"I'll come with you, Mademoiselle Alix." Roland stepped into his pants, slid his hands into the pockets. "How could I forget?" he said, pulling out a gold wedding band. "Monsieur Mountain's blessing." He bent over and kissed Ginny, slipped the ring on her finger. Then he took Claire in his arms and went downstairs, leaving her alone.

Ginny turned the ring on her finger. The gold band added a subtle weight to her hand, made her aware of her own pulse, the blood that ran from her hand to her heart. Then she opened the letter. From the first word, she could hear her mother's voice.

> I know, Virginia, that you think you love a man and are loved by him, and that this is enough. But to value another person so highly is to put him above Jehovah, to make of him a false god, and you know well that we are commanded to have no other gods before Him. You think I do not know what I am talking about, but I once made this very mistake.

Even now her mother could not bring herself to name her mistake—Papa Ben.

> So I know what I am saying when I warn you that, like the great city Babylon, you are riding for a fall. Daughter, return your allegiance to Jehovah and to his wise and faithful servant.

Ginny paused. When she had been in grade school, Pastor Russell was the wise and faithful servant. Now that he was dead, Ginny wasn't sure who her mother thought was the wise and faithful one, maybe herself.

Failing that, I ask you at least to keep your heart open to Jehovah, so that I may say truthfully in my reports that my daughter is among the sheep, not the goats.

Ginny read on, glad, for now, that there was an ocean between them. Her mother's tone had not softened as much as she had hoped. She counted sixteen direct or indirect Biblical quotations. But at the very end of the letter, Claire had scribbled a line, as if trying to write quickly before she caught herself:

P.S. I am worried. Please write.

Ginny found herself crying. A postpartum patient is often overly emotional, she imagined Papa Ben saying.

Ginny wrote to her mother about giving birth. That, at least, they had in common. She told her that she loved her, that Claire should come to see her grandson in Le Puy. She made herself seal the letter without rereading it, afraid she might despair and tear it up. For now, it was the best she could do. She also wrote Fanny, told her about seeing her at her party. *You should dance more often,* she wrote, *if it makes you so happy.* Roland returned while she was writing Mrs. Corbet. He put Claire down beside her on the bed and stood at the window while she finished.

"This pattern," he said, running his hand down the curtain, "is too much of the same." He made a face. Ginny looked at him. "Like eating nothing but carrots day after day."

"What do you mean?" Ginny asked. Roland hummed five notes, then hummed them again.

"Like that. Don't you see?"

Ginny put down her pen.

"Look at the pavement in the courtyard," she said. "How may stones can you see, see individually, at one time?"

Roland leaned out, looked down. "All of them."

Somehow, even before he spoke, she knew Roland was going to say that, but still she pressed him. "All of them?"

"Yes," Roland said, turning to face her, surprised at her questioning. "One thousand and forty three."

"I think," Ginny said, "you should go downstairs right now and talk to Madame Sabatier. She's been waiting for you." Ginny smiled, satisfied. Roland looked puzzled. There was a knock on the door, and Sister Luc came in carrying a medical bag. She looked at Roland, cleared her throat.

"I was just leaving," he said.

Sister Luc made Ginny lie flat on her back to change her bandage. Then she hung Claire in the cloth sling of her scale and weighed him in at 2.5 kilos. "Better than average for a baby born so prematurely," she said, smiling. "He must be sucking you dry."

"Hardly," Ginny said, pointing to the trickle of milk that leaked from her breast, dampened the sheet, "but I am sore." Sister Luc rubbed some lanolin on Ginny's nipples, left her the jar.

"Wait until he has teeth," she said. Roland knocked and came in with Calixte on his arm.

"Look, dear," Calixte said, holding up a sheet of white paper made almost gray by a swarm of tiny black dots. Looking at it, Ginny sensed, more than saw, an underlying order, as if the dots were worker bees in a hive. "Have you ever seen anything like it?" Calixte kissed Roland on the cheek. "In fifteen minutes, a completely new pattern."

"Is there anything else I can do for you, Madame Gillespie?" Sister Luc asked, packing up her bag.

"Yes," Ginny said, sitting up. "Could you hand me my suitcase, Roland? It's in the armoire." Roland laid the suitcase across her legs. Ginny opened it, took out 25,000 francs, one tenth of what was there, and gave it to Sister Luc to give to the hospital. After all, it was Paul's money. She printed his name, Paul Gillespie, on a slip of paper. "The name of the donor," she said, "for the memorial wall." She'd been wrong in Paris, thinking of Paul's money as oxygen, something she couldn't live without. Their work—hers, Madame Desnos's, Odile's, and Roland's—was building a new life. She closed the suitcase. She would keep the rest of Paul's money for Claire, a gift from one generation to the next.

After Sister Luc left, Ginny took Paul's urn and set it upright on the bed. Calixte touched the green marble, drawn to it as if it were a shiny, spinning top. "Her dead husband's ashes," Roland explained.

"I don't know what to do with them," Ginny said. "I've never known."

"Well, dear," Calixte said, "you could donate him to the museum." She smiled at Ginny's shocked look. "But it would probably be more practical to lay him to rest in the Alix family tomb. After all, I'm the last Alix, and the tomb isn't nearly full." Calixte paused, touched the urn again. "Do you think he'll get along with my mother and father?" Ginny opened her mouth to say no, but then she caught a flickering glimpse of Paul as a baby, tossing and then catching a blue ball.

"I think so," Ginny said. At least in the Alix tomb, Paul wouldn't be alone.

"Good," Calixte said. "Now all three of you should rest.

By the next evening, Ginny, Roland, and Claire were ready to go out. Ginny felt oddly unbalanced going down the stairs. She kept leaning back too far, compensating for her now missing belly. When they got downstairs, Roland handed her Claire, and Ginny found that a baby in her arms was the perfect counterweight. The dining room of the inn was dark except for the light of one lamp near the kitchen door. Ginny could make out rows of chairs. Most were full of people from the town, but she spotted Odile sitting in the fourth row with her duck farmer. "Honoré Rouchette," Odile said, introducing the farmer, "my grandson, Roland Keppi."

"Your grandmother," he said, "is an uncommon woman." Roland and Honoré shook hands on that. Ginny found empty seats in the third row, sat down with the baby, and Roland sat beside her. At the front of the room, barely visible in the gloom, two undecipherable shapes, one slightly larger than the other, sat side by side draped in white sheets.

"What do you suppose . . ." Ginny started, but just then she saw Madame Desnos standing in the kitchen door talking to a stranger. From the white lab coat he wore, she guessed it was Dr. Reynaud. Madame Desnos pointed to the larger of the draped shapes as she spoke, and Dr. Reynaud nodded vigorously. When she had finished whatever it was she had to say, he pecked her on the cheek. Madame Desnos spotted Ginny and waved, made her way down the aisle to join them, and sat down.

"Well, hello there," someone said to Roland. "We were wondering where you were." Ginny looked up and saw the young African cameraman she remembered from their trip to the clothes market in Paris. Calixte had him by the arm.

"May we sit with you, dear?" Calixte asked Ginny.

"Please," Ginny said. Calixte and the young African took the last seats in the row.

"Isn't this exciting, dear?" Calixte said.

"Ladies and gentlemen." Dr. Reynaud had taken his place in front of his veiled shapes and was holding a flashlight high in one hand. He pulled the sheet off the larger shape, revealing a square glass screen, a little smaller than the paper one Dr. Love had shone lantern slides on in the assembly hall. Was it, after all, going to be only a moving picture show? Then Dr. Reynaud pulled the sheet off his second, smaller piece of equipment and shone his light on it. Ginny leaned forward, trying to see. Whatever it was, it didn't look like any projector or movie camera she'd ever seen. A round metal disk the size of a car wheel was mounted in front of some sort of engine. The disk was perforated in a spiral pattern, the holes starting a few inches from the edge and swirling into the center.

"Television!" Dr. Reynaud shouted, pointing the light so it shone on his face. "Do you know what that is?" The audience shook its head no. "First," Dr. Reynaud held up a finger, "let me tell you what it is not. It is not the viewing of distant events by a telescope, nor is it the projection," he looked back at the African, "of moving pictures transported by truck over a great distance. It is, simply," the doctor paused long enough for the audience to draw a breath, hold it in, "the transmission from one point, by electrical means, of moving scenes to be viewed at another point simultaneously with their original occurrence." The audience exhaled.

A bald man with a handlebar moustache walked down the aisle and out the door, and after a moment, Ginny heard a motor start up in the courtyard. The front of the room was flooded with brilliant electric light. Ginny blinked, spots floating before her eyes, and she saw Zoé move out of the darkness of the kitchen door into the light. She stood next to the machine, dressed in a black top and tutu with light blue hose, her lips and cheeks painted an amazing dark blue. She looked with great longing down the aisle at the bald man who had reappeared at the door. Her Harris, Ginny guessed.

"This," Dr. Reynaud said, placing one hand on the machine with the metal disk, "is a television camera. With these little eyes," he touched one of the holes in the disk, "it will scan Mademoiselle Saby head to toe twenty times per second and send the images through this," he touched a thick black wire with his foot, "to an identical device, synchronized to receive and amplify the signal, that is hidden behind this screen of fifty parallel glass tubes. On this screen, in just a few minutes," he paused, "you will see Mademoiselle Saby dancing as clearly and gracefully as she will simultaneously be doing in person." The doctor turned to make some adjustments to his apparatus.

The African tapped Ginny on the shoulder. "You know, the Doc says television will let a wife back home watch her husband fighting at the war, right as it happens. See him going over the top. Do you think we'd have any more wars if mamas could see their sons getting shot?"

"I don't know," said Ginny. "Mothers can be cruel sometimes." She thought of her mother's vision of the future, the ancient prophets returned to rule the world from Jerusalem, talking on the radio, flying in dirigibles, leading the fight at Armageddon. Had the *Watch Tower* predicted even this?

Doctor Reynaud threw a switch on his apparatus and the disk on the television camera began to spin. He nodded at Zoé. With one last look at Harris, she began to spin too. "Faster," the doctor said, and Zoé spun faster, trying to outdo the whirling disk. Dr. Reynaud left the camera, went to the screen, and turned a knob on one side. One by one, the tubes behind the glass screen flickered, lit up, bathing him in a bluish white glow. Ginny shifted Claire off her legs, which had fallen asleep, into Roland's lap. Zoé turned and turned, spinning her heart out, sweat flying out from her like rain.

Then there she was, up on the glass screen dancing. Or at least a shadow of her, distorted, wavering. Ginny leaned forward. All around her, she heard chairs squeaking as others did the same. Only Roland sat back, unmoved, as if he saw such things all the time. The picture of Zoé began slowly to scroll upward, until her feet were dancing on top of her head. Ginny closed her eyes, no longer looking at the screen. She felt Roland sitting inches from her in the darkness, Claire asleep on his lap.

"Isn't it wonderful!" Calixte said, clapping her hands together. "The future is close enough for us to reach out and touch."

AFTERWORD

This spring, I returned to Paris. My husband, Dan, was with me and our two children, Max, four, and Magdalena, eleven. I was stunned by how much time had passed since I'd been there. I knew I hadn't been in Paris since doing the research for *The Museum of Happiness*, but saying that out loud—it has been *twelve* years, more than a decade, since I was here—was a shock. The last time I'd been in France, I'd been nobody's mother. When I wrote about the birth of Ginny and Roland's son, about her labor and childbirth, I'd never experienced any of those things. When I finally did go through pregnancy and delivery with Magda, I had a distinct feeling of *déjà vous*—as if I had done it all before in Paris and Le Puy.

This spring, as we traveled into Paris from Charles de Gaulle, as we walked around our first jet-lagged day, I was overwhelmed by a sense of how much the city had changed. I said so to Dan. Then said so again. And again. He agreed—to a point. Yes, there was more graffiti. Paris seemed to be undergoing one of those periodic graffiti plagues that sweep every city. Yes, more *boulangeries* sold cold Coke and Fanta in addition to baguettes. Yes, there were now busy Chinese take-out shops next to the *pâtisseries* in nearly every neighborhood. There were also the *fin de siecle* additions to the city Mitterand had made—the glass pyramid at the heart of the Louvre, the corporate pomp of La Défense with its Grande Arche built to echo the Arc de Triomphe. But even on the far side of the ocean, we had read about the controversies surrounding these last two additions to Paris.

Still, Dan's sense was of minor variations on the theme of Paris, of a few notes added for a new century, while I felt like a disoriented time-traveler. Then, riding the Métro from Gare St. Làzare to Les Halles, I looked around at the passengers filling the yellow plastic seats of the rocking car, and it hit me. I felt Paris had changed drastically because the last time I was there, with Dan beside me, I had been so deeply involved with Ginny and Roland, that while Dan was in Paris in 1990, and had every right to assume I was too, I was really in Paris, 1929. I walked the city with a 1929 Baedecker in one hand, my notebook in the other, and no matter what was there, I'd seen only what would have been there for Ginny and Roland to see. I was back in Paris after an absence of not twelve years, but seventy-three.

Of course, there were not as many of the gilt-mirrored storefronts or rows of odd shops selling used shoes. They had been a fading presence, really, in 1990. Now many of those tattered remnants, too, were gone. But Paris was still Paris. The inner arrondissements had not really changed since Haussmann's great revisions, the outer arrondissements were still the home of the working class. But, in addition to my odd misplaced nostalgia, I also felt a deeper grief that took me a while to identify. I missed Ginny and Roland. I am in no way an author who thinks she is writing about her previous lives or who believes she is channeling forgotten dead who long to speak. I make up my characters. I give them names, invent the color of their hair, and the stories of their childhoods. Yet I'll admit when I was in Paris working on *The Museum of Happiness*, walking the boulevards, riding the Métro, Ginny and Roland had been so real to me, I felt if I just turned my head quickly enough—*there, there*. I would catch them turning a corner or stepping through the sliding car doors onto the waiting platform. Now, they were gone. It was almost impossible to imagine them in this Paris. I found it just barely possible to imagine them still alive. If they were, Roland would be ninety-six, Ginny ninety-two.

One night, walking a meandering route down from Sacre Coeur where we had sat watching the sunset, the children and I passed over the Montmartre cemetery. *Oh*, I thought, looking down at the dim white tombs, *Roland and Ginny are buried here*. It even crossed my mind that I should come back in the morning, when the gate was open, and find their family tomb. Then sense of a sort returned. I say "a sort" because I did not think, *Ginny and Roland are not buried here, because characters in fiction are not buried anywhere*. No, I thought, *They're not buried here. Paul is buried here. I sent Ginny and Roland safely out of Paris*.

Okay, I was tired after a long day spent climbing everything high in Paris—the Eiffel Tower, Notre Dame, Sacre Coeur—with my daughter.

I was still on Wisconsin time, and my mind a barely tethered balloon, floating from thought to thought as my feet bumped down the steep hill. But this moment of confusion, of the real world blurring together with the fictional, did start me thinking about where the novel left Ginny and Roland. The jacket copy on the original hardback edition reads "*The Museum of Happiness* is a . . . novel with a gloriously happy ending." Much to my surprise, nearly all the reviewers took this on face value and agreed that the end was, indeed, happy. Most reviewers thought it was good for a novel about so much dislocation to have a happy ending. One or two disapproved of happy endings in general or this one in particular.

But no one said "Contrary to what the publisher of *The Museum of Happiness* seems to believe, the ending is not 'gloriously happy,'" or wrote that the end was only partly happy or that its happiness was tinged with shadow—which is the way I have always seen it. After all, I left them—Ginny and Roland and baby Claire, the whole cast of what sometimes seemed to me an enormous opera, ending with everyone on stage—in France, poised between one world war and the even more terrible one that was coming.

What had happened, I found myself musing, to Roland, a stateless person, or to Ginny, an enemy alien, after France had fallen? Had they been deported to Germany? Did my story, as did so many real ones, end in Hitler's camps? I'd meant the mad detention center where Roland is held to foreshadow what was coming, but surely, so deep in Vichy France, Roland and Ginny stood a chance of passing the war, like Gertrude Stein and Alice B. Toklas, unnoticed or, at least, undetained. I had the sudden impulse to abandon our family travel plans—we were to be a week in Paris, then head to Brittany, reputedly the ancestral home of Kerchevals—to board a train with Dan and the children in tow and go south to Le Puy in search of the answer. Maybe I should have. I know I had a keen longing to see the red iron Virgin standing above the town again, and to climb her spiral stairs and look down on the world through the eyes of the Mother of God. My daughter, always eager for heights, would have loved the climb, and all the others in that land of rock pillars topped with chapels and gigantic statuary. But part of me thought I would not find my characters there, not even in an imaginary way.

I was suddenly quite sure that the coming war had cast them adrift again, that the whole odd, extended family had closed the circle, returning to the north Florida of Ginny's childhood. DeFuniak Springs had served as my model for Ginny's imaginary hometown DeSoto. I'd driven through the town earlier in the year when we'd been in the Florida panhandle visiting Dan's mother. DeFuniak in the new millennium was no ghost town, but it had grown away from its old center. The new buildings flanked I-10, that artery of commerce, and the stores facing the town's old life blood, the rail line, stood mostly empty. Still, efforts were clearly being made to restore the old Victorian houses that circled the lake. The house I'd always imagined as Papa Ben's had scaffolding all around it, clear evidence of care. Though, to be honest, the scaffolding looked as if it had been there for a while, and only one side of the house was scraped and primed, ready for new paint. There were large, lush pots of ferns and impatiens hanging on the shady porch, but front steps sagged, clearly rotten under an old gray coat of paint. Did Keppis live there? Or if not there, in one of the other complicated gingerbread houses? Or were they buried in the same hot and sandy cemetery as so many of my husband's relatives?

If Roland and Ginny were dead and buried in DeSoto, as suddenly seemed likely to me, I wished them rest in a cemetery both imaginary and shady. But what of Claire, Ginny and Roland's son, Odile's grandson? Maybe, just maybe, Claire had, like us, just arrived in Paris as a tourist, an *émigré* come back to visit. If so, then surely he was riding the Métro just as we were, strolling the gravel paths of the parks under the horse chestnut trees. Maybe he too ventured out to La Villette to see the new science museum built on the foundation of the old slaughterhouses. Like me, he would be looking at Paris through his parents' eyes, hearing their stories echoing in his ears. Wouldn't he be thinking, feeling, what I was? That Paris was exactly what we expected. That it was not at all as we had imagined. That it was less, and then again much more. My children fed the birds below Sacre Coeur. They stood under the Eiffel Tower looking up as Ginny had done. They were learning to love Paris. And so would he.

In that way, the story ends nearly where it started. Ginny went to France and the world opened for her. Paris has that effect so often, in fiction and in life, it is a cliche to say it, but that doesn't mean it isn't true. Whether it is an imaginary Ginny or Claire, or a flesh and blood Magdalena or Max, every generation discovers its own Paris, and their lives go on from there.

I made the first tentative start on what became *The Museum of Happiness* when I was finishing my MFA at the Iowa Writer's Workshop. An excerpt was published in a magazine, then picked up for an anthology, and one morning I was awakened, to my complete astonishment, by a phone call from Italy. An editor there had seen the excerpt and wanted to publish it in his magazine. He said he loved it because it reminded him of his time in Paris. "Ah Paris," he said in his lilting, Italian-accented English, "those were the days. But now I am stuck in Milano." I laughed. He might be stuck in Milan, but I was talking to him from a basement apartment in the middle of a sub-zero January in Iowa City, Iowa. Still, I felt the same way he did about Paris. So did many of the people I met when I traveled to give readings from the book, even those who had never set foot there. Nearly everyone, it seemed, longed to cross the Seine on a warm spring night and was grateful that I'd brought the city to life for them.

After I returned from Paris this time, I got down my own copy of the novel and reread it, rediscovering the characters and scenes I created, but which now had a life of their own in the world. So if it is true that *The Museum of Happiness* brings Paris, and France, to life for readers, then this year, Paris returned the favor and brought *The Museum of Happiness* to life again for me. And I will always be grateful for that.